The Ghost of Cattingham Hall

Amber A. Cross

To Jess
Love
Amber 8/4/16.
xxx

ISBN: 978-1-326-54585-7

www.publishnation.co.uk

Prologue

It was July 1807. She had lost her voice with her screaming. She had scratched and scratched at the blistered wood, but she couldn't break through it.

Why hadn't someone come? Why hadn't they heard her cries? Before she had lost her voice she had sung nursery rhymes to herself, banged, kicked, and wailed: anything to make as much noise as possible. With the witches now gone she had felt safe, thinking she would soon be found. But still no one came.

When she heard Antrabus call to her it heightened her distress. He thought she was his mother. The bird's rattle became more agitated from outside as he continued to call for her filling the air with his plaintive, echoing croaks. The rasps continued with short, repeated calls. Finally his frantic calls died down. Then there was silence.

Salty tears dripped down her cheeks. Her red, raw face had started to burn. She was thirsty, but she was unable to wet her dry, cracked lips. Things now were getting confused ... she kept drifting in and out of sleep.

She cursed the witches for doing this to her, and whispered out all the words in that book she had found. Let them suffer for what they had done to her. She would make them pay for this.

Her breathing became laboured. But then she heard something. What was it? It sounded like a bang on the door. Her ears had grown accustomed to different sounds in the pitch black. The rats didn't make noises like that. It gave her hope. Had someone found her?

She smiled.

"Of course," she thought. That was it. She had been found. She was going home. At first it sounded like scraping, then a light rapping becoming louder. Finally she realised what it was.

The door was being bricked up.

Chapter 1

The ghost of Cattingham Hall been only been seen by a few people. The haunting had really begun at the beginning of a rain-sodden week in August 2014. Those who had seen the ghost remembered a tall girl wearing what looked like a white gossamer dress and a long trailing cobweb shawl.

But it was the high-pitched shriek they remembered the most. It was almost ear-shattering – banshee-like –as the phantom came running down the long, sweeping corridors of the Hall, her hands stretching out in front of her. Dark, wet hair dripped water down her shoulders as she stared malevolently out of blue orbs rather than eyes.

She was a frightening sight.

On several occasions she had also been sighted being followed by a huge black raven soaring above her head. The last person witnessing this manifestation had been the Accountant's wife. But it was not in the gallery, where she was usually sighted. It had been in the kitchen. It was only now that the woman had had the courage to leave her house, but she was still in shock. Her hair had turned starch-white overnight.

The current occupier of the Hall had never seen the ghost. Lydia heard the strange tapping and groaning noises, but dismissed this as either the ancient heating system or families of rats nesting inside the walls of the Hall. What she found worse was the sickly smell that made you clasp your throat, which would permeate the Hall when it rained.

Things then took a turn for the worse when Lydia Underville's niece Maddie Johnson came to stay.

Cattingham Hall in Northumberland had been in the Underville family since the 1700s. During the Second World War bombings the Hall had taken a hit on the roof (the bomb had been intended for the explosives factory nearby). Unfortunately the old tower had been destroyed in this attack. The Hall had then been patched up by dishonest cowboy builders.

The Hall had been built in 1704. Even with its ancient murky water-damaged family crypt it still had a commanding presence. The arched marble entrance led visitors past a huge white stone deer resting on mottled grey stone pillars to the wide oak front door. The house however was riddled with dry rot, and the basement walls were covered in mushroom spores.

The decline in the house had been gradual process. It was if the house's heart was slowly dying from the inside. The beat of it was getting weaker every year. But Lydia didn't have any money for the house's upkeep. It did not help that her funds had dwindled due to bad investments and financial ineptitude.

Now and again rain would come in. A large grey plastic bucket lay beneath the drips collecting the droplets of water as they fell. Lydia had been trying to write cheques out for bills, irritation written all over her face.

The recent heavy rain in Northumbria had been disaster for the Hall. The final straw had been when the family crypt had flooded a month ago. The bricked-up wall covering it up had collapsed under the strain of heavy rainwater. Some of the coffins had floated out into the walled garden and had had to be dried out and returned back to the crypt.

All the coffins had remained intact except for the coffin of Ursula Underville, an ancestor believed to have been a notorious witch. It was during this time that the haunting of Cattingham Hall really began. The flooding had then brought further damage to the Hall.

Lydia had even had to move the six-foot oak and walnut grandmother clock in the library, nearly putting her back out in the process. The weather had never been this bad before, and certainly not in August.

"It's as if a black cloud seems to rest permanently above the Hall," thought Lydia. She sighed, scratched her head, and rubbed her shoulders wearily as she went through the bills. What was in the current account just about covered these bills. Then what? Further bills would be coming in shortly. If she dipped any further into the 'only to be used for emergencies account' she would be heading for trouble.

Lydia was an attractive woman in her sixties with short, silvery blonde hair. Her face was small and thin. Today she had her glasses perched on her nose, which half covered her dark blue eyes. She had been slim but weight had now gathered round her hips and legs, caused by years of eating home-baked cakes and her favourite Belgian chocolates. She called herself a connoisseur of chocolate.

But Lydia could never decide which of them she preferred: white chocolate marzipan cuvettes with their combination of raw cane sugar, ground almonds, and creamy strawberry and coffee fillings … or orange truffles made from rich milk chocolate and tangy orange-flavoured zest dipped in melted thick milk chocolate. Mostly she gave up trying to decide, and wasted no time in scoffing the lot. Fortunately she always had a good emergency supply, and there was always plenty of choice from the larger boxes she ordered from Bryonies' of London.

After watching her aunt Maddie helped go through the bills she too sighed as she felt her aunt's anguish. She would have much preferred to have been outside practising her cricket with Titch, the estate manager, but felt guilty because she had smashed a glass panel in the rear greenhouse window while playing cricket. It was not nice to see her aunt worrying about money. She also knew her aunt missed Uncle Akkoubian.

He had died recently. He had always been smiling, and you couldn't help but like him. But his weight had ballooned up as he got older, which had chronically affected his health. The numerous diets he had been on had failed despite Lydia's efforts to get him to lose weight. He had usually worn fine-quality woven tweeds, but he had often got the colours of the suit jacket and trousers mixed up because he was colour-blind. This had resulted in a daily mismatch. Unfazed, he would roar with laughter if it was pointed out to him. He was not in the least bit embarrassed: instead, his brilliant blue eyes would be full of mirth. Maddie had been very fond of him.

The Hall had a sad, empty feel about it without his extrovert presence. Since he had died most of the family heirlooms had been sold off to pay death duties. Nearly all the paintings had now gone.

The furniture left was well made but worn. The Hall had eight bedrooms, but only a few rooms were furnished.

Lydia was looking after her niece, Maddie – who was fifteen years old – during the school holidays. Her mother, Julia Johnson, was a journalist working in Africa, covering the news of a political prisoner in Kandala. The woman was due to be released, and Julia was hoping she would be one of the first to get to interview her and then get full coverage. She would not be back in England until after the school holidays.

Maddie and her mother lived outside Cattingham in a quiet village called Meadowfield. It was decided it would be better for Maddie to live with Lydia at the Hall for the six weeks rather than stay with her mother's friends or at Uncle Julian's. The suggestion she stay at the house of her uncle was met with a stubborn refusal. Even thinking about staying with him for even one day was enough to make her want to vomit.

Maddie Johnson was quite small, very thin, and slightly pear-shaped, with tiny shoulders (jumpers would hang off them). Her shoulder-length, tousled honey brown hair framed an oval-shaped face, the long fringe half covering her deep-set grey-blue eyes. Very much a tomboy, she had not changed as she grew older. When she was younger locals had thought she was a boy. There was not much difference to her looks even now.

Sitting in the library was not particularly pleasant. Today there was no heating on. It was freezing cold. The fireplace was stacked up with kindling, but the fire was unlit. Lydia was attempting to budget by only warming one room at a time. The icy chill whistling through the house made sure you had the sense to wear warm clothes. Maddie had put on a thick-ribbed grey wool cardigan. The pockets hung down, straining under the large number of things she had stuffed in them. Underneath this she had on her black and white long-sleeved spotty tee-shirt over faded black skinny-leg jeans. Her small feet were encased in her grey owl lace up slipper boots with their bird foot print soles.

Lydia never said much about her clothes. She just hoped Maddie would become more ladylike as the years went by. Well, she lived in hope. Lydia signed another two cheques and, after glancing at the front page in the local newspaper, said,

"Oh, no. Listen to this. Five more cats have gone missing. I wonder if we should keep Hodge in until they find what is going on."

"Why, what's happening to them?"

"The newspaper report just says they are going missing. It is not known why. Do you think we will be able to keep Hodge in?"

"I doubt it, Aunt Lydia. You know what she's like. She will only try and escape."

"Yes, I suppose you are right. What a nightmare she would be if she was locked in. She would screech her head off," came the worried reply.

Lydia suddenly remembered the trauma of Hodge climbing up on the roof when they had tried to take her to the vet's, then the embarrassed call to the fire brigade.

"Well, we will have to watch her. I will mention it to Titch. This village seems to have a terrible history of cruelty to cats and women. Can you remember the story about Sage Cottage?"

Maddie looked blank, so her aunt reminded her.

"Oh ... maybe it was your mother I mentioned it to. When the builders were renovating the property they found some old leather diaries under the floorboards. The Bickleberry Post then researched the history of the cottage. The diaries gave details of hundreds of women who had been accused of being witches all over the village. It was said that a woman called Martha Barnfather had in I think it was 1805 lived in the house during that time and had recorded what had happened. You would have thought that witchcraft would have died out then but according to these records her niece had accused her of being a witch."

"A witch ... She was a witch?" asked Maddie excitedly.

"No, she was not. The newspaper said she had been just a midwife. A baby had died, and she was blamed for its death. There were a lot of infant deaths in those days. Anything could have caused it. The newspaper said she was taken by a mob, placed on a ducking stool, and thrown in the river. She then drowned. They were wrong about her being a witch, of course. According to local superstition she would not have drowned if she had been a witch. Poor woman. Her niece moved in shortly afterwards. Then – if that was not enough – the niece and the villagers then chased the woman's white cat out of the cottage, claiming it was a witch's familiar."

"Why did they do that?" asked Maddie.

6

"It was a hysterical time. People were very superstitious in Cattingham. They believed that removing the cat would protect the inhabitant of the house from evil. But then there had been a lot of illness in the village. It was the days of the white plague. Witches were believed to be behind it. Many young girls and women were placed on the ducking stool at Low Row Bridge to test them to see if they were witches. Most of them drowned. The ones who didn't drown just disappeared. People in service at Cattingham Hall were even tried as witches."

Lydia swiftly changed the subject after realising it was not a pleasant conversation to be having with her niece. But she made it worse by saying,

"Of course in the village they have been saying there is an outbreak of giant rats round here now, and that might be why the cats are going missing. No one has ever caught one, though. I really hope Hodge doesn't attack one. It could really hurt her."

"Wow ... giant rats. Do you think we will get to see one?" said Maddie, getting excited.

"I sincerely hope not. We are already riddled with ordinary rats as it is. So don't go looking for giant ones. You would get a nasty bite, from what I have heard about them. They also will have ... what's that disease? It's Weil's disease from rats' urine, isn't it? What with you telling me about the skeletons of giant dogs being dug up in the woods with cloven feet – and now the witchcraft and the rats – this is turning into a very strange village ... Anyway, I think it's about time I changed the subject." Lydia cleared her throat and continued.

"This is more important: before I forget to mention it we will need to go to your house on Monday to check everything. We can bring back anything else you may need."

Maddie nodded back in reply. Her house was tiny compared to the Hall, but it was very cosy.

Listening to this was Hodge, who was sitting on the leather recliner dozing. Now and again she would lift her high-arched eyebrow whiskers in what appeared to be mild curiosity. She was the family cat: a big black short-haired cat with narrow pale yellow eyes. She had appeared out of nowhere, and had slowly begun to trust the family. She would not let anyone near her apart from Maddie, Lydia, and late Uncle Akkoubian, and she had eventually turned into a bit of a diva.

"Maddie," said Lydia, clearing her throat. "Another thing … on Sunday Uncle Julian and Cousin Phillip are coming for Sunday lunch. It would be nice if you could put something pretty on." Her niece groaned and pulled a face, twanging at the laces on her slipper boots as she listened to her aunt.

"Oh, Maddie, don't be like that. Your uncle has done a lot for us since your Uncle Akkoubian died. He sold all those paintings for us, and got us good prices. Heaven knows how he managed to do that. After all, remember how he said some of them were worth nothing. We were lucky to get anything at all."

Maddie didn't answer. He may have done that, but in her view Uncle Julian and his son Cousin Phillip were a really obnoxious pair. How could Aunt Lydia not see through them for what they were? Time and time again Uncle Julian had tried to buy Cattingham Hall from her aunt for what Titch had said was a knock-down price. Her aunt had refused each offer.

Maddie was worried that if Aunt Lydia didn't manage to get any more money in future she might take the latest offer out of desperation. Maddie loved Cattingham Hall. Her uncle would ruin it and turn it into a sideshow. Solidly built in his sixties, short in height, with a barrel chest and halitosis breath. He was always dressed in a tobacco-smelling light brown tweed jacket which he matched with everything he wore. He had huge hands with pink sausage fingers. When he ruffled Maddie's hair in a pretend playful gesture she always felt she was going to get her ears boxed. He was not an attractive man. He was red-faced, had rheumy blue eyes, and was bald … well, apart from one long grey-brown strand of hair, which appeared to wrap around his head like a turban. The lone piece of hair seemed very important to him. Maddie often wondered if he had hair sprayed it on, the way it stuck round his head so tightly.

Cousin Phillip, his son, was also very much a peacock – with dyed white-blonde hair which he had teased into what looked like a high bouffant, gelled to perfection. He was round-faced. He had inherited his father's complexion, and had a beak-like nose and small hazel eyes. But of course the first thing you noticed about him was his extremely sulky mouth, which even at his age had pout lines round the upper and lower lip. He always dressed in the latest fashion. He would look at Maddie and her clothes and laugh. Sometimes when he came to visit Aunt Lydia he would make kicking gestures at her when Lydia wasn't looking with his highly polished pointy leather boots.

Chapter 2

Sunday was exactly as Maddie thought it would be: a complete nightmare.

Maddie had watched from one of the upstairs windows as Uncle Julian drove at full speed into the grounds of Cattingham Hall in his new silver Porsche, as usual waiting until the last minute to put the brakes on. On this occasion he narrowly missed Titch, the estate manager, who had been in the process of planting a hydrangea bush. The estate manager glared at him and did not say anything to him, but the expression on his face spoke volumes. If you could lip-read you would see that he had mouthed the word 'prat'.

Julian did not appear to notice that. He did not like Titch. He felt that he should be more servile to him, and know his place. He would – he thought, when he finally persuaded Lydia to sell the Hall to him – sack him immediately. This filled him with undisguised relish. Then he would move into the Hall and live the way he felt he should be living. But of course the main reason he wanted the Hall was because it held many carefully guarded secrets, and he wanted to make sure they never came out. The stuff needed to come out of the Hall. He had not had time to get it. There was also always the fear that nosy Titch would discover it.

"That plastered wall was just a temporary measure," he said to himself. In desperation he had offered to pay to send Lydia on a free holiday while he looked after the Hall, but the stupid woman wouldn't go. Somehow, he thought, he had to get her out of the way.

Julian had shown no grief when his older brother Akkoubian had died. In fact it was better it had happened. His brother had begun to ask too many awkward questions, which would have caused big problems for Julian. Akkoubian had been well liked by the locals, but had had no idea how to run the Hall. It had filled Julian with rage when his brother had inherited the Hall and all its possessions after his father had died, while he had to make do with – as he termed it – 'just inheritance money', and nothing else.

Now 'Stupid Lydia' (as he called her) had it all, but it would not – in his opinion – be for long. He smiled to himself and patted his deceased brother's turnip watch –something he had purloined on the day of Akkoubian's funeral – which was concealed in the side pocket of his coat, and climbed out of the car. This puzzled Titch, who thought he was smiling at him.

Cousin Phillip followed him out to the car and looked disdainfully at Titch, who was used to his rudeness. Lydia answered the door. The smell of roast lamb wafted from inside. She kissed Julian on the cheek. She smiled at Phillip, but had long given up attempting to kiss him. He had always moved out of the way, horrified if she made any attempt to show any sign of affection towards him …

After walking them into the sunflower-yellow sitting room, with its huge cream sofas littered with pink fuchsia needlepoint cushions, she poured them each a glass of red wine. The oak log burning on the fire gave the room a warm welcome as they came in. As they proceeded to sit down Maddie came downstairs dressed in a navy blue floral tunic, blue skinny-legged trousers, and ballet shoes. She had even used hair straighteners and teased her unruly hair into a shaped bob.

"Maddie, you look lovely," said Lydia, beaming in admiration at her niece.

Uncle Julian stopped talking, turned round, looked her up and down, and said nothing. He then proceeded to continue talking to Lydia about the money she would make if she sold the Hall to him. Aware of Cousin Phillip watching her, Maddie ignored him and walked over to Hodge and began to stroke her. The cat was balanced precariously on the top of a large cardboard box crammed with books for the jumble sale.

"I hate cats," said Phillip.

Knowing he was trying to get a reaction from her, Maddie said nothing. He was horrible but at least he had not brought Deborah, his black-haired Goth girlfriend. She was almost robotic, and tended to speak in monosyllabic tones. Her face was ivory-white, set off with blood-red lipstick – which sometimes smudged, making her often look like she had a gigantic Cupid's bow mouth. Born with no eyebrows, she had painted on in their place black high-arched eyebrows – which gave her a look of disdainful mockery. Never smiling, and not possessing any sense of humour, Deborah would sit completely upright in her chair and look down on Maddie in snooty disapproval – and she would listen to Maddie's every word, as if checking to see she was speaking correctly.

Maddie was convinced that it was only a question of time before she was found to have a long-life battery planted deep inside her back. Her friend Sam had nicknamed them 'The Twins of Evil'. The pair played mind games with Maddie. They would look at each other if Maddie spoke to them, and smirk when she replied to any of their questions. Sometimes they would play 'good cop, bad cop'. Just when she thought one was being nice to her the other would be horrible to her. The next time she saw them they would reverse roles. One thing was for certain: when she grew up she was determined to have nothing to do with them, and would not be forced to see them the way she had to now.

Cousin Phillip had an equally horrible best friend called Nathanael. He must have – she thought – been trained by them in their ways of nastiness, and had some really disgusting habits. One was pulling his underpants out of his bottom when he spoke to her, and another was picking at the spots on his chin. Yet another unpleasant thing was that a faint smell of sulphur tended to follow him in his wake. Even worse, Nathanael seemed to fancy her.

To break into her thoughts Phillip said,

"Filthy creature should have been put down. I bet it's full of fleas."

Hodge stared at him through half-closed yellow eyes, and appeared to understand what he was saying. She swished her tail and gave him a cursory glance of contempt, and began to lick the soft fur down on her belly. This action, however, caused her to fall off the box, much to her annoyance. The cat haughtily regained her composure and looking Phillip up and down angrily stomped off in a huff.

Lydia, however, on hearing this remark about her cat in mid conversation, turned her head to Phillip and annoyed said,

"Don't be so rude."

Phillip looked as if he was about to say something to her, but on seeing his father's expression said nothing and began fiddling with his silver belt buckle. Lydia then got up and went off to check on lunch. It was then that the noise started up, almost like fingers rapping. Then it became louder ... drum-like. It became even louder. It started to reverberate round the whole room. You would have thought a train had thundered past by the noise it made.

"It's about time your aunt did something with the heating system," said Julian. He was getting irritated, but he had finally acknowledged Maddie's presence.

"She had it checked. They could find nothing wrong with it," came the reply.

"Huh. When I come to live here I will not let the Hall go to ruin the way it is now. It's a disgrace, the state it's in. Your aunt has no idea how to run something of this size."

Uncle Julian's tedious voice continued on with the usual repetitive stuff. Maddie was saved further rants by Lydia popping her head round the door and telling everyone that lunch was ready. The heating continued to rumble.

Maddie knew it wasn't the heating system that had caused all the strange noises. She had given up trying to tell her aunt what it was, or how objects appeared to move by themselves in her bedroom. Even books came out of the bookshelf for no reason. Of course it never happened when her aunt was around, so she had stopped running to get her. As soon as Lydia had returned with her on previous occasions the books were back in their places. But something bad was happening to the house.

Since Uncle Akkoubian had died whatever had seemed to protect them appeared to have gone with him. No fresh flowers now survived for more than two days if they were brought into the house. Putrid moulds had begun to appear on various walls round the house. Small red flies would gather in clusters on them. Attempts to catch the flies proved to be unsuccessful. No one knew what species of fly they were, or where they had come from. It made Maddie feel uneasy, almost as if there was a calm before a storm. She did not know why she felt like that. Strange whispers in her head seemed to warn her of something about to happen, but what? Sam had suggested they hold a séance, but each time Maddie had chickened out. She had delved into the history of the Hall, but it had not produced any record of a ghost at Cattingham Hall until recently.

The only dark history, of course, was that of Ursula Underville. Maddie needed to find out more about her. But her laptop was being repaired, and she could not get it back until Monday. Of course she could always find out stuff from the library, but with her mum going away she had been distracted. Maddie thought about Uncle Julian. If Aunt Lydia sold Cattingham Hall it really would be a nightmare. This was Lydia's life. Where would she live? She was sure that if Uncle Julian got his hands on it he would, in his words, 'modernise' it.

His house was a huge white monstrosity. It was modern: a flat-roofed building in chalk-coloured stone. It did not match the Northumbrian countryside. The drive even had white gravel leading up to the house. Once in the house you were met with hunting trophies. Sad-eyed stags and wild boars' heads were mounted on the walls, and a zebra skin rug led you into the smoky sitting room. Inside the room by the fireplace was a stuffed moth-eaten lion. Its glassy, golden eyes gazed out at you ominously. Julian was very proud of his collection of stuffed animals – all, he boasted, that he had shot himself – which was something that Maddie hated hearing him say.

Uncle Julian's wife had left him years before. Cousin Phillip had been brought up by a stream of nannies. His mother now lived in Adelaide, Australia. She never contacted Phillip, and he now only thought about her with anger. Encouraged by his father, he had grown to hate her memory.

It was a relief when Sunday lunch was over and Uncle Julian and Cousin Phillip decided to make tracks. At least now on this occasion Aunt Lydia had not agreed to sell the Hall. Uncle Julian, stony-faced, had got back into his car, and did not even say goodbye to them.

Chapter 3

The minute they had gone the phone rang. This did not surprise Maddie. She knew it would be her best friend Sam Street, who lived with her brother Josh and her parents. Her friend lived in the village of Butterdale, not far from her. Sam would want to know how she had got on with her obnoxious relatives. After answering the phone she proceeded to tell Sam. Both girls then started giggling down the phone.

The six-week school holidays had started four weeks ago. The school Maddie attended was Mount High Senior School at Riding Mount. She had some mixed feelings about it – sometimes loving it, other times hating it …

But six weeks away from Julie Painter and her gang, the school bullies: that would be something she would not miss. She was picked on because her aunt lived at the Hall, but what they didn't know was that their families were probably a lot better off than her aunt. The school holidays had not been a real holiday, what with schoolwork over the period and helping her aunt pick the fruit from the vast gardens. The produce was then sold at the farmers' market. It did bring in a little income, but not a lot. Her aunt also organised cream teas in the sun room. Maddie helped out with them. How much they made was dependent on the weather.

The amateur photographers' club had now also booked one of the furnished rooms once a month. They had booked it one day every month. This was good, as money would come in sooner for her aunt. The club wanted full use of the house and gardens to take photographs, which was not a problem. Aunt Lydia had no objections as long as they kept on paying to hire the room.

Maddie also made a bit of money for herself. She did a cat-sitting job with her friend Sam once a month for Margaret and Ophelia Dee, who lived at the end of the village. They were retired schoolteachers, who lived in a large Swiss-style wooden house. It was a strange-looking house with a wide sloping roof, with precariously supported eaves set at a right angle to the front of the house.

The house had been painted in olive green and had brown shutters, which encased the large dusty windows. Cascading curls of wild ivy poured down the front of the house, and a family of grey squirrels had taken up residence nearby as the property was surrounded by large oak trees and a monkey puzzle tree, which kept it in a permanent gloomy shade.

The Dee sisters had retired from teaching after forty years – a relief to the school, as they had started to become very odd. They had looked after their parents, and had never married or had children. The house, though, was overrun with cats. They were all breeds: a nightmare for the bird world, as they had decimated the bird population in the area. Even the outside of the house had claw marks on the window sills.

The Dee house needed a good clean. This was something Maddie tried half-heartedly to do, but was put off by the cobwebs which brushed against her face. This made her squirm. Lights also did not appear to be something the sisters believed in. Light switches were ignored. Most of the rooms were lit up by candles. But sometimes when Maddie was cat-sitting dark shadows on the walls would fuel what her aunt called her overactive imagination …

It seemed in her mind that the shapes were gradually moving towards her. Often it seemed to her as if they looked like long black fingers wrapping round the back of the furniture and coming towards her. It also didn't help when now and again one of the cats – Timmy, a brown tabby with a bent tail who looked moth-eaten – would let out a strange wail, and would appear to be looking at imaginary objects in front of his nose.

Maddie should have been used to this because Hodge did this all the time at the Hall, but she wasn't.

One Friday afternoon, when Maddie was due to be cat-sitting with her friend Sam, something happened. The sisters had left their usual note on which cat was fed which meal. It was a very detailed note. Maddie had to follow it word for word, or face the wrath of the sisters. As usual she had to separate some of the cats when she fed them, otherwise they would fight.

She had to feed a few of the cats in the basement. It was horrible going down there. There was only a small amount of lighting down there, so she had to screw her eyes up to see. It spooked her, and she had a gut feeling telling her someone was watching her. The basement smelt musty, and the powdery-smelling dust tended to make her sneeze. If the money wasn't so good she would have packed the job in, but jobs were difficult to find in the village for someone her age. So she put up with it.

Friday afternoon had not been good. Sam had not come with her, as her brother Josh was coming back from university and she was excited about seeing him. A big family lunchtime meal had been organised. Sam said she would come later that afternoon. But Maddie did not like being in the house on her own.

Friday at the Dee sisters' house had started off as normal. The Dee sisters were going to an afternoon theatre performance of Le Petit Hubert, which was all in French. Margaret had told her it was about a boy who travels throughout France looking to find the perfect baguette recipe. This play sounded sheer torture to Maddie, who was lousy at French. She didn't let on to the sisters in case they took her under their wing and gave her French lessons.

For the play the sisters had dressed in their trademark Laura Ashley floral velvet dresses, matched with green and purple shawls. On their feet they wore cream leather pointed shoes, which did not match their outfits. They were seemingly oblivious to this – or maybe, Maddie thought, they did not care. Their wiry, white hair had been scraped back into French plaits and they had powdered their faces. Once again they had applied too much rouge because of their short-sightedness, then plastered their thin lips with garish red lipstick.

Every time Maddie looked at them she had to look away. An image of a pair of ventriloquist's puppets came into her mind. But she had to go through her duties with Margaret Dee so she kept her eyes down and pretended to be engrossed in the duties list.

Margaret was the more frightening of the two sisters. She was hatchet-faced with narrow brown eyes, which always appeared to look at her disapprovingly. Maddie had brought a book with her to read later called Lacey Jane. The corner had stuck out at an angle from her satchel. Seeing it Margaret's disapproving, prune withered face grimaced as she then plucked it out of the front pouch of the bag and, after reading the first page, dismissed it and said disparagingly,

"You should not be reading this rubbish. We have plenty of books in our library. I will prepare a reading list for you next time you come." Maddie inwardly groaned and stammered back,

"B-b-but, Miss Dee, this is the book the school has given me to read for my homework. I have to do a review on it when I've finished it."

"Well, then, it shows how your school has gone so downhill. I will have to speak to your school about your reading material. Put the book away and do not continue reading it. Child, now look what you have done. You have lost me in thought ... Where is Samantha?"

Maddie explained that she would be coming later in the afternoon. This did not please Miss Dee. The understanding had always been that the girls would be together. Two for the price of one was the real reason. She was not happy. The sisters were notoriously mean, even though they were believed to be very rich. They owned various houses in Northumberland, some of which they rented out. Maddie then had to listen to Miss Dee's lecture about how teaching standards had fallen since she had left the school. She was only saved from this by Margaret's sister telling her the taxi was outside.

She waved the sisters goodbye, and Maddie gave a sigh of relief as she went back up the stairs. The temperature had dropped very quickly. She had started to feel very cold. A strange thick green fog had begun to envelop the house. This was very odd because it was the afternoon, and the sun had been shining brightly. It also seemed to be turning frosty.

Maddie shivered and quickly opened the door. She came back into the sitting room and stuck her thin white arms into her thick navy cardigan. The wood burner needed stoking up, so Maddie quickly piled up wooden sticks from the basket of kindling. The room quickly became cosy, if a bit smoky. It would have been lovely to stay in this room all night, but the cats had to be fed. Besides, one of her favourite cats, Oscar, the tortoiseshell was already wrapping herself round her jean-clad legs with bursts of ecstatic purring.

Maddie began to read Margaret's spidery handwritten notes. She fed Oscar first. Then she fed a short-haired black cat called Tobias, then the ginger tabby cross Clementine, then Timmy, the mackerel tabby ... then finally, Thomasina, the oldest cat, a long-haired calico cat with two protruding front teeth. Maddie took five silver bowls, a bucket filled with dried cat food, and some packets of sealed cat food pouches, and made her way down to the basement.

There were already some clean cat bowls down there. She opened the basement door, switched the light on, and went gingerly down the stairs. The sudden excited wail of the cats in the basement when they heard her almost deafened her.

The cats in the basement came in from the downstairs cat flap. They were nearly all ginger, apart from one black one. She could not handle these cats: previous attempts had ended with her being covered in scratches. The sisters had had the majority of them neutered but there were still two intact tomcats, who were completely wild. Margaret had not managed to get hold of them to get them castrated.

Finally, with all the cats fed, Maddie filled their water bowls for them. But curiosity once more got the better of her.

The basement was large, with a small side room with another door leading on from it. You were then met with an overpowering smell of cat pee, which would make you gasp for your breath. No matter how many times Maddie bleached the floor the strong smell of urine still lingered.

The cellar was on left-hand side of the basement. She had never been in there, because she had always been too nervous. It tended to look a bit creepy. This time bravery took over, and she opened the small white dirty wooden door. It creaked ominously when she opened it. It was empty inside, but a network of hexagon-shaped cobwebs covered the inside the door. A dripping noise seemed to be coming from inside it, but she could not see any water. Disappointed, she went to close the door. Almost immediately a scratching noise started to come from inside the door, then what sounded like feet coming up the cellar steps with something being dragged behind them. As she slammed the door shut all she could think was that there had been nothing there when she opened the cellar door.

"Who is there?" she shouted from the outside the door.

Alarm bells were now ringing inside her ears, and her voice was almost strangled with fear as she shouted the same question. But she received no reply. The footsteps sounded heavy-footed, and appeared to still continue to come up the cellar steps. Then came the sound of dripping water again.

"Who is there?" she shouted once more.

But no one answered. Terrified, Maddie made to run back up the stairs. But she tripped over Raven, the only black cat in the basement, and came half sliding back down the wooden steps with a bump. As she struggled to get up she felt something touch her. It was a hand, which then wrapped itself round her ankle and held on to it tightly. The fingers round her ankle felt cold and wet. Then came strange whisperings in her ear. She screamed as she broke free from whatever had held her. Half racing up the stairs in terror, she turned round to see who had done this.

There was no one there.

Shaking and her heart hammering she locked the basement behind her and ran to the telephone, but stopped suddenly when she got to it. If she phoned the police they would think she had imagined it. Had she? The hand on her ankle had seemed so realistic. When she rolled up her trouser leg and looked at her ankle she saw that an outline of fingers round her ankle had appeared, but the red marks slowly started to disappear.

When she looked back at the cellar door she saw nothing. The cellar was not very big.

"Surely I would have seen someone trying to hide in there," she thought.

Instead of telephoning the police she phoned Sam and explained what had happened to her. Sam said she would come round with her brother. They had finished the family meal, so Josh would drive straight up. Sam would get him to check the basement for her.

In the meantime Maddie went outside the house. Her heart was still hammering. It was freezing cold outside. The fog had lifted, but it was better than being inside. She sat and waited for them, and sat on the two-seater pink floral sofa that had been left next to the

20

dustbins because it was now threadbare. It seemed like an eternity until Sam and Josh arrived in Josh's battered red Fiesta.

Josh gave her a concerned look as he got out of the car with Sam, and he asked her if she was all right. She nodded and said,

"Josh, you haven't said anything to your mum, have you?"

"No, of course not," came the reply.

"Josh, I was in the basement and I thought I heard footsteps from the cellar. I became frightened and ran up the stairs, but tripped over Raven. I felt something grab me. I honestly don't think I imagined it. It was as if a hand had grabbed my ankle. It was really frightening."

Instead of rubbishing her story he told Sam and her to stay outside, and he would check the basement. Ten minutes later he came out of the house.

"I couldn't find anything, Maddie, apart from some rat droppings, so there is nothing to be worried about. No one could have escaped from there if you had locked the basement door. The cellar is tiny. It must have been rats brought in by the cats scratching about the place."

"But I could hear someone coming up the stairs, Josh, and what touched my ankle? It couldn't have been a rat. Surely it would have bitten me if it had been. My ankle had red finger marks on it."

"It's just rats, Maddie. Maybe one brushed against you. They are rife round here. As to your ankle … maybe you did that yourself, and were unaware that you had done it.

"And don't you think the cats would have gone crazy if there had been someone in the basement?" continued Josh, his Adam's apple bobbing up and down as he spoke.

"I never thought of that," agreed Maddie. "Yes, you are right. They would have been demented if anyone had been in the basement, wouldn't they? Well, it spooked me. I have never been so frightened. I really thought something was trying to grab me. Those marks on my leg really did look like hand marks."

"You have imagined it. Forget it. Anyway, what time do the Dee sisters come home?"

"Seven," Maddie replied.

"OK. I'll drive you both back home when they come back."

"Thanks, Josh," replied Maddie.

"Hey, Josh … it does seem odd, though, don't you think?" said Sam.

Not wanting to encourage her in case she started her 'ghost stuff' again, Josh ignored his sister's comment.

Sam shrugged. She had expected him to do that. He always did. But to her it seemed really strange, so she had no intention of letting her theories lie dormant …

Maddie felt a lot better after hearing what Josh had said. He was like a brother to her. Currently he was going through a growth spurt. He was now six feet two but still growing, with the build of a basketball player. His feet were also growing, and were now a size fourteen.

Sam and Josh were very alike: green-eyed, with long, thin faces and wavy, slightly reddish-brown hair. Sam was much taller than Maddie, and carried her height well. She could wear any clothes and they would suit her, unlike Maddie, who was sometimes swamped by clothes because of her tiny frame and height.

They went back into the house. Three of the cats circled them affectionately. With Josh and Sam stroking them Maddie went into the kitchen to make coffee. She filled the kettle with water and glanced over at the basement door. Then she went over to it and checked it was still locked, only relaxing when she saw that the rusty grey key was stuck firmly in the lock.

The kitchen was in an old-fashioned 1950s decor. It was painted white, with light blue wooden units. The shelves were rounded at the end of the units for extra storage. The larder was white. Inside it was filled with tins and preserves. Large food items were covered in see-through plastic containers. There was food wrapped in waxed white paper, which looked grubby, and was something that Maddie thought only the sisters would eat. The only good thing was that there were no mice in there which was surprising considering the poor hygiene...

Maddie would eat her chocolate digestives at the house, which she brought from home with her. The sisters tended to never throw food away, even if it was past its sell-by date. Maddie came into the cluttered sitting room, handed out the drinks and biscuits to Sam and Josh, and asked them,

"How is your mum?"

Sam answered,

"She is getting better. Dad is getting her out of the house more. Her hair is still white. The doctor says it might never get back to its normal colour."

Maddie felt gloomy at hearing this. If Sam's mother had not dropped off clothes for the village jumble sale for Lydia at the Hall she might never have seen the ghost. Sam and Josh's mother had seen the apparition when she had gone into the kitchen to find Lydia. Her mother had been found unconscious on the stone floor of the kitchen. Efforts to revive her had been unsuccessful.

The doctor had then been called. He had at last managed to wake her up, but she had bruised her hip when she had fallen. Once she was fully conscious again she had then recounted what had happened.

On entering the kitchen at Cattingham Hall she had heard someone humming, but when she looked around she could not see where it was coming from. Thinking it was Lydia she shouted "Hello," but received no answer. The kitchen at Cattingham Hall was huge, with a large wooden table made of pine in the centre of the room. Half-chopped vegetables and peelings lay on the table, but there was no sign of her friend. The kitchen door had been open so the accountant's wife went outside, but could not see her.

As she looked out of the window all she could see was an enormous black raven perched on the fence post outside. It was such a beautiful bird, with inky blue eyes. She soon became fascinated by it and looked at admiringly. Time went by and she forgot to look for her friend until she became aware of someone standing beside her, humming. Thinking it was Lydia, she asked her where she had been without turning round.

When Lydia did not reply Valerie turned round, smiling, but the amused look on her face turned to horror.

Staring back down at her was a ghostly apparition. In place of eyes were electric blue orbs. It was a tall young woman with a white, angular face and long thin nose, but the skin on the left side of her

23

face was hideously disfigured. Uneven scar tissue ran in thick tramlines across her face, and down her shoulders dripped long wet black hair. Droplets of water from the ghost then began to gather in puddles on to stone floor.

Valerie Street, could only look back in shocked horror and listen to sound of the water dripping on to the floor. She became fixed to the spot and unable to move her body, then one of the apparition's long dripping wet fingers stretched towards her. A wet finger slowly touched her mouth. Valerie's lips almost immediately went icy cold. Then they began to burn.

That was all she could remember. Much later, when Lydia had come in from the garden after going out there to pick some bunches of tarragon for her baked chicken recipe, she had tried to open the back door – but an object was blocking it. Lydia had then given it a final thrust with the side of her body, and it had opened. Behind the door she found Valerie Street lying on the stone floor of the kitchen. Her body had been blocking the door. When Valerie finally opened her eyes she came face to face to Lydia staring anxiously beside her, with the doctor speaking to her in a gentle tone. She remained in shock for some time.

Josh had never seen the ghost. He was not sure if he believed in them, and thought his mum had imagined it … Sam, on the other hand, did – and revelled in anything like that, even saying that she had seen ghosts. She had told people of her theories, but no one took her seriously. Hooked on programmes such as Just Haunted, or anything with a ghostly theme, she strongly believed there was an afterlife.

Maddie, of course, believed in ghosts. Too many things had happened at the Hall to her for her not to believe in them. She had told Sam about objects moving about in her room at the Hall when she was in bed. When she did drop off she would have broken sleep and hear voices whispering and then strange scratching noises, but on opening her eyes and putting the light on there would be nothing there. Even the library seemed to contain a ghostly presence.

Hodge had raced out of the library once because the books had begun pouring out of the shelves. There had been no wind in the room to cause the books to come off them. She did not even bother mentioning this to Lydia. Hodge, however, never forgot this. Wary now, she would only go in the library if the door was wide open.

After Josh and Sam had had their coffee Maddie started grooming Thomasina, which was one of the jobs on the list. As she was talking Sam stretched her long legs and took off one of her frog-patterned socks. She twirled it round her finger and let Thomasina swipe at it with her paw, and said, yawning,

"You know all these strange things that are happening at the Hall – don't you think it might be the ghost trying to tell you something? Whenever I go to your house I always feel there is some type of presence there. I even feel something is watching me."

"You sense it as well ... I even feel it in here now," said Maddie suddenly, in a half whisper.

Sam, on seeing the interested look on Maddie's face, seized the opportunity and said quickly,

"Sorry, I didn't really want to say this to you ... but don't you think things are getting worse at the Hall?" Josh, who had been engrossed in the local newspaper, looked up annoyed and retorted,

"Oh, Sam ... you and your imagination. Don't frighten her. You say you are psychic, yet you haven't even seen the supposed Cattingham ghost."

"Well, Josh ... Mum has, hasn't she? Anyway, you have to admit there are weird things happening in the village. The Historical Group even found some animal skeletons in Brocket Woods. Can you remember that they said the skeletons were of two enormous dogs with cloven feet? The villagers said they were believed to have been phantom hellhounds summoned by the witches from the Underworld, as far back as the 1400s. Their skeletons were, they said, at least seven feet in length."

Josh sighed in reply he had this story numerous times from his sister and said,

"Oh, here we go again. You are always talking about that story. It's like an old record. What a load of codswallop. It's just hearsay. If it was true surely we would have had the press round here. How come nothing else was ever said about it? With all the talk going round the village about the Hall everyone's imagination has gone in overdrive. If there were skeletons of that size why are they not in some museum now? And the ghost stuff is utter rubbish. Remember, I used to help Titch with the gardens at the Hall all the time before I went to Uni. I was always in the kitchen. I never saw anything."

"Well, maybe it doesn't want to talk to you because you are so mind-blowingly boring. If you saw the ghost you would give it a lecture on conservation. Hang on, there's an idea … it would leave the Hall after it heard your ramblings. You would bore it senseless."

This made Josh and Maddie laugh. Their laugher half woke Thomasina, who now – thoroughly groomed – had settled on the arm of a chair. Maddie, while they spoke, raked the thick tufts of cat fur out of the comb and placed them in the bin. Sam, however, was now in overdrive and continued,

"I know what we should do – hold a séance at the Hall."

"You are out of your head, Sam," came Josh's now irate reply. "That is a stupid idea. Those crazy programmes about the paranormal are soaking up into your brain, and taking what little you have of it."

"Oh, shut up, Josh. I am talking to Maddie, not you. So mind your own business. This is what we should do. If we don't, more things will happen at the Hall. The ghost is trying to make contact. It's obvious. Don't you agree, Maddie?"

"I don't know, Sam. What if the spirit tries to hurt us? And Aunt Lydia would never agree to this."

"Well, it didn't hurt my mum, did it?"

"I know, but it did make her hair go white – and it might make things worse at the Hall. My aunt would go mental if she found out we were going to do that."

Sam could not persuade Maddie to hold a séance and – annoyed, and not having backup from Josh – stomped off into the dining room, exasperated with the pair of them. Maddie went to go after her but Josh stopped her and said,

"She'll be fine. You know what a miserable git she is when she doesn't get her own way. Leave her a bit. She will come round to our way of thinking."

"OK. I suppose you are right, Josh."

Maddie should have been used to her friend's mood swings. Fortunately Sam always bounced back after she was left on her own.

To take her mind off it she went into the kitchen and proceeded to go through the sisters' jobs list. It was not just cat-sitting. She had to fold all the towels, tea towels, and jumpers out of the drier, along with the underwear. The first time she had done this it had made her laugh. The sisters' identical cream woollen vests and big knickers were all practically falling apart. But the sisters rarely threw anything out, and had even stitched their names in them so there was no cause for confusion. The bins also had to be emptied in the kitchen and the sitting room.

But the worst bit was that Maddie now had to go and groom Raven. He was in the basement.

"Josh," she shouted, "Can you come with me into the basement? I have to groom Raven."

Josh nodded and came out of the sitting room, and they unlocked the basement door. He walked ahead of Maddie as she walked hesitatingly after him down the steps.

Raven was easy to find. He appeared out of one of the many scattered wicker baskets and made kitten-like meows in response to her calling him. The basement had a white plastic cat flap on the coal chute. The outdoor cats would only stay in this room, and would panic if any attempts were made to get them into other rooms in the house. Raven came running to her, but on checking her hand he was disappointed that there were no cat treats there for him. As he started nudging her hand to get some attention Maddie produced a green wooden cat brush out of her pocket.

In the meantime Josh had a thorough search of the basement once again, and said,

"There's nothing here, Maddie. Look: the cellar door is open, and there is still nothing there."

"I think I'm going to have to put that episode down as my imagination then, I suppose, Josh."

She smiled, giving a small smile while taking the loose hairs off Raven. It was a long job. He was long-haired and had a habit of getting bits of twigs stuck in his tail and legs. She worked quite well until she came to a well-sucked knotted piece of fur on his tail, and worked gently round it. The wet, sticky fur came away as she gave a final tug. But this action annoyed Raven and, losing patience, he bit her hand. In surprise Maddie dropped the brush, and it bounced off the stone floor. As she bent down to pick it up she noticed that the floor was quite dusty, and she had to pick it out of bits sawdust and wood chippings.

Then her eyes picked up something else: a footprint in the sawdust on the bottom of the stairs. It was quite distinct, and showed a footprint much bigger than her size fours by at least two inches … It was long and narrow. But there were six toes on one of the feet. It was a very clear imprint.

"Josh, look," she shouted to him, almost screaming the words.

He came over and as she looked at it in stunned silence, said,

"What?"

"Look. The footprint."

"Where did that come from?"

"I don't know, but that proves someone has been in the cellar. See: I'm not going mad, Josh. It is a footprint I am looking at, isn't it?"

"This is mad stuff. It looks like one … more of a woman's footprint, because it is quite narrow. But look at the six toes. What person has six toes? How the hell did it get in here? There is no other way out apart from the back door in the basement, and it is locked. The key must be with the Dee sisters."

Maddie started to feel cold inside. So she had not imagined it. The footprint was on the bottom of the stairs. The Dee sisters' feet were much smaller. So it certainly wasn't theirs. Had the foot belonged to the person who had tried to grab her? And, if it was, why had she not seen them when she turned round? Then another thought came into her head, something she had been trying to blot out.

"Josh, I think the ghost has followed me from Cattingham Hall to the Dee sisters' house. What does it want with me?"

The sheer frustration of it all became too much for her, and she started to cry. She had bottled up her feelings for so long without telling anyone how really frightened she was. She hadn't said much to Lydia in case she ended up having to stay at Uncle Julian's. Warm tears poured down her face. She could not stop crying. Josh put his arm round her and said,

"Maddie, I am sure there must be a rational explanation to all this." But he was at a loss to say what the answer was, and looked helplessly at her.

"I know what the answer is," came a voice at the top of the basement stairs.

It was Sam.

"The answer is that the ghost wants to contact Maddie. She has to do a séance and speak to it, or it will never leave her alone."

"Sam, don't start all that again. Can't you see Maddie is upset? For Christ's sake leave it alone, and stop going on about it."

A tear-stained Maddie broke into their conversation and said,

"Josh, don't you see? She's right. I have to do this. If we find out what the ghost wants, or if there is someone it wants us to contact, it may then leave me in peace."

Maddie wiped her damp eyes and gave Josh a weak smile. It wasn't just the ghosts that had upset her. It was the fact her mum was in Africa, and she wouldn't be seeing until after the school holidays. Her mum used Skype to contact her twice a week, but it wasn't the same as seeing her and being able to have a hug when she needed one.

She loved Lydia. But she really missed her mum. It was the longest time they had ever been away from each other. Her father had died when she was born, so her mother and her Aunt Lydia and her late Uncle Akkoubian were the only relatives she had ever been close to. There were no grandparents still alive on either side of the family. They had all died a long time ago. She had an Aunt Persephone, but she lived in the Scottish Highlands and she hardly ever saw her. Since moving to Meadowfield recently she had not made any friends, apart from Sam and Josh. She had not told anyone apart from Sam about Julie Painter bullying her.

Without Sam and Josh she would have been very lonely.

After coming out of the basement Maddie and Josh, following Sam, walked back up the basement stairs. When she went back into the sitting room a troubled Maddie gave Oscar a stroke, but he was fast asleep and unaware of her. His nose snuggled deep into the hand-knitted throw on the light brown leather recliner. She brightened up after stroking the dozing cat. Maddie then did a last check of the Dee sisters' list.

The only remaining thing to do was empty the waste bins and drag the dustbin down to the front of the house. Then, last of all, she had to rinse the milk bottles and place them on the doorstep. So with the jobs all done she settled to watch television on the settee, hoping Josh and Sam would join her and pack in their arguing. She started to feel a bit better. Josh and Sam came into the room chatting to each other in a friendly fashion. They must have had a ceasefire, thought a relieved Maddie.

"I've finished the jobs off. I've got some more biscuits if you want them," she said to the pair.

"That's OK," said Josh. "I'll get something when I go home. Chocolate digestives with cat hairs on are not very nice. I think I still have one of Raven's hairs lodged in the back of my throat." He pulled a face as he spoke.

Sam – seemingly oblivious to this remark – took the packet, took some biscuits out, and then greedily munched on them, washing them down with a can of Sprite she had taken out of her purple leather messenger bag ...

Nothing more was said about the séance.

But Maddie had already made her mind up. She was going to do the séance. It was best, though, she thought, to speak to Sam with Josh not there. The only question would be when they were going to do the séance. Maybe they could do it when Aunt Lydia was out, or in Maddie's bedroom. Sam could have a sleepover at the Hall, Maddie thought.

The Dee sisters then arrived home. They were annoyed Josh was there until Maddie explained that she thought she had heard something in the basement. She only gave them the most basic of details, knowing they would not believe what had really happened. As she spoke Margaret rudely butted in and asked Maddie if Josh was her boyfriend. This made Maddie go bright red.

"I don't have a boyfriend, Miss Dee."

"You haven't been kissing and cuddling him in the house, have you?" replied Margaret, sharply glaring at her, which resulted in the teacher's nervous squint in her right eye coming back. Maddie was so embarrassed that she could not look at Josh, and only mumbled answers back to Margaret's interrogating questions.

Luckily Ophelia, who was bored with the cross-questioning, came to Maddie's rescue and said she would look in the basement. She opened the basement door and went down the stairs, returning a couple of minutes later.

"Well, there is certainly nothing down there," she said impatiently to Maddie. "You must have imagined it."

"Yes, I suppose you are right. No, wait. There is a footprint down there. I'll show you."

She went down the basement with Ophelia and pointed at the ground. To her annoyance the footprint had gone.

"It was there. Josh saw it."

Ophelia just looked at her and sighed. Then, rolling her eyes, she went back up the basement steps.

Upstairs Ophelia asked Josh if he had seen anything. He said that he too had seen the footprint, but he was given the same unbelieving look. Maddie shut up quickly, not wanting to talk about the matter further or answer any more questions about Josh. Being accused of kissing and cuddling Josh had been gross. Why, he was like a brother to her. Ugh. What a horrible thought. The thought of it made her squirm inside. She put her coat on as Ophelia handed the cat-sitting money over and asked,

"How is Hodge?"

"Fine, Miss Dee. She sleeps most of the time."

"Hmm. She needs stimulation. You need to spend more time with her," Ophelia reprimanding her, and added,

"The way people treat cats is disgraceful. If I had it my way people would be vetted before they were allowed to own a cat."

The rant did not seem to be aimed at Maddie in particular, just aimed at all cat owners in general. The younger sister, Ophelia, was not such a frightening presence. Her face was much softer.

She had (according to Titch) been stunning when she was young – and there had even been talk of a romance with a soldier, but it never came to anything. Her mother had been overbearing, and had wanted the sisters to look after her and not get married. Titch had

31

hinted that the mother, according to village gossip, had been the reason why the romance between Ophelia and the soldier had failed.

Still embarrassed about the boyfriend incident, Maddie hurriedly gathered her things together and went outside with Sam and Josh. Just as she was getting into the back of the car she turned as she felt Margaret's cold gaze on her. It felt very intimidating, and she had to look away.

Chapter 4

After Josh and Sam dropped Maddie off at the Hall her aunt opened the door and hung Maddie's coat up. They then went into the kitchen and Lydia started preparing their tea. Telling Lydia that Margaret Dee had accused her of kissing and cuddling Josh made Lydia burst out laughing.

"Oh, Aunt Lydia, it was embarrassing. I am sure she didn't believe me."

"Well, who knows? Maybe one day you might want to kiss and cuddle him," came her aunt's response through tears of laughter.

"That is never going to happen. It is so gross. I don't even want to ever think about it again," said Maddie, as she went red and shook her head in undisguised horror.

"Oh, Maddie, I am only joking. Come on, then. Let's see what's on the television," said her aunt, deciding not to tease her niece any further on the subject.

Later, after watching a strange science fiction film, Maddie felt tired and climbed up the stairs leading to her bedroom. The attic room bedroom was on the fourth floor. It was a large double room with a walk-in oak wardrobe which filled the length of one wall. At the top of the room was a washbasin in the corner. There was a bedside table and a large rosewood chest of drawers in the corner. A white wicker rocking chair lay with its back to the window, to its right was an old dining room chair sat on by Maddie when she worked on her laptop.

The bed was an enormous brass four-poster covered in a hand-knitted pink patchwork quilt and layers of wool blankets. It had been Lydia's bed when she was a girl. Hanging on one of the bed knobs was a little blue polka-dot bag that Sam had filled with dried lavender and sewn up for her.

After washing her face and cleaning her teeth Maddie changed into her pyjamas. Her eyes were half closed as she walked to the bed. Because she was not looking where she was going she nearly tripped. To steady herself she grabbed one of the brass bed knobs but as it was old it was worn and, through the years, had developed a sharp edge. It cut into her thumb.

"Ouch," she shouted to herself.

It then started to bleed, so she quickly ran it under the tap. It seemed as if it would bleed for ever. As far as she could see it just looked like a paper cut, so was nothing serious. She grabbed some tissues from a box on her bedside and wiped the watery blood away, then wrapped her finger up in some tissues that she had folded in two. Finally she tied a spare tissue round it, hoping it would stay on. Fatigue set in and she could not be bothered with it any longer, and just wanted to go to sleep.

Once in bed with the light switched off she was soon asleep.

Nearby the silent figure of a young woman watched her in the doorway. Her long dark hair fell down her shoulders. She was very tall, and her profile bewitching. It was only when she turned round that you could her face looked like it had been slashed down one side of it. She remained there for a long time, only disappearing in the early hours of the morning.

Oblivious to this, Maddie had fallen into a deep, hypnotic sleep, which developed into nightmares.

In her dream she was trapped in a dark, wet place. It was pitch black, and there was a strong smell of damp wood. She could hear voices, which became louder. They seemed to be talking, but she could not understand what they were saying. This did not feel like a dream. It felt real. Her fingers scratched at a wooden lid, which she found was covering her face. She tried to force it open, but it would not open. The lid was too heavy.

Her voice in the dream then became hoarse from screaming. She wiggled her toes. She was starting to get cramp. The dream had her wearing a white dress, which was damp. She could not move around in the tiny place she was trapped in.

"Help me, someone. Please help me," she shouted.

But no one came.

Then she lost her voice completely. She had a feeling of helplessness and utter desolation. That was when the loud banging started. In her dream she tried screaming again, but her voice only came out in whispers. Her despair made tears pour down her cheeks. It was in the early hours of the morning that she woke up with a jolt. Her pillow was wet, and tears were pouring from her from eyes.

"This is crazy," she thought. "It is only a dream.

"Ouch."

The side of her face really hurt. It burnt her finger when she touched it. She raised herself up and got out of bed. She switched the light on and touched her face. She felt drops of blood on it, and thought she had scratched it in her sleep. She ran the cold tap and splashed it with water … When she peered in the mirror there didn't seem to be anything there. It was odd.

But the strange dream had been very unsettling.

Drying her face with the rough towel on the side of the basin was painful. She became aware of an object on the soap dish that she had never seen before. She picked it up. It seemed to be a lace bouquet, filled with what looked like dark green leaves of parsley. On sniffing it she could smell a strong smell of celery.

"What is that?" was her immediate thought. "How did it get here? And why is it wrapped in strange-looking lace?"

She cleaned her room. Aunt Lydia rarely came in her room, so where had the bouquet come from? With the cold water soothing her face she started to feel a bit better, and she decided she would ask her aunt about the strange object in the morning. She remembered her bleeding finger and glanced at it. The tissue paper had come off, and had probably stuck somewhere in the sheets. Tomorrow she would have to remember to look for it in her bed …

At least her finger had stopped bleeding. It had a nasty cut, but there was no antiseptic in her room. She did not want to wake her aunt up by looking in the medicine cupboard for antiseptic. Lydia would give her some in the morning, she thought. Then she climbed back into bed and switched the light off. This time she slept soundly. When she woke up at 8 a.m. and got up and glanced in the mirror she laughed. Her hair was sticking up all angles. Flattening it down with her hand was a wasted effort.

She shivered, and put on the purple spotty fleece dressing gown her mother had bought her. It had the comforting smell of her mother's perfume on it. Feeling it she nuzzled the thick fleece shawl collar to her face and breathed in the faint smell of bluebells. As she picked up the soap to wash her face she remembered the lace bouquet …

It had not been a dream. This time she studied it more carefully. The lace looked old. It was not white but yellow, with unpleasant-looking black spots on it that looked like mildew. After washing and drying her face she put the object in her dressing gown pocket and put her slippers on.

As she came downstairs she could smell bacon. When she went into the kitchen Aunt Lydia kissed her on her cheek and continued turning the double-yolk eggs that she was frying in the pan. Aunt Lydia said,

"Good morning, Maddie. I heard you getting up. I thought we would have a fry-up before going back to your mother's house today. Whatever have you done to your hair?"

Maddie giggled. Every morning her hair always stuck up, no matter how many times she brushed it the night before to flatten it down.

"It always seems to stick up like that in the morning. I'm not sure why."

"I think you have inherited your Uncle Akkoubian's hair," answered Lydia drily, and they both laughed. Lydia then said,

"Maddie … take the teapot into the breakfast room, will you, and come back for the milk?"

"OK," said Maddie, her mouth-watering at the smell of the sizzling bacon.

After placing the teapot on its brown ceramic teapot stand on the breakfast table she went back into the kitchen, gathered up the plate of buttered bread and the milk jug, and put both on the table. Lydia then came in with two steaming helpings of sausages, eggs, bacon, mushrooms, tomatoes, and beans, which filled the plates. Even a triangle of fried bread lay on the side.

"Aunt Lydia, this is so good," said Maddie.

"That's exactly what Akkoubian used to say," her aunt replied. "But I had to stop cooking breakfasts like this for him because of his health."

As they tucked into breakfast Maddie took the lace bouquet out of her pocket.

"Look what I found in my room. I don't know where it's come from."

She handed it to Lydia, who turned it around and replied by saying,

"What a strange thing, Maddie. It is very old, by the look of it, and that looks like lovage."

"I thought you might have found it and put it there to show me."

"No, I didn't. I have never seen it before. But whatever have you done to your finger?"

Maddie's thumb had started to go purple, and was extremely swollen.

"I scratched it on the bed knob," replied Maddie, as she tucked into mouthfuls of mushrooms.

"Oh, it looks quite sore. It will need cleaning, and some antiseptic put on it. We'll clean it up after breakfast. Actually the lovage in the bouquet would have been good, as it is a good herb to prevent infection. It's a shame it's so old and dirty. We could have rubbed some on your finger. Did you know that in medieval times lovage was used to cure various ailments? But you can't use this, of course. It is filthy. I'll put it in the bin after breakfast."

As she reached out to pour the tea into the cups the table started to rattle. Out of nowhere came a thin wind that blew over the table and caused the milk jug to bounce up and spill, resulting in a river of milk being poured over Lydia's wrist.

"How on earth did that happen?" said Lydia, dabbing at the spilt milk with her cloth napkin. "Where did that wind come from? The windows are shut."

It was puzzling. As she helped her aunt to mop up the milk Maddie didn't reply. She just thought the answer: the ghost was up to its tricks. If Aunt Lydia didn't know anything about the lace bouquet then the ghost must have given it to her as a present to heal her cut. Surely that was good, as it meant it meant her no harm. Well, that was that. She was going to hold a séance with Sam no matter what.

She picked up the lace bouquet and said to Lydia,

"I'll throw the bouquet away," and she picked it up and put it back in her pocket.

But she had no intention of doing this. If the ghost wanted her to rub this on her finger that was what she was going to do. The room suddenly seemed to go back to being calm, and they finished breakfast.

After Maddie had cleared the dirty dishes from the table and placed them in the sink she covered them with soapy water. Lydia then started washing up. Maddie dried and put them away.

Being small, she had to stretch to reach the china cupboard. At home they just used the dishwasher all the time but her aunt refused to have one, and all crockery was washed in the sink. This could be a real pain when a lot of people came, and Maddie could not understand why she would not get one.

After drying the dishes Maddie felt inside her pocket for the bouquet. She rubbed her sore finger against the herbs. The lace felt harsh against her skin. She would have continued rubbing her finger against it if Lydia had not noticed and said,

"Maddie what are you doing? Have you still got that filthy thing in your pocket? For heaven's sake, throw it in the bin."

Maddie did as she was told, and reluctantly threw the lace bouquet into the kitchen bin. In the meantime Lydia went out of the kitchen and came back with some antiseptic and a plaster. She then bathed and dried Maddie's finger.

"How strange ... the purple swelling seems to have gone down, and it doesn't looks as bad as I thought. Still ... we'll give it a good clean and dry it, and put some antiseptic and a plaster on it. That should do the trick."

Once the plaster was placed on Maddie's finger Lydia told her to get showered and dressed so they could check on her mother's house and then left the room.

Chapter 5

Half an hour later Maddie was ready, and waiting for Lydia. She hated being in Lydia's car, which was an old blue Hindustan Ambassador. The trouble was that Aunt Lydia was a terrible driver. Behind the wheel her aunt became a snarling beast, with her anger directed at motorists who – she felt – did not follow the Highway Code correctly. Fortunately this would not be a long drive.

Maddie's house was not far – about three miles from the Hall. Maddie lived at no. 3 Horse Croft Cottages. It was a small white stone-built cottage in line with the other cottages next to it. Lydia parked outside the cottage and, after removing the key from under the fifth grey stone under a planter by the front path, opened the door. As they entered it the yellow primrose air freshener gave off a sweet smell.

There was some post on the horsehair mat but Lydia, on quickly glancing at it, saw nothing for her sister Julia (it was just advertising). Maddie immediately ran up the wooden stairs to her room and picked out two books, and placed them in her rucksack. Then she added a strawberry lip salve and two fleece tops from the top of her wardrobe, as it was getting so cold at the Hall.

The bedroom was completely different from the Hall. It was very modern, and her quilt was a blue tartan with lilac sheets. In the corner of the room there were boxes of different crafts piled up in a wooden tea chest that Maddie had completed. The furniture was in a milk toffee-coloured wood. The room was filled with a huge chest of drawers, a single wardrobe, an ottoman, and two bookshelves. There was also a furry blue recliner that Maddie loved to swirl herself round on, and a white portable television was perched on a small wooden table. The pale blue curtains gave the room a feel of freshness and neatness. Maddie had always been a tidy child, which was something completely alien to Sam. Sam's bedroom always looked as if it had been burgled.

As she came out of her bedroom she peered into her mother's room. A new black angora cardigan was draped casually over a green

Lloyd Loom chair. Recognising it as she sniffed at the air she breathed in the overpowering fragrance of the Jo Malone's scent Red Roses in the room. As she closed the bedroom door quickly she gulped back raw hot tears which clung to the back of her dry throat. But a common sense voice in her head soothed her telling her that it would not be much longer before her mum came home.

By the time she came downstairs Lydia had emptied the out-of-date food items from the fridge and placed them in a black bin liner. Dettol was sprayed quickly on the surfaces, and she then vacuumed the house. With everything done Lydia asked Maddie if she had everything she needed.

Maddie looked down as she nodded back in reply, still thinking about her mother. However, it was obvious by her face that she was upset. This did not go unnoticed by her aunt, who said,

"Come on, let's go to The Maltsters now we've finished up here," and she gave her niece a gentle hug as they went out of the door.

The Maltsters was regarded as the best coffee shop in the village. Maddie and Sam loved it. The cakes were home-made, and enormous. With the door locked and the key placed back under the stone they walked out to the car. While her aunt was getting her car keys out of her bag Maddie turned and looked to her right when she heard a loud croaking. Perched on the apple blossom tree on the communal green facing her was an enormous black raven. She pointed this out to Lydia, who was now opening the car door, and said,

"Look at that bird. I think it's watching us."

"No, it's not, Maddie. It's looking at the bread Mrs Ferguson has put out." But the bird was not looking at the bread. It was looking directly at Maddie. The bird's head turned to one side. The blue-black eyes seemed to gaze without blinking at her.

"Come on, get in the car," said Lydia, now losing interest in the bird. Maddie gave one last glance at the bird, got in the passenger seat of the car, and closed the door behind her. When she got to the door of the coffee shop Lydia bumped into her friends Kitty and Ava. The talk in Maddie's mind appeared to be all about the fancy dress charity night and the Women's Institute bake-off ...

Ava was an amazing cook, and belonged to something called The Secret Cake Society. It seemed to Maddie to involve a group of furtive men and women who met every two months in a secret destination to parade new cake recipes to each other. It was extremely competitive, and Ava would get very angry if anyone appeared to be anywhere near as good at baking as her. Maddie tended to switch off and just nod now and again when required whenever Lydia met her friends.

However, this time the conversation turned to the crypt being flooded so her ears pricked up.

"That's a bad sign," said Ava.

"Whatever do you mean?" asked Lydia.

"Well … it's supposed to bring bad luck, isn't it, Lydia?"

"I've no idea, Ava. Wherever did you get that idea?"

"Just talk in the village – and, of course, the heavy rain has brought an onslaught of those giant rats, from what I heard," was the reply.

Lydia just shrugged it off.

"The rats are a nuisance, but they are hardly going to attack anyone, are they? They are probably more frightened of us than we are of them. As for all the gossip about the Hall … I should be used to that, what with the wailing ghost that everyone appears to have seen – well, apart from me.

"Still, I have more important things to think about. I have a hungry niece to feed, so we'll have to get going … Lovely seeing you both. Shall we make arrangements for the fancy dress charity night? How about coming round next Thursday … say 11 a.m.?"

Kitty and Ava nodded in unison as they said goodbye to them.

"What did Ava mean about the crypt being unlucky because it had been flooded?" Maddie asked.

"Oh, nothing. It's the usual gossip. Forget she said it. The weather has been atrocious, and that's why the crypt flooded. There is nothing supernatural about that."

Maddie would not be swayed, and continued asking,

"Do we have giant rats at the Hall?"

41

"Well, yes. There were some very large ones that Titch came across when the coffins were placed back in the crypt, but it was just their skeletons that he found. They looked very old, so I doubt that we have any live ones there. Giant rats were rife at the Hall at one point, but they died out a long time ago. They never harmed anyone, though."

"Aunt Lydia, do you think the ghost has appeared since the crypt flooded?"

"Oh, Maddie, of course not. It's all rubbish, the talk that's going on. Do you not think that if anyone had seen the ghost at the Hall it would have been either your late Uncle Akkoubian or me? But we have seen nothing in all the years we have lived there."

However Maddie continued to argue the point and said,

"But other people have seen the ghost. Mrs Carstairs from the antique shop did. Remember, she came to value some of Uncle Akkoubian's book collection. She saw the ghost in the gallery when she went to look at the old photograph on the walls. And Sam's mother saw her."

"Maddie, it is all hearsay from people with overactive imaginations. I really wish Ava hadn't mentioned the crypt … Come on, let's forget about it and go and get something to drink. Let's get you one of those cakes you love so much."

Maddie gave up discussing it any further. Her aunt would not believe any weird goings-on at the Hall, no matter who had spoken to her about it. It was so annoying,

"All right," said Maddie, breathing inwardly and admitting defeat. Once again, her aunt would not be drawn into any conversations concerning ghostly goings-on at Cattingham Hall. She felt that even if her aunt woke up in bed with a ghost sleeping beside her she would ignore it and go back to sleep. It was just so frustrating.

But she soon cheered up once inside the coffee shop. You were met with a neat array of dark brown wooden tables all with pale green check tablecloths. The walls were all in cream, and decorated with enlarged sepia photographs of a 1920s actress. The aunt of the coffee shop's owner had been a silent movie actress. The photographs were a homage to her.

Lydia and Maddie sat down at a table in the middle of the coffee shop. Within seconds the waitress came to take their order. Maddie ordered a double chocolate Viennese pastry and a vanilla latte. Her aunt ordered her usual apricot slice with fresh cream and a green tea. Their orders arrived quickly. Their cakes were enormous. This was heaven for Maddie, but Lydia looked at hers clucking disapprovingly. Still, however, she managed to eat all of it up.

While they were sipping their drinks Maddie looked across the table and could hear familiar voices. One of them became very loud and argumentative. Then it was if all her nightmares had come together.

She tried to avert her gaze but it was too late. The Beast of Mount High School had spotted her, and with glee said in a loud voice,

"Hello, Maddie. How nice to see you. Is that your aunt you are with?"

Julie Painter beamed across at Lydia from a table further down the coffee shop. She was with her sister, and the girls came across to them. Lydia seemed to be unaware of the sarcasm in her voice and smiled back at her.

"Aunt Lydia, do you remember Julie Painter? She is in my registration class at school." Maddie spoke through gritted teeth as she said this.

"Hello, Julie. It's a long time since I last saw you. I hardly recognised you. My, you are so tall now. I often see your mother in Cattingham. I hope she is well."

"Hello, Mrs Underville. Yes, me mam is fine. I remember you. I can remember playing at the Hall while me mam worked in the kitchen."

"My word, Julie, I can't believe how grown-up you look now. It's nice to see you. I don't get to see many of Maddie's friends. I didn't even know you two were friends."

"Oh, yes, we are great friends. I would have spent more time with her but I have been so busy studying." This answer was met with a delighted smile from Lydia.

"What a load of rubbish. Her, studying? What a liar- more like spending time bullying," thought Maddie, but didn't say anything.

"This is my sister Linda," added Julie sweetly.

"Hello," Lydia replied to Linda's grunt. Linda was another school bully. Her nickname at the school was 'Troll'. She looked nothing like her sister, and had only inherited her nature. She had a wide face and long brown coarse dark hair. Her very obvious freckled snub nose with enlarged bowling ball nostrils had given her the nickname "Troll". She was not particularly bright, and because of this she enjoyed making the lives of who she termed 'swots' a living nightmare.

"Well, it's very nice to meet you both. You must both come to tea some time."

"That would be lovely," said Julie. A smug crease formed across her mouth as she looked at her sister at her side, who was trying to smother a laugh. Lydia failed to notice this.

"Well, we will have to go. I will mention to me mam that I spoke to you. Goodbye, Mrs Underville. What a nice cardigan you have on. Is it a twinset?"

Lydia nodded and smiled in reply. Then Julie added,

"Maddie, if you give me your mobile number I will give you a call."

"I haven't got it on me," said Maddie quickly.

"Well, give me your home number and I'll phone you on that. Write it on this napkin. Here's a pen," said Julie helpfully, getting a pen out of her brown leather bag, which was strapped across her body.

Julie was a tall girl who towered over Maddie. Her straight blonde hair was tied in a thin, wispy plait. Fake tan covered her face, giving her an unnatural orange glow. She had painted her fair eyebrows – which had been plucked to high crescents above her eyes – black, which gave her a slight look of a raccoon. Her eyebrows would raise slightly when she spoke, making you wonder if she had practised this movement in the mirror. When she spoke she stared catlike at Maddie, her large hazel eyes not blinking, and gave Maddie deep, penetrating looks.

If you looked at Julie you would have thought her a pretty girl, but her neglected uneven yellow teeth ruined the effect.

Maddie scribbled the number on a napkin with the pen and gave it to her.

"Thank you, Maddie. See you soon," said Julie.

Maddie nodded back, and as Julie and Linda left the coffee shop she could hear them laughing as they went out of the door. Lydia smiled at them, and did not appear to notice this.

"Such pleasant girls. It will be nice for you to see them over the holidays."

"Yes, Aunt Lydia," said Maddie, smiling only now the girls had gone.

The telephone number she had given Julie was wrong. She had made it up. If it ever cropped up that she had given Julie a dud number she would say to Aunt Lydia that she had accidentally got the numbers mixed up. But there would be trouble when she went back to school. It would be the usual hair-pulling and being tripped up, then the name-calling. Julie Painter would often shout out gleefully at Maddie as she went past her at school, usually saying the words,

"Oh ... look, everyone. It's that boy-girl. Maddie, are you a boy or a girl?"

Maddie would look down and say nothing. Julie would then repeat the question, and then look around and make sure everyone was laughing. Everyone around Maddie would then laugh nervously on cue, hoping they would not be the next target of the bully. Julie would then would burst out laughing spitefully, and ask the same question again and again.

To Maddie it seemed as if the bullying would last a lifetime. She even imagined being bullied by her when she had left school. Why wouldn't Julie leave her alone? Why did she hate her so much? She could not understand it. She had never done anything to Julie and her sister, but they always seemed to target her.

After Julie Painter and her sister had left the coffee shop Maddie and her Aunt Lydia finished their drinks. Lydia placed their empty cups on the trays and Lydia said,

"We can check in Computermax and see if your laptop has been repaired. I know you want to go to the library, but we can do it afterwards. Did you say it was for your school project?"

"Yes. I'm doing a history of Cattingham Hall."

They got their bags together. Lydia paid at the till, and they came out of the coffee shop and walked across to the high street.

The village of Meadowfield was a larger than average village. It had a library, a church, a computer shop, two clothes shops, and a newsagent's, as well as a small supermarket and a charity shop. On the third week of every month there was the usual farmers' market. It was from here that her aunt sold a large amount of fruit and vegetables from the Hall.

They walked into Computermax, and Lydia checked with the assistant whether the laptop had been repaired. Lydia asked if she could pick it up in an hour and the assistant said that was fine, as the shop didn't close until 5 p.m. They walked across the narrow high street across the road to the library. It was a Victorian library, and up the steps dark brown wooden gargoyles were carved on the front of one of the banisters. Paintings of the founder, Oliver Crawford, and his family hung on the walls.

They all looked quite austere to Maddie because they had the usual frozen-in-time expressions that so many Victorian black-and-white photographs tended to have. Plus Oliver Crawford always appeared in pictures to have a huge carbuncle on his nose, as did his son. This was something that Maddie had mentioned to Lydia, which made her smile. Lydia told her that it was just the shape of their noses.

The library was split into two large rooms: one for the museum and one for the library. Maddie and Lydia split up. Lydia went to look at crime novels while Maddie went to look at history of the Hall. After finding the books she wanted she singled out anything to do with Ursula Underville. For some reason the woman fascinated her even though, by all accounts, she sounded as if she had been a really frightening woman. The history of her went back to the 1800s. Maddie found a whole section dedicated to her.

Chapter 6

At the age of eighteen Ursula Sacrisen been married off to Thomas Underville. He had been in his fifties. His first wife had died eighteen months before, after a miscarriage, so it was imperative that he remarry quickly to ensure that the family line was not broken. Ursula had begun to get quite wild prior to the marriage, and her family married her off quickly so they did not have to bear the burden of her. In one chapter of the book Maddie was reading she found an oil painting of her.

She looked quite delicate, with a tiny pale heart-shaped face, and almond-shaped green eyes with long dark eye lashes. Small in stature. The historical account said she was barely five feet tall. Her hair was a silky chestnut brown, with neat brown sausage curls which fell down to her shoulders. Her face had a rosebud mouth, which was small and turned up at the corners. It would have been a beautiful picture but for the expression in the eyes, which seemed to have no light in them. They were almost like a doll's. Her pupils were unnaturally dark ... She was dressed in a white jewelled Grecian-style dress, with a gold scarf draped across her shoulders. The more you looked at her the more fascinated you became with her face.

Ursula had a son called Robert. Her husband Thomas had died of tuberculosis within five years of their marriage. Her son appeared to have been placed in the care of one of the Underville relatives later: Katharine, Thomas's sister. Katharine already lived at the Hall at the time of her brother's death, and was believed to have taken over the full care of Robert.

There were further accounts of Ursula Underville, apart from her being involved in dark practices. Katharine Underville had detailed in a journal in one of the library books that there had been wild parties at the Hall after her brother had died, and that she could not control Ursula's behaviour. Fearing for the safety of Robert, she told the family doctor of her concerns.

It was only after one of the servants had been found half beaten that Ursula was placed, as a temporary measure, in an asylum. But her mental health had deteriorated, and she died within weeks of arriving there. Her son Robert remained at the Hall and was looked after by Katharine. Katharine had never had children but appeared to have lived at the Hall and acted as the female head of the household, living with her late mother at the Hall even during her brother's first marriage. However, she did not appear to have lived at the Hall when Ursula was first married to Thomas. Her death twenty years later was from a heart attack.

Robert, the son of Ursula and Thomas, had been well liked, and had provided jobs for the locals and given money to the poor. He married Constance Whitelaw, a commoner, and had two sons. When he died half the villagers attended his funeral.

Ursula Underville's coffin, however, was placed in the family crypt at Cattingham Hall. Her death held no such ceremony. In fact at one point her coffin had had to be placed under guard because the villagers had threatened to burn her coffin because of her links they said she had had with witchcraft. At that time the crypt had already been bricked up, and had to be opened up again to place Ursula in there. This time a good job was made of it, and it stayed bricked up until 2014 ... Ursula's notoriety, however, ensured that she was never forgotten.

But the description of Ursula Underville did not match the description of the ghost of Cattingham Hall. The apparition was that of a tall woman.

"So it wasn't Ursula Underville trying to contact her," thought Maddie. "But who then who was it ...?"

The last account that Maddie had found about Ursula Underville detailed a book she had written on medicinal herbs. It had been more of a pamphlet, by the look of it, but anything she could find on it, she thought, would look good in her project. There was also evidence that Ursula had shown an interest in the architecture of the house, and that she had made substantial changes to the rooms in the house.

Ursula had been ahead of her time and highly educated.

"How frustrating it must have been for her to have been married off so young," thought Maddie.

According to the records her father had made a pledge to Thomas that Ursula would marry him. Maddie was fifteen and she didn't even have a boyfriend – not that anyone was remotely interested in her ... well, apart from Nathanael. Ursula had not been much older than her when she had got married.

It was a horrible thought that Ursula had had to marry at such a young age. For some reason – and despite all the bad history about Ursula – she felt sorry for her, but why? The illness Ursula had was detailed, but the physician at the time had said it was 'an attack of the demons'. Accounts of her at a young age said that she appeared to have suffered seizures, which continued as she grew older.

Her family doctor Erasmus Lockhart had finally declared her 'insane in mind'. Ursula had been taken away from the Hall because her behaviour was too wild in manner. She had been accused of cruelty to servants: hitting them with a wooden cudgel that she kept by her bed. There was even a human cage, which she had apparently used to discipline the servants. Her sister-in-law had found it in the basement ... It was believed to have been called her punishment room. The safety of Thomas had been paramount, and there had been the danger that she would seriously harm her son.

Maddie was so engrossed in writing down notes on her pad that she didn't notice Mrs Welmort the grey haired librarian glancing over her shoulder and reading what she was writing.

"Hello, Maddie. How are you getting on? Your aunt said you were doing a project on Cattingham Hall."

"Oh ... hello, Mrs Welmort. Well, more on Ursula Underville, Mrs Welmort. I am trying to gather as much information as I can. Are there any more books on Cattingham Hall?"

"I'll check," said Mrs Welmort smiling.

She came back a few minutes later armed with books and said,

"Here are some reference books on Cattingham Hall. Ursula Underville designed some of the rooms of the house. They might be useful. My great-aunt's grandmother used to work at the Hall, and told me the usual gossip passed on by generations of staff." The librarian lowered her head and spoke in what she hoped was a conspiratorial tone to Maddie.

"I am afraid there was nothing nice said about Ursula Underville. The talk had been that Ursula had been referred to as a white witch by the servants. That might be something your friends would like to hear about."

Mrs Welmort smiled again as she spoke to Maddie.

"I think they would," replied Maddie, returning the smile. Mrs Welmort then went away as a woman and child were now beckoning to her at the counter.

Maddie looked through the first reference book. The architectural drawings of the Hall and the library had been completely changed, and so had Ursula's bedroom. That was quite interesting. She would photocopy the plans and show her aunt so they could compare the changes over the years at the Hall.

Checking the books out she thanked the librarian and went to look for her aunt. It didn't take long to spot her. She was walking up to the counter with a bundle of books, all of them the usual serial killer stuff, she then handed them to the librarian to stamp.

"For such a gentle woman she certainly loves the blood and gore books," thought Maddie shaking her head in amusement.

They then crammed all the books into Aunt Lydia's shopping bag and they headed towards the computer shop. The car was not too far away and the laptop was fairly light, so carrying it would not be a problem. Lydia handed the order form to the Anthony, who ran the computer shop, and Lydia paid and placed the laptop handed to her into its carry case passing it over to Maddie. The small car park was next to a clothes shop selling clothes that were of no interest to Maddie. They were in the category of more for comfort than for any fashion. A flutter of wings made her look up. It was a raven.

"Look, Aunt Lydia. It's that raven."

It was a noticeable bird because of its size and huge wingspan. Again it seemed to be looking at Maddie. This time it was quite noisy, and was making a gurgling croak from the back of its throat. The noise seemed to echo around them.

"I suppose it has a nest round here," said Lydia. She didn't look round, and uninterested was now busy opening the car door.

Maddie opened the boot and placed the laptop in it, then closed it and got into the passenger seat. She then looked over her shoulder to look again at the bird which, after a few moments, flew away. Seeing the bird again made her feel uneasy.

She was now convinced it was seeking her out, but why?

Was it something to do with the ghost of Cattingham Hall? Didn't someone say they saw a huge bird when they saw the ghost? That was it, she remembered now. The ghost of Cattingham Hall was always followed by a huge raven.

Lydia was shouting abuse at motorists as they arrived at the supermarket, which took Maddie's mind off it. With all the shopping collected they loaded it in the car, and they went back to the Hall. After putting it away it was already 3 p.m. Maddie took the laptop up to her room. Her Aunt Lydia went to seek Titch out to help her pick the fruit and vegetables. It was agreed that Maddie would come down later and help out after working on her project.

With the laptop plugged in Maddie removed everything from her bedside table and rested the laptop on it, then dragged a chair from the back of the room and placed it behind the table. She then placed one of her pillows on the chair to sit on.

For a change she did not have to wait long to get into the computer. Usually the reception on her laptop at the Hall left a lot to be desired. Amazingly, this time it was instant, so she went straight into Google and typed in 'Cattingham Hall'.

She found various references to the Hall but Edward Wragg, a nineteenth-century historian, appeared to have recorded the most information, especially about Ursula. As she scrolled through the earlier history of the Hall she eventually came to Thomas Underville. He had come from the family of Undervilles who had made their money in spices.

But, even before he married, he was plagued with ill health. His second wife, Ursula Underville, appeared to have nursed him when he had suffered from various ailments in the early years of their marriage. In fact she created ointments, which were applied to his bloated legs with great success. She was believed to have kept these potions in Delft pots in the kitchen on a special wooden shelf, which were never allowed to be touched anyone but her. This only increased the suspicion about her being a witch. At one point there had been an account when all the housekeeping staff had left the house because of claims about Ursula Underville and witchcraft.

There had been an outbreak of tuberculosis in Cattingham. Ursula had also been blamed for this. The account from a maid – Hettie Gargowin – in 1804 had given details of a dead cockerel, its blood drained. The blood of the cockerel was later found in the master's bedroom in a silver spittoon. The Justice of the Peace investigated the matter but the Undervilles were a rich and powerful family, and the case was dropped. All the staff were then sacked, and new staff were employed.

After that no one questioned the activities of Ursula Underville.

But her husband's health continued to deteriorate, and early in the marriage he died. She then had a free rein over the house and developed ranges of herbal products, which appeared to make her a lot of money … not that she needed it. Her husband had left her well-provided-for.

There had been proposals of marriage but she had refused to marry again, and lived quite an introverted life. But her mental health deteriorated. Her sister-in-law then took control of the Hall.

On scrolling further down the page Maddie saw that there was a painting of Katharine, her sister-in-law. The painting must have been done, thought Maddie, when she was middle-aged. A bloated blotchy face looked out at you from the painting. She seemed to have one long eyebrow, but on looking closer Maddie could see it was because a cluster of warts were in between them, which gave a false image. Her eyes were small and pale blue in colour. A cruel-looking Roman nose hung over small and thin parted lips. Her broad chin appeared to show the faintest suggestion of a beard.

"I bet she wasn't pleased when that painter painted those warts in," thought Maddie. There was certainly nothing flattering about it. Katharine's mouth appeared to turn down with criss-cross lines round the corners, very much like Cousin Phillip's.

"Maybe that's where he got his permanently sullen expression," wondered Maddie. Katharine's hair was completely covered by a lace cap and she was dressed in a plain grey dress with no adornments, apart from a dark brown cloak round her shoulders. She seemed to have had a very long body and, judging by the painting, looked quite a big-boned woman. According to account by an Edward Wragg she belonged to a religious body called the Drakens. This order did not believe in any form of medicine for illness. Prayers were said five times a day. They fasted one day in the week.

As she looked at the bulky, well-nourished body of Katharine Underville Maddie doubted whether she had ever fasted in her life.

"What complete opposites Katharine and Ursula must have been," thought Maddie.

An image came into Maddie's head from nowhere of two women who were totally different from each other. It was if a voice was whispering to her that they hated each other. So why did they live together at the Hall after Thomas had died? Was it because of Robert, Ursula's son? There did not appear to be any record of Ursula's family coming to the Hall.

But when she attempted to scroll further down the screen the print went into white zigzags, which made it completely impossible to read. The screen then began to make crackling noises, which was something it had never done before. There was no computer message on the screen for Maddie to be guided by, so she waited a few minutes. Then the screen went off completely.

"Oh, bugger. Here we go again," sighed Maddie agitatedly.

Her laptop never played up at her mother's house. She then did what Lydia always told her not to do. She switched the computer off, and then put it on again. But again there was nothing. It was so infuriating. The school project had to be finished by the time she went back to school, so she only had a couple of weeks left to complete it. Her paperwork consisted of scribbled notes she needed to type up. All she had was the pamphlet, and some photocopies of plans of the house.

Fortunately she had some library books, but she needed to print off Edward Wragg's historical accounts of Ursula and Katharine. The work had to be done, so she would therefore have to use Aunt Lydia's computer in the library. Her aunt would be picking plums from the trees and berries off the fruit bushes, so she wouldn't need it for the moment. Maddie unplugged the laptop and left it on her bed. She would try it again later with Lydia. There was no time to mess about with it: she had to get more of the project done.

Armed with the library books, her project folder, and her pencil case, she made her way down the narrow stairs to the library. It was a shortcut to the library if she went down the old servants' stairs. This was the oldest part of the house, so she always rushed through it. She was always half expecting a ghost to come rushing out and float and wail before her, but it never did much to her relief. Opening the library door. It was quite warm in there, for a change.

Hodge was sitting on the old books for the jumble sale, quite content and quietly purring to herself. However, on seeing Maddie, she jumped on the computer table and demanded to be stroked. Maddie stroked the warm black fur and was rewarded with her hands being kissed and her chest head butted. Then the cat's purring became louder and more excitable. Maddie switched the computer on, and at the same time tried to stop Hodge from parking her black furry backside on the computer keys.

Maddie was now back on the search engine on the computer, and she printed off the historical accounts from Edward Wragg on Ursula and Katharine while half stroking an over excitable Hodge at the same time. The printer in the library printed quickly, but the paper shot out of the tray erratically. This annoyed Hodge, who then finally jumped off the computer table in disgust.

The search brought more history on Ursula and Thomas Underville. Maddie even managed to print off another copy of the pamphlet Ursula had written on holistic medicine. Things were getting better, and she was enjoying looking through the history of the Hall. She unzipped her pencil case and took her yellow felt tip out. She would mark points of interest out on the printed material.

A crashing noise of books falling made Maddie turn round. Hodge had fallen off the cardboard box filled with books. The box had turned sideways, and books had spilled out of it. Hodge was obsessed with card board and seemed to make a habit of falling off books she thought as she went to pick them up a lone rubber fell out of her pocket and rolled in Hodge's direction. Hodge, with lightning speed, started to push it along with her left paw. The rubber bounced over to the bookcase near the fireplace. Hodge then sat on the offending item. Maddie had to pick Hodge up, who shouted angry cat abuse at her as the rubber was retrieved from under her belly. She then placed the cat – who continued to shout at her – down gently.

As she stroked the accident prone cat to calm her down her eyes caught sight of a book she had never noticed before. It was half sticking out between two books in the bookcase. She pulled it out. The title of the book was Household Cures. It looked very old, and it was only six pages long. She had never seen it in the library.

The paper was yellowed with age. It was made of thick parchment, and the spidery writing on the title was difficult to read. The title had a second title under it. It said Cures of the Head and Body.

She opened the first page. It was like looking at a medical journal. Hand-drawn pictures of arms and legs were sketched on the side of each cure, with the name of a plant as a cross reference to it. The front of the book had a picture of a man in bed with a servant by his side.

This was a fantastic thing to find. Maddie was excited. If she photocopied each page it would look good in her project. Also, Lydia would be interested in it if she had never seen it before. It looked old.

When she looked closer she could see that on the back of the book the name of Ursula Underville was written on it.

"Maybe Lydia could sell it and get some money for it," thought Maddie.

Uncle Akkoubian must have known about it, but why did he never mention it? She glancing through the rest of the books, but there was nothing else that looked particularly old.

Lydia would look up the types of plants used for each cure. She might even find some of them still growing on the estate. It was an exciting thought.

Another thought in Maddie's head was,

"If Ursula was so evil then why did she have a book to cure ailments? Why would she want to help people?"

It did not make sense. Her coffin was in the family crypt. That would be something to look at. Maddie decided she would write the words on the coffin out and place it in the project at the end, then sketch a picture of her beside this. She did not want to look at it on her own, and thought she would ask Aunt Lydia if she could look at it. Maddie hoped she would let her because she knew she was doing a school project, but she would probably come with her. That was fine by Maddie, as she most certainly did not want to go into a crypt on her own.

She placed the book in her pocket and went out of the kitchen door to find Aunt Lydia. It did not take long to find her. She was wearing a multi coloured cardigan. She was stuck in the middle of two strawberry bushes, and a strand of her highlighted short blonde hair had blown over her face. A brown wicker basket lay beside as she tossed in the strawberries. Hearing Maddie shout for her Lydia waved one of her red-stained hands at her in reply.

"Aunt Lydia, look what I have found," said Maddie loudly as she ran over excitedly.

She fished out the book from the huge pocket in her cardigan. Lydia brushed a stray hair off her face to look at the book. She picked it up and glanced through the pages.

"I found this in the library," said Maddie. "It was in a book at the bottom of the bookcase near the fire. It looks very old. See, there is a date on the back of it. It looks like Ursula Underville's book on healing."

Lydia pointed at it with her finger, looked at the back page, and then turned it over.

"Yes, you are right," she said." You say you found it in the library. Whereabouts?"

"It was on the bottom bookshelf next to the fireplace. It was between two books."

"I have never seen it before. I am surprised Akkoubian never mentioned to me, especially because of its age. Before your uncle died we separated the old books for valuation. Were there any more of these books?"

"No, this was the only book there. Maybe we could go through the library and see if there are any more books. We might find some really valuable books."

"Oh, Maddie, that would be wonderful. But I don't think that we will find anything else, and you have to consider the amount of time it would take to do this … Your uncle went through the library with a fine-tooth comb. It must have just been missed."

"Do you think the book is valuable?"

"I doubt it, Maddie. The pages are too yellowed, and they are slightly ripped. Also … it is quite a small book. The age would interest a library, though. We will take it to the library next time we go there."

Maddie was disappointed. She so wanted the book to be worth something so that it would help her aunt. Why couldn't she have found a whole hoard of old books that would have been worth a fortune? Then her aunt would not have to worry about money or selling the Hall.

"Aunt Lydia, can I photocopy the book for my school project?"

"Certainly, Maddie. Just be careful with it though."

"I was reading more on Ursula Underville. Don't you think it is strange that she lived with her sister-in-law Katharine, what with her being so religious?"

"Well, in those days – due to the age of Ursula – the family of the Undervilles may have felt she needed looking after."

"But they were so different."

"Yes. But you have to remember that Ursula had a son, Thomas. With Ursula's ill health the heir to Cattingham Hall would have been put before Ursula's needs. She was, after all, very young. Women were regarded as second-class citizens in those days. I can remember your uncle talking about her when he went through the family history. He said her father had remarried after her mother had died.

"Apparently Ursula did not get on with her stepmother. That might be the reason why she was married off so young. I am sure Akkoubian had some papers on the Underville family, which we can look at. Remember, I told you we could look for them. I just wish I knew where he had put them. They would be really useful to you."

Maddie placed the book gently back in her pocket.

"Can I look for them?"

"Of course you can. The only rooms they could possibly be in would be either the library or Akkoubian's bedroom. Your uncle was a creature of habit, so those are the only places they could be.

"Sorry, but I really haven't time to have a good search for you at the moment. I want to get as much fruit picked in case we have any further rain."

Chapter 7

Maddie went back in the Hall while her aunt carried on picking fruit. When she went back into the library she looked through the mottled grey lever arch files propped up on the computer table. All she could find was bill receipts and orders for fruit and vegetables.

There was a large red diary on the table, which she moved as she placed more files from out of the drawers on the table. Again, she could find nothing. She sighed and looked across at the vast bookcases. They lined all the walls, and were crammed with books. Some were spilling from where they had been wedged into corners. There must have been at least 2,000 books in the bookcases. Looking for them would be a nightmare task.

"Surely Uncle Akkoubian didn't stuff the documents in there," Maddie thought. Looking through them all would have to be the last resort. She decided to look in her uncle's bedroom instead.

Aunt Lydia and her uncle had had separate bedrooms. The bedrooms had an interconnecting door between them. Lydia had said to Maddie she had not been able to stand Uncle Akkoubian's loud snoring. Maddie did not want to go in her late uncle's bedroom, but she had no choice if she wanted to have more subject matter for her school project.

As she entered the bedroom the door jerked unsteadily open, which only set her nerves on edge. Her uncle's bedroom looked very much like the library in Meadowfield. It was painted in dark wood with oak-panelled walls. She could even smell his pipe tobacco as she came into the room. His large four-poster bed still had the mint green candlewick cover on it. His book, The Man Who Mistook His Wife for a Hat and Other Clinical Tales, lay abandoned on it. He had often carried it about with him, but she had never seen him read it.

When she picked it up to look at it she found a leather-bound Bible underneath it. Inside it were the names of previous family members. The list was long and she would have looked at the Bible in detail, but she wanted to find Uncle Akkoubian's paperwork first.

It was such an odd feeling being in the room. You almost felt that you would hear his whistling, and that he would come in any minute.

As she looked at The Man Who Mistook His Wife for a Hat and Other Clinical Tales Maddie thought, with tears pricking at her eyes, that it must have been the last book he picked up ... On top of the book was a small tube of his eucalyptus chest rub, which lay half open. It had been well used, and had strong thumb indentations in it. In the corner of the room was an enamel washbasin with a cupboard under it. Her uncle's sandalwood shaving soap lay neglected on his pewter shaving dish.

She went further into the room and opened the rosewood wardrobe. Rows of suits hung in military fashion on wooden coat hangers. There was a strong smell of mothballs as she opened the drawers in the wardrobe. As she opened each drawer she found they had been emptied.

Just when she thought there was nothing in the drawers she came to the third drawer. It was difficult to open. Something was stuck inside it. She wrestled with it and finally managed to open it. Two hand-knitted cardigans were wrapped tightly round something square-shaped. She unravelled the arms of the cardigans and unbuttoned the final cardigan. In it was a brown leather-bound Radio Times journal. Inside the journal were some A4 sheets of printed pages. It was Uncle Akkoubian's history on the Hall ... exactly what she was looking for.

"I wonder why he kept it in here, and not the library?" she wondered. "Oh, well. At least I have found it ..."

She took it out of the drawer. As she did so some papers fell out of it on to the floor. As she bent down to pick them up she saw a white postcard. It had a long number on it, which looked like a library reference number, with 'Ursula' scribbled in pencil beside it. She placed it inside her pocket. She would get the librarian to look for it for her when she was next in Meadowfield. The journal was crammed with other papers, so she placed them on the bed and spread them out. Her uncle had had a plan of the house. He had written in capital letters in red,

"Where is this room? Is it another room? And who is Anna Blackstock?"

It meant nothing to Maddie. It just seemed to be a plan of the library, but Anna Blackstock? That was a name that she had never heard before … She would see if Aunt Lydia could shed some light on the room and this Anna.

The other papers were a history of the Hall. Thomas Underville had moved into the Hall with his first wife Sarah, his sister Katharine, and their mother. Thomas and Sarah had a child, and they named her Alice. At the age of five she died from pneumonia. Sarah also died within ten years of this tragedy.

Katharine and her mother appeared to continue to live at the Hall with Thomas until Ursula married him. Katharine's mother died prior to Thomas remarrying.

In the documents there was a small black diary. Maddie opened it. The name Sarah Underville was handwritten inside it. On the first page it simply said,

My darling Alice died today.

Nothing else was written on that page. A small dried flower was embedded in one of the pages. An account a few days later said,

Why won't Agnes and Katharine leave us with our sorrow?

There was only one page left with writing in the diary. All it said was,

We will have no rest until they are gone from us.

So there had been no love lost between Sarah and Agnes and Katharine. It was getting exciting. More of the story of what had happened was now enfolding. This was something that Maddie did not think she would have found out.

A typed document said that Agnes had suffered some form of paralysis three years after Sarah died. She remained bedridden in her bedchamber until the day she died. Maddie wished she had not found this out, as the bedroom she eventually died in was her bedroom. A photocopied portrait of Agnes in the paperwork was not flattering.

When she looked at it she saw a heavy-jawed, thickset woman, with a quite a mannish-looking face. She was very similar in looks to her daughter. Her drooping eyelids covered almost colourless blue-white eyes. Her mouth was small and pinched with her daughter's criss-cross lines embedded round the corners, making it look as if someone had taken a pastry cutter and crimped round her mouth.

In the painting she was sitting on a chair dressed in a shapeless black dress, and appeared to be smoking a pipe. Like her daughter, she was a very broad woman. A gold hexagon-shaped necklace lay tightly around her thick neck. Draped over her legs was a black shawl, but it could not conceal how large, red, and swollen her lower calves were.

"Ugh. She looks almost witchlike," thought Maddie and shuddered.

Platinum-white hair hung down from a white lace cap she was wearing. In one of her hands she held a book of some sort. The writing on it was too faint to decipher.

Agnes had surprisingly long curled-up fingernails on her huge hands, which were holding the book in the portrait. It was like looking at the talons on a large predatory bird. It was not a pleasant image. It was one you would not wish to remember.

"I wish I hadn't seen that," thought Maddie. "I will have nightmares tonight, especially now I know she died in my bedroom. I wonder what Sam will make of it."

When she took a closer look the painting of Agnes it looked as if it had been painted in the gallery room beside the stained-glass window. Maddie picked up more A4 printed pages. One of the pages said that Thomas had worked away. It seemed as if Sarah had spent a lot of her time alone in the house with her sister-in-law and mother-in-law.

"I suppose Sarah's coffin is in the family crypt somewhere," thought Maddie. The family crypt had been bricked up for as long as Aunt Lydia could remember, and had only been opened because of the recent flooding.

Maddie's uncle had been buried at Cattingham Church. Lydia had wanted him to be buried there rather than the crypt, which had a tainted history. At first Cattingham Hall had appeared to have a quite boring history, but Maddie was discovering more and more things. It was almost as if an enormous jigsaw with more pieces were being fitted together.

She was so deep in thought that she did not hear the strange tapping coming from the bedroom window. If she had been more aware she would have noticed something that would have turned her blood cold ...

A hand was trying to open the bedroom window but it was jammed, so it would not. The wood on window had had a lot of rain damage, and this meant that the window could only be opened with great difficulty. Heavy lily patterned brocade curtains were drawn across the window, which blocked out the intruder. Long curled-up fingernails scratched impatiently at the latch as they tried to force it open. They then raked the glass, leaving claw marks down the glass. It was not as if whoever was outside wanted to get in the room: she just wanted to get the window half open, just enough to drag the girl through the window. Once she had the window open the rest would be easy.

The woman was a great mimic. A trapped bird would get the soft-hearted girl racing to the window to free it. But it was no use. The woman could not open the window. She would have to try some other method of getting the girl. Cursing she disappeared into thin air.

Maddie felt a light breeze come from the window, but did not look up. She just touched the back of her neck absent-mindedly. She picked up the loose A4 pages and placed them back in the journal, and then she went down downstairs and placed it in the library so she could show Lydia later. Going out into the vast gardens she found Lydia picking strawberries and placing them in baskets.

"Aunt Lydia, I found Uncle Akkoubian's journal in his bedroom in a drawer in his wardrobe."

Her aunt did not answer to this, and just stared at her. She finally said,

"Maddie, how long have you been here?"

"I have just come here straight from the house. Why?"

"I must be imagining things. I was sure you were standing beside me. Would you believe that I thought I was talking to you? I heard humming. When I turned round there was no one there." Lydia shook her head slightly and continued,

"Oh, forget it, dear. With all this ghost hysteria I think I am beginning to imagine ghosts myself. That's great news – finding the journal, I mean. We'll look at it later, but let's finishing picking the fruit and veg first. If we get this all out of the way there will be less to do later," Lydia replied as she wiped the sweat from her brow.

She looked tired, and although Maddie wanted Lydia to look at the papers now she knew that her aunt would want the fruit picking done first so she didn't say anything further on it. She just said,

"Sure. Which patch do you want me to start on?"

"You can finish down here. If you could finish the last of the strawberries and the raspberry bushes that would be great. I'll pick the rest of the plum from the trees. Titch has nearly finished the digging up the potatoes." Her aunt smiled at her and handed her a half-filled basket.

The only thing Maddie didn't like about the fruit picking was the large fruit spiders that would gather in the baskets. They tended to crawl in and quickly spin webs in the baskets. As she glanced across she could see that there were still empty baskets that needed filling.

The afternoon went very quickly. Fortunately the weather wasn't too bad. Maddie had her head down as she picked, and she was completely oblivious to the fact that she was being watched by a huge raven perched on a tree.

Hours later she took the filled fruit baskets back to the kitchen and placed them on the draining board. She felt hot and sticky. Her palms were stained purple, and she was sure she had a spider in her hair. After shaking her head vigorously she hoped she had dislodged it.

"Yuk," she said. She was sure she could still feel a spider brushing against her face, but it was just its light cobweb.

"Ugh. What if it had gone in my ear?" she thought.

She finally thought she had shaken it off her head.

She ran the tap in the sink. The water removed some of the fruit stains on her hands, but not much. The whole kitchen smelt of it. It was quite a nostril clenching smell. Maddie had long stopped sampling the fruit because she had eaten too many strawberries in the past. Gorging on them had only made her feel sick.

As she sat at the kitchen table Titch came in with the vegetables. She stood up and helped him place the trays on the kitchen floor. Then she mentioned the documents she had found in Uncle

Akkoubian's bedroom to him. Titch thought they sounded interesting and said he had some photographs of his great-grandmother, who had been in service, in an old biscuit tin.

"You can use them for your project so long as I get them back," he offered.

"OK. Thanks, Titch," came her reply.

Maddie adored Titch. He would often tell her stories of when he had been a sergeant in the Northumberland Fusiliers. He had worked under Uncle Akkoubian, who had been a colonel in the army. It was great that Titch was now going to give her some of his family photographs. Her project was going to have a lot of information in it. When she mentioned the plans to the library she said that she could not understand why her uncle had highlighted in red the information about a room.

"Do you think there is a secret room?"

Titch laughed.

"Do you not think if there had been one we would have found it? Don't get too excited, pet. We'll look at the paperwork later. How about a drink before we start washing the fruit and veg?"

"OK," she replied.

Titch put the kettle on and Maddie took three large brown earthenware cups from the tree mug. One was for Lydia. Just as she was getting the green cockerel biscuit barrel out Lydia came in breathless, with baskets of plums. Titch took them off her, and she sat on a kitchen stool.

"Just in time," she said, and smiled as she looked at the coffee being made. She took the chocolate biscuits being handed to her.

"Michael will collect the vegetables," she said.

Maddie and Titch nodded in response. They were more preoccupied with the contents of the biscuit barrel. Lydia started eating a biscuit, then took off her shoes.

Michael worked for one of the hotels. He was a delivery driver. The Hall supplied some of the fruit and vegetables. It was a regular contract. It was not a lot of money, but she also had other customers – such as Clara, one of the locals, who had a chutney-making business.

"You've done a great job, you two," said Lydia.

"Nah … team effort," said Titch, smiling.

After he had drunk his coffee he started placing the strawberries in bowls. He then removed clumps of soil off the vegetables in the sink and started placing them back in the trays.

"If you do those, Titch, Maddie and I will sort the room for the photography club."

Maddie pulled a face and sighed. She had forgotten about that room. Her disappointed expression must have been noticeable to Lydia because she said to her,

"It won't take long – and afterwards we can walk into the village and get some fish and chips. Do you want some, Titch?"

"No thanks, Lydia. Our lass will be making me dinner. But thanks for the offer, pet."

After finishing their drinks Maddie and Lydia left Titch in the kitchen. Armed with dusters, cleaning materials, a small kettle, and biscuits, they went up the small steps leading to the room for the photographers.

The room was small, and there were horizontal lines of indentations on the walls. The walls were a murky porridge white. Lydia looked at them and winced. She wished she had had the walls painted by a professional decorator.

A Victorian cast-iron radiator stood in the corner. To warm the room up Lydia had been putting it on now and again, but there was still a smell of the cold in the room. It was not well furnished. Since all the bookshelves had been removed the walls looked quite lumpy. But it was too late for the room to have a makeover now. Maddie's Uncle Julian had painted the room but he did not appeared to have been skilled at painting, and it was very surprising that he had actually volunteered to do this in the first place.

While Maddie vacuumed the room Lydia dusted and removed cobwebs. They then removed the wooden chairs from the gallery and the dining room. Fifteen people were coming.

The final touch to the room was a large table. Lydia then wheeled in a small trolley with the kettle filled with water, and placed some coffee cups on the table. A tin of shortbread was placed beside the cups. They would bring the milk in tomorrow before the meeting started.

65

The photographic club had booked the room between 9 a.m. and 5 p.m. If they were happy with it they would use the room every month, so Lydia had her fingers crossed about that. With all the work done and the cleaning materials put away they went down out of the room. Lydia ruffled Maddie's hair affectionately and said,

"Fish and chips ... Come on."

She then shut the door behind her, and they walked downstairs and put on their coats. The fish and chip shop was a ten-minute walk from the Hall.

Titch had now gone home. Maddie had wanted to show him the plans to the house. She would show them to Lydia instead later. The house was silent now. Only their footsteps on the tiled floor made any noise.

Chapter 8

To get into the village they crossed the main road leading up to the Hall and cut up the narrow lane lined with hedgerows that went into the village.

Cattingham had not changed much since the sixties. Most of the villagers wanted it kept that way. The village was built out of local sandstone. The tarn, which was named The Talkin' Tarn, was less than a mile from the village. Small boats would rest on the icy blue waters. There was a talk of a medieval village having once existed under the tarn, but as it was general hearsay no one had ever investigated it.

The Talkin' Tarn was used by the village's dog lover brigade. Wet dogs and the ice cream van were attracted to it like magnets. As they passed the white stone-built police station they met some of the villagers. Mrs Longbone the postmistress beamed at Lydia as she went by. Everyone had liked Lydia and Akkoubian and there had been a lot of flowers sent to the Hall when Akkoubian had died, which showed deep respect for him. The villagers did not, however, have the same respect for Julian Underville.

Walking into Mr Baird's fish and chip shop set a small bell off, and a little man appeared from another room, which led to the counter. Lydia ordered Maddie's usual cod and chips. They did not order anything else. You did not need to. The portions were enormous. The piping hot chips hung over the sides of the white greaseproof paper as they were wrapped up. Once they were placed in her shopping bag Lydia paid for the order and they went out. Maddie giggled and Lydia, who was trying not to smile, said,

"Don't start that nonsense again."

"Oh, Aunt Lydia, Mr Baird adores you. You should see the way he looks at you."

Maddie imitated a lovesick Mr Baird, and they both burst out laughing. Mr Baird might be a bit boring for her aunt but he had a much nicer nature than her mother's last boyfriend – Greg Julian, a chemistry teacher – whose only words to Maddie had ever been,

"Fab stuff," and, "Super." He had showered her mum with compliments and presents. With Maddie it was a different story. He tended to have a bored, glazed look in his eyes if he attempted conversation with her. It had been a relief when her mum had split up with him.

As they started to walk up to the cut leading to the Hall they met Mrs Endean, one of the church volunteers, who then began her usual outpouring of local gossip. Maddie was bored, and looked around her. Even Aunt Lydia had a trapped, helpless look in her eyes as Mrs Endean then proceeded to tell her about fundraising.

That evening there was a fancy dress night in the village to raise money for Help for Heroes. Maddie had managed to get out of it, but only because she knew the Painter Sisters were going and wanted to avoid them. She, had, however sold some raffle tickets and had given the money to Mrs Endean.

Some of the children, who were excited about the fancy dress night, were already wearing their costumes in the village. Three children came down from the cut. Only one person remained. It was the slender figure of a tall girl, who was wearing a long white dress with a white shawl draped loosely around her shoulders.

"I wonder who she is going as?" thought Maddie.

She could not see the girl's face because she was walking up to the cut with her back to her, and with her long, dark hair hanging loosely down her shoulders. There had been some light rain during the day. Maddie was curious to see that the long dress was not muddy.

Lydia had finally managed to extricate herself from Mrs Endean. The relief on Lydia's face was evident, even though she did not say anything. They looked across to the cut, where they were now heading. The girl quickly disappeared into it.

"That was quick," said Maddie to Aunt Lydia, who also had noticed the girl. "Did you see how fast she was walking?"

Lydia nodded. She was curious, and she hoped that the girl would turn round so she could see her face and look at her dress again. She did not recognise her from the back, and could have sworn that her dress was soaking wet. She thought that the girl would catch a chill wearing such wet clothes. As they came halfway up the cut, which was a straight walk up uphill to the Hall, they would have been able to have seen anyone who was at the top it. The girl was not there. She was nowhere to be seen. It was bizarre. Maddie looked at Lydia and said,

"She's gone."

"No, she hasn't. She must have gone up the hill more quickly than we thought. Perhaps we will see her when we get to the main road," came her aunt's reply.

Maddie didn't say anything. Too many strange things were happening lately. They walked up the hill leading to the main road. All they could see was a lone pool of murky grey rainwater. The top of the hill gave you a clear view of the main road. There was no one there. It was if the girl had disappeared into thin air.

"Aunt Lydia, where has she gone?"

"I don't know," came the puzzled reply. "There must be a shortcut."

But there were no shortcuts to take. They glanced over at the road ahead and screwed their eyes up to see if there was a figure in the distance. The girl's long white dress would have stood out.

Lydia quickly changed the subject and said,

"Come on, Maddie, let's go home. These fish and chips will be stone cold."

Still completely baffled, they walked in silence back to the Hall. But Maddie could not keep quiet for long and finally blurted out,

"Aunt Lydia, do you think we saw a ghost?" Aunt Lydia was nonplussed, and she just shrugged.

"I honestly don't know what we saw. We can't both have imagined it. It's a complete mystery."

But she did not dwell on it further, and talked about Mrs Endean's fundraising instead.

Once home they had their tea and cleared up. Maddie went to her bedroom to phone her friend Sam. Lydia had gone into the sitting room to listen to the news on the television. A patter of tiny feet made Maddie turn round. It was Hodge. The cat leapt on her bed and head-butted the phone, and purred loudly as she phoned the number. Maddie tickled the soft down of the cat's tummy as the phone rang out Sam's number. Sam answered the phone, and Maddie told her what had happened.

"When can we hold a séance?" Sam asked, butting into Maddie's garbled 'ghost girl' conversation. "How about tomorrow?"

Maddie replied,

"OK. The photography club is coming, so Aunt Lydia will be busy with them. We could do the séance in the library. That's where all the strange noises and things moving by themselves started from. I'll ask Aunt Lydia if you can come round and work on our school projects. She will be fussing with the photography club, so will not be in the library. That's the best time to do the séance."

She felt guilty telling lies to her aunt, but she knew she would not agree to a séance if she asked her.

"We won't tell Josh. You know what he thinks of séances, so if you bump into him don't mention it," said Sam.

"OK. Let me speak to Aunt Lydia, and I'll phone you back."

Maddie switched off her mobile and placed it in her pocket. Hodge, her tail wagging, had jumped off the bed and was now sitting on the chair.

"Come on, Hodge," said Maddie, trying to appease her, but the cat ignored her and proceeded to stretch out on the chair.

"What a grump you are," she added.

The black cat lifted her head and looked at Maddie up and down. Her tail was moving from side to side. Any attempts to stroke her were wasted. The cat was now sulking. Hodge would get jealous if either Lydia or Maddie spoke to anyone on the phone, and she normally mewed loudly to try and get them to come off the phone.

Maddie left her on the chair and went downstairs into the sitting room. Her Aunt Lydia was knitting a jumper, but it did not seem to be going well. A line of undone grey wool lay on her lap as Maddie came in to speak to her.

"Aunt Lydia, is it OK if Sam comes for tea tomorrow? I thought we could work on our projects in the library afterwards."

Lydia was amused and said,

"Of course, dear. Tell her to come early ... say five o'clock?"

70

She knew that once the girls got together they would not be talking about their projects. But she did like Sam. It was nice to see Maddie finally having a close friend. Maddie, she felt, had been lonely for quite a while, and it was obvious she was really missing her mother. Lydia adored her niece.

The same could not be said for her nephew Phillip. How could the pair be so different? Any attempts Lydia had made to get closer to Phillip had been a disaster. It had made her very sad. She had never been able to have children – much to the rage of her deceased mother in-law, who had cruelly expected Akkoubian to get rid of Lydia because of this. But she hadn't counted on Akkoubian adoring his wife and it being a very loving marriage.

Maddie's mother phoned at 8 p.m. that night. Lydia had answered the phone first. Maddie was excited and would have loved to have taken the phone off her, but knew she would have to wait her turn. Finally her aunt came off the phone and handed it to her.

"Hello, Maddie. Is everything all right?" asked her mum.

"Yes, Mum. Fine," replied Maddie.

"I am in Kamala, Maddie. It looks as if the prisoner we are covering is going to be freed. I might be home sooner than in two weeks' time, but don't take my word for it. Things change here all the time.

"It is amazing what is going on here. The prisoner has been imprisoned for her political beliefs for nine years. She is an incredible woman, and it has been a roller coaster. But I am missing you so much, and have been worried about you … I know Lydia will have spoilt you rotten."

"She has, Mum, but I have been helping her … and Titch is so nice."

"How is your schoolwork going?"

"I have a lot of homework. I have done most of it. There's just a project I now have left to do. Before you ask I am eating fine. Don't worry about me. Aunt Lydia has been great, and I love her food."

Maddie continued her account of what she had been up to almost without stopping to breathe, and said,

"It's better than yours. She takes me to The Maltsters nearly every week. You'll have to take over doing that when you come home," said Maddie.

Her mother laughed down the phone and said,

"Cheeky monkey. Wait until I come back … I will have to sort you out. It will be back to gruel for you, my girl."

"Mum, Sam is coming round for tea tomorrow … and guess what? Aunt Lydia got the contract from the photographic club. They have booked a room, and are coming on Wednesday."

"That's great news about Lydia. I am glad you are spending time with Sam. I have some lovely presents for you and Lydia. You will love them."

"Oh, Mum, the most important thing of all to tell you is … I found a file in Uncle Akkoubian's room in a wardrobe drawer. It's all his history on Ursula Underville. I can't wait to show you it. My project is going to look great."

"That will be really interesting to see. I am looking forward to seeing it when I get home. Darling, I am so sorry, but I have to go. The rest of the team are shouting for me. Look after yourself and make sure Lydia is OK. Love you …"

"Love you too, Mum," said Maddie. The line went dead. A lump formed in her throat.

"Are you all right, Maddie?" asked Lydia anxiously.

"Yes, fine," gulped Maddie, her eyes watery. Her aunt went up and hugged her.

"Not long now before your mother comes home," she said gently.

"I know," came the choked reply, as her niece began rubbing her eyes with the sleeve of her jumper.

"Come on, Maddie … your programme will be on, won't it?"

"Yes," said Maddie nodding back gulping back tears. "It's The Assassin's Throne. Sam and I love it."

"I know you do. I just wish I knew what it was about," said Lydia, pulling a comical face and making Maddie grin.

It was a great sacrifice for Lydia to sit with her while she was watching the programme, as she just couldn't understand what Maddie saw in it.

"Aunt Lydia, can I show these papers I found in Uncle Akkoubian's drawer to you first? They are in the library."

Maddie went in there, followed by Lydia, and handed her the journal and the loose papers. Her aunt went through them and read from the papers.

"Your uncle writes with such great detail. He should have been a writer. Do you know that he has never shown me these papers?"

Watching Lydia gently handle the papers was a touching sight. She said,

"Why, you can even smell his Green Fern cologne."

Maddie hadn't noticed it before, but now it was very strong and she could now smell it. It seemed to linger in the room.

"Aunt Lydia, look at this." Maddie gave Lydia the details of the plans of the library.

"See where Uncle Akkoubian has written in red … what do you think that means? Do you think there is a secret room somewhere?"

"No. I think he would have found another room if there had been one."

"But, Aunt Lydia, he took ill when he was going through the history of the Hall. Maybe he never had time to look. There might be treasure somewhere."

"Oh, Maddie … you're dreaming again. If only there was … Things like that only happen in films. If only to curb your curiosity I will have Titch have a look at the plans tomorrow. I know you want to help me."

Her aunt smiled brightly at Maddie, but Maddie knew she was only humouring her.

"Thanks," said Maddie. She was feeling disappointed.

Titch wasn't there to look at them yet. They left the papers in the library and went back into the sitting room. Maddie began to lay more kindling on the fire. Lydia then lit it, and they settled on to their favourite sofas to watch the television. Lydia picking up her knitting and undid more lines, which were full of holes. She was terrible at knitting, but Maddie and her mother never said anything. They would wear the misshapen scarves to please her. They had hoped she would give up knitting, but she never did. More and more knits appeared as presents for them. Every Christmas she presented them with these knits. It would not have been Christmas if she had not done so.

The next morning, as Maddie was washing the breakfast dishes in the sink, Titch came in.

"Titch, can you have a look at Uncle Akkoubian's stuff for me? I just need some help on something."

She removed her hands from the soapy suds and dried them with the tea towel.

"They are in the library."

Maddie ran to get them and came back. She placed all the papers flat on the kitchen table. Titch looked through the papers carefully and finally said,

"Your uncle was such a clever man. Why, look at all the detail on the history of the Hall. He was well respected in the army. The men loved him. I was proud to serve under him in the army. You and Lydia are not the only ones who miss him, you know."

"Yes, Titch. I know a lot of people miss him," said Maddie quietly.

"These are those plans Uncle Akkoubian had ... but see what he has written in red. Do you think there is another room in the library?"

Titch studied the plans but then looked puzzled and said,

"These are not the plans of the main library. See ... look, this is the plan of the small library. I should know, pet. I had to move the bookshelves and the dresser out of it so Lydia could make it into a room for the photography club. It was a worry, because I really thought at one point that one of the walls would come down.

"That room seems to be badly built, from what I can see. I don't think you could even hang a picture on one of the walls without plaster coming off. No wonder they had the large dresser covering that side. I know it's the small library because it has that small side door. The main library does not have a side door, and is much larger than this. Look, he had more plans. See there ..."

"Oh, Lydia and I didn't see those plans," said Maddie. "This means that the secret room may be in the small library."

Titch replied,

"From looking at the state of the walls anything could be behind there. Your Uncle Julian did a rubbish job painting them walls. I don't know what possessed him to paint them. It is such a mess. But I doubt your Aunt Lydia will let that room be touched. The wall could come down at any time. I have warned her about it. It's a shame the photography club chose that room."

Maddie sighed. He was right. There was nothing she could do, what with the photography club using that room.

"What if we touch the walls? Do you think we might find a secret door that will open up into a room?"

"No. Probably nothing will happen, pet – apart from your aunt having to get the builders in to replace the lumps of plaster that will come off. So don't get your hopes up, and don't try."

"I suppose you are right. I won't mention it to her," said Maddie, frustrated once again.

It seemed as if there was always something trying to block her attempts to find out more about the Undervilles.

Chapter 9

Maddie went back to the kitchen and finished the dishes. Lydia began sorting out the laundry. Maddie, at her aunt's request, did a quick vacuum and general tidy-up. Then she then went back to look at her school project. She could not find anything further on the Undervilles.

The day went quite well. She sketched pictures of the Underville family, and did a family tree. She stretched, then she yawned and rubbed her neck. She decided to walk to the shops. When she looked out of the bedroom window it looked like a nice day, for a change. She went into her walk-in cupboard and took her camera off the shelf. Then she went to find Lydia, who was busy polishing some silverware.

"Can I go to the shops, Aunt Lydia?"

"Of course you can, dear," came the reply.

"Do you want anything?"

Lydia fished her tapestry purse out of her handbag and handed her a five pound note.

"Can you get me a copy of The Lady? Do you need any money for yourself?"

"No, Aunt Lydia. I still have some of the money Mum left me – and, remember, she said she had wired some more over for you. It should be in your bank account."

"Your mother really didn't need to do that, but it was nice of her to do it," said Lydia, sounding embarrassed.

Maddie put on her blue Jack Wolfskin coat, grabbed her bag with the camera in, and walked into Cattingham. She did not know many of the people of her age living there.

It was at Meadowfield where she had a few friends. But one person who she would prefer to not live in Cattingham was Julie Painter. She knew where she lived. It was in Albany Street, in a small Victorian terraced house made of brick, so Maddie avoided going anywhere near there like the plague.

After walking into the newsagent's she bought Aunt Lydia's magazine. The front cover had the head and shoulders of Colin Firth in a bubble bath.

"My aunt will certainly like looking at him," thought Maddie as she giggled to herself. Then she bought her own magazine and a birthday card for her mother.

The woman in the newsagent's was called Jane. She was a well-known nosy parker. She was tall and thin, with closely cropped blonde hair and a big nose. Loving her holidays abroad, which involved siting on a beach and not moving, the result of which had now produced extremely wrinkled and sun-damaged skin. This made her look older than her forty-six years. She was also man mad. Any good-looking male who came into the newsagent's was bombarded by flirtatious attempts to get them to go out with her.

As she took Maddie's money Jane's large nose seemed to almost quiver with nosiness as she tried to get her into conversation about the Hall, but she did not get much out of her. After Maddie had gone out of the door Jane, who was disappointed, craned her neck and watched her walk up the street. Then she turned to her assistant, who was marking off deliveries, and said,

"What a quiet one she is. Why, I could hardly get a word out of her. Her friend must be as shy as her, because she waited outside the shop."

Her assistant Elaine, a curly-haired girl, said in reply,

"I think she is lonely ... such a nice lass."

"A bit stuck-up, I think. Well, what you can expect, with her jet-setting mam going off halfway round the world and then dumping the lass on Lydia at the Hall ...? Still, at least she has made a friend now in Cattingham I suppose she will be posh as well?" replied Jane, cattily now busy and going through her orders.

"Aye but it will be good for her. Oh, I must have missed seeing the friend she was with. Do you know her?"

"No, I don't know who she is. She was outside waiting for her dressed in some white costume. Strange time in the morning to be dressed in that get up, but that's young girls for you."

Maddie had come out of the newsagent's completely unaware that the ghost was following slowly behind her. The church was now facing her. She looked across at it and crossed over the cobbled street towards it. She thought she might be able to take some photographs of it, and remembered that some of the old household staff from Cattingham Hall were buried there. The history would with any luck bulk up her school project out if she ran out of ideas.

The church was thirteenth-century, with a vaulted stone roof with rusty iron railings surrounding it. It was shaded by three huge yew trees, one of which looked as if it was dying. The leaves had an unhealthy, discoloured look about them. A lone wood pigeon strutted across Maddie's path and excitedly grabbed a purple-coloured worm then flew off.

Maddie walked up the well-weeded path towards the church. To her left was a carved stone angel, its wings outstretched as if in flight. In its praying hands the angel held a musical instrument. The stone sculpture rested on a white plinth. Maddie took a picture of the outside of the church with her camera. Then she walked round the back of the church to look at the graves.

She decided she would make notes of the names of the staff and see if she could find anything connected to the Hall. Some of the graves dated back to the sixteenth century. One of the graves caught her eye.

Normally she would not have taken any notice of such a plain, completely unadorned stone headstone. There was one tiny white rose carved in detail on it. It said simply the dates of the births and deaths of Mathew and Agatha Blackstock … They had died in 1830, and had been faithful servants to Thomas and Ursula Underville. Underneath this inscription it said,

Beloved daughter Anna Blackstock
Lost but never forgotten.
There were no birth or death records on the headstone.

"Who was Anna Blackstock?" That was the second time that name had been said. Perhaps she was a relative. But why did it just say,

Lost but never forgotten?
And hadn't her uncle mentioned that name?
"Strange that the name should come up here," thought Maddie.

It seemed too much of a coincidence. Maddie quickly photographed the grave and reminded herself that she would look on the Internet when she went back to the Hall to see if she could find any further information on that name.

"Hello, Maddie. I thought it was you."

On glancing up Maddie recognised the friendly Scottish voice. It was Colin, the vicar of Cattingham Church.

"Hello ... I am looking for information on the Undervilles. I came across Mathew and Agatha Blackstock. See this gravestone here. It says they worked at the Hall. I was curious about Anna Blackstock. I have heard of that name before. Look at what it says here."

The vicar bent down to have a look at the headstone with her and replied,

"Well, it is a strange inscription. How strange that I never noticed it before. If it was their daughter Anna it would have said the year she was born and the year she died. I have never seen a grave here just saying lost but never forgotten. It is the family burial plot. She would have been expected to be buried with them if she was unmarried.

"If you come with me we might find something in the parish records. The books in the church are so old they date back as far as the sixteenth century. I did know there was a tuberculosis epidemic around the date the Blackstocks died in Cattingham. She may have died from tuberculosis from what at the time was called the white plague. Come on, let's check the registers and see what we can find."

Maddie followed him as he went into the church. He was a heavily built man with a pleasant, round face and blue eyes. He was fortunate in his middle age to be in possession of a full head of hair, which was pepper-and-salt brown with a side parting. His broad face was quite white apart from his cheeks, which were a pink red that had been caused by mild rosacea ...

He was dressed in a faded navy blue crew-necked jumper that strained over his belly. His matching faded blue corduroy trousers were struggling to stay up, and were held up by a leather belt. A pair of dusty brown suede shoes completed the image. The only way you would have known he was a vicar was by his dog collar, which poked unceremoniously out of the neck of his jumper.

The wooden church door was heavy. Inside it was a smaller door leading into the church. The church gave off a sparkling turquoise light caused by the dark green-coloured glass of the leaded windows. The windows of the church were decorated with stone angel heads mounts;

Maddie moved past the walnut pews. As she walked she looked at the walls, which were covered by faded religious tapestries. There was a chalky, classroom smell about the church. Maddie trainers made an embarrassing squeaking noise on the wooden floor as she walked across it. Colin did not appear to notice or, if he did, was too polite to say anything.

A brand-new church organ gleamed from the far left of the church. Mrs Mountside, the church organist, took her job very seriously, according to Titch. She would press her fingers down on the keys with a great flourish and raise her hands high in the air after each note, and look at the congregation for approval. Titch had said to Maddie and Lydia that, from the way she played, you would have thought she was Liberace. Lydia had laughed but Maddie hadn't, as she didn't know who Liberace was. When she was told who he was she was still none the wiser.

Maddie and Colin walked to the side door of the church, and Colin asked how Lydia was. He then said wistfully that he was sorry that Akkoubian had died.

"He did a lot of fundraising for the church," Maddie said in response, and told him that her aunt was being kept busy running the Hall, with Titch helping her.

"She has a contract with the photographic club now," she said.

"That is good, Maddie. It is best that she keeps busy in her time of sadness. She will have her good days and bad days. Help look after her," he said kindly.

"I will," said Maddie. "So will my mum. She is back from Africa soon. She spends a lot of time with her."

"Excellent. I have not met your mother, but she appears to have a very exciting life as a journalist. She must have great tales to tell," replied Colin.

"She has. I am going to be a journalist when I grow up, so I am trying to learn as much as I can from her," said Maddie seriously.

Impressed by her maturity, the vicar smiled fondly at her. As they walked through the door of his study the first things you saw were a bookcase, some filing cabinets, and an old computer and table with a wobbly computer chair. A cup of stale, curdled tea rested on a newspaper. The milk had gathered at the top, giving it a spotty custard-like top. Next to it was a crumpled-up packet of Nice biscuits.

"What date did you say that inscription read?" asked Colin.

Maddie repeated it. He went through a heavy records book, and his finger went down each page.

"Ah, here we have it. Agatha Blackstock died from tuberculosis, shortly followed by Mathew Blackstock in the same year."

He went through the book further on in the years and said,

"Well, there is no death recorded of Anna Blackstock. She may have been a baby who died at birth. But I will first check in the register of births. I will start at the earliest date she may have been alive."

He once again did a detailed search. His face scrunched up with concentration.

"I've got it here. There is a birth of an Anna Blackstock, who was born at 5 Low Row Cottages, Cattingham. Her parents were Mathew and Agatha Blackstock. Of course, when she was older she may have married and moved away from the village. There may be another parish that holds her records. But the inscription on the headstone is strange. I might be able to check further on this for you, but it may take a bit of time. Leave it with me, Maddie."

"Thank you, Colin, for going to so much trouble for me. The other thing I need is ... have you any information on the Undervilles?"

"Yes. There is a separate book on the Undervilles. Here it is. They were an eminent family. They provided most of the work for the villagers round here. It's sad now to see that the village has changed so much, and that a lot of the locals have moved away.

"Ah, here's some early information on them. Thomas Underville was married to Sarah until her death. They had a young daughter, Alice, who died young. Thomas Underville's mother was, I have heard, a religious woman. It says here, however, that she belonged to the order of the Drakens."

Colin wrinkled his nose in disgust as he said this.

"Do you not like the Drakens, Colin?"

"No. They are not to my taste," he replied tersely. "They are a fanatical religious group. I'm afraid to say that I have always found them cruel and unforgiving. There are people who still belong to the group, but they tend to be more secretive about it these days. They still use the old Masonic Hall at Bickleberry. I do not, I am pleased to say, have any current dealings with them. There have been problems in the past with them."

He shuddered when he said this, but would not add anything further on the matter. Instead he continued through the book on the Undervilles and said,

"Thomas married Ursula Underville. She died before his sister, so she was very young to have died. You do know she is in the family crypt at Cattingham Hall, don't you?"

"Yes, I do know that. I have not been in there. But I think I will go just to see if there is more information there."

"Well, just be careful, Maddie. Make sure you go with someone if you do. The recent flooding caused a small landslide, from what I have heard. Some of the stonework could dislodge itself, and it might hurt you."

"I will," she replied. "Thank you for all your help." Colin smiled back and said,

"I will try and get more information on Anna for you. There must be parish records that show she moved from the village."

He quickly wrote down the information from the parish records and handed it to her. She placed it in her breast pocket and said goodbye and went out of the church. When she thought about what Colin had said about the Drakens she did not like the sound of them. They must, she thought, have been very nasty people.

Chapter 10

Low Row, where Anna and her father and mother had lived, was not far. Maddie decided to take the long walk home through Brocket Woods. Low Row was on the way to the woods.

When she turned the corner from the church she came to the farm. To the left side of it was Low Row Cottages. There were only three cottages left standing, and only one looked intact. The others looked as if they were on the point of falling down … A blinding curiosity made her, for some reason, go up the path to the Blackstock family house.

The ramshackle whitewashed cottage was in need of a lick of paint. It would have been a very pretty cottage once but now the white paint, which now looked like porridge, had peeled off in flakes on the front of the house. There was a well-worn grass path leading to it, and clusters of daisies grew among the tough-looking weeds …

As she walked up the path it felt surreal.

She was sure that it reminded her of something in some of the dreams she had been having lately. Cardboard boxes of broken tiles and rubbish lay propped up against the front of the cottage. A stone planter was filled with old school textbooks and broken, abandoned Christmas decorations.

When she peered in the window she could see only an old fireplace, but no furniture. Bits of scaffolding were strewn about the floor. It was not how she had imagined it. It would have been a long time ago when someone had last lived in the house. The door appeared to be the original door. More boxes of rubbish were piled up by the dustbin. The sound of a door opening made her jump, and a voice said,

"Hello. Can I help you?"

As she turned round she saw it was the games mistress from her school, Miss Price.

Maddie started stammering and felt embarrassed at being caught snooping. She blurted out,

"Sorry ... I just wanted to see what the house looked like. My school project is about Cattingham Hall. I went to the church and saw the headstone of the Blackstock family. They were in service at the hall. I believe they lived at Low Row Cottages."

On seeing her discomfort her teacher gave her a reassuring smile and said,

"It is OK, Maddie. I didn't think you were trying to break in."

"Miss Price, do you live here?"

"Heavens, no," came the amused reply. "The houses are on the point of being pulled down. Bill Robson, the builder, has bought all three of them. He is just waiting for completion to go through. It was the land he wanted underneath them. The end house was my aunt's ... She passed away. I have been clearing the house. It is very sad to see the houses in this state. But they are not habitable any longer, and will need to be pulled down. Bill is going to build some new houses on the site."

As the teacher paused Maddie could not contain herself any further, and burst out with,

"Miss Price, did your aunt know anything of the history of the Blackstocks? I just want to add information to my school project, what with them working at Cattingham Hall."

"Well, yes, my aunt did mention them. The local gossip had been passed down to her from the previous generations. The father was a gardener at the Hall, if I remember rightly. The daughter Anna was, according to my aunt, known in these parts as a natural healer. There was some mystery about her, though, from what I have heard. It was if she had completely vanished into thin air. Her family tried to look for her, but never found her. The mother died of tuberculosis, but my aunt said – from what she had heard – that it had been of a broken heart, not from that. She never got over Anna disappearing. Her husband died shortly after her. Anna was their only daughter. She was, I have been told, great friends with Ursula Underville at the Hall."

"Oh, was Anna friends with Ursula Underville?"

"Yes, Maddie. Best friends. But the friendship would have been frowned on by Ursula's family because of Anna's low social status. Commoners like Anna were not regarded as having equal status to the Undervilles, and were expected to know their place. Anna was an unusual girl, and would have stood out in the village. She was also very striking and was believed to have been at least six feet tall, which would have been something unusual in those days."

"Miss Price, I bet they would have been friends because I read that Ursula had written a book on natural healing," replied Maddie.

"I didn't know that. It looks like you have been doing your homework on this one. Oh, this might interest you … The builder has stripped the cottage to its bare bones to see how it would have looked originally. I have keys to all the cottages, and I check on them for him when I come up here. Do you want to have a look in Anna's cottage?"

"Oh, yes, please. That would be great."

"Well, let me get the keys. They are in my aunt's kitchen. I'll be back in a minute."

The teacher smiled at her and went back into her aunt's cottage. She was a very slim woman, and was wearing her usual trademark navy Nike tracksuit and trainers. Her long red wavy hair was tied back in a tight ponytail.

Maddie had not been that good at sport but Miss Price had been patient with her, and had spurred her on with her running and swimming. Maddie had then gone on to achieve some athletic prowess on the running field. It was only because of Miss Price's faith in her that she had come second on sports day this year in the 100 metres and in the 200 metres.

The teacher was back out of the house and marching down the path within seconds. The stance of gym teacher was taking over.

"Come on," she commanded Maddie.

The door appeared to make what sounded like groaning noises as she unlocked it, and they both went inside the house. The house was not built for tall people that was for sure.

"Josh would have had to bend his head all the way through it," thought Maddie. She wondered how someone as tall as Anna had fared when she had lived in the house.

The door of the house led straight into the sitting room. The room was bare. The only adornment was an old inglenook fireplace. Black, half-exposed beams ran in lengths across the ceiling. The wooden floor looked very uneven, and the bare boards creaked as you walked on them.

It was very dusty, and there was a smoky smell about the place. Maddie sneezed a couple of times. Fortunately she had a hanky. She did not think Miss Price would have been impressed if she had wiped her nose on her sleeve. The windows in the sitting room were quite small, and not much light came through them. The next room they went into was the kitchen. It had a door leading off it. Behind the door was a small toilet.

"The toilet, of course, would not have been in the house around the time of Anna and her family," said Miss Price. She added, "The builder is selling the old kitchen range to an antiques dealer."

The range had been taken out and was propped against the wall. Everything else had been taken out of the room, and it was difficult walking around the kitchen because there was so much rubble. A white object was stuck in among the rubbish. Maddie bent to pick it up. It was a lace posy, and it was exactly the same as the one she had found in her room at Cattingham Hall. Maddie let her teacher see it.

"Someone must have been into healing. It is full of herbs – very old herbs, judging by the colour of the lace. I am surprised it is not black after lying in the rubble," said the teacher. She turned the object over in her hand, and then dismissed it by throwing it into a cardboard box full of rags. She then looked at the oven and proceeded to talk about it.

"This looks like one my grandmother had," she commented.

Maddie half listened. She was straining to hear something in the background. It sounded like a humming

"Did you hear that?" Maddie asked.

"Hear what?"

"That noise."

"I can't hear anything," came the teacher's reply. She was now too busy opening the old oven door and peering in.

"Yes, it's exactly the same as my grandmother's," she said excitedly. Then came a whisper in Maddie's ear.

"Maddie," said a voice from behind her.

She jumped, but Miss Price did not notice. She was still talking about the oven. When she looked behind her there was only Miss Price in the room with her.

"Let's look in the bedrooms. I hope this is not boring you," Miss Price suggested.

"Oh, no, miss," Maddie replied, still shocked by the voice she had heard.

They went up the tiny flight of stairs. The first bedroom was tiny. It was a narrow-shouldered room with a beamed ceiling and a window in the eaves. There was no furniture in it. Maddie had a strong feeling that this had been Anna's bedroom.

Almost immediately after entering the room a light tapping began at the window. Maddie turned round, her heart in her stomach, but saw that it was just ivy growing outside the window and trying to creep its way into the house. Miss Price was completely unperturbed by the tapping and said,

"This fireplace does not look as old as the fireplace downstairs. Look at the style of it. What a big fireplace ..."

Maddie smiled stupidly. She was not able to discuss this matter as she did not know the history of fireplaces or their sizes, so instead she said,

"I like the shape of the bedroom," just for something to say, but thought Miss Price probably had decided she was a bit stupid.

To avoid any more conversations on fireplaces Maddie looked out of the window of the bedroom. The garden was small but beyond that it led to a field, and then to Brocket Woods.

"Anna must have loved playing round here," said Maddie to herself. On hearing her say this Miss Price said,

"It was not an easy life if you were poor. Children had to work in those days. I do know she could read and write, and was taught by nuns at St Saviours School. In fact she helped to teach the young pupils, so she was quite bright. But she would have been expected to go into service and give up any ideas about being a teacher."

"Where is the school? Maddie asked.

"Oh, it's not a school now, of course. It's in the village of Bickleberry. I believe they use the school for parish meetings. You can get to it through Brocket Woods. Anna would have walked through the woods to get to her school. It's about a couple of miles away."

Miss Price walked briskly out of the small bedroom saying,

"Come on, Maddie. Let's look in the other room."

Maddie came away from the window. As she did so she could hear a rumbling sound coming from the fireplace. She went over to it. Soot poured down from it into the grate and on to her feet. Then something hit her foot. There was so much soot that she could not see what it was. It felt heavy, and she hoped it was not a dead bird. When she moved her feet she saw that a small, soot-covered book lay on the ground.

For some reason instinct told her not to tell Miss Price about this, so she placed it in the breast pocket of her coat. She then wiped her hands with her now-blackened handkerchief just as Miss Price came running into the room. On hearing the noise and seeing the fireplace she said,

"Are you all right, Maddie?"

"Yes, Miss. Look what happened to the fireplace. The soot just came down. I didn't touch it," said Maddie quickly, thinking she was going to get told off. But Miss Price just said,

"Oh, don't worry about that. Old fireplaces tend to do that … although it would have been a very long time ago when the last fire was lit in this house."

"Who were the last people who lived in this cottage?" Maddie asked.

"Well, my aunt said that an elderly couple lived here, and before that another old lady lived there – if I can remember from my childhood – but she died, and it was empty for a long time after that.

"Oh, Maddie, look at your shoes. They are thick with soot. We'll get you shoes cleaned up, though. Your hands are black. There is still water in the cottage, but it will be cold water. On the plus side there are plenty of old rags to clean your shoes with."

She was being so nice to Maddie, even though the bedroom floor now looked a blackened mess as more soot poured from the chimney on to the floor.

Maddie felt guilty about not telling her about the book, but it was almost as if a voice in her head was telling her not to give the book to her teacher. So she said nothing, and did not look in the other bedroom.

Instead they went downstairs, and Maddie brushed herself down in the garden while her teacher wiped Maddie's shoes with a piece of a wet towel in the kitchen sink, then she washed her hands.

When she looked out into the garden she realised that it was very small. There was a tired-looking blackcurrant bush and what looked like rows of slug-eaten lettuces and a few runner beans, but there was not much else growing out of the hard clay soil. The only adornment to the garden was an old wooden trellis with dried dead flowers draped ceremoniously around it that lay there abandoned. Flowers were growing about the garden, but Maddie did not know the names of them. More boxes lay propped against the dustbin, which was filled with newspapers, old curtains, and towels.

"Well, I'm afraid there is nothing much more to see now, so that's the tour over," said Miss Price, smiling.

"I hope you enjoyed it."

"Yes, I did. Thank you, miss." They went back through the kitchen and out of the sitting room door.

"Bye, Miss Price," said Maddie, wishing she could have been more talkative. She thought that her teacher must have thought her very boring.

"Goodbye, Maddie. I hope your project goes well."

The teacher waved goodbye to her, locked the front door, and then went back into her aunt's house.

It was August, but there had not been much sun. As Maddie walked down the path she noticed that it was now littered with what looked like polystyrene beads. As she looked back at the boxes of rubbish she saw that a black bin liner had blown open and had released them along the garden. It felt slightly hard underfoot as she walked on a carpet of the beads, and she enjoyed hearing the crackle as she trod on them.

Maddie did not dare to have a look at the diary yet. She thought that she would wait until she got to Brocket Woods. To get there she had to cross a stone bridge. A fast running stream ran underneath it.

Maddie hated walking across the bridge. It always made her feel uneasy, and she ran across it to get over it quickly.

Her history teacher, Mr Pulman, had told the class the that bridge had been used in the sixteenth century – and even up to the eighteenth and nineteenth centuries – as a test to see if any suspected local women were witches. The women were thrown into the stream with one hand and one leg tied. If they floated down the stream they were guilty, but if they drowned they were innocent.

Maddie thought that the women did not have a fair chance either way. On the days she sometimes walked across the bridge with Lydia she would race down even then. Her aunt always told her that she had an overactive imagination, and to forget about the story. But she never could.

Chapter 11

As Maddie came up to the entrance to the woods it was very dark. Lines of Norway spruce grew in regimental lines as she walked through into the woods. They led on to new planted Scots pine. As she walked there was a stream to her right side, and overgrown fern and knotted duckweed spilled out of it in twisted clumps. Uncle Akkoubian used to take her fishing there. She blinked away the sad memory that came when she thought about him. The wood was heavily shaded. The crowded trees were full of huge buzzards' nests.

Maddie did not have to go much farther to get to the old splintered wooden seat in the woods. There she would be able to read the diary in peace. She hoped that she would not bump into anyone she knew.

She pulled the small cloth diary out of her breast pocket. It was still mucky. She wiped it with her hankie. Written on the front of it in embossed gold spidery letters were the words Anna Blackstock. There was no date inside the diary. The first page said,

Monday. It is a sickly time at Cattingham Hall. She gave her a pill, which made her sick just as the others had done. She tells me she makes her take the pill every day. There have been a lot of funerals here. Ursula has not got better from her sickness. I miss my friend.

The entry for Tuesday said,

They will not let me see her. I can make a posy with herbs to make her well again. I offer my posy to them but they do not take it to her. I must help Ursula, or she will die. Miss Burnham has told me I can take my posy to her. I go tomorrow night to take it to her. I must not tell Mam and Dad I am going to do this. The villagers are calling me a witch because of Ursula.

There were no further entries in the cloth-bound diary. The only things in it were dried herbs and leaves, which were in between the pages of the book.

"Why were there no other entries in the diary?" Maddie wondered. "What happened to Anna after she had delivered the herbs to Ursula? Would the school at Bickleberry show where Anna had gone?"

The air seemed very cold around her, and she became disturbed the more she thought more deeply about it.

"Did a terrible thing happen to Anna, and is that why she disappeared?" If only there had been dates in the diary she might have been able to link up the dates when Ursula ended up in the mental institution.

Maddie was now becoming more aware of her surroundings. Alone in the woods she felt spooked. The only sound was the rustle of water coming from the stream. How she wished she hadn't opened the diary in the woods. The dark, grey trees lining the woods cast malevolent shadows round her, which sent her imagination into overdrive. It was in these woods that the seven-foot-long skeletons of the dogs had been found, or something. Maddie remembered Sam telling her about it. Didn't she also say that they had been servants to the witches who lived in the woods? Villagers had often said that when cutting through the woods they could hear strange howling noises.

She was now feeling nervous, and she took her mobile out of her pocket to phone Sam just to hear her friendly voice. Sam answered immediately. Maddie told her about the gravestone and the diary.

"Wow ... you have her diary. That's great," said Sam.

"Not really. I feel guilty about not telling Miss Price."

"Oh, don't worry about it. We'll think of some way to return it to the house."

"Don't you think it strange how Anna disappeared?" Maddie went on.

"Yes, it does seem creepy. Can you imagine if she had been murdered, and her body was under your Aunt Lydia's hydrangea bush? Titch would go crackers. They are his pride and joy."

"Don't say that, Sam. I am frightened enough as it is. I am in the woods on my own, you know."

"Oh, I am only joking. She probably took off with a village boy. I bet that's the reason. I am sure the ghost will contact you if we hold a séance."

"Oh … guess what? I found my Ouija board. Did you say to come round at 5 p.m. for tea—? Oh, Mum's calling me. I have to go."

"Yes, I did. See you then. Bye."

Maddie placed the mobile in her coat pocket and the diary back in her breast pocket. Then she continued walking through the woods. Something strange caught her eyes. It looked like a pile of old brown woollen rags piled up in a messy heap. She wondered if they had blown over from somewhere else. For a moment her eyes played tricks on her, and she had a crazy idea that it was a figure rising up from the ground. On realising her mistake she laughed nervously to herself and walked past it. She now wished someone was there with her so at least she would not feel so alone.

As she began to walk fast she had a strange feeling that something was not right, but she did not know why she felt this. Her heart started to beat very fast. Something in her head warned her not to turn round in case she saw something she did not want to see.

"This is silly. Why am I so nervous?" There is nothing there," she kept repeating to herself.

To comfort herself she remembered what Uncle Akkoubian used to say when she became frightened in the woods when she was little. He would say that the tall trees in the wood were not trees, but a large family of African elephants that came out at night to play. He had said they played football and had a large red ball hidden in the woods.

Sometimes he would look behind bushes and peer up trees and say he was looking for their football, and would ask her if she could help find the football. She had loved that story … But it did not feel like there were elephants in the woods now.

In her mind she had the distinct feeling someone was behind her, and she ended up breaking into a run to get out of the woods. Then came strange whisperings in her head telling her to get out of the woods quickly. Once she got to the edge of the woods she turned and looked back.

In the distance was a figure, but she could not make out what the person looked like. He or she seemed to be dressed in brown, and was wearing what seemed like monastic clothing. The person certainly did not look like a villager from Cattingham. That was enough for her to continue to run at full speed all the way back to Cattingham Hall without looking back. The unexpected run made her breathless when she arrived there.

The photographic club were still taking photos of the gardens. Lydia was outside talking to Mr Robin Stanford, who was the head of the photographic club. As he went away Maddie managed to compose herself and catch her breath as Lydia said,

"Titch won't be pleased if they touch any of the flowers. You know how blunt-speaking he is."

Maddie nodded in agreement. Some people would say he was sharp-tongued but to her he was just plain-speaking. You knew where you were with him.

An image of Titch came into her head. He was of average height and slim build, with silvery-white hair and blue eyes. His skin was permanently weathered, due to always being outdoors. He had the typical gait of a person who had been in the forces, in Maddie's mother's opinion.

He had been born in Bickleberry to parents who had run the local cafe until they had retired. Now his parents lived at the Sunny Lodge retirement home in Bickleberry. He had not had any children with his wife, but doted on his niece. She was at Sheffield University doing a degree in fashion and design.

Lydia would have been lost without Titch. She gave him what she could afford, and he would turn up in all weathers to help her. Maddie would have loved to have shown Titch the diary, but decided to get it photocopied then return it to her teacher. She tried not to think what her teacher would say about her having taken it in the first place.

"Great news, Maddie. I have another room booking. The Fine Arts Group have booked a room once a month. They want Saturdays, so it will be all day from October. Things are looking up." Lydia's eyes were shining, and they sparkled as she spoke. Relief in her voice.

Maddie was pleased to see her not looking so worried.

"When the photographic club are finished Mr Stanford is going to take the projector back to his car. We'll keep the door wide open because a lot of the group members have brought their own equipment with them."

Maddie looked across at Mr Stanford, a tall and thin dark-haired man. He had won quite a few photographic awards. In fact Lydia had an enlarged photograph of a sunflower field he had taken hanging on the kitchen wall.

"Aunt Lydia, I've got your magazine. I'll take it into the sitting room."

"Thank you, dear. Maddie, this will please you. I have made my special pasta sauce for when Samantha comes tonight, and I have done a lot of baking."

Lydia emphasised the word 'baking'. A broad grin came across Maddie's mouth. "That will please Sam," thought Maddie. Sam loved Lydia's cooking.

The baking usually consisted of either nutty tray bakes or jam coconut squares. As she went into the sitting room she brushed against one of the photographers coming out of the hall.

"You might be an interesting subject to photograph," the man said to Maddie.

Embarrassed, she smiled back shyly at the heavily bearded man and hurried into the sitting room. She thought that probably meant she was plain and boring.

Once in the sitting room she placed the magazine on the coffee table. On realising that she still had her coat on she went to take it off, but the diary thumped at her chest as she did this. So she removed the diary from out of her pocket and proceeded to have another look at it. The fabric looked more like a dull brown, and some of the pages were stuck together. She had not noticed that before. Her thin fingers gently unstuck them, and to her delight she realised that two of the pages had further entries written on them. Annoyingly though there was no year mentioned in any of the entries.

The first page read,

December 3. For Mam and Dad I plant the witch bottle. Please help them. God protect them.

They call me a witch. Mam says I must go to Bickleberry to be safe.

95

The second page had what seemed like some sort of rhyme on it. It said in spidery handwriting,

I will fill a bottle of my pee filled at midnight to make sure the magic do work.

In it I fill my fingernails, hair, and bent nails, and my leather I will wear.

I bury it outside the house so that the evil will go back to the witches.

I will fill a bottle for Ursula. I must go from the village and take Ursula with me. It is not safe.

Reading it gave Maddie goose bumps.

So Anna was not a witch. She was trying to protect her family from the witches. So who were the witches?

"And a witch's bottle ... I wonder what that looks like," thought Maddie.

She put the book down and went into the library and switched the computer on, and typed the words 'witch's bottle'.

On Wikipedia it came up that this was used as a form of protection against witches. The bottles were usually made of glass, with a cork stopper. A person would place urine, hair, or nail clippings, and bent nails in it. Usually it was buried somewhere in or outside the house. The witch's bottle was supposed, it was said, to capture the evil – which would then be impaled on the bent pins.

"Ugh ... urine in the bottle. That would not be nice to handle," thought Maddie.

Her eyes were wide open as she read more detail. Anna was leaving the village, it seemed, because the villagers were calling her a witch. But then she could not be a witch, they were wrong because she was trying to protect her family against witches herself.

Maddie placed the diary back in her coat pocket. The door opened, and a strange face peered at her.

"Oh, I am so sorry. I think I took a wrong turning." It was a lady from the photographic club.

"Oh, don't worry about that. I do it all the time, and I live here," replied Maddie.

The woman got over her embarrassment, and noticed that Maddie had on her computer screen the words 'witch's bottle' displayed on it.

"That looks interesting."

"I'm doing a school project and I came across this word. I just wondered what a witch's bottle was."

"What a coincidence," the woman replied. "My name is Sandra Duffy, by the way. I have been doing a family tree. It goes back as far as the 1700s. None of my family moved from Cattingham, so I suppose that's why all the family history remained intact. They were farmers … nothing too high-class, unfortunately. I had hoped that I might belong to some wealthy dynasty, and could claim my inheritance. Instead I find that an ancestor of mine stood trial for witchcraft."

Maddie gave a shy smile and responded by saying,

"That sounds really interesting. It's very nice to meet you. My name is Maddie Johnson. I am the niece of Lydia Underville, and I am staying here for a couple of weeks. I have been reading about witchcraft in Cattingham … It is hard to believe there were witches in Cattingham. What was the name of your relative who was accused of witchcraft?"

"Mary Blackbird. She was an innocent woman. They would have called her a midwife in these days. A kindly body well known for making potions for women with childbirth problems to help alleviate the pain. This was mistaken as witchcraft. It was shameful, what happened to her," Sandra Duffy shook her head, as if imagining the injustice of it all, and continued by saying,

"My family history gave details of innocent women and young girls being drowned under the bridge at Low Row. There was never enough proof that there were any witches. The Drakens, from what I have read, appeared to have orchestrated all the witch-hunts. There was a lot of misery and fear brought to this village by them.

"My aunt mentioned another lady, too, who had been a midwife, who had been accused of being a witch – a Martha Barnfather."

"I heard about the Drakens from Colin at Cattingham Church," Maddie said in response. "Do you know anything of an Anna Blackstock?"

"Why, yes. She was one of the villagers they tried to drown at Low Row, wasn't she? I know the names of three of the women who stood trial. There were two women and a girl who stood trial for witchcraft. That was not Anna. This was some other unfortunate. Anna appeared not to have had a trial, but the villagers tried to drown her. However, she escaped then disappeared. She must have got out of the village ..."

"Have you seen the grave of the parents of Anna Blackstock at Cattingham church?" asked Maddie.

"No, I haven't, but I will look out for it now. I might have some papers you can have on the Blackstock family. I'll pop them in an envelope through your aunt's letter box. It's not a lot of information, but I was trying to find out about women accused of witchcraft ... bearing in mind I was related to one," said Sandra.

"Thank you so much. Any information you could find would be great."

"OK, dear. Well, I must go. I am helping a couple of new recruits. They will be wondering where I am."

"Oh well it was nice meeting you .If you go out of this door turn right round the corner, and the front door will be facing you," said Maddie.

Chapter 12

After saying their goodbyes Sandra went out of the door and Maddie had another look on the screen at 'witch's bottle'. There was nothing much to add about them. But she now knew Anna had placed one outside her house ... not that she could tell Bill Robson the builder, and she still had the diary. She switched the computer off and made her way up to her bedroom, hoping her laptop was still working. But she had to go past the small library, so she peeped in to look at the photographs on the walls.

On some of the tables there were light boxes with pictures on stands. Most of the photographs tended to have a gloss finish. There was some amazing photography. The one she liked the best was one of Brocket Woods in early morning, with a lone grouse walking along to the stream. The sun shining directly on the trees had made the woods really come alive, and it took away their normal dark and uninhabited look.

One of the photographers had taken a picture of Titch digging. But he did not look happy, and had more of a grimace than a smile on his face. But there was something to the side of the picture, and Maddie had to look closely to make it out. It was the girl dressed in white she had seen the other day in Cattingham. It was a side profile, and she even had her white outfit on. Her face was quite blurred, so Maddie could not get a good look of her face in detail.

It startled Maddie, and she stared in shock until a voice said,

"Hello, Maddie. I see you have been looking at our photographs."

"Hello, Mr Stanford. This picture here ... do you know who took it?" asked Maddie.

"I think, if I remember rightly, it was Anita Cummings."

"Do you know who the girl in the photo is?

"No. I'm afraid you will need to ask Anita."

"Ask Anita what?"

Maddie and Mr Stanford turned round in reply to the voice.

"Hi, Anita. Do you know who the girl in your photo is?" Mr Stanford said in response to a small, fair-haired woman wearing a polo neck jumper that appeared to be two sizes too big for her.

"No, I didn't ask her name. Titch distracted me by asking me how long he had to hold his shovel, and when I turned round she had gone. I asked him who she was, and he said he didn't even notice her beside him. It was a complete mystery. But the most annoying thing was that my photograph did not come out very clearly. You can see Titch's face very well, but the girl's face is extremely blurred. If you knew how expensive my camera was you would know it's not the type of camera to give that type of image. I was really close up to them both, so there was no reason why that should have happened."

Maddie was tempted to say to her,

"Do you believe in ghosts?" but whenever she had said that people looked at her like she was a bit of a loony, so she decided to say nothing. When Sam had said she had actually seen ghosts people tended to look at her in the way they looked at Maddie when she said it. No one ever took them seriously. It was so annoying.

More photographers, who were talking excitedly, arrived in the room. The photographic shoot appeared to be going well. Maddie edged past them and went up to her room. She mulled over what had happened. It was obvious that she was going to get some contact from the ghost. Now she did not feel frightened of her. But it was the robed person she had seen in the woods who she did not like the look of.

"Who was it?" she thought. She was sure this was also a ghost. One ghost was bad enough, but another …

"Ugh. It doesn't bear thinking about," she said to herself.

As she went into her room she noticed that the door was wide open. She had shut it when she had left the room. A quick glance round the room showed there was no one there. She switched the laptop back on and prayed it would work. The light came on and she signed in with her password. The icons appeared, and she got into the Word documents she had created for her project. After looking through the papers she had collected she began typing. She was so engrossed that she did not hear Lydia come into the room.

"Maddie." She jerked up from the computer in surprise and saw it was her aunt.

"Sorry. I didn't hear you come in."

"I said I am making tea now. It's 4 p.m. Can you give me a hand, please?"

"It's never 4 p.m. already, is it?" said Maddie. She was amazed. She had completely lost track of time. "I'll just finish this sentence off."

"OK, dear," replied Lydia.

"Lydia, I had a few problems with the laptop earlier and I couldn't get into the net. It seems to be working OK now."

"Well, that's a relief. Computermax have made a small fortune out of me, what with the television constantly needing to be repaired – and the computers. But it's where we live. For some reason we keep losing the signal. It is so annoying. The neighbours do not appear to have this problem."

She gave a long sigh as she said this, then went out of the door. Maddie finished off the sentence and closed down the computer and switched it off. A text pinged on her mobile. It was Sam. It read,

Got OB. Parents will kill me if they find out. See u 5 p.m.

Maddie responded,

OK, and went downstairs.

She set the dining room table with the dinner things in the kitchen. Lydia was always precise about where meals should be eaten. That was something Maddie didn't have to worry about at home. They only had the kitchen and the living room. Her mother preferred eating out, or had ready meals. Cooking was not her speciality, but they did go to lovely restaurants.

It was a great treat, her aunt being a terrific cook. Lydia sometimes set a table in the garden room, or on the terrace. Maddie placed a wicker basket of home-baked bread on the snowy-white linen tablecloth and began to lay the wooden place mats. A well-layered green salad on a white china plate painted with buttercups lay in the centre of the table, with a jug of fruit juice by it. Lydia's bottle of South Eastern Australian red wine stood uncorked. The smell of the bolognese sauce and the home-made bread stuffed with garlic wafted through to the dining room.

Lydia came in with more dishes and laid them on the table.

"Once we have had tea can you clear up for me, please, so I can go in with the photographic group?"

"Will do," replied Maddie.

"I just want to see who will win the photographic prize this year. Charles Stephens will be arriving shortly. He is doing the judging."

Charles Stephens had been a celebrity fashion photographer in the eighties. He lived with his Canadian wife Esme in the Lake District. Lydia produced a picture of him from her pocket. Maddie saw the face of a tanned middle-aged man with spiky white hair and dark brown eyes who was dressed in a black polo neck and trousers. But in Lydia's eyes he was all but a film star.

"Aunt Lydia, do you know what happened? I went into the small library, and one of the photographers had taken a picture of Titch. In the picture standing beside Titch was that girl in the white dress in the photo we saw. But it was quite blurred. The photographer came into the room, and she said that the image should have been clear because it was an expensive camera."

"Does Titch know the girl?"

"No. He didn't even know she was beside him in the photograph. The lady photographer said that when she looked round to talk to the girl she had disappeared."

"I honestly don't know what to say, Maddie."

She quickly rearranged the dishes that Maddie put out. To Maddie it seemed that she was nervous.

"I'll get the water," said Lydia.

She returned a couple of seconds later and placed the jug of iced water and glasses on the table. Nothing else was said about the matter.

At 4.45 Sam arrived. She hugged Lydia, and Lydia took her coat.

"Do you want me to take your rucksack?" asked Lydia.

"Er … no, it's got my studying stuff in. I'll put it in my room, if I may," Sam replied guiltily.

What was in her bag certainly wasn't anything to do with studying. It was the Ouija board.

"OK," said Lydia, and went back into the kitchen.

Maddie grabbed the bag from Sam, took it upstairs, and placed it under her bed. At teatime Lydia mentioned that the Antiques Roadshow might be coming to Cattingham, and how she had written to them to say that they could hold the show in the grounds of Cattingham Hall.

"That would be great. They might pay you lots of money," said Maddie.

"They might," said Lydia shrugging "But we will have to see whether they think the Hall is right for them."

"It's the biggest place around here," said Sam. "They are bound to use it. There is nowhere around here they could use to hold it apart from the Hall."

"I know, Samantha. We'll just have to see, and keep our fingers crossed," said Lydia.

"Oh, Lydia, I am in heaven. This Bolognese is fabulous," Sam said. She closed her eyes in an exaggerated gesture, and threw her arms about wildly as she tucked into the rich garlic sauce.

"Oh, and listen to this. I can't believe I haven't told you," said Sam between mouthfuls of food. "It's about Mum. Can you remember that she had a lump on her tongue, and the hospital took a biopsy? Well, they did. If you remember they found that it was not cancer, but they were going to do a further biopsy as a precaution. Well, she went back to the hospital ... and you will never believe it. The lump has completely gone from her tongue."

"That is wonderful news, dear. Did they say why they think it disappeared?"

"No, Lydia. They just said that they had never come across anything like that before. Mum is so much better. The colour of her hair is coming back, and she is feeling normal again. This has all happened in a space of two weeks."

She mopped up the rich sauce with chunks of garlic bread and beamed at Maddie and Aunt Lydia.

It was lovely seeing her friend so happy. Sam had not talked much about it, but Maddie knew she had been very upset about her mother being unwell. They then celebrated this news with helpings of Lydia's coconut tray bakes. They were completely full and content. Sam responded by making gestures to show how big her belly had now got.

"Well, I am going to have to get back and talk to the photographers. It won't be long before the competition winners are announced," said Lydia, and stood up.

"Maddie, I tell you what … Leave the dishes, and go and get your studying done." She said these words carefully, and tried to keep the amusement out of her voice.

"Oh, no, Aunt Lydia, we'll do them. We have plenty of time to study," said Maddie, as she tried to avoid Sam's gaze. Sam was groaning inwardly. Lydia started clearing the table while the girls took the china into the kitchen.

"Come on, Sam," said Maddie out of earshot. "It won't take long."

"Why did you say we would do them?" sighed Sam.

"Well, it's not fair on my aunt, is it? Come on, the sooner we do it the sooner we can do the séance."

"It would take less time if we didn't have to do it," responded Sam, but Maddie ignored her.

They then began the task of washing up. Maddie took the Bolognese pan, which was thick with congealed sauce. Rather than listen to Sam moan any longer she washed it herself. Finally, with the dishes washed and put away, she said,

"We will have to use the Ouija board in my room, not in the library. People might walk in there by accident. A lady photographer did that today to me."

"But wouldn't it be better in there? That's where it started."

"No," replied Maddie. "We can't take the risk. Come on."

"That's a pity. Oh well. Oh— we will need candles and matches."

"There are some in the dining room. Hang on a minute."

Maddie went off and returned with the items. Sam followed her up the stairs into the bedroom. Once in the bedroom Maddie looked under her bed, and on seeing the black Ouija board sticking out she removed it from Sam's bag. It was a circular object with alphabetical letters round it. At the top corner of the board were gold symbols of the sun and moon. Attached to it was a moveable indicator, which Sam said it was called a planchette.

"We will need to sit on the floor with our knees together and facing each other. It's best if we place the board on them to keep it level," said Sam as she took it from Maddie.

Maddie started to feel nervous about the whole thing, and it didn't help when Sam said,

"I'll light a candle. You draw the curtains. It will need to be dark in here."

"Do we have to draw the curtains, Sam?"

"Yes," came the reply.

"It will be all right. Don't be nervous. If you get spooked I will put the light back on straight away."

Reassured, Maddie drew the curtains.

The room was very dark. Her bedroom window was very small, so there was not much light to start with. The candle gave the whole room a glow. Around it strange shapes appeared round the furniture.

They sat cross-legged, with their knees touching. Sam placed the board on top of them. She then held the planchette in place.

"Right, concentrate when I ask the board questions." Maddie nodded back, and bit her lip in reply. They both held on to it nervously. The first question Sam asked was,

"Is there anyone there?"

She gently slid the planchette to the centre of the board. Nothing happened.

"What happens now?" whispered Maddie

"We wait. Shush."

They waited five minutes, but still nothing happened.

"I think I will ask another question," said Sam.

Just as she said this the planchette moved in their hands.

"Sam, are you doing this?" asked Maddie.

"Of course I'm not, Maddie," came the agitated reply. The planchette then stopped abruptly. They looked at each other, shocked.

"Are you male or female?" asked Sam of the board.

The board started to rattle which made their knees vibrate, then the planchette started to move erratically across to the letters of the alphabet. It finally spelled out the word,

Girl.

"Ask her if she is Ursula Underville," asked Maddie.

Sam asked the question. The answer came back,

No.

"Are you Anna Blackstock?" said Maddie taking over the questions.

The planchette stopped and started. It wobbled from one side to the other and eventually spelled out the word,

Yes.

"How did you die?" asked Sam.

"I can't believe you asked that," whispered Maddie.

"Well, I had to. We have to know." Once again there was silence. Then Sam and Maddie's hands appeared to have been taken over by some presence. They could only look at each other as the planchette spelled the words,

The witches did it.

Then the planchette rocked with such force that it spun off the board.

"Oh, my God," wailed Maddie.

"Shut up," Sam snapped back.

The planchette had bounced so wide that it had landed under the bed. Sam quickly retrieved it. She sat down again on the floor. The girls faced each other with their knees touching again, and their hands on the planchette.

"Ask her something nice," pleaded Maddie.

Sam ignored her.

"Where are the witches now?" she asked.

The candle started to flicker, and the planchette once again moved under them. Their hands were stuck firmly to the planchette. They had no control over it. Something touched Maddie's hair. She screamed, her heart racing.

"Something touched me."

"It will be all right, Maddie. It's nothing. I can't see anything."

"Sam, there is something behind me. I can feel them breathing. Stop this. I am getting really frightened."

They tried to move their hands but could not, and could only stare at each other. The planchette raced across the alphabet and spelled out the words,

The witches killed me. Go. They mean you harm. They are here.

"Come on, let's get out of here," said Sam as she desperately tried to free her hands.

But when she looked at Maddie she saw that she was gulping. Sam then realised then she was now breathing strangely. Maddie pointed at her shoulder and whispered the words,

"Something is hurting me."

Her eyes were getting dilated, and her head was starting to flop.

"Maddie!" screamed Sam. "Keep awake."

She pushed at the planchette with all her force. Finally she managed to move their hands. The Ouija board flew over Maddie's head as she slumped forward. Sam grabbed hold of her. But something was holding her down and stopping Sam from dragging her to her feet. Unseen hands ripped at her hair.

"Get off" she shouted wildly as she tried to pull the unseen force away, while her hair was being dragged out by the roots.

Sam was still screaming but, with one last effort and holding on to Maddie's hand, she dragged her limp friend along the floor by the arm. Maddie lay unconscious on the floor.

Chapter 13

Sam attempted to open the door, but it was stuck. She pulled at it with all her might, and it finally opened. With tears streaming down her face she placed Maddie gently on the ground. Maddie lay there with her eyes closed. She was deathly pale.

"Oh— please, please wake up. I am so sorry," Sam cried. "Please wake up," she repeated to her friend. Slowly Maddie's eyelashes flickered, and her eyes opened.

"What happened?" Maddie asked.

Sam cradled her head and stroked her hair.

"Are you all right?" Maddie nodded, half gulping in reply. She pointed at her shoulder and said,

"Someone hurt me."

She pulled down the front of the neck of her jumper. Red marks were visible across her shoulder as she pointed, but they slowly started disappearing. Sam looked as tears streamed down her face.

"I will never do anything like this again. I am so sorry. These are evil spirits we are dealing with."

"No, I don't want to stop. I want to help Anna," said Maddie. She was now sitting up weakly and regaining her composure.

"I think the witches have trapped her. That's why she can't move on. She needs our help."

"It is too dangerous, Maddie. You could end up getting badly hurt, or something worse."

"Sam, I am going to use the Ouija board again. We need to do it now. It's the only time we can do it. I go back home soon."

On seeing Maddie's determined face Sam replied,

"You are crazy. This could be very dangerous. I am sorry I ever did this … But if you are going to do it we are going to have to be better prepared. We need protection from the witches. Have you any crosses, or a Bible?"

"Yes. There is a Bible in Uncle Akkoubian's room. I saw it last time I was in there … as for a cross, I have one in my drawer. Aunt Lydia gave me it."

"Well, put the cross on. That should give you some form of protection, but we need the Bible."

The girls got up nervously and went back to Maddie's bedroom. Sam opened the door. The Ouija board had been ripped in two. The planchette was across the other side of the room.

"Someone didn't seem happy that we were using the Ouija board," said Sam grimly.

"Oh, my God ... Look, there are scratches on the top of the board. Someone with very sharp nails did this."

"Ugh, don't say that," said Maddie as she shook her head and shuddered at the deeply embedded claw marks.

She opened her top bedside drawer and took the cross out. She handed it to Sam and said,

"You wear it. I will be all right."

"No, Maddie. You were the one who was attacked. Put it on, and don't be a pain. They attacked you, remember."

Maddie took one look at Sam's face and realised it wasn't worth arguing about. She placed the small silver cross round her neck.

"I'll go and get the Bible. Hang on ... maybe its better if you come out of my bedroom with me."

Sam nodded, and they went into Uncle Akkoubian's room.

"Wow. How posh is this?" said Sam, visibly impressed, and trying to get Maddie to forget about what had happened. "It's like something out of Downton Abbey. Look at the monogrammed dressing gown," she said as she touched the sleeve of the green silk dressing gown hanging on the back of the door. Uncle Akkoubian's initials were embroidered in gold on the chest pocket. Maddie, who was looking distracted, removed the Bible from under the book on the bed. On opening it she said,

"It's the family bible. It's been passed from generation to generation."

"Yes, but have you read the earliest entry in it?" said Sam, who was now looking closely at the book.

"No. Why?"

"Look at the signature."

In beautifully exaggerated scrolled handwriting it bore the name Ursula Underville.

"How did I miss that? Well, that proves it. She was never a witch. She believed in God. So if she wasn't a witch ... who were the witches?"

"If we pursue this any further I have a feeling we are going to find out sooner or later," replied Sam sombrely.

They went out of the room and walked back into Maddie's bedroom. The bible was clutched firmly in Maddie's right hand. Sam picked up the ripped Ouija board.

"Ouch," she shouted, and dropped it very quickly. "It burnt my hand."

Maddie tried to pick up the board this time. It felt cold to the touch. Puzzled, she looked at Sam.

"Must just be you," she said, but got rolled eyes from Sam in response.

Maddie then opened the bottom drawer of a large rosewood chest of drawers.

"Oh, don't tell me you have a stationery drawer," said Sam.

"Of course," came the reply.

The drawer was filled with stationery, which was all neatly set out. The pens and pencils appeared to be in colour order. Even her rubbers stood up like a platoon of soldiers alongside various sharpeners, which were lined up in order of size.

"You are seriously weird, Maddie. I am sure there is a name for this disorder."

"Yes, I think I know what it is. I think it's being tidy ... something you wouldn't know about."

Sam pulled a lopsided face at her, but Maddie was right. They were exact opposites. Sam's bedroom usually had all her clothes all over the bed. Sometimes she slept with various clothes on the bed, having not bothered to remove them or put them away when she went to sleep. She would stuff her shoes under her bed rather than place them in the wardrobe. Her long-suffering mother had given up nagging her about this. So long as it was clean she let Sam leave her room in a state of disorganised chaos.

Maddie quickly wound strips of Sellotape round the ripped Ouija board so it was firmly back in one piece.

"Let's hope it still works," said Sam.

"Right. Let's recite the Lord's Prayer first,"

They both knelt by the bed and recited the words, with Maddie holding on to the Bible.

Maddie closed her eyes, but Sam kept hers open and looked round the room as she recited the prayer. Sam then lit the candle again and they switched off the light.

Once again the flicker of the candle gave out unnatural amber shadows round the room. They both sat cross-legged on the floor with their knees touching once again, and together they held the planchette once more.

"Is Anna here?" Sam asked. The planchette moved quickly and replied,

Yes.

"Why are you at Cattingham Hall?" responded Sam. The planchette moved from right to left and spelled out the words

I am trapped.

"How can we help you?" asked Maddie, interrupting Sam.

Find where I lie.

Further questions brought no further response. They waited thirty minutes. Nothing happened.

"How can we find out where is? I'll ask another question," said Sam.

"Where you are ... is it at Cattingham Hall?"

The planchette moved under them uncontrollably, and spelled out the word Yes.

"How does she not know where she is?" said Sam.

"It's a huge place. She could be anywhere," replied Maddie.

"Right. Third question ... I hope this gives us a clue," said Sam in answer.

"Where you lie ... What does it look like?"

The planchette quickly responded,

Cold. In a cellar. I am wet. Help me. I want to go home.

In the background they could hear crying, which then turned into loud sobs. Maddie felt tears coming into her eyes. It was heartbreaking to hear.

"She wants to go back to her home. She is lost between two worlds," said Sam.

111

"Anna … is there a window in your cellar?" asked Maddie.

The planchette spelled out the word Yes.

"What do you see out of the window?"

The planchette moved. The words it made said,

I see nothing. I hear water. I am hungry, but my friend the raven do feed me seeds from the medlar tree. The rats scratch at my door.

Despite Sam asking more questions no further answers came. The ghost had gone. They eventually gave up.

"Well, there is a clue. She hears water, and it's a cellar, and there is a medlar tree, and there are rats. If it's a cellar it must be somewhere under the house. She said the raven feeds her seeds from the medlar tree," said Sam.

Maddie, as she uncrossed her legs, picked up the Ouija board and placed it on the chest of drawers as Sam added,

"I think that should be enough for tonight, don't you? This is spooking me out."

Maddie agreed, apart from saying,

"I wonder what a medlar tree looks like."

"Are you sure you are all right?" Sam asked, ignoring her question.

"Well, my shoulder is a bit sore, but it is OK now. Don't worry. One thing is for sure: I am never taking that cross off."

She rubbed her shoulder and sighed. She opened her stationery drawer and took out a large lined A4 notebook and a black felt tip pen. Then she wrote down everything Anna had said.

"She mentioned a medlar tree. I don't know what they look like. I am going to look them up on Google. Don't you see, Sam? If we find a medlar tree we will find where she has been trapped."

"Yes, I suppose so, but as your aunt's estate is vast it could be anywhere."

"Well, we will keep looking until we find it," replied Maddie excitedly. She then went to her bedside table and turned her laptop on. It only took a couple of minutes to come on, with her crossing her fingers, in case it conked out. But luckily she got in straight away and typed 'medlar tree'.

Wikipedia described a medlar tree as having fruit that was orangey-brown in colour. It was an apple-like fruit that was favoured in the Victorian era, which was good for making jelly. It was a small tree, less than eight metres high. The photograph on the screen was quite clear.

"We should be able to recognise that if we come across it. We could walk round now – round the estate, I mean. It won't take long."

"It won't take long, Maddie," repeated Sam. "It will be dark, and freezing cold. We won't be able to see anything."

"Sam, we are not going to be out that long. If it gets too dark I can look for it in the morning," said Maddie.

Sam did not look happy.

"You can stay here if you want," said Maddie.

"No, I'll come. But if it gets dark we go straight back. Deal?"

"Yes," replied Maddie.

"No worries."

They went downstairs quietly, past the small library. It was jam-packed with people about to watch the presentation.

Aunt Lydia had her back to them, which was good, so there would not be any awkward questions from her about where they were going. They put their coats on, and Maddie grabbed a small hand torch just in case they needed it. They then went out of the kitchen door. Once outside the cold air hit them. Sam shivered and pulled a face, which Maddie ignored and said,

"We'll just go round in a circle. The outside light should give a good amount of light to start with, and the torch should help if it gets too black."

Sam didn't reply. She was hoping they would not be out too long.

Chapter 14

As they went round the faded walled garden there were only small shrubs and areas sectioned off where Titch had been digging.

They next came to the abandoned stables and outbuildings facing the Hall. So far they had not seen anything that looked like the medlar tree. They continued round. Sam, with her arms folded, burrowed in her coat. Now and again she blew cold air out of her mouth to show Maddie how cold it was getting. This was wasted on Maddie. She was in a world of her own, determined to find the tree.

Finally, round the last lap, Maddie said,

"Well, there's only the crypt to look at. Then we can go home."

"Well, only look at," said Sam. "We will not go in it. Understand?"

"Yes. I am not stupid ... but it would save us time if we found it. Come on."

The air became colder as they walked, and a thin fog seemed to engulf them.

"It's freezing now, and look at the fog. Where did that come from?" said Sam,

Maddie ignored her moaning. She was now too busy looking at the crypt.

It had a medieval look about it. Engraved round the sides were flowers, with a small archway leading up to it. A wooden door then led you into the crypt. There was still rubble around it where the original brickwork blocking up the crypt had caved in. Bushes paved the way but they were overgrown, with one growing amongst another in a tangled heap.

Maddie shone her torch on the bushes, and pulled at part of one of the bushes.

"Look behind this one. There is one that could be it," she said excitedly.

The torch shone on the bush in question. It was twisted round the stonework, and there were dark berries growing on it ...

"It's too dark to know whether it is the medlar tree, but I bet when I look at this tomorrow it will turn out to be the tree," said Maddie.

A rustle in the bushes made them both turn round. Out of a bramble bush came what appeared to be a black cat, its long body hunched. Sam screamed and moved backwards away from it, almost falling over in her fear to get away from it.

"Oh, my God, it's a rat. Look at the size of it."

It was a rat. It was much, much bigger than your average rat, and it did not seem to be frightened of them. Its dark eyes glinted in the dark as it stared, unafraid, at them. It was wet and shiny black in colour, and was at least two feet long. Its two front teeth protruded out of its mouth as it bit into a berry.

"Ugh … it's horrible. Let's get out of here. It might jump us," said Sam nervously.

"Don't be stupid. Look at it. It's more interested in eating its berry than in us. If it had wanted to attack us it would have done it by now. Having said that, it is right near the tree I want to look at. But I don't fancy looking at it with that thing watching me. Come on, we'll go. I will check it out in the morning," replied Maddie.

They walked away from the crypt. But Sam continued to look over her shoulder as they walked to make sure that the rat didn't attack them. Once out of sight from the crypt she relaxed. Dark eyes peered out from the bushes. Following in the footsteps of their ancestors, a huge family of rats had made nests in the overgrown bushes. If you had looked closely to the entrance to the crypt you would have seen hundreds of years' worth of teeth marks in the stone, uneven soil scattered, and a great many rat droppings leading to the door.

Down under the bushes a faint voice could be heard.

"Please help me. Someone please help me," the distressed voice called out.

She had been hopeful. She was sure that they would find her now, but why hadn't they come and set her free?

Then came the sound of sobbing, which made a group of the rats look up in the direction of the sound. A flutter of wings sent the rats

115

scrambling to safety. Then a huge black raven settled on the medlar tree to watch over its mistress.

Sam raced ahead of Maddie. She wanted to get out of the dark and back into the house. If that's one thing that made her squeamish it was rats.

When they went back into the house they were not exactly warm once they had taken off their coats and shoes. Maddie hung them up.

There was a lot of noise coming from the small library, followed by clapping. After walking into the sitting room Maddie lit the fire. Sam switched the television on and looked at the television guide and said,

"I'm a Celebrity...Get me out of here?"

"OK," replied Maddie. She wasn't particularly bothered about what they watched. Her brain was now in overdrive from thinking about the medlar tree.

The wood in the fire started to crackle, and its warm orange glow spread all around the room. Maddie then drew the thick curtains, and they settled in separate chairs to watch in glee as a horrified celebrity on the screen tucked into a plate of mealworms. It was only later that Lydia entered the room.

"Well, that's everyone gone home now. Everything went fine. How are you two doing?"

"Fine," replied Maddie, and asked, "Who won the competition?"

"The same person who has won the last two years: Miriam Brightwell. I wish it had been a new face, but even photographic clubs are shrouded in politics. Anyway, what would you like to drink?"

"Hot chocolate, please," both girls replied in unison.

Later Maddie and Sam started yawning, so they made their way up to bed. Lydia was half reading her magazine, but even she was nodding off. It had been decided that they would tidy up the rest of the things in the morning. Maddie, Sam, and Lydia had already cleared away the leftover food and china. But there was still a lot to clear up.

Sam was to sleep in one of the guest rooms – not Uncle Akkoubian's room, which was to remain untouched. After saying goodnight to Sam Maddie turned the handle on her bedroom door, and decided she would keep the light on. When she saw the Ouija board on the chest of drawers it seemed to rock. It stopped when she went up to it. She picked it up, opened the stationery drawer, and quickly placed it in there. She reminded herself that she would have to give it back to Sam tomorrow, it was something she did not like now having in the house.

Then, with her face washed and teeth brushed and having changed into her pyjamas, she climbed into bed. The blankets were a huge weight, so she pulled a couple off and threw them on the floor. Sleep came very quickly, and she drifted back into her haunting recurring dream.

This time she was in the room and sucking at some strange fruit seeds. The room was not completely in darkness this time. A jagged strip of light through the tiny window gave off some faint light. She threaded her hand through a bar in a window and cupped a bird's beak in her hands. She stroked the soft and sooty black feathers and whispered gently,

"Antrabus ... how I have missed you." It was not Maddie's voice that came out. The bird clucked as she spoke to it.

The door opened suddenly. She released her hand, swallowed the last seed, and quickly turned round.

Two women walked into the room. The women were Katharine the sister of Thomas Underville and another woman... On entering the room they almost immediately began to chant strange words at her, then said,

"Say the words, then sign the document Anna, and we will let you go."

The older woman screeched this at her, and shoved a large piece of parchment in her face.

It was if Maddie was not in her own body. She was now in Anna's body. The voice that spoke back to the women had a Northern accent.

"I will not say those words. Let me go. My family will look for me. They will be worried."

"Anna, your family will never find you here. You are one of us now. The villagers would kill you if they found you. They know you as a witch. You have the sign. Look."

Katharine Underville lifted up the hem of the white dress Anna was wearing to show her feet. This was the dress that Maddie always seemed to wear in the dream.

"See. It is the sixth toe. It is the sign. Give your soul to the Drakens. Turn your back on your God, and you will live as us and be spared. Do you want your family to be tried as witches and warlocks?"

"Leave my family alone," screamed Anna back at them, but this made her cough violently. "They are good people. It is you who are witches."

She continued to cough. The older woman cackled with contempt. Irritated by the girl's lack of respect, she poured a bucket of water over her. The icy water dripped off Anna and her white dress and made it soaking wet.

"This will teach you some manners, and stop with your pretence and your coughing. You are not a Christian. You are a witch. Your God will not want you. Why would he want a witch? Out Lord has brought you into the world to serve him. Accept what you are. Join us, and your loved ones will be spared."

Anna answered again and said,

"I do not believe you. Others have joined you, and still you have had their families drowned as witches and warlocks. It is you who should be drowned. If people knew it was you – the Drakens – who were involved in witchcraft you would all be drowned. What you do with me I no longer care about. If I am to die I am to die."

She began coughing. Her head was spinning. She just wanted to close her eyes and go to sleep. But back came a withering response from Katharine,

"Girl, you will not die. He will not let you die. Ursula thought she was stronger than us, but she was wrong. You will not win, Anna. Stop this infernal coughing, and show your powers to us. If you are indeed ill make yourself well. I have seen you do it to others. See what is written. All you have to do is read out what is written, and sign it. Do that and you will be free."

"If I sign this paper I would be signing my soul over to you, and I would be eternally damned. Just let me go, and I will tell no one what you have done. If you have hurt Ursula I promise you this: I will lay a curse on you, and you will be damned for ever. That is a promise."

Anna's angry voice wavered as she spoke, and Maddie could feel her grief.

"Ursula and I were like sisters," a sad voice whispered out to her.

The dream appeared to have moved further back in time. This time she was in the small library at Catting ham Hall and dressed in a scratchy caramel wool dress. She was sitting on a wooden chair with someone. Maddie recognised her from the historical pictures as Ursula Underville. Ursula whispered nervously to her,

"Oh, Anna, you are so brave. But you must be careful they do not catch you. I wish it were like this all the time. This is when I am most happy. No one is watching me. I wish my husband was still alive. He would have not let Katharine behave the way she does to me. She tells people I am a witch. It is all lies. The villagers are frightened of me. I am trapped in this house. They keep me prisoner. I am watched wherever I go. Why did we ever let the woman come into our house?"

Anna's voice replied,

"I will get you out of here. That I promise. Do not be afraid, Ursula. Here, take this … I have made it for you to protect you. It is my witch's bottle. Bury it safe in the house. The evil Katharine does will go back to her if she casts a spell on you."

Taking the glass object from her Ursula said,

"Oh, Anna, you are my only friend. There is so much cruelty in Cattingham because of the Drakens. I fear even that the Doctor Lockhart is in league with them. I am sure he has tried to drug me. I have tried to throw away his pills, but they are forced in my mouth by the servants under his orders. When I wake up I am in a strange room. I know not how I came there in the first place. The doctor says it is for my own good, and to stop me harming my child. I love my child. Robert is all I have. Why would I harm him? It breaks my heart that they keep him away from me. They will turn him into a Draken. That I am sure of."

"Do not upset yourself, Ursula. I will get you away from here, and that is a promise. We will make a plan. Let me think. Be brave and keep safe."

They hugged each other. On hearing footsteps Ursula, who was full of fear, whispered?

"The hiding place, quick. You must go. They will kill you if they catch you."

Ursula pulled a small lever on the bookcase. A small room appeared. Anna went behind the bookcase into the room and sat down, hardly daring to breathe. The door was closed on her and she was in darkness.

"I thought I heard voices, Ursula. Who was it you were talking to?" came the sound of a woman's voice.

"I was talking to myself. You have said I am a witch. If that is so then I must then surely try and behave like one."

"Insolent girl. What is it you have in your hand? Show me it ... A witch's bottle. You have a witch's bottle. Proof, to be sure, that you are indeed a witch. I must tell the Justice of the Peace. He will have you burnt."

"How, Katharine, do you know that this is a witch's bottle? Unless you are, as you say, indeed a witch."

"Give me the bottle, Ursula."

A noise sounded from the library. It sounded as if there was a struggle going on.

Anna felt helpless. She could not help her friend, and could only pray that she was safe. Then came the sound of breaking glass. She knew what had happened. The witch's bottle had been broken. There was nothing to protect Ursula from the women. Then the spiteful voice came again and said,

"No one can protect you, Ursula. You will be going away, and I will then take over Cattingham Hall and teach your son the ways of the Drakens."

"You are pure poison, Katharine," Anna replied. "You have no power to send me away. You will not take my son. If you try and take my son I will curse you to eternity. I do not want him twisted by your evil. This is my husband's home. This is my home now. I will have you taken away not I."

"Ursula, you fool. Do you think you can send me away? Everyone thinks you are a mad witch," said Katharine, laughing spitefully. "Even Doctor Lockhart has said you must be committed. He fears for your son. I have shown him how you have harmed him. Your family are frightened of you, and keep away."

"I have not touched my son. It is all lies, Katharine. No doubt you have told lies to my family. You are full of evil and bile, and have made the servants turn against me. Your brother would have been disgusted by the way you have treated me. You have dishonoured his name. You cannot do this to me. My brother will come for me. You will see," said Ursula.

"My brother was a fool marrying Sarah, and then you. I should have inherited the Hall. I would have run it the way it should have been run in the first place. I was just to be married off. That was something that was not going to happen to me. I have waited and waited, and my time will be very soon. I will have it all.

"Your son will be easy to train. He is very young. As for your brother, he is abroad and may never return to England. Your father is only interested in his new wife. You will be forgotten. No one cares what happens to you".

"Martin, take her to her bedchamber. I fear she will attack me. Doctor Lockhart will be arriving soon. I will have to tell him that she has been having her attacks and how she tried to hurt me again."

Anna could hear the door open. She recognised the deep, gruff voice. It was Martin, the stable lad. He was six feet five, and as wide as he was tall. Ursula would be no match for him. All the kindness Ursula had shown to him, and this was how he repaid her …

Anna bit into her hand, and tears fell down her cheeks. She could only listen helplessly. The voices became raised. Ursula bravely refused to go. There was a scuffle outside the secret chamber – dangerously close, Anna feared, to the chamber itself.

"Ursula … before you go … tell me, where is Anna?" asked Katharine.

"I do not know," came the reply.

"You are a liar. But do not worry. We will find her."

121

Then came a scream from Ursula, then silence. To Anna it sounded as if Ursula had been slapped.

"Take her to her bedchamber and put her on the bed. I will send her maid in to undress her," commanded Katharine.

The door sounded as if it had been shut, but there was still someone in the room. Anna could hear them talking. Another person spoke and said,

"We have not been able to find her."

"Well, look again – and do not come back to me until you find her. Anna must be somewhere round here. The witch's bottle will have been from her. She will come to help Ursula. That is when we will catch her."

"Why is it so important that you have Anna?"

"She has the gift. She has had it since she was a child. I knew she had it the first time I laid eyes on her. We will make her join with us. Our group will be stronger. Go and look for her, and get out of my sight."

The door closed. Anna could hear a rocking movement

"Katharine must be still in the room," she thought. Then came some chanting. Katharine began muttering to herself.

"If ever there were any witches in Cattingham one of them must surely be Katharine Underville," thought Anna despairingly. She hoped she would leave the room, as she was beginning to feel claustrophobic. Not being able to see in the darkness was beginning to frighten her. For some reason the pitch dark filled her with a spine tingling fear sensing almost as if one day she would powerless to protect herself.

Chapter 15

Katharine remained in the room a long time. Cramp had set into Anna's legs. If she moved an inch she was terrified she might be heard. There was another room leading off from where she stood, but she dared not move. She would have to be patient. If she was captured she would never be able to help her friend.

Katharine had said that Ursula was going to be sent away. If Anna managed to rescue her Ursula would not leave without her son. The situation seemed hopeless. This gift they spoke of that Anna had ... what did they mean? She had no gift?

She could help make potions which would make people better, but it was because she knew about herbs: always had done. This did not mean she was a witch. Why did they think that?

Katharine remained in the library for a further hour. She appeared to be going through the books, but did not seem happy. It was if she was picking books out, then there was silence. Then there was a shout from her and a thud, as if a book was being thrown down and then another one picked up ...

Finally she left the library grunting, and there was silence. Anna waited a couple of minutes, and then came out of the darkened chamber. But it was painful. She was hardly able to walk, and her whole body felt stiff. She rubbed her legs, then her eyes.

There was still a dimly lit candle burning in the library. Books were scattered all over the floor. Anna picked one up. They were historical books.

One of them was the history of the Drakens: another was a silk threaded book on the black arts. As she looked through the large black embossed book one of the spells caught her eye. It made her shudder as she read the frightening words in it, but she was instinctively drawn to them. She memorised them by heart. Something in her head telling her to do this but she did not know why.

Then she placed the book back on the floor. She did not have time to waste by looking at any more of them. Today the doctor might commit Ursula to an asylum. She had to act now. Remembering where Ursula's bedchamber was she opened the library door and went cautiously up the stairs.

A stair creaked. She waited. But no one came out of any of the rooms.

She finally reached Ursula's bedchamber, but it was locked on the outside. She slowly unlocked it. Ursula lay in her bed. Her ghostly white face was shining with sweat, but she was fast asleep. Anna gently went up to the bed so as not to frighten her.

"Ursula," she half whispered. "It's Anna. Wake up."

Ursula sleepy eyed woke from her drowsy sleep and said,

"Anna."

But she did not appear to come completely out of the slumber she was in. Anna reached into the pocket of her dress. She took out a small bundle of green leaves and pressed them to Ursula's face. Ursula's eyes opened, and she half smiled. Then she screwed up her face and sniffed at the leaves, pulling a face.

"Ugh. What's that?"

"Leaves to wake you up. Come on, Ursula, we have to go. They might come back for you and take you away. Wake up! You are falling asleep again."

The urgency in Anna's voice made Ursula open her eyes wide. She started coughing, but Anna placed her hand over her mouth to stop her.

"What happened? Where am I?"

"They drugged you. My herbs will keep you awake. Come on, get dressed. We have to go."

Ursula got up unsteadily. She went to her chair and put on the clothes that had been laid out for her by her maid. From her wardrobe she produced a green cloak. She then took some money out of a wooden box and placed it in the pocket of the cloak. Hesitating she turned to Anna and said,

"I cannot leave without my son."

Anna replied "We will go to the Justice of the Peace's house at Bickleberry. I have heard that he is a good man. We will tell them how Katharine has drugged you. But we cannot take your lad with us. The woods to Cattingham are a dark place. It is no place for a bairn. He could get a chill. It will be too cold. We can come back for him after we have been to the Justice of the Peace."

To Anna's relief Ursula didn't argue, and agreed to go with her. Anna thought it might have been the drugs she had been given, which had made her too weak to argue. They went out of the bedchamber and walked quietly down the stairs. There was a smell of cooking fat coming from the kitchen.

"The staff, no doubt," thought Ursula, "are preparing dinner for the doctor's arrival."

Every creak on the stairs filled them with fear. Their hearts were racing. They felt that they would surely be caught, and that there was nowhere to hide if someone came out of the many doors.

They eventually reached the front door. Anna turned the brass handle, opened it quietly, and they went outside.

There was no one outside.

Anna turned to Ursula and whispered,

"We have to go to me mam and dad's first, and tell them what we're doing. The woods are behind the back of where we live. It's a two-mile walk to Bickleberry from there."

Ursula nodded weakly in agreement, and pulled her cloak further over her face in case she was recognised. Then they ran out of the Hall. Once outside it they crossed a small field that went past the church. The clock in the church struck the sixth hour. After looking at the clock Ursula said,

"No one will wake me yet. Doctor Lockhart will not arrive until seven. We should have plenty of time to get to Bickleberry and tell the Justice of the Peace what has been happening."

"Let's go to the back of me mams and dad's cottage," said Anna. "We are less likely to be seen that way."

They scrambled round the back tentatively. Even a wood pigeon cooing made them both jump. Anna knocked on the back door of the cottage. Her mother answered.

"Lass, where have you been?" her mother asked her.

"Mam, I have Ursula with me. Katharine has been drugging her and keeping her prisoner at the Hall. We are going to the Justice of the Peace to tell him what's been happening."

125

"Anna, I don't like this. You should not be crossing Katharine. She is truly evil. I have seen what she has done to other people."

Her mother's face became etched in worry lines.

"Mam, don't worry yourself. The Justice of the Peace is a good man. He will help us. Where's my dad? Asked Anna, but then she started coughing violently and could not stop making her eyes water.

"That cough is not getting any better. You will have to have the doctor see to it. You've just missed your dad. He is helping out at the quarry now. It's good money. He should not be long. Do you not want to take something to eat?"

"No, mam, we haven't time. Tell Dad we will see him later. We'll come back and see you after we have come back from Bickleberry. Mam, if anything goes wrong will you tell the Justice of the Peace what I have told you about what Katharine has done to Ursula? She means to take the Hall, and to take her bairn away from her."

Anna's mother started crying.

"I don't like this. I feel nothing but bad will come of this. Lass, please stop what you are doing. You cannot hope to win against the likes of Katharine."

"Do not worry, Mrs Blackstock," said Ursula, trying to reassure her. "Once I have the Justice of the Peace on my side I will be able to get Katharine out of the Hall."

But Anna's mother would not swayed by this, and more tears fell down her face. As she wiped them away she said,

"Take care, the pair of you. You two will have me sick with worry. Your father will go mad when he hears about this. But if you have to do this then let God guide the pair of you." She held tightly on to her daughter's hand. Her own heavily veined hand covered the pale soft skin of her daughter's.

"Mam, it will be all right. Don't worry yourself," Anna hugged and kissed her mother goodbye.

Anna tried not to look back as they walked away, so that Ursula would not see her get upset. She had to be brave for both of them. They then made their way to the footbridge but Anna – almost immediately, on placing her foot on it – had a very bad feeling. Ursula, on seeing her face, said,

"Don't look so worried."

But a feeling of doubt in Anna's heart did not fill her with optimism. The small bridge they crossed was the notorious place where women had been placed on the ducking stool. To her it was a haunted place and an ill omen. She could almost imagine the voices of the screaming women who had been tried as witches.

As she tried to brush away her fears she took a deep breath and walked across it with Ursula. Her cough was still bad. She had had it for weeks, and could not seem to get rid of it. She thought she might have got a chill when she had gone to market in the heavy rain at Hexham a week ago and there had been a thunderstorm, and she had been caught in it. Despite using a number of herbal remedies she had made it seemed to have got worse ...

It was sheer nonsense to her that Katharine thought she was a witch. Surely if she had been a witch she would have cured this cough, wouldn't she?

They then cut across to the woods. It was getting dark, and they had no light to guide them. Once they entered the woods they came alive with noise, as if sensing their unwanted presence. In the distance came the frantic calling of a vixen to her fox cubs, as if the animal wanted to get away from them or someone. Something heavy brushed against Ursula's hair.

"Ugh. What is that?"

"It's only a bat, Ursula. They are harmless. It will not have seen you," answered Anna. Twisted tree roots came into view, their gnarled silhouettes making disturbing witchlike shadows.

The roots were wet and slippery, and there were so many of them sticking out of the ground that they had trouble stepping over them. Ursula half fell. Anna managed to catch her in time, and pulled her foot out of a deeply entwined tree root.

"Ouch. That hurt," said Ursula as they freed her foot.

"I use this path all the time. It has never been as wild as this. The heavy rain must have uprooted some of the trees."

"No matter. We will just have to follow the path and not come off it, or we will get lost in the dark."

They made their way past dense bracken, wiry hair grasses, and fern. An animal scuttled out of a hiding place and made Ursula scream, and she only calmed down when Anna pointed out that it was just a rabbit. Then came a familiar noise: dogs barking. They stopped in their tracks, not speaking but thinking the same thing. Had Katharine found out where they were heading? Instinctively they started to run along the path, Anna half dragging the tiny figure of Ursula along with all her strength because Ursula was still drowsy from the medication she had been given.

As the lady of Cattingham Hall she had never even been on country walks. This was something that Anna was aware of, but she had to be tough with Ursula to get her to move more quickly. It did not work. Ursula became breathless from all the activity.

"Please stop. I don't know how much further I can go, Anna," she panted, breathing heavily.

"Ursula, you have to keep going. If they catch up with us you will be sent away. Look, I can see Martha's old cottage. We are getting near to Bickleberry. We must be, I am sure, at least halfway there."

It would have been easier, Anna thought, if she had gone to Bickleberry on her own. She would have run there. But the Justice of the Peace would not have listened to the ramblings of a country girl. Having Ursula there would be a different story. It would be something he would have to investigate because of her social status.

Further into the woods Ursula pointed at what looked like white fluorescent chalk marks on the trunk of an old oak tree. They glowed eerily in the dark.

"What is that?" she asked.

"I do not know," came Anna's untruthful reply.

She knew what they were. Her late grandmother had warned her to beware of such signs as those. The cloven foot symbol was the sign of Satanists. She had never seen marks such as these in the woods before. According to her grandmother they represented the old world: the difference between good and evil. The woods had once been haunted. The ghosts haunting the woods were believed, according to her grandmother, to be the unbaptised souls who had committed evil acts, and who had never moved on to their next life.

When she looked more closely at the tree she could see that white stones circling the entire trunk of the tree were in a precise pattern. Anna moved Ursula away from it and tried not to show her feelings.

"It will be nothing. Come on … ready to run?"

"Yes ..." came Ursula's reply. She was worn out, but knew that to stop would result in them being caught... They ran further into the woods. The thick mud stuck to their shoes and made running very difficult. The sound of the barking dogs became faint, which was reassuring to them both.

"We are nearly there. Come on," smiled Anna encouragingly as she spurred Ursula on.

Ursula did not have the right footwear for the woods, which was something they had both overlooked in their haste to get away from Cattingham Hall. She was wearing green brocade slippers, which were now caked in mud. They also kept sinking deeper into the thick mud. A couple of times Ursula nearly lost a shoe and had to pull it out of the mud, which blackened her lily-white hands. Her silk handkerchief was now completely black in her cloak pocket.

"You will have to get out of those shoes later. Your feet will be soaking wet," said Anna.

"Yes, I will, indeed," said Ursula unconcerned. She yawned, and pretended to sigh.

"Do you think there are any wolves in these woods?" she asked Anna mischievously.

"Well ... I go to school every day, and I haven't seen any wolves. I would rather face a wolf than your sister-in-law Katharine any day. It would be a lot much nicer, I would think."

Ursula gave a wry smile in answer to this and then turned to her and said,

"You have been a great friend to me. Do not think I will forget this. My son and I owe you a great debt. You are more than a friend to me ... more like a sister."

Tears welled up in Ursula's eyes. She wiped them away with her hands, but only succeeded in leaving a black smudge on her cheek. Anna hugged her and wiped the mark off her face and said,

"You are a great friend to me too. It is strange. We are from different lives, yet it is as if I have known you all my life."

"Yes, I know," responded Ursula.

"Once I have spoken to the Justice of the Peace and Katharine has left the Hall with all her followers we and the village will be safe from her. Anna, I am so sorry. If I had known your mother had been dismissed from Cattingham Hall I would have stopped it. Please forgive me."

"Oh, don't worry about that. Me mam knew it wasn't you who did that. She hates Katharine. She knew it was her. Mam found a new job cleaning at the Widow Bracken's place, so don't worry yourself about that. Anyway, we can't stand here talking. We've got to move on. Come on."

Ursula stroked her hand affectionately and said,

"You know, if I had had help from my family Katharine would never have moved into the Hall. My father has been too busy with his new family and wife … My brother has been abroad for many years. He is a good man. If he had known about what has been happening he would have helped me, that I am sure of. I know he would never have deserted me. But it was in my husband's will that Katharine would be a guardian to my son and to me after my husband died. My poor husband did not know what trouble this would cause me." She stopped to wipe her misty eyes but then went on to say,

"In the event of my demise Katharine thinks she will take over the Hall and look after my son. It is true when they say that nightmares can come true. I have also prepared a will. My brother has it, and Katharine does not know about it. It is the only protection I have for my son. I will have to show it sometime to you when my brother comes home."

"Do not talk about wills. You are too young a lass to be talking about such things. Come on, we have to move more quickly."

Chapter 16

They now had not much further to go, and they climbed up the muddy brown hill that rose up and led from the trees to the edge of the woods. It was dark now but a brilliant yellow full moon shone brightly, giving them some light.

"The Justice of the Peace has the house on the corner by Jacob's Cottage, but first we must get you cleaned up. He will think you an urchin if he sees you like this, and will send you away."

Ursula's tiny shoes were a sorry sight. They were caked in mud and looked completely black, and the edging to her dress did not look much better.

"I tell you what we will do. The leaves from that hedgerow will clean them up," continued Anna as she pulled off some thick leaves that looked like dock leaves and wiped Ursula's shoes down with them. But the shoes were soaking wet and completely ruined.

"It is no matter, Anna. My long dress will hide them. You do not think I will be showing my ankles to the Justice of the Peace, do you? I do not think so. If I did he would think me a scarlet woman."

They both giggled at the thought. This made Anna cough. Ursula was worried and said,

"You must see a doctor. It is not getting any better."

"I will see a doctor, but not Doctor Lockhart."

This caused them to burst out laughing again. They were not frightened any longer, now that they were nearly there. They had almost reached the house. They would be safe.

The brilliant yellow moon had now lit up the stone village of Bickleberry. There were uneven, cracked cobblestones everywhere in the village. They were painful for Ursula to walk on, and she grimaced.

"It will be, if I remember, just round this corner," said Anna.

Ursula linked her arm in hers, and they walked round to the Justice of the Peace's cottage. They looked odd together, with Anna being so tall and Ursula being less than five feet. The light seemed to dim, and the darkness wrapped round them.

Anna gave an involuntary shiver.

It was then that the screaming started. It was Ursula. Their arms became unlinked. Anna could only see darkness. A sack-like cloth had been placed over her head. She heard another scream, more blood-curdling than the first.

"Ursula," she shouted, but her voice was muffled through the cloth. Then she could no longer hear, and the darkness continued. Her eyelids were heavy.

That was all she could remember.

When she opened her eyes later all she could hear was trickling water. Then there was a loud ringing in her ears, and she was finding it difficult to catch her breath. When she looked round she now knew what the noise was. It was a large crowd. Their faces were lit up in the dark by burning torches, which gave them an unearthly look. She was back in Cattingham. The crowd then started screaming and throwing rotten fruit at her.

"Witch ... witch," droning voices shouted at her with hatred in their eyes. What had happened? How had she got here? Where was Ursula? She had never felt such terror. Her heart was in her mouth.

She knew where she was now. She was at the bridge at Low Row. This could not be real. She had not had a trial, so why was she here? A man placed her on a ducking stool.

"I am not a witch," she shouted back at the crowd. She saw people she had smiled at in the street who were now looking at her with hostile eyes.

"Thou shall not suffer a witch to live," shouted a voice.

She recognised Parson Paltmore. He was with a group carrying candles. Water hit her in the face. Someone had poured a bucket of water over her head. People began laughing at her cruelly. She could not escape. Her left hand and foot were then tied together and a rope attached to her waist. She was lifted from the chair, and she turned to see Martin from Cattingham Hall.

"Sink or swim, stinking witch," he smirked nastily at her.

He lifted her up, to the excitement of the baying crowd, and then threw her over the bridge. She had no time to scream. It happened quickly. Water covered her body, completely submerging her into the inky black ice-cold water. The strong current pushed her from the small stream into the river, where sharp rocks cut into her face. The pain was agonising as she glided by.

She floated up to the surface, kept her head back, and spat out the water that had poured into her mouth. Then she frantically tried to untie her foot, but this met with no success. It had been securely tied. The force of the water made the rope from her waist come off. She was at the mercy of the unforgiving river. Her foot and arm were still tied together. A voice in her ears cried out to her,

"Anna, be brave." It sounded like her grandmother's voice.

"But how could that be?" she thought. "She is dead."

The water then seemed to gently caress her, and it guided her body to a corner of the riverbank. A strong hand grabbed hold of her. It slowly dragged her out of the river. Her body banged against the muddy bank as she was dragged up. She looked up at her rescuer in thanks, and gave a grateful smile into the amused face of Katharine Underville. The shock was too much for her, and she fainted.

The rest of the night was a memory she tried to block off, but eventually she had to open her eyes.

She found herself in a candlelit room. Sitting up she was lying on a small wooden bed, and no longer wearing her brown dress. She was now wearing a fancy white gossamer dress, something she had never seen before. Then her racking cough started up again and she could not stop sputtering until a glass of water was pushed unceremoniously into her hand.

"Drink it, Anna," came the familiar voice of Katharine Underville. "We thought we had lost you at first. But my test proved right. You are indeed a witch. You did not drown. You floated."

Anna looked into the mad eyes of Katharine Underville. Her face was shining with undisguised triumph.

"You did this to me?" said Anna's incredulous voice.

"Yes, of course if did. I had to know. Of course, if you had drowned it would have been a disappointment. You have been the only girl who has passed my test. All the others died. But my test proved right.

133

"I knew you would try and rescue Ursula. We let you escape. It was so easy. Once you were in Bickleberry we just lay in wait. I told the villagers that you were in the woods, and that you had taught Ursula to lay spells on their children. The villagers were waiting for you in Cattingham. Everything went the way I wanted it to. I now have you, and you must see now that you have no other choice but to join with us."

"Where is Ursula?" asked Anna.

"She is safe, back where she belongs. Doctor Lockhart has taken her to the asylum. I would have liked to have had her tested as a witch, but it was too risky. If she had been proved to be a witch it would have been no good to me. It would have affected my position at the Hall. It is better that she is mad rather than a witch."

Anna could have strangled Katharine, whose cruel voice became full of mirth. Instead she asked fearfully,

"What are you going to do with me?"

"Why … test you further, of course. It is a shame about your face. We have bathed it, but it will never be the same. Still, no matter," came the reply.

"My face. What is wrong with my face?" asked Anna, touching her face, which stung as she touched it.

"I think you may have dashed it on the rocks. You will be scarred, but my followers will not be concerned about that. So long as you have the power … that is all we need."

"Where am I?" asked Anna, still dazed.

"In your secret room. Don't you recognise it, Anna? I found it by accident after you had escaped. It must have been a room to hide priests in. It is now serving our purpose perfectly now."

"My mam and dad will be worried about me and will look for me," Anna responded.

"Why do you think I placed you here? They will never find you. . However, if you join the Drakens I will allow you to see them. The choice is yours. Be grateful. I saved your life. You are not safe with the villagers. They believe you are in league with the devil, and that you have turned Ursula's mind. If I let you out now they would lynch you, or even have you burnt."

"The Justice of the Peace would not allow that without a trial," came Anna's weak reply.

She would have said more, but she started to cough violently. Yellow phlegm poured out of her mouth. She wiped it away with the piece of cloth by her glass of water and took a sip. She touched her face again but it once again stung, and blood poured off it.

"Wipe it with the water and cloth, girl. Huh. The Justice of the Peace is at Bickleberry. Do you think he cares what happens at Cattingham? He has turned a blind eye for years about what has been happening. Money keeps him sweet," responded Katharine. She sounded highly amused.

Anna picked up the glass and dabbed water on her face, then wiped it with the cloth. Watery streaks of blood stained the cloth. Once again she began coughing. Her eyes started to water and she started coughing convulsively, which made her ribs hurt.

"Stop coughing, girl. Heal yourself. Do not play games with me. I know you can make yourself well. Do it. I know about your healing powers. Did you not cure Mary Blenkinsopp's purple swollen legs with a spell? Did you not make Farmer Markham's sheep die?

"I know about you, girl. I have watched you since you were a child. The Drakens need magic. Prayers have never helped us. We have now begun to believe in the old ways. The dark arts will give us the recognition we want. People will listen to us, and girls like you will help us. You will frighten the villagers into believing in us." Katharine's voice was cold. She showed no concern or tenderness to the sick girl.

"Mary Blenkinsopp's swollen legs …" thought Anna. "A spell? What rubbish. Why," she thought, "all I did was grind up some horse chestnuts and place a poultice on her legs. These were not spells, just country ways."

She knew it would be pointless to argue, so she let Katharine continue talking about all the so-called spells she thought Anna had made.

"I will let you sleep, but I will return. Think on it. If you do not join us and read out what is written on the paper I will lock you up in this room, and you will die in here. No one will ever find you or know you are there. The choice is yours. I have left you a pen and paper. Write your allegiance to us on it. All you then have to do is to say the words."

Katharine looked Anna up and down as if mentally calculating what her answer would be. Then she opened the small door that led out into the library. The door closed behind her, leaving Anna in semi-darkness.

"The woman is pure evil. I have to get out of here," thought Anna, panicking. "I must tell someone about her." But her strength was exhausted.

The harsh river water had knocked the stuffing out of her. She grabbed the pen and scratched her name, Anna Blackstock, on the wall. Someone had to find her or know she was in here. Underneath she wrote in desperation,

Help me.

Help would have to come, surely. But if the worst happened to her then at least her words would tell someone who she was. Her eyes then closed, and she sank back into exhausted sleep.

Chapter 17

Maddie once again came out of her dream. She was now not Anna but Maddie, but she was going in and out of troubled sleep. There was an immense burning heat pouring into her lungs. Red hot she started throwing the covers off her bed, as if to get out of this terrible nightmare she was having. But she was unable to shake off the story that appeared to have her as the main character, and it would not release her. It forced her to re-enact everything that had happened to Anna.

It seemed that the ghost would not rest until the whole story was told. But the story moved back and once again she was Anna, and was now in a fever. Sweat poured off her, and her body began to shake. The dry cough turned into a rattle. She was hallucinating, and she imagined she was soaring up to clouds in the brilliant blue sky.

It was broad daylight. She was flying above Cattingham Hall, and seeing sun-drenched ploughed yellow fields and horses and carts moving round the village. Her whole body had a feeling of weightlessness. Finally she reached Low Row Cottages. On entering her house she could see her father sitting in his chair with her mother holding his hand.

"Hello," she shouted to them.

They did not respond. She shouted again and ran to touch them, but her hand did not seem to touch them.

"I am here, Mam … Dad. Look. I got away from Katharine." But her mother did look up, and appeared to be crying and wiping her eyes on her old blue pinny.

"Mam, it's all right. I am here. Don't cry. Look, I'm here … see." She ran to her father and touched his hand, but she only felt air.

"Dad, speak to me," she said, almost screaming the words at him. But there was no response.

Instead he placed his head in his hands and gently sobbed. A crumpled piece of paper lay on the chair. She blew at it. It moved and fell on to the brown-patterned carpet. Anna blew it again.

"Look at that. Where is the wind coming from? All the doors are shut," said her mother to her father.

But he continued to have his head down. His hands were over his eyes and he did not answer.

"Why can they not see me?" she thought. She shouted to them again, but still there was no response.

There was a bright light like a doorway which seemed to beckon to her, but she could not make her way to it. It was if she was being pulled backwards from it every time she tried to enter it.

"Help me, someone," Anna screeched. Her voice echoed through Maddie's ears, and made her finally wake up from the nightmare.

Maddie put the light on and looked around the room. She was back in her bedroom. Relieved, she went to the mirror and touched her face. It was smooth. There was no pain. Maddie now knew that Anna was telling her the story of what had happened.

"Anna," she whispered to the empty room. "Tell me the rest. What happened?"

A voice spoke to her softly in her head.

"I never saw my mam and dad and Ursula again. I am trapped. I want to reach the light. But I am between two worlds. You must help. Set me free."

"How do I do that?" asked Maddie. Anna's voice spoke back and said,

"Find where I lie."

Maddie asked another question but there was silence, and Anna did not speak to her again. She kept trying, but still Anna did not respond to any more questions. But it was as if there was a voice telling her that she would have to go back to the medlar tree, and also to the crypt. That's where the key to this puzzle lay, she was sure of it. But she would go back in daylight, definitely – not at night-time. She did not want to bump into that strange brown-robed figure she had met in the woods.

Maddie glanced at the clock by her bedside. It read 6 a.m. The dream had exhausted her, but she could not rest. Her mind was now too active.

Getting up she switched the light on, then ran the cold tap, and washed her face as bursts of ice cold water poured into the sink. The water made her skin sting. Her face in the mirror above the sink was very pale staring back at her, with what looked like the beginnings of a large red spot on her cheek.

"Oh, great," thought Maddie. "My whole face is now being taken over by one large spot instead of two small ones on my chin." She sighed and dried her face.

The dream had been so clear that writing it down would be the best way to go over it. She walked over to her chest of drawers, opened her stationery drawer, and took out a large A4 pad and pencil. It took a while to write everything she remembered down. Her head was full of questions, including,

"What had happened to Ursula? Wasn't she believed to have ended up in a mental hospital? But what happened after that, and how did she die?"

Maybe the Sacrisen family could give her that information.

Sacrisen Hall was near Brampton, about seven miles from Cattingham. It would be a bus ride to get there. Sam might want to come along. She would ask her after breakfast. Of course her laptop might be able to shed some light on it in the meantime. She had not looked up the Sacrisen family. She placed the black laptop on her bed and plugged it in, then opened up the lid once more.

Typing the name produced a list, so she keyed in 'Sacrisen Hall'. The dates of the Sacrisen ancestors came up in chronological order. Sacrisen Hall was open to the public from 10 a.m. to 4 p.m. The Sacrisen family still owned the Hall, but they now lived in France. The Hall was run by what appeared to be museum staff.

The photographs showed a house from the 1800s with a sweeping marble staircase and a look of sheer opulence. There was even a museum attached to the house. This was certainly not run-down, unlike Cattingham Hall, Maddie thought. She scrolled down the list of ancestors, and came to Ursula Underville.

There was no dark history on Ursula on this website. It detailed that she had been a loving wife and mother to Thomas and Robert respectively but, because of ill health, had had to have medical treatment. There was no account of her mental illness. All it said was

139

that she suffered from fits. She had been nursed through ill health by her brother and her family. The final piece read that she was buried in the family vault at Sacrisen Hall. This did not make sense. She was supposed to have been buried at Cattingham Hall, wasn't she? Why did it say this?

If she was not buried at Cattingham Hall then who was in the coffin of Ursula Underville?

Aunt Lydia would have no objections to her going to Sacrisen Hall. She had been to Brampton by bus before. Fortunately Sacrisen Hall was easy to get to. It was just a slight walk uphill from the bus station, if she remembered rightly. But first she needed to check out the medlar tree. Not wanting to wake Lydia or Sam up, she decided on having a shower after checking the crypt. Surely, she thought, in the early morning it would not be spooky.

She put on a grey fleece from her wardrobe over her pyjamas, and slipped some socks on. She then she picked up her bracelet watch and placed it round her wrist and went out of the bedroom door. There was no sound from Sam's room as she walked down the flight of stairs. From the second landing she could hear the gentle snores of Aunt Lydia. So Maddie tiptoed down, while hoping the stairs would not creak too loudly and wake up Lydia.

When she walked into the kitchen she was cold even with her fleece on. The stone floor held no warmth from the house for her feet. Her outdoor shoes were by the back door, so she sat on a chair to put them on and laced them up. Then she went out of the kitchen door. It was light outside. The large community of sparrows perched on the ancient rose bush sounded as if they were they were having an argument. Listening to their chatter felt strangely reassuring. But a thought came into her head. Should she not have left a note on the kitchen table to let Lydia and Sam know where she was?

Thinking further about it she gave in to laziness, however, and decided she would not be long in the crypt, so it was not worth leaving a note. Surely she would be back before they got up, wouldn't she? It did not make her nervous about going into the crypt. It was morning, so she felt that surely any spooks would be asleep by now.

As she came round to the crypt she looked out for rats. There were none in sight.

Now she could see it in full detail the medlar tree seemed to stand out from all the other bushes in the daylight. Its large green leaves draped over the slightly crooked branches, which were laden with orangey-brown fruit. This explained why the rats had been round there. Some of the fruit lay scattered at the base of the tree, and there were teeth marks in some of the half-eaten fruit.

"The rats must use this tree as a pantry. Let's hope they don't use me as one," she thought wryly.

As she opened the door to the crypt it gave out a stomach churning creak. Maddie then shook her head and argued with herself about her stupidity.

"Whatever possessed me to come to the crypt on my own?" she said as she berated herself.

The water-damaged door was difficult to open fully, so she gave it a further push to get it open. There was a smell of earth inside the crypt. As she touched one of the stone walls it felt wet, and it was covered in marks of cloying decay. Intricately patterned cobwebs brushed against her face. It was not pleasant.

Once inside it was not how you imagined it would be. There was no over-the-top splendour inside. Instead it was quite plain, with coffins on either side of the vault. Maddie came back out of the door and wedged it open with a large tree branch and a rock. The thought of it slamming shut and no one knowing where she was filled her with horror. As she walked over to the coffins which had all been placed side by side she read the inscriptions.

She knelt down. The first coffin she read the inscription of was that of Sarah Underville. It was made of white marble, with carved, praying hands round the sides of it. A remnant of faded red silk stuck out of one of its corners. It made Maddie shudder. Was this the dress of Sarah Underville sticking out of the coffin?

"Ugh. Why am I doing this?" she thought. "I have been in the crypt barely a minute, and I am already nearly wetting my pants."

The second coffin was that of Thomas Underville. It was not so delicately carved. This was a large mahogany coffin with brass handles. A pattern of small horizontal lines ran down it.

The third coffin was completely different from the other two. It was made of what looked like unvarnished pinewood. A brief inscription simply read Ursula Underville. It was longer in length than the other two coffins.

"How plain the coffin is for Ursula Underville," Maddie thought.

Some of the splintered wood had come away, and the coffin now appeared to be on the point of falling apart. Something was not right.

Maddie stared and stared at it, and then she stared at the other two coffins.

Then it came to her.

"Why is the coffin so much longer than the other two? Haven't I read that Ursula Underville was less than five feet tall? Why, then, is it so long?"

A noise at the door made her look up. Then she heard footsteps and a voice.

"Maddie, lass, what are you doing down here?" Titch came into view. He was not smiling, and he was looking very angry.

"Do you not know this is not a safe place to be in?"

Maddie jumped up and replied,

"Sorry, Titch. I just wanted to read the inscriptions. I wedged the door open so it would not shut on me. I was not going to be long," she said, hoping he would not be so angry.

"Did you tell Lydia where you were going?"

"No," said Maddie and put her head down, knowing she was now going to get a right rollicking from him."

"That was a really daft thing to do. You could have been locked in here, with your aunt frantic with worry and not knowing where you were. Bloody stupid, I would call it."

"I know. I know I should have said. Please don't be mad."

Titch could not be angry for long after looking at Maddie's downcast face, and muttered something under his breath instead.

"Titch, I have discovered something. I don't think Ursula is in that coffin. The coffin is too big. She was a tiny woman. If she is not in the coffin someone else is."

Titch stared back at Maddie and gave her a strange look.

"Who do you think is in the coffin?"

142

"I think it may have been an Anna Blackstock. Her parents were in service at the Hall. I read on her parents' headstone about how she went missing and was never seen again. I think I know what happened. You won't believe me, but I think the ghost of Anna Blackstock has been trying to tell me this. The only way I will find out is if we open the coffin lid. Anna Blackstock was believed to have been six feet tall. If there is a skeleton that long in the coffin I will be proved right."

"Do you really want me to open a coffin lid so you can look in it? Think again, pet."

"Please, Titch. If you do not want me to look in you could look in and tell me if the skeleton is at least six feet long. Please ... I won't ask for anything else."

Titch scratched his head and pursed his lips. He gave a deep sigh.

"I suppose, hinny, if I don't do this I will not get any peace from you until I do it. I will do it, but I want you to look away. You do not look in the coffin. Is that understood?"

"Yes, yes. I promise I won't look," Maddie replied, unable to believe that Titch was going to open the coffin.

"Right. Turn round with your back to me and I will look for you ... and no peeking. Understood?"

She did as he said. She heard his footsteps as he got nearer the coffin, then the sound of scraping, and then of the lid being opened and Titch coughing.

"You said that Ursula Underville was only five feet tall, didn't you?"

"Yes. She was believed to be only five feet."

"Then this is not Ursula Underville. It looks like the skeleton of a person who would have been well over six feet tall, judging by the length of it, with what looks like white fabric around it. I am now going to put the coffin lid back on. You can turn around now."

Maddie turned round.

"Well, Lydia is going to have to be told about this. If Ursula is not in the coffin then where is she?" asked Titch, and added,

"The main question she will be asking is, 'Who is in the coffin?' I think we should get out of here now, and we'll speak to Lydia when she gets up. Come on, lass."

143

Maddie began to follow Titch, and wondered if her aunt was going to tell her off for going into the crypt on her own. Something touched her face, and she suddenly became aware that it felt like a light kiss on her cheek. She smiled and whispered,

"Thank you, Anna."

"What did you say?" Titch turned round.

"Oh, nothing … just talking to myself," came her response. But on touching her face she could feel it was slightly wet, and she smiled to herself.

Titch shut the crypt door and they walked back to the house.

"How will they prove who is in the coffin, Titch?"

"I don't know. Lydia will know what to do. The skeleton looked old, so I don't think it is going to be a murder enquiry. But it is a mystery. I am surprised nobody had found out that Ursula was not in the coffin before," said Titch, perplexed by the whole thing.

Chapter 18

After coming out of the dark crypt Titch shut the door closing it firmly behind him. They walked back to the house. Hodge appeared and gave purrs of delight as she led them into the kitchen.

"She'll want her breakfast, no doubt," said Titch as they listened to the cat mewing with delight. Then, on hearing Lydia's voice talking to Hodge, he added, "Sounds like Lydia is already sorting that out."

Lydia continued having a conversation with Hodge as they came in.

Hodge did not now bother looking up. She was too busy tucking into her favourite beef-flavoured cat food. Lydia looked surprised at seeing Maddie up so early and asked,

"Maddie, what are you doing out outside? Where have you been?"

"I think I had better tell you about that, Lydia," Titch responded quickly in reply. "I found her round at the crypt. She was looking at the names on the coffins."

"Maddie, what on earth were you doing there? You should not have gone to the crypt on your own. The flooding has caused some damage in there. It could have been dangerous – and to go there and not tell us where you had gone … It was a really stupid thing to do. For a bright girl I am really surprised at you."

Lydia continued to speak angrily, and Maddie meekly kept her head down.

"Lydia, we found something in the crypt," said Titch, jumping into the telling-off and coming to Maddie's rescue. Lydia immediately stopped the tirade and asked,

"What did you find?"

"Ursula Underville is not in the coffin we thought she was in. There appears to be another woman in there."

"Oh, my God … Are you saying someone has been murdered?" responded Lydia, horror-struck.

"No, no nothing like that. I fancy it's an old skeleton. Maddie thinks it may be the skeleton of an Anna Blackstock. Her parents were in service at the Hall around the time Ursula was the lady of the Hall. Anna Blackstock appears to have gone missing around that time. This may be the mystery solved. But the problem is ... We don't have proof that it is the lass is in there, or where Ursula Underville now lies." Lydia replied,

"Good heavens. Well, the first thing is that we will have to let the police know. I imagine that they will have to age the skeleton. I will also contact the curator at Sacrisen Hall. The Sacrisen family live abroad now. We will see if the curator can shed any light on the matter concerning Ursula."

"Aunt Lydia, I really believe that the skeleton is Anna Blackstock. She was friends with Ursula, and she disappeared. According to the history of the Sacrisen family Ursula was buried at Sacrisen Hall. I found that out on the Internet."

"Maddie, we don't know if this is the case. Hopefully this will be cleared up shortly, but it is a very strange thing. If Ursula was buried at Sacrisen Hall then why does it state in our historical records that she was buried here? I will, as I have said, contact the police. I'll do that now. While I am doing that, Titch, help yourself to breakfast".

"No, thanks, Lydia. I will get on with my jobs. I have had my breakfast. I am going to cut back some of the trees at the back before the bad weather sets in. The weather forecast said there would be heavy winds today."

"Well, Maddie, I imagine you will want some breakfast." Lydia asked not really listening for the reply. Her thoughts everywhere.

"No, I will just have a drink and a banana. I can't wait to tell Sam what we have discovered."

"Well, I am now going to have to call the police. And as for Sam ... I think you may have to wait to tell her, but make sure she has something to eat when she gets up" said Lydia. "She is not one of life's early risers so it may take some time."

"Aunt Lydia, she will wake up for me. I am good at getting her up."

That was true, but it wasn't with a gentle rap on the door. It was usually Maddie bellowing at the top of her voice in Sam's ear. Lydia had now lost the serious look on her face, but Maddie thought she would quickly have a drink and eat her banana. If Lydia had to phone the police she did not want to be around, due to her causing the problem in the first place.

Lydia went out of the door into the sitting room and Maddie quickly drank her tea. Grabbing a banana from the fruit bowl she crammed bits of it into her mouth and gulping it down. She was far too excited to eat, but just went through the motions to please her aunt. Eating it like this was something that would have disgusted Lydia. Maddie raced up to Sam's bedroom. Excitement had taken over, and she banged on Sam's door. She did not wait for a reply, but barged in. Sam was half hanging out of the bed with her red hair fanned over her face and a lily-white foot sticking out of the gathered clump of bedclothes.

"Sam, wake up. You will never believe what has happened."

Sam groaned and pulled the bedclothes further over her face.

"Go away, Maddie. I don't care. Let me sleep. It's freezing in here."

"No, Sam, you have to wake up. I have got lots to tell you." But she would not get up, so Maddie pulled the covers off her.

"Maddie, you are a cow," came Sam's angry response.

"Oh, shut up and listen to what I have to tell you. Here, put on your dressing gown."

Maddie handed her a pink dressing gown. Sam was shivering. She grudgingly sat up got out of bed and put it on.

"Go on, then. Tell me this exciting news," said Sam grumpily.

"I went to the crypt this morning, Sam. Titch found me and gave me a bit of a bollocking, but I noticed something. The coffin Ursula Underville was in was too big for her. Ursula Underville was less than five feet tall. I managed to persuade Titch to look in the coffin."

"Oh, my God, Maddie. Did you get to see the skeleton?" said Sam, getting excited.

"No," said Maddie disappointedly. "He wouldn't let me see it. From looking at the body in the coffin he said it was a woman with a white dress. But ... you will never guess. It was not Ursula in the coffin. It was a much taller person. Ursula Underville was barely five feet tall, so it could not have been her. I think it was Anna Blackstock.

"Remember your mother saw a girl wearing a white dress? Anna Blackstock is the ghost. Titch said the skeleton in the coffin had something white on. You know I have been having those dreams, and they have been so realistic? I really thought I was in them … I think Anna wanted me to know what happened to her, and after the last dream I had pieced it all together."

"What did you dream?" asked Sam.

Maddie told her all she could remember.

"That Katharine sounds like a monster," said Sam.

"I think she was," replied Maddie. "She wanted Ursula out of the way so she could have her son and the Hall, and keep Anna as some sort of mystic."

"Do you think Katharine killed her?"

"I don't know, Sam. I felt in my dream that Anna was already very sick. If she had died Katharine would have had to hide the body. Maybe that's why her parents never found out what had happened to her. In my dream Katharine kept saying that Anna had special powers."

"Katharine may have had servants loyal to her who helped her put Anna in the coffin. If she was that tall it would have taken more than one person to carry her and place her in there," said Sam.

"Well, if Aunt Lydia contacts Sacrisen Hall we may find out more. Come on, get up. Aunt Lydia was asking what you wanted for breakfast."

"OK," said Sam wiping her eyes and yawning. "Tell her I'll get a shower first. Then I will have some cereal. Of course I may have to shower in my dressing gown, though. Maddie, how can you stay here? It is so bloody cold."

She blew her breath at Maddie. A white wisp of air came out her mouth.

"See. Freeezing."

"You get used to it, Sam," replied Maddie, smirking, then said,

"I think I will get my shower as well, and use Aunt Lydia's en suite. What time is Josh picking you up?"

"He said about eleven," came the reply.

"You can stay as long as you want, you know."

"Thanks. But I have to get my project done. It's all right for you, you swot. I haven't even started it. I still don't know what I am doing yet. I might do what you said. Women suffragettes."

"Sam, knowing you it will be brilliant. You always come up with something really good right at the last minute, while I have to slog my guts out. You are so lucky. It is effortless for you. Oh, look. Your toe is really swelling up. What did you do to it?"

"I don't know. It's just my big toes. They seem to be getting bigger. All the other toes are fine. Mum says I will have to be looked at. It's almost like there is a lump on top of it. It has always been odd, but seems to be getting worse as I have got older. Putting my shoe on is a real pain. The smaller toes are OK, but I think the other big toe is exactly the same."

They both looked at the toe. It looked quite bulbous, like a huge white onion, and it didn't match any of the other toes. Sam got embarrassed from Maddie staring at her feet in fascination, so she quickly put her slippers on. On sensing her discomfort Maddie went out of the room. As she watched her go out of the room Sam could hear her whistling.

"Maddie is such a tomboy but so pretty, and not in the least bit interested in her looks ..." thought Sam, "and she doesn't have deformed feet."

Maddie's feet were half the size of Sam's. Her own ritual was make-up and hair straighteners, the latter which her mother said appeared to be fastened to her hands like an umbilical cord. She wished she looked like Maddie, with all her natural prettiness. It was so unfair ...

By 11 a.m., just as Josh arrived, the weather was getting worse. The sky was black, and some of the old oak trees looked as if their branches were about to snap off. As she opened the front door to Josh Lydia remarked on at how bad the weather was.

"Do be careful driving, Josh. Are you sure you don't want to wait until the weather is better?" Lydia asked.

"No, we will be all right. We have to get to Newcastle."

Sam butted in and sniggered as he came into the hall, and said,

"Yes, we know why he is so desperate to go to Newcastle. He has a date with Emma."

"Oh, put a sock in it," said Josh angrily, his face beetroot.

"Sam, don't tease him. It's cruel. If he has a date then it's none of our business. So don't be so nosy. Josh, does she live locally? And who are her parents?" asked Lydia.

"Lydia!" replied Josh.

"Sorry, Josh ... Couldn't resist it," said Lydia, winking as she said it. Josh, still embarrassed, placed Sam's weekend bag in the boot of the car.

"See you soon," he said, smiling at Maddie. Then Sam and Josh climbed into the car seats. Maddie felt strangely lonely.

She wondered what Emma was like. Lydia seemed to read her mind as Josh and Sam drove off.

"You don't have to worry, Maddie. Just because Josh has a girlfriend it won't stop you all being friends."

"I know, but she might really get on with Sam," came Maddie's jealous reply.

"Well, I am sure as you are her best friend she will not neglect you. So don't worry. Come on in, anyway. It's getting cold and windy. I think I will move those planters into the hallway. I don't like the way they are blowing about."

"I'll give you a hand," replied Maddie.

The stone planters were heavy and wet. Lydia put black bin liners under them as they placed them near the cloakroom.

"When the weather improves we will bring take them back out," said Lydia.

Just as she said that there was a loud rumbling noise.

"What on earth—?" said Lydia, not even having a chance to finish what she was about to say.

They looked across at each other and raced to where the noise was coming from. They found it coming from the small library. After opening the door they could only look in shock. The floor was inches deep in water, and it was pouring towards them. A voice behind them answered Lydia's unspoken question.

"I think the radiator has burst. Get some towels," shouted Titch.

Maddie raced off to the airing cupboard on the second floor and armed herself with old towels. When she came downstairs Titch was using an old curtain to mop up the flow. He took the towels from her. The water seemed to have stopped pumping from the radiator. Titch waded over and immediately switched the valve off on the radiator. Within minutes Lydia was on her mobile to the plumber.

"The plumber will be here in half an hour, but I am going to be charged a fortune as it's an emergency ... I wish I had never put that radiator on to warm it up. I just did not want the photographers to be cold in here. What a mess. Heavens knows how much it will cost to put right."

Lydia raised her hands in the air in agitation as she spoke. She said,

"Oh, no ... and look at the wall."

The plaster was now breaking off in thick pieces on the wall.

"Get out of the room," shouted Titch as he realised what was about to happen. "The wall is coming away."

They all moved to the door as pitted white plaster crumbled off the wall. However, it only appeared to come off one side of the wall. The plaster fell down in huge chunks. It crashed down and made a damp, dusty cloud.

Chapter 19

When it had subsided a powdery white door faced the three of them. Titch walked towards it, the legs of his trousers now soaked in steaming water. A small doorknob was visible. He turned it. More plaster fell lightly on his head. In front of them was what looked like a room?

"Don't go in, Titch. It might be dangerous," said Lydia.

"It's all right. The rest of the wall looks strong enough to hold."

He walked into the room. They could hear his footsteps. He came out with a painting under his arm.

"It's the painting of the Duchess of Barchester. What is it doing here? Julian sold it to some auctioneers in London and gave me £250 for it," Lydia said, puzzled.

"Lydia," said Titch quietly. "There are more paintings in there."

"What? Which ones?"

"The Duchess of Pargrove, The Hunt Supper, The Reaper, and The Duke of Meadowfield," said Titch, as he tried not to sound disgusted.

"Sorry, pet, but I think I know what he has been doing. The Hunt Supper and The Reaper are the ones he gave you money for. The Duchess of Barchester and The Duchess of Pargrove and the others are the ones you thought were stolen, remember, after Akkoubian died?

"What do you mean, Titch?" replied Lydia, completely puzzled.

"I think those paintings are worth a lot more than you think. He has been ripping you off. I bet he has a deal with one of them fancy auctioneers in London, and is waiting for the price to increase on them. No wonder he helped me in the library. He even plastered the wall himself because he said he was worried about the wall collapsing. Well, we know why now. He was not doing it to help you. He was doing it to make sure that the paintings were safe so he could sell them later. It was only recently that he mentioned to me about paying for you and me and me wife to go on holiday. He wanted us out of the way, and I know why now."

"Titch, I can't believe what you are saying. There must be some mistake."

"I very much doubt it, Lydia. These paintings might be worth a lot of money."

Lydia's shocked face said it all.

"Do you think that the row Akkoubian had with him before he died was something to do with this?" Lydia asked.

"I don't know, and we will probably never know. But Akkoubian was a very sick man, so I don't think a row would have caused his heart attack. Remember the doctor said that Akkoubian had an enlarged heart. He could have gone any time. So don't upset yourself about that."

Lydia's eyes had misted up, and Titch and Maddie, who were concerned, looked at each other.

"Don't worry. This will all get sorted. Do you want me to have a word with Julian?" Titch asked.

"No. I will sort it out," said Lydia quickly. "You could sort the plumber out when he comes, though. That would be a great help. It's only mid-morning, but already we have an unknown skeleton, the radiator has burst, and my brother-in-law appears to have been robbing me." She gave a sad smile and shook her head, as if trying to banish the images from her head.

"Come on, Maddie. Help me mop up the rest of this water before the plumber comes. We can keep towels over the floor because, no doubt, there will be more water coming out later."

"I will get the rest of the paintings out," said Titch. "Lydia, look on the bright side. If Julian has been hiding these paintings then they are worth a lot of money."

Lydia looked deeply into Titch's eyes as he spoke, and said,

"It's not a question of money. It's how he has deceived me. I will be speaking to him, don't you worry about that. I will get the other paintings valued – but not, on this occasion, with any help from him. I can't believe that Julian would rob his own brother's family. What did we ever do to be treated this way by him? We trusted him."

Her navy blue eyes darkened with hurt and anger as she spoke. She said,

"I have phoned the police about the skeleton. They are sending someone along. Let's hope that I don't get charged with murder on top of this." Titch and Maddie did not reply to this. They just looked at each other.

Titch then went back into the secret room and came back out and gently placed the pictures on the ground outside the library door.

"What a strange room. There is a bed in it, and what looks like a chamber pot and jug. There is something else. Scratched on the brickwork is the name Anna Blackstock. Maddie, I think you may have been right."

"Titch, please can I look at the room?" She didn't wait for an answer, and raced into the room.

"Maddie," shouted Titch. "Get out of that room. It's dangerous." She ignored him and went in.

As she looked round the room she had a feeling of terrible sadness.

"This is where they had kept Anna Blackstock prisoner. It will be Anna in the crypt," thought Maddie. A lump formed in her throat at the horror of it all.

Deep in thought at what she imagined had happened to Anna she said,

"Look, at the wall, Titch. See what she has scratched under her name: Help me. She was locked in here, I am sure of it," said Maddie to him.

Titch was now too interested in the room to be angry. He looked at what was written and shook his head and said,

"Yes, I see it. The poor lass. The room is tiny."

There was something desperately sad about the room. Standing in there made the hairs stand on the back of your neck. It was if you could almost feel a sense of sheer hopelessness, and that Anna knew she would never get out of the room alive.

"I am going to tell Colin," said Maddie. "Do you think she can be buried in her family plot? I think this may bring her peace, and then there will be no more hauntings."

"We will have to see," said Lydia. She had just appeared in the room, which made it very cramped for Titch and Maddie.

154

"To think this room has been here for heavens knows how long. Your Uncle Akkoubian would have been amazed."

The long bed was quite sparse, and was covered in cobwebs. Faded strips of an unknown fabric clung to it. A dirty glass, which had been misted up by its black contents, lay on a small table.

"Look," Maddie said. From under the bed she produced a brown leather shoe.

It was very long. The size was much larger than Maddie's or Lydia's. The front of the shoe appeared to have been widened at one of the toes.

"I bet this was stretched because of Anna's six toes," said Maddie as she placed it down on the bed.

"What an incredible room, Maddie. I am amazed about how much you know about Anna Blackstock," said Lydia.

"I dreamt it, Aunt Lydia. Anna wanted us to find her. This is her shoe. Look at the small window. This is all in my dream."

As they looked the three of them became aware of a bird peering from outside at them. It was a huge bird. It was a raven. The bird looked directly them and then, before their eyes, disappeared into thin air.

"Did you see that? It was a raven. But where has it gone? It's disappeared," said Titch.

"Yes, it has, hasn't it?" said a shaken Lydia.

"Aunt Lydia, can you remember the accounts of the ghost of Cattingham Hall? They said the ghost was followed by a raven. That will be it," said Maddie.

Lydia and Titch just continued to stare at the window in stunned silence.

"Come on, we will have to get out of here," said Lydia finally. "The police will here at any minute."

Just as she spoke the door knocker banged loudly. She hurried out of the room and went to answer the door. It was as she said, but it was a policeman on his own. Lydia took him into the sitting room. Titch and Maddie continued to mop up the water.

"What a bloody mess. It is going to take ages to dry this room out. I would like to wring Julian's bloody neck. He has broken your aunt's heart."

"But, Titch, it was better it happened. Aunt Lydia has now found out what he was really like, and the paintings that she did not sell to him might be worth a lot of money."

"Aye, I know it is for the best. If I had my way I would have called the police and had him arrested, but that is something your aunt is not going to do. So he gets away with it. It is not right. People like him always walk away scot-free. The man is nothing but a conman."

"I don't know about him getting away with it. Lydia looked very angry," replied Maddie. She was trying to calm Titch down, as his voice was now becoming raised.

It was a relief when the plumber arrived not long after the policeman. Titch took him into the small library. The policeman had now come out of the sitting room with Lydia, and they had then gone to the crypt. They were there a long time, which worried Maddie.

"Surely the policeman would know it was an old skeleton, and not think there had been a murder?" thought Maddie. She was getting so worried that she sat chewing at her nails until Lydia came back into the kitchen.

"Where is the policeman?" Maddie asked her aunt.

"Oh, he has gone now. He is going to instruct a forensic archaeologist, who will determine the age of the bones." On seeing her niece's face Lydia said,

"You don't have to worry. It's not a murder enquiry. Those bones are most likely to be more than a hundred years old."

"They're older than that, Aunt Lydia," came Maddie's reply.

"Well, we'll see. The next thing I need to do is contact the curator at Sacrisen Hall. I am still intrigued to know if they know where Ursula Underville is buried," said Lydia.

"What about Uncle Julian?"

"Maddie, I really don't want to think about him at the moment. I haven't decided what I am going to do," came Lydia's reply. She now sounded quite irritated.

When she saw the look on Lydia's face Maddie was pleased that she was not in Julian's' shoes. Her aunt, judging by her severe expression, looked like she would eat him alive when she saw him.

"Right. It's now 10.15 a.m. The curator should be at the Hall by now. We'll see if we can solve this mystery. Maddie, can you put the washing machine on? Stick it on the delicate wash. All the washing and the soap powder are in. I just forgot to switch it on."

Maddie murmured, "Yes," as Lydia went off to the sitting room to phone him.

Once Maddie had switched on the washing machine she went into the study to get a notepad. It was not worth phoning Sam yet, because she would be getting her eyebrows threaded. This was something that sounded thoroughly unpleasant to Maddie, who hardly had any eyebrows. All she had was a fine brown line of hair where they should have been.

After picking up the notepad Maddie wrote all the new information down while it was still fresh in her memory. Then she tapped into her laptop and looked to see if she could find further information on the Sacrisen family.

Maybe she had missed something when she had been scrolling down. According to one website Ursula's brother had come back from abroad after three years of being away. His father had died, and he had moved into Sacrisen Hall with his new wife. He then appeared to have also run Cattingham Hall and taken charge of the care of Ursula's son. Katharine then left the Hall. To Maddie it sounded, from reading between the lines, that the brother had appeared to have cottoned on to Katharine's activities. But there was no further account of Ursula.

Maddie would have liked to have gone into the secret room to see if there was anything else she might find. The lone shoe under the bed was a poignant reminder, it seemed to Maddie, that Anna had been kept prisoner there. How claustrophobic it must have been.

"Why had no one heard her cries? Or had the servants turned a blind eye to this?" she thought. Maybe she would have another dream, which would tell her more. As she was still mulling it over she could hear Lydia's muffled voice coming from the sitting room.

The telephone conversation appeared to have stopped and Maddie, unable to contain her excitement, raced into the sitting room to see Lydia. Her aunt, who was smiling, spoke before she had even had a chance to utter one word. She said,

"Well, according to the curator, it was a family secret that Ursula had been taken out of the asylum and moved back into Sacrisen Hall. Her brother came back from abroad, having married out there, and found his sister in the asylum. His father had signed over Ursula's care to a Doctor Lockart. Ursula's father had died during the period Ursula was there. Her brother found that she had been heavily drugged. She was kept in secret at Sacrisen Hall. The drugs at the asylum used on her had an adverse effect on her health, and she died at Sacrisen Hall."

"So that's what happened to her," said Maddie.

"Yes, Maddie. But there was so much hysteria about her being a witch that it was decided she would be buried at Sacrisen Hall in secret. A fake coffin was placed at Cattingham Hall in case anyone tried to damage it. Ursula's brother, in his grief, had a complaint made against Katharine and Doctor Lockhart. The doctor left the area, and Katharine was removed from the Hall.

"One thing Katharine was unaware of was that Ursula had made a will before she became ill, which she had sent to her brother. This seems to have been to protect her son. She appears to have done it after her husband died. She had placed the protection of her son in her brother's hands. Cattingham Hall was then shut up for quite a number of years until Ursula's son was of age. He then moved back into the Hall."

"That must have been a surprise for Katharine to find that Ursula had made a will in favour of her brother," said Maddie in response.

"Well, there is no further account of what happened to Katharine. We are probably unlikely to find out anything further," replied Lydia.

"Well, I hope something horrible happened to her," said Maddie.

Maddie didn't say anything else. She hoped that Anna had heard what she had said. It was so sad that although Ursula's brother had rescued her Ursula had not told anyone about Anna because she was too ill to speak so she could not ask what had happened to Anna. She also wondered if Anna's parents had gone to the Justice of the Peace and they hadn't believed what Anna had told her mother to say to him in the event of anything happening to her. Or did her parents not tell him thinking their daughter had drowned. But what would happen to Anna's skeleton. Just hoping and hoping there would be some proof that would be found which would confirm that it was Anna in the crypt. Maybe once that was discovered Anna could be buried in her family burial plot, and would be at peace for her at last. She would ask Colin if he could do this.

"Aunt Lydia, can I go into Cattingham?"

"The weather is still bad. It is windy at the moment, but it might pour with rain again. So no, I don't think so."

"Oh, please … I just want to buy some more stationery and want to go to the library again. I won't be long."

Lydia was so distracted with all that had happened that she could not be bothered to argue. She sighed and said,

"Well, I suppose so. But you must wear your thick coat with the hood, and I do not want you cutting across to the woods. A tree could come down. Understood?" Maddie nodded.

Lydia then said,

"It would be a help to me if you went, actually. I missed adding a few things on the shopping list. Could you get them for me?"

"OK," said Maddie.

Her neck suddenly felt itchy, and she remembered she had the cross on. But her neck continued to itch so she took it off and put it on a chair, and she decided to put it on later. But the cross slid off the chair and lay by the skirting board.

Lydia disappeared into the kitchen, and returned ten minutes later as her niece was putting on her thick padded purple coat and beanie hat on. She said to Maddie,

"Winter is coming early. I can't believe this weather. We have had no summer to speak of. The way it's going we may have heavy snow in early November. Here is the list— Oh, and use this bag. It's quite sturdy."

A red tartan shopping bag was thrust into Maddie's hand.

"I have my school bag. I'll take that for the shopping," said Maddie. She looked at the old-lady shopping bag with undisguised horror.

"No, this is a much stronger bag."

No amount of arguing with Lydia would persuade her otherwise so, defeated, Maddie took the bag.

"It's either that or the shopping bag on wheels," Lydia said, knowing that her niece hated the shopping bag on wheels.

"No, no. I'll take this bag," came Maddie's reply. Her immediate thoughts were that the shopping bag on wheels would be even worse. What if someone from the school saw her with it?

She brushed away this image of sheer horror from her mind and took the hideous tartan shopping bag.

Lydia's eyes began shining with amusement at the disgusted expression on her niece's face as walked away. She tried with great effort to stifle a laugh. She knew Maddie hated the bag, but it was the biggest one she had.

Chapter 20

As Maddie opened the front door the sheer strength of the wind nearly blew the door shut. Hanging on she managed to get out of it. It was a fierce wind, and the cold bit into her face. Attempting to put her hood up was a wasted effort, as it immediately came down again. After a few further attempts she gave up. The wind pummelled her tiny frame and blew her and the shopping bag along the drive.

"I wonder if the wind will blow this bag away," thought Maddie hopefully, but an afterthought made her hold on to it more tightly. If she lost it then Lydia would make her take the loathsome shopping bag on wheels out. She had better not accidentally lose the bag.

It was a struggle walking through the cut to Cattingham. She narrowly avoided being hit in the face by a wooden vegetable box that had been blown up into the air.

The real reason she wanted to go to Cattingham was to see Colin the vicar about Anna. There was hardly anyone about – which was hardly surprising, because of the bad weather.

Maddie was surprised that Lydia had agreed to let her go into Cattingham, and thought that if her aunt had not had so much on her mind, what with the skeleton, the burst radiator, and Uncle Julian, she might have not let her go. In Maddie's opinion the only good thing seemed to be that the paintings could be worth a lot of money, and this would help her aunt financially.

She half walked and was half blown to the front door of the church. When she opened it there was no one there.

She walked into the church and to Colin's office where she found him bent over his laptop with a puzzled expression on his face. As he looked up he said,

"Hello, Maddie. What are you doing here?"

"Hi, Colin. I just wanted to ask you something, if you are not too busy," Maddie replied.

"I don't suppose you know anything about spreadsheets?" he asked hopefully.

"A bit. We have been doing them at school."

"Can you help me? I have the 'week commencing' dates on my spreadsheet but they don't match the months, and I can't get the cell with the border to match it."

Maddie looked through the spreadsheet, and then picked up the mouse and started working on the spreadsheet.

"There. I think this is right. I've made your date the last week in July. You were missing that. It should work now."

Colin picked up the mouse and gave her a smile of relief.

"Well done. You are marvellous. See, it's working now. I have spent an hour going round and round with the dates and getting nowhere. Thank you ... What did you want to ask me?"

She told him what had happened.

"My word, Maddie. That sounds exciting stuff."

"What I was wondering, Colin, was – if it is established that it is Anna Blackstock in the crypt – can she be put back in her family burial plot? I am sure she will be at peace if she is laid to rest with her family."

"How do you know that?" Colin asked.

"I don't suppose you believe in ghosts, do you? Well, I do – and I am sure that the hauntings at Cattingham Hall have been caused by her not being properly buried."

Maddie told him about her dreams, and then looked at him. She wondered if she should have mentioned it to him, hoped that he didn't think she was mad. He listened very carefully without interrupting her.

"I think you may have had a sign from God, but I do not understand about ghosts as it is not in my faith. If it is proved that it is Anna Blackstock I am sure her family would wish her to be buried in the burial plot. I did find out that the last surviving relative of the Blackstocks lives in Bickleberry," said Colin.

"Do you know where they live?" Maddie asked.

"It is an old lady, Jeannette Raby – a distant cousin. She lives at the retirement home at Bickleberry. You could write to her if you wanted to see her."

"I will do. Thank you. The other thing I wanted to ask is about Katharine Underville. She left Cattingham Hall ... I just needed to know if you would have any information about when she died."

Colin went through the old parish records. After ten minutes of scanning through them he looked up and said,

"There is nothing here about her death. Of course you might find some information from the Drakens. The modern day group is still in existence. Their place is at Bickleberry. I know one of them is a retired teacher. I can phone him. The Drakens are very conceited about how far back their religious order goes. There is bound to be information on her. I think a visit may be in order, but I think I should go with you. These people are always keen to initiate young people, and are extremely manipulative.

"We can go today, if you like, and afterwards I will drop you off at your aunt's. Check with your Aunt Lydia first. I just need to finish updating this spreadsheet. This is what I call my Sunday, so I have all the time in the world." He smiled back kindly at Maddie.

"Oh, Colin, that would be great. I'll just give her a call." She phoned her aunt from her mobile and asked if she could go. Lydia said it was fine to go, but reminded her to get the shopping first.

"Colin, I just need to get Aunt Lydia's shopping. Can I put it in the boot of your car when I get back?"

"No problem, Maddie. While you are out I will phone Martin at the Masonic Hall at Bickleberry," said Colin. He scratched his head and frowned as he went back to finish his spreadsheet.

Maddie walked to the paper shop. The shop was selling half-price jars of sweets. She picked up a large jar of humbugs that were sitting on a shelf as nosy Jane began talking to her.

"I see you haven't got your friend with you today."

"What friend?"

"Why, your friend with the long white dress. Does she live round here?" Maddie tried not to look shocked. Anna must have followed her the last time she had been in Cattingham.

"But how come I didn't see her?" she thought.

"Er, no. She lives at Stocksfield. I don't get to see her much," Maddie replied, but she was lying.

"Oh, that's a shame ... It's always nice to have a lot of friends. I bet you get very lonely up at the Hall. How is your Aunt Lydia, by the way?"

"She is fine," Maddie replied, not willing to say anything more to Jane.

To get out of talking further she hurriedly picked up the jar of sweets and placed them in the carrier bag that Jane had handed her.

"Thank you," she said, smiling at her and hoping that Jane was not going to ask her any more questions. She then walked quickly out of the shop before Jane could say anything further.

After going out of the shop she whispered to herself,

"Anna, why didn't you let me know you were following me? Talk to me."

At first she thought it was the howling wind, then a voice whispered gently. She looked behind her. There was no one there. She could then hear the voice in her head saying,

"I was following you to keep you safe. My power has not yet come back strongly enough for you to be able to see me. Only people who see ghosts can see me. I was helping you. One of the witches was following you."

"Who was following me, Anna?"

"Her."

Maddie asked another question but got no reply, then another one. One of the witches had followed her. How many witches were there? She wondered.

Maddie began to feel queasy.

"Why is she following me?" she thought. "Oh, my God. A witch has been following me in the woods." She repeated this to herself, but this only made her only more terrified. Well, one thing was for certain. She would not be going in those woods again.

By going to all the shops on the list she got all the shopping her aunt wanted. As she walked back to the church the wind continued to howl and give high-pitched shrieks, which sounded almost wolf-like and unearthly.

Something touched her shoulder. It felt as if something was digging into her skin with deep thrusts in order to hurt her. It reminded her of the séance.

164

A rasping voice then began to whisper in her ear. It spoke in a low threatening tone,

"We will be coming for you, girl." It then chuckled evilly.

The voice croaky, like an old woman's. It continued to utter whispered threats to her. Maddie placed her hands on her ears, trying to block out the words. Her whole body froze, and the hairs on the back of her neck stood on end. Terrified, she began to run back to the church – her shopping back banging into her right knee as she ran.

Chapter 21

Due to the bad weather there was no one around who could see her distress. As she opened the church door the wind was against her, and the door nearly shut in her face as she tried to open it. She heard something that sounded like a short, cruel laugh.

The sound went deep into her bones. It was terrifying. She was pushed by invisible hands and almost fell into the church.

Colin came to the church door. He was shocked by her face.

"Maddie, whatever is the matter?"

Tearfully told him she had heard a whisper in her ear and what they had said to her, and that something had pushed her.

"The wind can make strange noises that can sound like voices. Do not be frightened. As for being pushed … it will have been the strong winds."

"No, Colin. It was a voice, and something really did push me. I felt it. I can't expect you to believe everything that has happened to me. But I do not know what to do. How can I protect myself? Please help me."

Because he could see her getting more and more distressed as she spoke Colin rubbed her shoulder and said,

"Young lady, God will protect you from any evil. You must believe in him."

Colin took off a small cross and went to put it on her.

"No, Colin that is yours."

"Maddie, do you not think that I would have more than one cross in a church? Here you are." He smiled as he placed it round her neck and fastened it.

"Touch it whenever you feel frightened. Promise me you will do that?"

"Yes, Colin," said Maddie as she wiped away the tears that had fallen down her cheeks with her sleeve.

"Come on, Maddie. We have some investigative work to do, don't we? I phoned Martin Willis, the historian I told you about. He will see us at the old Masonic Hall. Here, let me take that shopping bag off you. It looks heavy. That's a nice bag. It looks very strong."

Maddie gave a small smile.

"If you like it maybe my Aunt Lydia will let you have it. Oh, I almost forgot. This is for you."

She produced the jar of humbugs from her bag.

"Just a thank you," she said as she handed it to him shyly.

Colin laughed as he was handed the large jar of sweets and said,

"No, you keep the bag. It's a good shopping bag. Look at these lovely sweets. My word, the last time I ate humbugs was when I was at school. Thank you very much. I will enjoy eating those. I shall keep them in the office when I am on the computer messing up my spreadsheets."

Colin took the jar into his office, and was still beaming as he came out with his coat on. He pulled a bunch of keys out of his pocket.

Maddie waited outside the church as he locked the door, then placed her shopping in the boot of his battered green Mini. He appeared to use the inside of the car as some sort of dumping ground: toffee wrappers and odd pages of old sermons were strewn across the seats. He brushed them on to the floor as they sat down. It did not take long to get to Bickleberry in the car.

The village was even more basic than Cattingham, and it had hardly any shops. The grey Masonic-style hall they drove up to, Maddie thought, looked like something out of a horror film. It was ugly. The path had been concreted over, and small red bricks acted as a tiny wall round the property. There were what looked like cell windows with small bars on them. They walked up the mud-encrusted concrete path. Colin lifted up the ornate brass door knocker, which was in the shape of an eagle, and knocked on the door. The noise seemed to reverberate all around them, which made Maddie jump.

A man opened the door. He was very pale, with brown greasy hair, and was wearing a brown suit that had seen better days. It hung down off his painfully thin frame. His off-white shirtsleeves were frayed, and looked dirty.

"Hello, Martin," said Colin quickly. "This is Maddie, as I mentioned. She is doing a school project on Cattingham, and was interested in learning more about the Drakens."

"Hello," came the toneless reply.

Maddie found herself looking into watery eyes the colour of brown mud. The man looked as if he had never seen sunlight. His anaemic skin was the colour of milk. On looking closely she could see that his nose was covered in red spider like blemishes. As he opened the door wider to let them in she noticed he had dirty fingernails that were almost bitten to the quick.

"Follow me," he said with no emotion in his voice as he shuffled ahead of them.

Colin went in first, and gave Maddie an encouraging smile.

Once inside they saw that there appeared to be a flight of stairs to the left in a large, tiled hallway. Martin Willis went up the stairs. They followed him.

The dark red wool carpet they walked on was faded, and held in place by pairs of solid brass clips. The distressed wood panelling on the walls of the stairs had carvings of goat-like figures on it, and a strange half-human horned creature.

Maddie caught sight of Colin's side profile as he looked at them. His expression appeared to show shock, and then disgust. Once up the stairs Martin guided them into what looked like an old-fashioned gentleman's reading room and pointed to some leather seats that they could sit down on.

As Maddie sat down all she could see was the dark wood panelling and the bookshelves that went round the room. The carpets and curtains were in dark red. For a reading room Maddie thought that there was not much light in there.

Colin turned to Martin and pointed to the painting on the wall set in a carved gilt wooden frame. He asked him if it was of Katharine Underville.

"Yes," came the ecstatic reply.

It was a portrait done when she was much younger and slimmer than in the other painting that Maddie had seen of her, and it had perhaps been painted when she had been in her twenties. You could, however, see the beginning of hardness about the mouth. The eyes gazed hypnotically from the painting at you. Maddie imagined that they would follow you round the room. The figure was dressed in brown ceremonial robes, and carried a black handled dagger in one of her hands.

"That's not a particularly jolly painting," said Colin lightly, much to Martin's anger.

"Katharine was committed to our cause. She was strong, and did not have any of the weaknesses of your Christian faith. She was responsible for putting the Drakens on the map. She did not have time to be jolly," said Martin, almost spitting the words out in contempt.

Colin shrugged, and did not voice any further opinions in case it led to an argument. Martin looked across the vast bookshelves and indicated at a book behind a glass door.

"A lot of her work is catalogued in these books."

Colin would have loved to have asked Martin's views on the early witch-hunts the Drakens had organised against innocent women in the village but did not, in case they were asked to leave.

"What further information can you give me about Katharine Underville? There was nothing in the parish records about the date of when she died," Maddie blurted out. After seeing Colin's discomfort at being in the house of the Drakens Maddie almost shouted out the words nervously.

Martin went over to one of the bookcases and picked up a book. He frowned and put it back on the shelf. Then he picked another one out.

"This is it. I already knew what had happened but I wanted to be precise … For all her work, the people of Cattingham treated her very badly. A new Justice of the Peace was appointed, and he conspired with Ursula Underville's brother to have her removed from the village. She spent the last of her days a recluse in Stocksfield. It was a travesty of justice for such a remarkable woman."

As he said this Maddie felt she was being watched. She turned and looked into the eyes of the painting of Katharine Underville. Maddie could have sworn that the expression on the portrait had changed, and the woman now appeared to have a sneer on her face.

There was also something else about the painting that appeared to have changed, but she couldn't put her finger on what it was. She was unsettled and looked away from it, but then kept looking back it. What was it that was different about it?

"Where was the house she used to live in at Stocksfield?" Maddie, who was now quite shaken, asked Martin.

"It's Wycombe House, just opposite the swimming baths. We, the Drakens, bought the house in memory of her. We rent it out to get income for our society," came the reply.

"Oh, I know where that is. I know a lady who lives round there. She is in my parish. Who do we contact if we want to look at the property?" Colin asked.

"It is Wallhead, Grey, and Aitken, who handle our tenancy. Why do you want to know?" Martin asked. He was starting to get quite agitated. Sensing this Colin said,

"Maddie is, as I mentioned, doing a school project. She needs to gather as much information as possible. Don't you think it would be a good thing if her school could see information on Katharine Underville and learn the history of the Drakens? If she had a photo of the house that was Katharine's final resting place it would round the project off."

For the first time Martin appeared to smile. Unfortunately, however, he directed his smile at Maddie. It was not pleasant. He had black tombstone teeth. Maddie shuddered inwardly. She now recognised the strange smell he had on him as mothballs.

Martin started talking to himself while looking fixedly at the painting of Katharine Underville. He turned to Maddie with a strange look on his face and said,

"What school do you go to?"

Maddie told him, but for some reason felt she wished she hadn't. He then bombarded her with more questions about her school but Colin did not like the sound of this and said quickly,

"Well, thank you, Martin. You have been a great help." Colin now stood up and gestured to Maddie to do so as well.

"It has been a pleasure," said Martin. He changed his tone and said, "The library we have here has many books on the Underville family. If you wish, Maddie, you can go through them now. I would be happy to help you. I am sure, Colin, that you have parishioners to see to, and you could collect Maddie later."

"Thank you very much, Martin. We have another appointment to go to," responded Colin quickly as he answered for Maddie. She could have hugged him for saying that. Ugh. She most certainly did not want to spend an afternoon in the library with creepy Martin.

Martin did not seem happy with this, but Colin and Maddie walked towards the door before he could say anything else. Maddie, relieved they were getting some fresh air, banged into the door in her haste to get out. The door closed on the library.

Maddie had been right about the painting. There had been a change in it. Katharine now appeared to be clasping her hands together. The black dagger she had previously held was now missing.

Martin escorted Maddie out of the front door. He continued to look at them as they got into Colin's car. He only went back to the Masonic Hall when he was satisfied that they were driving away.

"Colin, thank you so much for rescuing me from Martin. I would not like to have to spend an afternoon in there with him. He is seriously weird. Do you know that he was talking to that painting of Katharine?" said Maddie.

"Yes, I noticed that. I think his mind – poor man – has become unhinged. Oh, you had no fear of having to spend the afternoon with Martin. I had no intention of allowing that. I could not understand why he would suggest it. What I cannot believe is the great change in him. He was always introverted, but he appears to have gone quite strange. I would say he is almost like a total stranger."

"Wasn't he weird, the way he talked about Katharine? You would have thought he knew her personally ... and why was he so interested in my school?" said Maddie.

"I am afraid he has been brainwashed by the Drakens. He might have thought the school would be a good place to initiate recruits. I was not happy that he kept asking you so many questions about your school. If I find out that he attempts to initiate pupils I will put a complaint in with the Head of Governors of your school," said Colin. He looked serious, and was not smiling.

"Thank you for taking me, Colin."

"I am not sure if I did the right thing there. He was asking you too many strange questions … My word, look at the sky. It has gone completely black." Colin pointed up to the sky. It had. It was almost as if someone had placed a blanket over the sun. Then came the heavy rain. The windscreen wipers had to go into overdrive to cope with the amount of rain on the glass.

The journey back to Cattingham seemed to take ages. Finally, once they had driven up the long entrance to the Hall, Colin stopped the car. Maddie got out with Colin. They were being pelted with hail as Colin opened the boot and retrieved the shopping.

"Thanks again," she said. Her face was dripping rainwater as she took the shopping bag off him.

"Maddie, promise me you will never take that cross off," said Colin. He was suddenly unnaturally sombre.

"I promise I won't," said Maddie. She wanted to get out of the rain, so she waved goodbye and ran inside with a shopping bag that was now wet.

"Aunt Lydia," she shouted, but there was no reply.

Shaking off loose rain water from her shoulders she laid the dripping wet bag on the kitchen table, opened the fridge, and took a carton of orange juice out. Then she poured half the contents into a glass and sat at the kitchen table and gulped at the cold orange liquid. Quickly taking the shopping out of the bag. It did not take long to put it away.

After pushing a soaking wet tendril off her forehead and taking her coat off she took a clean hand towel out of one of the kitchen drawers and dried the wet parts of her hair. A sound made her look towards the kitchen door.

A ghost stood facing her.

Chapter 22

For some reason Maddie was not in the least bit frightened. She felt as if the ghost had been waiting for her.

"Hello. Who are you?" she asked finally knowing what the answer would be...

"I am Anna Blackstock," came the reply.

The apparition had a lovely face – narrow, with high cheekbones. In place of the ghost's abnormal blue orbs were sapphire blue eyes. A terrible scar ran down her face, but it could not take away her loveliness, it was unforgettable. The spirit gave her a gentle smile and said,

"I can now make you see me ... finally. It has taken a long time. I must be getting stronger. Take heed of what your vicar has said. Wear your cross at all times. They are out for revenge, and will now hurt you."

"Why?"

"Because you have broken the charm. I am all but free to get into the light. The witches are now trapped in this world in limbo. They need souls so they can be freed ... Their master is making them collect more souls for him. You saw what happened to me in my dream."

"I did, but it did not show how you ended up in the crypt," said Maddie.

"I do not know how I got there ... I woke up in there and was trapped. I could hear banging. It was then that I knew I was being bricked up. I tried to open the coffin lid. It would not open. I could not breathe. I scratched my name on the inside of the coffin with a coin in my pocket. I knew I was going to die, but I wanted to know that if I was ever found they would know who I was.

"Because I was not able to get out I died there. It was only later, after that had happened, that my spirit could leave the coffin. I could get out of the coffin. I had been ill for a long time. I remember seeing me mam and dad after I died, but they did not see me and I just gave up ..."

Anna had a lovely Northumbrian voice. She accentuated certain vowels when she spoke. To Maddie her voice almost sang to her.

"Do you mean to say that you think you were buried alive in your coffin? Oh, Anna, that is awful. How you must have suffered," said Maddie, shocked.

"I do not know. I remember being very thirsty, but death came quickly because I was so ill. I think Katharine thought I was dead. I could hear her angry voice when I was in the coffin, but then I heard the door being locked. I shouted, but I do not think she heard me. I had lost my strength and kept passing out.

"Every time I awoke I just remember shouting for my mam and dad. But no one came. I must have cried a thousand times. I just shouted and shouted, but nobody heard me. I heard Antrabus – my raven – call for me, but I could not answer back. He stopped croaking, and that was when I knew he had given up looking for me. He thought I was his mother.

"When the crypt was opened and my coffin was disturbed by the flooding and I took it as a sign and began to haunt the Hall. I was finally with Antrabus, but I could not get you to see me because you were not able to see the dead."

"How frustrating that must have been for you ... although you didn't half frighten some people," said Maddie?

"I never wanted to do that. The lady I frightened could see me as a ghost, but she fainted and I lost contact with her. I tried to help her sore mouth. All the people who saw me just ran away. I came into your dreams to tell you what had happened. That was the only way I could talk to you. It was after my coffin was opened that the charm had been broken, and now I have become stronger you can see me."

Maddie got closer to the ghost. She would have loved to have touched her – to see what it felt like to touch a ghost – but she did not want to do anything that would upset Anna.

Her mobile phone was in her pocket. If only she could have a taken a photograph and shown proof that she had seen a ghost. She decided against it, and decided that she did not want to take the risk of the ghost leaving her. But why couldn't the ghost, Maddie thought, have appeared when her aunt was around? It would be proof that there was a ghost.

"Anna, I think the final thing that will set you free is to have you buried with your parents. You said you scratched your name inside the coffin. I hope that will be enough proof that it is you in the crypt. Your last remaining relative is at Bickleberry: a Jeannette Raby. Once I have the proof I will go to her and ask permission to have you buried with your mum and dad."

"If only that could be so ... I see the light and I want to reach out to it, but something stops me going into it," said Anna.

"You will go into it, I am sure of it. Did you hear my aunt say what had happened to Ursula?"

"Yes, I did: that she died with her family. I feel better hearing that her brother came for her, and that she saw her son before she died.

"But since I have returned Katharine Underville and her followers have come back. I found a book on the black arts and remembered the words of a spell. When I was in the crypt I said those words against them, and placed a curse on them that if I died and if my coffin was ever opened Katharine and Agnes would be brought back to pay for what they had done. I did not know that the way to break my curse would be for them to find other people to take their places. How I wish I had never said the curse. The witches will take souls in order to save themselves.

"But I must be getting stronger. When I died I came out of the coffin but could only wander round the crypt at first. That was before the coffins flooded with the rain. After that I could get round the Hall and outside. But I can feel something bad is going to happen. It is almost as if I feel history will repeat itself. Please take care. I have a bad feeling that it will be you they will take."

The sound of Lydia shouting for her made Maddie turn round. Her aunt was now behind her, but Anna had disappeared. She decided not to tell her aunt about having seen a ghost. She regained her composure and smiled at her.

"Ah, there you are, Maddie. I was looking for you. Oh, no, dear. You look like a drowned rat. That towel is far too thin to dry your hair with. I told you the weather was too bad to go out in. If I had not been so distracted I would not have let you go out. I hope you don't get a chill."

Lydia looked concerned. She went away and returned moments later with a thick bathroom towel, and proceeded to dry Maddie's hair.

Maddie told her about the Masonic Hall. Lydia pursed her lips. She was not happy hearing about Martin, but when she saw Maddie's pale face did not comment further. Instead, satisfied her niece's hair was dry, she then ordered Maddie up to her bedroom to get out of her clothes and to change into dry ones.

Once again it appeared to Maddie her aunt was ignoring the strange goings-on around her. Why couldn't she see what was happening? It was so frustrating. Maddie felt she would never get through to aunt about what was going on at the Hall.

Once upstairs Maddie half-heartedly changed into a faded grey sweatshirt and jeans and put her thick slipper socks on her feet. She was thinking about so much. As she came back into the kitchen her aunt handed her a cup of hot tea and a buttered scone and asked her,

"Oh, Maddie, where is your costume for the fancy dress party?"

"Sam has the frock coat and the bowler hat. I have a tweed waistcoat that I bought from the jumble sale, remember? And my old black school shoes are upstairs."

Her Aunt Lydia was holding a fancy dress party in support of Stocksfield Children's Hospice. Sam was going as Sherlock Holmes, Maddie was going as Doctor Watson, and Josh was going as Professor Moriarty. Who they were going as had been Sam's idea.

"Maddie, make sure you get the costume from her in plenty of time."

"Ok," came Maddie's reply. She was still dazed by the encounter with Anna, and only half listening to Aunt Lydia because she was deep in thought about Anna.

"Ava and Valerie are going to help me with the food. We will have the party in the gallery room. There is not much furniture in there. We have plenty of time to get it organised. All I need at the moment is to know how many people are coming. I have spoken to Samantha's mother, and she has organised the band. It has been a long time since we had a band playing at the Hall," said Lydia.

"This is not as exciting as people might think," thought Maddie. The band was going to be playing folk music. Not her cup of tea …

"Oh, Maddie, ask your nice friend Julie and her sister. I forgot to ask them." After gulping back her look of horror Maddie replied quickly,

"I'll phone her." She crossed her fingers when she said this. Phone Julie Painter? She had no intention of doing that. Hell would freeze over before she phoned her.

Outside a hooded figure stood by the trees. Although she was gazing silently at the house the woman made no effort to enter. She needed to be invited in. She would bide her time.

Chapter 23

The week that followed seemed to fly by. A forensic archaeologist had determined that the skeleton in the crypt was female, and had dated it back to between 1800 and 1850.

DNA had been taken from Jeannette Raby, and it had been established that the skeleton was a direct ancestor of hers. Maddie had asked if the inside lid of the coffin could be checked. She had remembered Anna saying that she had written her name on the inside lid. Titch had checked it and said that she had, because the name scratched inside it was indeed Anna Blackstock. It was decided that the skeleton was almost certainly the Anna Blackstock who had gone missing. Jeannette Raby agreed that the skeleton could now be placed in the burial plot at the church with her family.

Maddie had visited Jeannette Raby quite a few times at the home. The old lady was quite frail. The last time Maddie had seen her she could not believe her likeness to Anna. It was quite uncanny.

When she was young Jeannette Raby had been at least six feet two, but now in old age she had shrunk, and she stooped when she walked. This made her look much smaller. The old lady loved talking to Maddie. It was nice to meet a young person who was interested in looking at her old photographs. Like Anna, Jeannette had been interested in herbalism. She only knew the history of Anna Blackstock from what she had heard through her family. She told Maddie Anna's parents had never given up their quest to find their daughter. It had been very sad.

"That poor lass was no witch, you know," she had told Maddie and said,

"When I was young my family said she was just a healer like me, Maddie. Did you know that she had a pet raven called Antra— oh, what was it ...? It was a funny name. Ah, yes: Antrabus. No one knew where she got such a fancy name for it. But it used to fly over her head as she walked around Cattingham ... such a strange sight.

"She had found it half dead as a chick and nursed it back to health. The bird thought she was its mother. Can you imagine such a queer thing? When she disappeared the bird pined away and died. Anna's father found it dead in his garden. That was when he knew his daughter was dead, and my great-aunt said she had heard that that's what finished him off. The bird never went anywhere but following Anna."

The old lady had started coughing and wiping her mouth with her handkerchief. She continued,

"He buried the bird in his garden, you know. He said that was what Anna would have wanted. He went downhill after that. People used to talk about Anna and that bird. No one else could go near the bird. It would go for them. Is it any wonder that the village thought she was a witch?

"But she had that strange way with animals. No matter how wild an animal was she could always tame it. Many a wild horse had been tamed by her. The farmers loved her."

The old lady had sat deep in thought pondering on this, but this set off a rattle in her throat that caused her to start coughing violently.

Maddie picked up a glass of water by her bedside table and held it as the old lady took sips.

"Thank you, dear," the old lady said, her voice croaking.

"The raven," Maddie said to herself. How Anna must have loved it. It had even fed Anna when she was imprisoned.

Things were moving forward so fast now.

It was wonderful news that Jeannette had agreed to Anna having a proper burial at the church. Colin would say a few words, and Anna would be buried in her family plot. Maddie now felt that everything was coming to a close. Anna would be at peace, and Maddie hoped she could then go into the light. This was something that Sam had often spoken of – about spirits who could not rest until they had gone into the light. If Anna was buried there Maddie hoped that the ghostly, monk like figure would end up disappearing as well.

But why had a voice whispered in her ear that they would be coming for her? It was worrying. She wished she could talk to her Aunt Lydia about it, but it was if she switched off when anything ghostly was mentioned.

The service for Anna was being held two days after the fancy dress party.

"Maddie, haven't you still got your book review to do?" asked Lydia suddenly.

Maddie gave a jolt and came out of her deep thoughts.

"Ugh. Oh, no, I had forgotten about it. Oh, no … I don't have much time to read it before I go back to school," she said to her aunt.

"Well, you are going to have to make time, Maddie, I'm afraid. If we switch the television off for the next couple of days you could get it finished. I have my books, so we could do our reading together."

"OK," said Maddie, and sighed inwardly.

Margaret Dee had been quite right about the book. Once she had started reading it the book had become so mind-blowingly boring. In the book Lacey Jane was always involved in some unfunny adventure, and she appeared to be a smug and irritating little creep who was always right.

Maddie thought that having to read the whole book all the way through would be torturous. But no television? That would be a real pain. She had an old DVD called The Dwelling Place on the Hill that Sam had lent her. It was supposed to be really creepy. Maddie had really wanted to watch it.

She knew that Aunt Lydia would not approve, that was for sure, and so she wasn't sure when she would watch it.

"Probably when my aunt is out, and only then with the light on," Maddie thought guiltily.

Maddie's mother phoned later that day. She had arranged to get an interview with the freed prisoner, and it had now been filmed and would be on the world news.

"Wow, Mum. Are you going to be famous?" Maddie replied excitedly. "When are you going to be on the news?"

"I think it might be on this Friday."

"Wait until I tell Sam. And Lydia is going to be so proud of you. She is outside, helping Titch with the firewood. Shall I go and get her?"

"No, Maddie. I will phone again later in the week. Tell me what schoolwork you have left to do now." Maddie told her.

Her mother seemed satisfied with her answer and didn't give her a lecture on doing more schoolwork, which was a relief.

Maddie was more excited about her mother being on the news. She could not wait to tell her aunt and Titch. She finally said goodbye to her mother and placed the phone down. Maddie picked up the Lacey Jane book.

She gritted her teeth, picked up her notebook, and started making notes. She was only reading the book to get it over with. Lydia was going out to Ava's tonight, so Maddie would stay in and get more of the book read. She would not be on her own. Titch was going to repair some of the fences round the back of the house so he would be around.

After tea Aunt Lydia went out. Maddie had, though, still not got used to being in the house on her own. To take her mind off this she occupied herself by adding more to her Cattingham Hall project, and made some more sketches of the ancestors of the Hall.

Chapter 24

The radiator in the small library had now been fixed. The library was still, however, drying out. The photography group had been persuaded by Lydia to use the gallery room. Twice Maddie had gone back to the secret room. Even with the door open it felt claustrophobic in the small bedroom. The sad-looking bed was still in the room. Titch said he was going to take it out.

Lydia had not decided what she was going to do about the room, and she was ignoring it for the time being. She had had other things on her mind. She was, unknown to Titch and Maddie, going to see Julian with her friend Ava that night. She had decided to sort the matter out herself. The only amusing thing was that Julian seemed to be under the impression she was coming round because she was finally agreeing to sell the Hall to him. His tone on the phone had seemed triumphant.

"Huh," she thought. "He is in for a shock when he finds out what I am really there to talk to him about."

After Lydia had gone out it had begun to get quite dark. Titch had popped round to his home to collect some tools. He had said that he would not be long. Being in the Hall on her own was a lonely feeling.

Maddie had decided to have a bath. She had enjoyed working on her project, but the Lacey Jane book had done her head in.

Having a bath at Cattingham Hall was a luxury. The huge Victorian-style bathroom was quite something to look at. It had a huge free-standing white bath with claw feet, and a basin. It was a very good reproduction. Uncle Akkoubian had even had the bathroom papered in what looked like genuine Victorian green wallpaper but was in fact a modern version. The flower motif with the metallic detailed leaves on the paper had been hand-painted by an artist years ago, and the paper was now quite faded. Thick green towels hung untidily over the towel rail. A dark green fluffy rug lay on the ground by the bath.

Maddie filled the bath with hot water and ran bubble bath into the water. Then she added two bath bombs. Turning off the hot tap she then turned on the cold tap. The bath water had quickly turned into a bubbly, turquoise blue – her favourite colour. She went to her bedroom and returned with clean underclothes and her pink and grey check cotton pyjamas.

The silence of the house seemed almost to absorb her every move. The high ceiling in the bathroom reminded her of the school assembly hall. After getting undressed she went to climb into the bath. Just as she was about to get into the perfumed water the brass door knocker thumped against the front door downstairs. The knocker had been made specifically to make as much noise as possible, so it could be heard anywhere round the house.

Maddie groaned and wondered what to do while she remained half suspended over the tub. At first she hesitated, but then the rich perfume from the bubble bath won her over. She ignored the door and immersed herself in the rainbow-coloured bubbles. The brass knocker continued to bang loudly. Maddie ignored it again. Whoever was at the door could come back later.

As she lay back into the bath suds something scratched at her chest. When she realised what it was she took off the cross Colin had given her and put it on the side of the bath. It fell off the side and fell under the bath. Maddie stretched her arm out to get it and put it back on. It was much nicer one than the one she already had. She had never really worn her old cross, just tending to look at it now and again. After the Ouija board incident and all that had happened she only felt safe keeping one on all the time...

Titch and Lydia each had a key, so it would not be them knocking on the door. She hoped it was not important, but could not be bothered to get up and answer it. Instead she closed her eyes and breathed in the scented vapours. Picking up the honey-yellow soap, she covered her arms in the lather.

It was sheer bliss.

Outside the front door the person knocking on the door was angry. The woman thought that it would have been easy to get the girl to open the door to her when there was no one about. The old

183

woman's face was contorted with rage and hatred. She did not have much time, but would have to try again. Time was running out.

It had been a surprise to find another girl like Anna. The girl had the same gift. Anyone stopping her getting this girl would have to be removed. The woman had listened to Sam's voice and practised it until she could mimic it perfectly. It would be quite useful. Then she walked from the door back into the trees and waited ...

Sam had been having problems with her mobile. Every time she tried to send a text the connection failed. Her dad had looked at it, and said they would have to go into town to get it fixed. This was a nightmare for Sam, as the phone was her life. Her dad had given her a spare phone that he had, but that didn't work either.

"It must be the reception here at the moment. Why that is the case is a complete mystery," said her dad. All the phones in the house were now playing up.

"Try your phone one more time," said her father hopefully. This time it worked, and all the others started working again too.

"Let me know if it plays up again," said her dad to Sam.

"OK," said Sam, half listening, but now engrossed in playing her monkey football game.

"Sam can you get the fancy dress costumes for me? I just need to see if anything needs altering," said her mother, who ruined her concentration in the game.

Sam put the phone down and went upstairs. She took both Maddie's and her own fancy dress outfits out of the wardrobe and went downstairs and handed them to her mother.

"What about Josh's outfit? Did you not think to bring that down as well?" her mother said, sighing at her daughter lack of common sense. "It should be in his wardrobe, Sam, shouldn't it?"

Sam groaned and went back up the stairs into Josh's room, which was just as tidy as Maddie's.

"There must be something wrong with him too," thought Sam. "How can they keep their rooms so tidy?"

On opening his wardrobe she found it immediately. The whole outfit was on one hanger. Just as she was about to go downstairs a text message buzzed on to her phone.

How are you, Samantha? I hope you are in good health today, the text message read from Maddie.

"What is Maddie playing at? She doesn't text like that. She must be bored and writing anything," thought Sam.

OK. Why r u bored? Sam replied.

Can we meet? Maddie replied.

When? Where? Sam asked.

Low Row Bridge. There is something you must see.

What? Sam replied.

Wait and see, came the reply.

OK. What time? Sam asked.

Twelve.

OK. See u then x.

She closed the messages and wondered what the exciting thing was that Maddie had found and wanted to show her? ... And why wouldn't she tell her? But a niggling feeling in the back of her mind seemed to claw at her and would not go away. Why was that?

Her mother shouted from downstairs and took it out of her mind.

"Sam, can you take Hamish for a walk, please?"

"In a minute," Sam shouted back. A warning light came on in her head. It looked as if her mum was about to start a nagathon, so it would be best to get Hamish out as soon as possible.

While she was brushing her hair the door opened, a rush of feet charged at her. Sam ended up sprawled on the bed. Hamish, the family collie, had knocked her on to the bed in his excitement. In his mouth he held his dark brown lead.

"All right, all right ... come on, let's go," said Sam as she laughed and stroked the soft black and white fur. His thumping tail was beating furiously like a drum on the carpet.

The dog's doll-like blue eyes watched her every move as she put her socks on. He was still leaping round her as she picked up her bag. Just as she went to close the door to go downstairs she heard what sounded like a shrill laugh come from the room. When she opened the door again there was only silence. She shrugged it off and went downstairs, with Hamish following half pushing her down the stairs in his excitement to go for a walk.

She took her coat from the peg and opened the front door. A rush of cold air hit her in the face that made her eyes water and made her reach for her gloves. Once outside she put the lead on Hamish, who was rearing up in excitement. She heard her mother's voice as she closed the door. She appeared to be speaking on the telephone to someone about finding a fancy dress costume for them. It had been a relief that her mother had got herself involved in so many things, but she had now gone a bit over the top with it all.

But it was so much better than before. Sam and her father and brother had seen her mother go into a dark depression, with periods of staying in bed and not getting up for days.

The incident at Cattingham Hall had been the catalyst that had made her illness spiral out of control. Her mother never spoke of the incident at Cattingham Hall … Now, though, she was hardly ever in.

As Sam closed the wooden gate behind her Hamish, with a rush of energy, began dragging her along the pavement. She struggled to hold him, and found herself arriving at the copse more quickly than she had expected to.

"Hold on, Hamish" she shouted, but he was in his own world and ignored her. She released him from the lead and he raced ahead of her.

The copse was quite small. Two rusty swings and a roundabout lay unloved and abandoned at the entrance. Dog poo lay at the front of the children's swings.

 Sam walked on to the bald, patchy grass. It was quite damp, due to some gentle rain earlier. Children never played here any longer. It was an eyesore, and was only used now by desperate dog owners.

Ahead of her to her and to her left she noticed a figure of what appeared to be a scarecrow wearing brown rags. When she got closer she saw that it seemed to be a dirty brown cloak with a hood. The scarecrow had a thick white stocking over its face. The face was quite broad, and it had small narrow eyes made from blue buttons and a painted-on black nose. The mouth was just a slash of red that turned downwards. It was not a pleasant sight, and it made Sam shudder. The more she looked at the face it seemed to look like a crude caricature of an old woman's face.

"What a horrible thing," she thought quickly as she walked past it. She wondered why someone had placed it there. She had never seen it before when she had taken Hamish for walks. On hearing a rustle behind her she turned round. The scarecrow seemed to have moved. She thought that her eyes were playing tricks on her so she walked ahead and shouted for Hamish.

The shaggy figure of Hamish appeared. He was dragging an enormous tree branch and wagging his tail excitedly. He looked happily at her. But his expression changed as he looked behind her. He dropped the branch, but then began giving low growls. Then he did something she had never seen him do before. He started snarling.

"Hamish! Hamish!" she shouted, but he would not stop. On turning around she could see nothing but the scarecrow.

"He must think the scarecrow is a man," she thought, and shook her head, while deciding the best thing to do was to run and get him to do the same.

"Come on, Hamish," she shouted at him.

But he had now started to give out a low whine. She stroked his head, picked up the tree branch, and threw it as far as she could. Distracted, he raced after it. When she looked behind again her eyes saw nothing. But then her head told her something else. The distance between her and the scarecrow should have lengthened. It had not. It had shortened. That was enough to have her running after Hamish, and to continue running with him until she came out of the copse.

The raven watching in the trees flew over her head. It knew the time would come when history would begin to repeat itself.

As they came back to the house Hamish walked very slowly. Sam thought about saying something to her mother but, on second thoughts, decided against it. She had only just recovered from being unwell. What Sam thought she had seen could only make her condition worse, and if that happened her dad and her brother would not thank her for it.

Once home Sam cuddled Hamish but he was withdrawn and very subdued, and constantly looked behind her. He then went into his basket with his head between his paws and sighed loudly. When

Sam's mother came into the room she shouted for him, but he remained in his basket.

"Whatever is wrong with him?" she asked Sam.

"He was chased by a large dog," Sam replied, feeling bad about lying.

"Come on, Hamish, come to Mummy. Let's get you a chew stick," said her mother while stroking him. She finally coaxed him into the kitchen. As he went sloping off her mother turned back and said,

"I forgot to tell you this. Can you believe it? Ophelia Dee has been arrested by the police."

"What for?" asked Sam.

"It has been her who has been stealing all the cats. The gossip about the giant rats eating them was all rubbish. The postman had been visiting his uncle, and saw her in one of the houses she usually rents out. He recognised his neighbour's cat Byron at the window of the house. It had gone missing two months ago. The only reason he knew it was Mrs Jameson's was because it had a brown checked collar – and the black mask-shaped markings on its face gave the game away as well.

"Ophelia was not at the house. So he had a look round the back, and when he peered in through the kitchen window he saw there were a lot of cats howling at the door. He then called the police."

"Why did he call the police? She would not have harmed the cats. He should have just asked her to give them back. She really loves cats," said Sam in defence of her.

"Well, he did not know when she was coming back. People who owned the cats would have needed to know. Wouldn't you have wanted to know if Hamish had gone missing and someone told you where he was?"

"I suppose so. But I work for her, and she really loves those animals. They are like her children."

"I know, Samantha. It is very odd. People do some strange things that they think are for the best. But sometimes their actions cause a lot of sadness for other people. Anyway, there will be a lot of relieved people when they find their animals are safe and well."

"I suppose so. But it's sad. I bet she only did it because she loves cats so much."

"Oh, well. Anyway, what are you doing for the rest of the day?"

"I thought I would go swimming with Josh," said Sam quickly, hoping her mother didn't have housework for her to do.

"That's fine. Make a sandwich for your lunch. There is some crabmeat in the Tupperware bowl, and I have prepared a salad.

"Oh, look at the time. I really have to go out now. I will see you later."

"OK," said a relieved Sam.

But as her mother went out of the door she turned round and said,

"You will need to work on your school project, so do that after the swimming. Understood?"

"Yes, I will," said Sam resignedly.

Of course there was something else Sam really wanted to do. That was to look at the book on ancient medicines that she had borrowed from the library. There were some great recipes that she wanted to try out. She had already made hand cream, some face creams, some bath oils, and all sorts with her other books. She had even asked her mother if she could do an aromatherapy course.

That had surprised Valerie. She knew that Sam dabbled, but did not know how enthusiastic her daughter really was about it. Sam knew all the names of plants and herbs. It was if she had known them instinctively. It was crazy stuff. She could not remember reading books on them, but she seemed to know about them nevertheless. At the moment she was looking for a cure for her strange shaped toe, but hadn't yet found anything.

Chapter 25

Cattingham Hall was a frenzy of activity leading up to the fancy dress party, and all Lydia's friends were in the sitting room discussing it. Valerie Street was coming round but had not yet arrived.

Maddie was getting bored with it all the fuss. She had been roped into getting the tables together in the gallery. Someone had lent Lydia a platform for the singers. Maddie had escaped from the sitting room when her aunt had produced her list, and ticked off who was bringing what food and which drinks.

The costumes had been discussed. Lydia was going to go as Miss Marple. She had borrowed a long grey wig from the local hairdresser's. She would make a bun out of it, and was even going to use her tapestry knitting bag as a prop. Maddie had been tempted to say,

"Why don't you borrow some clothes from Ava?" as she was sure she would have Miss Marple-type clothes, but didn't dare. Lydia was getting stressed about the whole thing, and might have bitten her head off for being rude about her friend.

Even Hodge had a red collar – not that she was going as anything, but Maddie did not want her to miss out. The small library was now at last drying out. Lydia had decided to show the secret room to people on the day of the fancy dress party.

The Bickleberry Post had even taken a photograph of the room and put it on the front page. People had been very interested. There was even a rumour that the history of the Hall would be on television.

"Good news," thought Maddie. "Maybe money is coming Lydia's way."

Titch had said that if the paintings Julian had stolen from Lydia turned out to be worth something then that would be good, and Lydia would not have to worry about money any longer. Lydia had still not told Maddie and Titch about her conversation with Julian and how it had ended with her telling him that she would not inform the police, but that she wanted nothing more to do with him. Then, after handing him the two painting he had given her money for, she had marched off briskly down the path – swiftly followed by Ava.

Seeing Julian's horrified face had been a great feeling for Lydia. She would no longer have to put on a false smile and arrange those unappreciated meals for him and his equally charming son any more. She hated the family gatherings as much as her niece, but she had felt that Cattingham Hall should be a welcoming home to Julian any time he wanted to come there.

Titch had taken the two other paintings up to the family valuer in London. Lydia had not had word yet about how much the paintings were worth.

Maddie had tried to email Sam, but time and time again here emails bounced back. It was a real pain, but she was not that worried. She was going to see her at the party anyway.

Anna could feel that she was getting closer and closer to the light. Sometimes she thought she could hear her parent's voices calling to her, but every time she tried to get nearer to the light something pulled her away.

She knew what it was. The dark forces were trying to stop her. The sly whispers, she knew, came from Katharine. Katharine was mocking her, and telling her that she was doomed to walk the Hall and never enter the light.

But Anna was getting stronger. The force was greater, and gentle voices were telling her to be strong.

However, she had been wrong about who the witches were after.

It was not Maddie. It was her friend Sam.

It was easy to see why they wanted her. She was a witch, just like Anna had been ... witch or herbalist, whatever you would want to call it. They both had the gift. It might be Sam they were after, but that would not stop them exacting their revenge on Maddie for trying to free Anna.

If she could just get into the witches' minds Anna would be able to protect the girls. Maddie had told her that she was going to be buried in the church with her parents. Once that happened she would no longer be able to warn her and lead her out of danger. If she did not save them the fear, she felt, was that the girls would suffer the torment that she had endured. It must not happen.

She had to protect them.

Katharine's mother was getting impatient. Her daughter had told her not to fret, but things had not gone the way they had planned. That interfering brat at the Hall had caused all their problems. She would have to pay for that.

The ceremony would have to follow, exactly as it had for Anna. If not, they would be trapped between the two worlds. Katharine now had the ceremonial dagger. The girl Sam would have to use it on her friend, as a sign of true allegiance to the Drakens.

The day of the party Sam was in full-on Sherlock Holmes mode, and had now taken to placing her pipe in her mouth on all occasions, only taking it out to hold it airily at a distance from her face when she was spoken to.

It was amusing to watch, her mother, father and Josh were well used to it now. Funnily enough, it seemed to suit her personality.

Sam was still curious about Maddie's text. Why was it so mysterious?

"Why didn't she just tell me what she had found? Why all the mystery?" Sam wondered.

She had thought about taking Hamish with her when she met Maddie, but her mother said she would walk him.

Sam could not shake off a dark feeling in her head that something wasn't right.

"Why is that? Why do I have this feeling?" she kept repeating to herself...

She had tried to text Maddie, but her phone was still playing up. Still, she would be meeting her in an hour, so she would find out what Maddie's great mystery was all about then. She did not mention any of the weird stuff at the copse because her mum was getting hyper about the fancy dress party.

She sat on her bed looked in the mirror, and fiddled with her pipe and practised more Sherlock Holmes gestures. Hamish came into the bedroom, but while she was stroking him out of the blue he started whining.

"What is wrong with him? He has been acting so odd lately," she thought.

Sam found his squeaky pork pie and threw it for him. He chased it, but suddenly turned around and cocked his head at her and started whining again. She picked up the squeaky toy and threw it again, this time halfway down the stairs. Hamish's lithe figure raced off to retrieve it. On hearing her mother's voice speaking to him Sam shut her bedroom door. It sounded as if her mother's friends had come. They would all spoil Hamish. He was so gentle that people tended to baby him when they met him. It was hardly surprising when you looked at those eyes.

"What a scaredy-cat he was at the copse," Sam thought. He had never behaved that way before. Snarling at the scarecrow was something completely out of character. Having said it she had been spooked by it even thinking the scarecrow had moved which she now realised was just her imagination. She was going to mention to her mum how weird Hamish was acting, but now was not the right time.

Her mum had snapped at her because she was getting stressed about the fancy dress party. Some of the people who were supposed to be coming to the party had contacted her to say they were now not coming. More of her mother's friends were now entering the house, which was a signal for Sam to get out …

The hair straighteners had warmed up so she worked on section of wavy hair, and then applied her favourite raspberry lip gloss. She looked in the mirror again and nodded in approval at her reflection. She went downstairs and quietly took her coat off the peg. She grabbed her leather satchel then left the house. Now her friends were here her mother would not even notice she was gone.

She had an hour to kill before she met Maddie: the bus took half an hour to get to Cattingham. But the newspaper shop might have her dance magazine in by now. The weather had been changeable in the last two months. The temperature had dropped. Most people were now wearing their winter clothes. She put her warm coat on.

It was disappointing. She had hardly worn any of her summer clothes. She tried once more to text Maddie, but once again the mobile was dead. She gave up with her phone, placed it in her pocket, and walked out of the house.

The newsagent's had the magazine in. Sam went to a dance class twice a week and was going through to dance finals. That was all she could think about at the moment. The school project had hardly been done. Over the last week of the holiday she would have to just work on that and do nothing else. Photographs would bulk up some of the project.

But why she had decided to do the suffragettes? Who was that woman who ran in front of the king's horse? Emily Dickson ... Emily Johnson ...? Bugger ... what was she called?

Irritated, she walked along the cobbled street reading her magazine, and nearly bumped into a woman pushing a pram.

"Sorry," she muttered, and placed the rolled-up magazine in her pocket.

There was no one at the bus stop apart from an old woman, who was muttering with her head half buried into her scarf. She never even looked up at Sam as she stood beside her. The 10B bus arrived on time. There were only two girls on the bus. Sam recognised them from Thorpe Grammar School at Hexham. They were too busy looking at an iPad to notice her.

The old woman sat behind her on the bus. Now and again Sam could hear her grunting and clearing her throat. It was not pleasant, and she seemed to smell very strongly of damp clothes and farts.

"Gross ... That woman is so vile," she thought, and felt the urge to purge.

Fortunately the bus ride would not take long. The bus passed her uncle's farm. Grace the retired racehorse was in the field, a striped blanket covering her elegant back. Sam's stop was the fifth one. She pressed the button and walked down the aisle. No one else got off.

It was quite a lonely place.

Sam crossed the road and took the shortcut to Low Row Bridge. She heard footsteps behind her and turned round. There was no one there. The small bridge was in sight, but she was early. She would wait on the bridge for Maddie, as promised.

The water looked tranquil. A family of ducks swam by and made a gentle ripple. There were some pebbles on the bridge. She picked one up and threw it into the water. The water shot up around the pebble and made a raised pattern on the surface.

She threw the second pebble further away and craned her neck to see how far she had thrown it, but this action made her drop her mobile phone.

As she bent down to pick it up and placing it in her pocket she became aware of a slight movement behind her, but found her neck had frozen. She could not move it. Something caught the back of her leg and she felt it wrap itself around her.

When she tried to turn round she found she could still not move. She could smell something, an animal-like musky smell. It filled her nostrils and made her feel sick.

Then something rough seemed to be placed round her legs. It was tight, and cut into her leg. Screaming she was lifted into the air.

Someone strong was holding her up.

Bony fingers with sharp nails dug into her flesh hurting her. She screamed loudly and tried to free herself from her attacker, but she went higher into the air. The hands then released her. She tried to free herself but she was hurled into the air. Only then did she realise that she had been thrown over the side of the bridge and was falling towards the inky black water below.

Chapter 26

Maddie was back and forward moving tables and chairs to suit her Aunt Lydia, who repeatedly changed her mind until she was finally satisfied.

The platform for the band had been erected in the gallery.

"She must have moved the table near the platform a thousand times over … Well it certainly feels like it," thought Maddie. Finally her aunt moved it back to the place where Maddie was sure it had been in the first place. She sighed inwardly.

Valerie Street had given Maddie her costume.

Maddie ran upstairs to her bedroom and dragged the cheval mirror out from her walk-in wardrobe. The pork pie hat was far too big, and hung over her eyes. She looked critically at herself in the full-length mirror, but pulled a face because she was disappointed at her reflection.

"Doctor Watson? I look nothing like Doctor Watson … more like the skinny one from Laurel and Hardy."

It would have to do. That was the only costume she had.

Sam, though, would look great as Sherlock Holmes. Maddie dropped the hat and stooped to pick it up. The mirror was Edwardian, and had lyre-shaped ends with carved mahogany finials. It was a heavy object but easy to wheel about, as it was supported on brass castors.

With just half of Maddie's body now showing in the mirror another face appeared above her.

The old woman stared out of the mirror. She was getting closer to the girl.

Julie Painter had a smirk on her face. It was the type of smile she reserved for when something unpleasant had happened to people she didn't like. Bumping into Maddie's Aunt Lydia with her mam was the reason for this. Lydia had been talking to Julie's mother about the fancy dress party at the Hall.

"I didn't know you were having a party, Mrs Underville," said Julie, pretending to look hurt.

"Julie, I am so sorry. I thought Maddie had mentioned it to you. Of course you can come. It starts at 7 p.m. tonight. Do you need a costume? Valerie Street might have something if you need it."

"No I don't. I have something I can wear, Mrs Underville. Can my sister Linda come?"

"Of course she can, dear," came Lydia's embarrassed reply.

A broad grin had then replaced Julie's smirk. Lydia was pleased she had bumped into Julie, but was surprised that Maddie had not invited Julie and Linda. With the girls coming to the fancy dress party she thought that this might now encourage Maddie to have more friends.

Julie seemed such a nice girl, and so sensible. She was always smiling. It was such a shame she had such terrible teeth.

But Julie Painter had a plan in her mind. It was a good job Lydia couldn't read her mind. Lydia had been putty in her hands.

"Such a stupid woman," thought Julie. The telephone number Maddie had written down for Julie had been wrong. She would teach her a lesson. A big lesson. One that would terrify the swot of Cattingham Hall. Linda would love it when she told her what she intended to do.

Julie's mother caught the look on her daughter's face. She didn't like it.

"What are you looking so pleased with yourself for, Julie?"

"Nowt, Mam. Just looking forward to the party."

But her mother knew her too well. The last two months with Julie had been a nightmare. The school had had numerous complaints about her for bullying. Children who had been too frightened to come forward had suddenly developed courage. The school said that if they received any further complaints Julie could be expelled. Trying to talk to her about it had been a wasted effort. She didn't take it seriously. The threats of taking away her mobile phone and grounding her were met with disdain.

Friends had told her she was too soft on Julie, but it was difficult being a single parent. Since her husband had her left she had been short of money and had had to take any cleaning jobs she could, which meant that she had to work a lot of evenings. This resulted in Julie being left to her own devices.

It was odd, her daughter wanting to make friends with Maddie. Julie called Lydia a stuck-up cow to her mother after she had walked away and said, as she laughed nastily, that Maddie looked like a boy.

"Don't be so rude, Julie. She is a nice lady, and Maddie is a bonny lass and does not look like a lad. I don't know why you said that, what with Lydia always being so lovely to you."

"So lovely that she gave you the sack."

"Lydia didn't give me the sack. She had lost a lot of money, and could not afford to keep me on. Anyway, she found me more work with her friends. Lydia has always been good to me, so stop being so nasty about her. Half of our house is furnished with things she has given us. So do not go upsetting Maddie. I am not sure why you are making friends with her. You said you didn't like her."

"Mam, I thought you wanted me to make new friends. You like Maddie, don't you? So stop going on."

"Well, yes, I do like her. But I wouldn't have thought you two would have anything in common," came the reply. But this only filled Julie with rage.

"Oh, so you are saying that I am not good enough to be friends with her because she is posh. Is that what you are saying?"

"No, pet, I am not. I just thought you didn't have the same interests as her. I worked at the Hall so I know a lot of what she likes and doesn't like, so don't get hurt about it. That's all."

Julie was angry. Her mam seemed to think that the Undervilles were a cut above them. Her mam was right about her not having anything in common with Maddie, though.

Why would she want to have anything in common with the boring little cow? It was all right for Maddie. She had everything: a big fancy dress party at the Hall, and her mam being on television. Then there was Lydia wearing clothes her mam could never afford, and even giving her clothes she had worn as hand-me-down presents.

Bored with her mother's lecture, Julie walked ahead of her to her house. Then, when her mother opened the front door, she ran upstairs and left her to carry all the shopping inside. As soon as she had gone upstairs she ran into her sister Linda's bedroom.

"You will never guess where we are going tonight."

Linda, who was busy applying blemish stick to a large spot on her cheek, looked bored and replied,

"Where?"

"The Undervilles' fancy dress party. Lydia has invited us. Maddie will wet herself when she sees us. I said to Lydia that we would surprise her."

"But I have nothing to wear," came Linda's reply.

"We'll find something for you. Nana wears rubbish stuff. There will be something there for you. I have been thinking about what we should do with Boy-Girl. Let's give her a fright she will never forget. What do you think about this?"

On hearing her mother come up the stairs she whispered her plan to Linda.

Maddie had gone into the garden to find Titch but really it was to escape from Aunt Lydia and Valerie Street, who were ordering everyone about. The band had also started to practise. If she stayed to watch there was always a fear that the professional dancers would grab hold of her and make her dance with them. One of the dancers had pointed in her direction to the others.

That was her cue to be off. Dancing to that hurdy-gurdy music was something too horrible for her to contemplate.

She found Titch in one of the greenhouses tidying up trays of seeds. As he looked up he said,

"Hello, pet."

"Hi, Titch. I am escaping from Aunt Lydia."

"Me too," said Titch, his mouth twitching into a smile.

"Are you going to the fancy dress party?" she asked him.

"Me? No. I can't see myself in fancy dress, can you?"

"No I suppose not," she replied as she returned his mischievous smile.

The smell of food from the Hall wafted up to them and engulfed Maddie's nostrils.

"Smells nice, though, doesn't it, Titch?"

"Aye, it does. What time is kick-off?"

"Seven," replied Maddie looking at her watch. "Oh, hell. Its six now. I'd better get a shower. I have to help Aunt Lydia greet the guests. Bye ... see you later."

She waved goodbye, ran back to the Hall up to the bathroom.

Titch tidied up the rest of the seed trays. As he looked down he could see the reflection of an old woman peering into the greenhouse. He dropped a packet of seeds and bent down to retrieve it. When he looked back up the woman was gone, and when he stood up there was no-one in sight.

He scratched his head. He thought he must have imagined seeing her, but he had not.

Just as Maddie was getting out of the shower Lydia shouted up the stairs,

"Maddie, can you give me a hand?"

"OK ... in a minute," she replied as she dried herself and her wet hair. Walking into her bedroom with a towel wrapped round her she shivered with the coldness of the room...

Quickly she put her fancy dress costume on. The shirt was wet under the waistcoat because she hadn't dried herself properly. The trousers were bit loose as she zipped them up, but not so big that they would fall down. With the waistcoat and coat now on she slipped into her shoes. When she looked at her reflection she still thought she looked like Stan Laurel.

"No one's going to guess who I am in a million years," was her immediate thought as she combed her tangled hair. But it would have to do. She didn't have another costume she could change into.

After running downstairs she found Lydia in the gallery in full costume. It gave her a shock. The grey wig her aunt was wearing made her look like a little old woman ... not so much Miss Marple, but one of the old ladies from Bickleberry Retirement Home. It was not a flattering image.

"Well, what do you think, Maddie? Do I look like Miss Marple? See, I even have my knitting bag over my shoulder." Lydia laughed as she spoke to Maddie.

"Er … yes, you do look old, Aunt Lydia," said Maddie as she struggled for something to say.

"Good. Come on, let's get these plates of food on the table," Lydia replied only half listening.

The long tables had been decorated with fruit sculptures, artistically done by Kitty. Ava and Valerie appeared to be having a heated discussion about the profiterole arrangement. Maddie quickly placed bowls of mixed salad on the tables away from them. Long tables had been placed by the band. All the chairs had come in handy. The rest of the furniture had been borrowed from the neighbours.

The band had left their musical equipment on the stage and gone for a cigarette break. The cold food was now out, and Ava started putting the hot food out on warmed plates. It was an impressive spread. The plates were filled with miniature pizzas, pork pies, and spiced hams. Other plates were filled with goat's cheese and rocket canapés, sausage rolls, lettuce wraps, and ham croquettes.

The open sandwiches had all different types of fillings. Other tables were filled with Indian delicacies. But the table Maddie liked the best was the cake and dessert table. A chocolate Smarties cupcake was hurriedly crammed into Maddie's mouth while Aunt Lydia was not looking.

"Maddie, the vegetarian feta bites are over there. Can you put them near the salads?" Lydia surveyed the table as if she was an army sergeant doing an inspection.

"OK," said Maddie as she quickly gulped down the last piece of cake. The final table had a huge punchbowl with wine glasses, fruit juice, and glass beakers on it.

"Oh, when is Sam coming?" Lydia asked.

"I'm not sure. Her phone has been down. She should be here soon, I should think. Josh is coming with his girlfriend, so I suppose she is getting a lift from him," replied Maddie. "I think she may have to walk Hamish before she comes."

"Maddie, remember you are on door duty," said Lydia, seeing two people coming into the gallery room.

"OK," said Maddie.

Lydia left her to greet the two smiling people coming up to her. One was Mrs Chamberlain, who was going to be doing the talk on the fundraising. A white clipboard was held tightly and purposefully in the woman's right hand. She believed it gave her an air of importance.

Now, left to her own devices, Maddie ate two feta bites as she went out of the room. The band were coming back in, so she had picked her time to escape just right. She then went off to do her door duty. The doorbell rang, and each time she opened it she half expected it to be Sam. Disappointed, she let the guests in. They were dressed in 1950s outfits, and seemed to be the neighbours from various houses not far from the Hall.

More arrived and, smiling, she ushered them all in. Time was moving on. In the background she could hear the band.

"But where is Sam?" she thought.

There was a further ring on the doorbell. She opened the door to a howling gale, which nearly blew her hat off. While she held on to it she saw that the person on the front doorstep was a woman dressed in a monk's habit.

"Are you Maddie?" the woman asked, unsmiling.

"Yes," came Maddie's reply.

"Are you inviting me in?"

"Yes," said Maddie, puzzled by the coldness in the woman's voice. As she looked closer she saw that the woman was much older than she had thought. She was not a bit feminine, and was almost mannish, with her broad chin. But it was her eyes that held Maddie's attention. They were small and pale blue, verging on white, and were devoid of any hint of emotion in them. It was unsettling.

The woman passed by her, and Maddie could smell what seemed like an earthy, mushroom smell.

"Ugh, she's creepy. I wonder who she is?" thought Maddie.

The woman turned round and looked at Maddie. The coldness in her gaze was intimidating, as if she had just read her mind.

Maddie quickly averted her gaze. As the woman walked away Maddie had a sneaky look at her. There was something vaguely familiar about her, but she could not think what it was. What long nails she had ... why, they were so long they curled up on the ends.

202

"I suppose," thought Maddie, "they must be stick-on claws. I have never seen stick-on nails like that before. I wonder where she got them from."

More people came to the door, and she soon forgot about the woman.

"Are you dressed as Charlie Chaplin?" a neighbour asked her as they came in.

"No," answered Maddie wearily. Three people had now asked her that. It was wearing thin. "I am supposed to be Doctor Watson."

The neighbour looked at her and smiled, but then said nothing further.

"Well," thought Maddie, "that is that." No one knew who she was supposed to be, and door duty was now getting quite boring. But it was 8.30 now, and Sam still had not arrived. Where was she?

Lydia appeared beside her and said,

"Maddie, you go and get something to eat. I will do door duty," and added, "I don't think there are many more people coming. Great news … we have had a lot of donations. Mrs Chamberlain did an amazing speech.

"Vicky is here from the Bickleberry Post, and after she saw the secret room she is going to write an article in the newspaper about it. She even hinted we might be on the television. Isn't it exciting? You would not believe the number of people who have been to see the room." Maddie smiled back, pleased that the evening was turning out to be a success for her aunt.

"Aunt Lydia, Sam is still not here."

"I expect she will be here shortly. Josh isn't here yet. They will probably come together."

More people came to the door, and Maddie went off to the gallery while Lydia greeted them. She filled her plate up and took a glass of orange juice and sat down at one of the empty chairs. The band had gone off for another break.

When she looked around she could see that there were some great fancy dress costumes. There were quite a few wizards, and plenty of witches. Maddie was glad she had not gone as one. Witches, after all that had been happening, left a sour taste in her mouth … plus all the people dressed in witch costumes made her feel uneasy. She knew she had no chance of winning the competition, as anyone who had seen her had not been able to guess who she was supposed to be. She thought that if Sam and Josh had been with her then people might have known who she was.

When she picked up her phone it looked as if it needed to be charged. After finishing her food she decided she would go upstairs and use the battery charger, then try and phone Sam again.

"Hi, Maddie," spoke a voice... Looking she saw it was Natalie Irwin, one of the pupils from her school.

"Hi."

"This is a great party, Maddie. We only just moved here yesterday. I have managed to escape my mum and all the unpacking. She is driving me nuts." Natalie rolled her dark brown eyes when she said this and gave a rueful smile and then said,

"We have just moved to Cummerville Drive."

"Yes, I know. My Aunt Lydia said it was being renovated. I didn't know it was you moving into it."

"Don't you hang about with Sam and Josh Street?"

"Yes, I do, but they haven't arrived yet. They should have been here by now."

"Maddie, you will have to come to my house once my mum lets me have friends round. She is really house-proud, and won't let anyone in at the moment because it's a tip."

As Natalie spoke her chocolate brown plaits moved to the sound of her voice, as if they had a life of their own. She was several inches taller than Maddie. Most people were. Her dark eyes were framed by long black eyelashes, which were something Maddie wished she had.

"That would be great. I like your costume," she said.

Natalie was dressed as Cruella de Ville, and even had toy Dalmatians sewn into her gown. As she smiled back Natalie looked puzzled at Maddie's costume.

"I am supposed to be Dr Watson. But no one knows who I am. Some people think I am Charlie Chaplin." Maddie gave a sigh as she said this.

"Oh, right," said Natalie, diplomatically not saying anything else about the costume.

"Maddie, if you give me your mobile number I'll give you a call."

Maddie read out her number to Natalie, who immediately typed it into her phone contacts.

"Oh, got to go. Looks like my mum has found me. See you later," she said, as she waved back at a very glamorous woman next to the stage.

"OK. See you later," replied Maddie.

After Natalie had gone Maddie looked back at her. She liked her. She thought that Sam would like her too, and that she would be good to hang around with. Maddie was thinking about Sam now as she finished off some tiny remains of food on her plate. She took it into the kitchen, and placed the paper plate and napkin in the bin.

She would charge her phone a bit and try calling Sam.

"But where was she? And where was Josh?" she wondered.

The house was now packed with people. Some were teachers from Maddie's school, and her jaw ached from having to beam at them. She did not know that her aunt was friends with them.

It had been a long time since the house had had so many people in it. In fact the last time had been for her uncle's funeral.

"So why do I feel as if I am all on my own now?" she wondered.

Chapter 27

As Maddie climbed the stairs up to her room her knee jarred because the stairs were steep. She always hung on to the banister as she came up to the last short flight because she had never got over a childhood fear she had of falling backwards down the stairs.

When she entered her bedroom she noticed that the wallpaper was ripped near the door switch. She touched the raised pieces of flocked wallpaper. She had not noticed it before, and thought that she would have to mention it to Lydia. She was sure she hadn't done it herself, and could not understand how it had happened. Hodge would never have been able to reach that high up. It was very odd … And the lighting in the room seemed very dim as she had switched on the light.

The phone charger was on the shelf in the walk-in wardrobe. The door was slightly open. Pushing it forward she found the charger wrapped in one of her old school jumpers. Patiently untangling the sleeves of the jumper she picked it up.

Hearing a strange rustle. The floorboards creaked behind her. She turned round thinking it was her Aunt Lydia. It was not. Then she became aware of a shooting pain in her head as she felt herself falling. Half unconscious, helpless, she was aware of being dragged along the carpet by her arm. Then all she felt was an engulfing darkness.

Josh arrived back at the Streets' house to pick up Sam. When he rang the doorbell there was no answer. He could hear Hamish whining. He took his key out of his pocket and opened the front door. The dog was in the kitchen, but when he tried to stroke him the dog moved his head and began to howl.

"Hamish!" he shouted at the dog, but he continued with his howling. Only when he had taken the dog out of the kitchen did the dog stop.

"Come on, boy, what's wrong?" He stroked the warm fur. The dog's nose was running and dripping on to the carpet. Hamish gave a gentle whine.

"Whatever is the matter with him?" And where is Sam? I am supposed to pick her up. Where the hell has she gone? She is such a pain sometimes," he thought.

He had to pick up Emma after he had picked up Sam. When he phoned his sister there was no answer, so he texted her instead. He then phoned Emma to tell her that Sam wasn't at the house.

"Well, just come to the party. She can make her own way there," said Emma huffily.

"No. I am going to keep phoning her. Once I've found out where she is I will phone you back."

His reply was met with a curt answer. Emma told him she would go to the party with her parents, and that he needn't bother coming to collect her.

"Fine. Suit yourself, but I'm not going until I find out where my sister is," he replied. The phone went dead. Emma had hung up on him.

Josh muttered under his breath and opened the back door. He had a look outside, but Sam was not there. There was a rush of feet behind him, and he was knocked over. As he tried to get up Hamish ran over his back. As Josh struggled to grab him his fingers slipped through the animal's fur. He dragged himself up and ran after the dog, but then Hamish jumped over the garden gate down to the front drive. Josh raced to get him, but the dog seemed to have developed some athletic prowess.

Hamish bounced then raced down the street. Josh swore and continued running after him, and hoped the dog didn't run into the road. The animal ran down past Cheatham View, and continued racing ahead of Josh. Hamish then built up his speed and disappeared further down the hill. Josh was not a runner, and had no hope now of getting hold of him. He would have to get his car and search for him. If anything happened to Hamish his mother would kill him. She treated the dog like a baby.

This was turning out to be one hell of a night.

"Sam is missing and Emma is not speaking to me, and now Hamish has disappeared. Everyone will no doubt blame me for all this," he thought full of self-pity.

It was getting dark, and it would be a nightmare trying to see Hamish. The biggest problem would be if he went into the woods. The woods stretched as far as Cattingham. It was only a couple of miles away, but the woodland could get quite dense in places. It was no good. He would have to phone his mum, but would see if he could find Hamish first before he got an earache from her. He sighed to himself and went back home to get his car. He looked a strange figure dressed as Professor Moriarty, with his coat-tails flapping behind him.

Hamish had entered the woods. He could sense that Sam was there even though she was much further away. Instinct told him he that was going in the right direction to get to her.

Katharine and her mother were now satisfied. The girl had not drowned. There had been no ducking stool, but Agnes had thrown her into the river instead, and she had survived. Sam lay on the muddy bank while she coughed and struggled to get her breath. Staring across at her were what appeared to be two women. Beside one of the women lay a small brown sack. A skinny white arm with a bracelet watch stuck out of it. Sam recognised the watch and began to cry. It was Maddie's.

The crying noise made the sack move, and Maddie's white face appeared out of it as she pushed the edges of the sack off her shoulders. When she saw Sam's frightened face she looked bewildered... As she looked up she recognised the faces from all her research. It was Katharine Underville and her mother Agnes.

"Sam, what's happening?" she whispered to her, but Sam shook her head at her.

"Be quiet," said Katharine sharply. The girls looked helplessly at each other – Sam even more than Maddie, because she noticed the knife sticking out of the pocket of Katharine's robe. It was black, with two carved entwined skeletons on the handle. The blade of the knife was hidden inside Katharine's pocket. As she looked around

Sam could see there was nowhere to escape. Maddie's feet were still in the sack. She would not be able to run.

"Are we ready yet?" Agnes asked, speaking with a deep, almost masculine voice.

"No. Why don't you listen, Mother? Have you no ears? You have to get the time right or the spell will not work," responded Katharine, irritated.

"So we have an hour when history will repeat itself – but this time the girl will be alive, not dead," said Agnes, her red bull neck quivering as she spoke.

The sheer coldness of her tone made Maddie and Sam shiver. The more frightening thing was that she had also spoken in the singular, as if there was only one of them there.

"So we will wait. You have made quiet the hounds with those leaves I have given you so they will not cause us any trouble, and you girls will not give us any trouble either... will you?" said Katharine staring at the girls.

They shook their heads fearfully.

"No," they said in unison.

Maddie had managed to get her legs out of the sack. She could only look dumbly at Sam, Neither girl dared to say anything. Sam looked at the sack and then Maddie, and kept moving her eyes up and down at the sack. But Maddie did not appear to understand what she was trying to tell her.

It was frustrating for Sam, because she now realised she would have to do what she was going to do on her own. Because Maddie couldn't understand her gestures it was the only way to save them both. She could feel her phone in her pocket but after it had been in the water would it work? There was no more talk from Katharine and Agnes, just total silence. This seemed to last a lifetime. Finally Katharine spoke to her mother and said,

"We go now. It's time." Then she said to the girls,

"Get up." Terrified, the girls did as they were told.

"Walk up the bank. You go first," said Katharine, pointing at Maddie.

She did so, half tripping over because she was still wobbly from being hit over the head. As Maddie walked up the hill Agnes followed behind her. There was a flutter of wings above their head, and on looking up Maddie saw it was the raven soaring above them. It made an action as if to dive-bomb the witches. The witches were distracted by this and it gave Sam the opportunity to grab the sack, which she then threw at Agnes. The witch turned round and screamed.

"Run, Maddie. Don't wait for me," shouted Sam.

Maddie half turned and began running up the embankment, her cut head soon forgotten. She knew she was running for her life, and desperately hoped Sam was doing the same thing. She sped up. Maddie did not dare to turn round, and could hear footsteps behind her and heavy breathing. Half sobbing, she kept running and looking for an opening in the woods.

A voice in her head kept telling her to keep running.

"Build up your speed," the voice said. She could hear Miss Price spurring her on. She then ran faster and faster, clawing the ground with her feet. As she ran on she felt her lungs would burst. The fear of the witches catching up with her gave her the strength to run as fast as she could. Because she had not had time to warm up her breathing became erratic?

Where could she go? There were just heavily shaded trees. But at least the sound of the heavy breathing behind had now gone. Something flapping above her head made her look up. It was a raven. It circled her. It had to be Antrabus, she thought. It continued to fly over her head. Then it began flying further ahead. As it croaked she looked across at it. There was an opening in the woods.

The raven had been guiding her. She whispered softly to the bird and said,

"Thank you, Antrabus."

She ran through the opening. It led on to the cottages on Low Row. As she ran past them her intention was to get to the church.

Colin would help her, and they would find Sam …

"Surely the witches would not attempt to go into the church, would they?" she thought.

Tears poured down her face. She now had the courage to look round. There was no one there. Thinking of Sam made her even more distressed. She prayed and prayed that Sam, too, had got away. When she looked ahead she saw that she was now in reach of the church. She raced to the door and tried to open it.

It was locked.

She hammered at the door. No one came.

Maddie was sobbing by now. She went round the back. Someone grabbed her arms, and she screamed and shrieked in terror as she looked into their face.

It was Colin.

"Maddie, whatever is the matter?" asked Colin, visibly shocked.

She tried to speak, but the words came out garbled at first. She finally managed to say,

"Oh, Colin, I think they have Sam. I didn't wait for her. I just ran. She told me to run." She was crying again as he guided her into the door of the church, but she tore away from him and locked the door. Only when the key was turned and she was satisfied that the key was in the lock did she follow him into his study. After sitting her down and waiting for her to speak Colin asked her if she wanted a glass of water. She shook her head. Finally she calmed down and spoke – she stammered at first – and said,

"We-we were taken by the witches, and we ended up in the woods near Low Row. I woke in a sack. Sam saved me. She hit one of the witches with a sack. I escaped. Sam told me to run and not wait for her. It was Katharine Underville and her mother. You have to believe me. Somehow they have come back. I think they were going to kill one of us. They were going to perform some type of ceremony."

"Have you got Sam's mobile number?" asked Colin gently.

"Yes, but I could not get through, and I went to charge it in my bedroom. My phone is still in the bedroom. That was where one of them was waiting for me, and she hit me on the head. Oh, my God ... Sam changed her number, so I don't know the number off by heart yet." She started crying again.

"Maddie, Josh will have her number, won't he? I have his number on my phone. Remember ... he did the charity boat race. Let us see if we can contact him, and I will call her." Colin squeezed the trembling girl's hand. He took his mobile phone out his pocket and phoned Josh.

"Hello, Josh. It's Colin Appleby. I have Maddie with me. Do you have Sam's mobile number?"

"Oh, you are looking for her as well," replied Josh. "She has disappeared, and Hamish has run off. I am in Brocket Woods at the moment."

"Well, Josh, give me her number and we will try and call her," replied Colin.

Josh read the number out to him and Colin wrote it on a piece of paper.

"She is not in trouble, is she?" asked Josh suspiciously.

"No. No, nothing like that. Don't worry. Josh, do you not think it's a bit dark to be searching for Hamish in the woods? I am sure the dog will be fine. I think you should come home."

"I suppose you are right but my mum is going to kill me, though. Oh, hang on. I can hear a dog barking. I have to go. It might be Hamish."

"No, wait, Josh—" But he had hung up.

Colin tried to phone him back but there was no answer. He then phoned the number on the paper. It rang for a couple of seconds and then he heard a voice.

"Sam, is that you?" he asked.

"Yes," came the faint voice.

"It's Colin Appleby. I am with Maddie. Where are you?"

"Hiding," said Sam. Her voice was soft and she was almost whispering, but then her voice started to sound strangled. "But I think they are going to find me," she said.

"Sam, where are you?"

"Low Row Cottages. I am going to hide in one of the cottages – the middle one. I can hear something like a scratching noise. It's a voice. Oh, my God, I think it's one of the witches. I have to go. I have to go and hide." Sam's phone cut out, and then there was silence.

"Aren't you going to phone her back?" Maddie asked.

"No. She has gone to hide. She will be safer without me phoning. I am going now to telephone the police. You stay here, and I'll phone on the way to Low Row Cottages."

"No. I am coming with you," said Maddie defiantly.

Realising it would be no use arguing – and he was also extremely concerned about Sam – he hurriedly put his coat on and phone the police. The story he gave the police was that two women appeared to have abducted Maddie and Sam but that the girls had escaped, and one of them was missing. He had managed to phone her, and she was now believed to be hiding in the middle cottage at Low Row.

Colin gave them Sam's mobile number, but told them he had not phoned her back because she was hiding. He told them he would be going to Low Row Cottages, and would meet them there. He was glad they were phoning Sam's parents. He didn't relish speaking to Valerie and trying to explain what Maddie had told her.

Maddie could not understand why he didn't tell the truth, so Colin explained.

"How could you explain to the police that centuries old witches appeared to have come back from the dead without sounding like a real fruitcake?

"Maddie, I will go to Low Row Cottages. It's better if you come with me, as I will be meeting the police there now. Just stick to the basic facts about those two women when you phone your aunt. She will be very distressed. Tell her you are safe and well, and are meeting the police with me."

"OK. Will do," said Maddie. She took the mobile off him as he locked the church door. After getting into the car she phoned her aunt's mobile number, but there was no answer.

"I bet she left it in her bag. She hardly ever carries it around with her," said Maddie.

"Won't she be worrying where you are?"

"She might be too busy. There are a lot of people at the fancy dress party."

"Well, after we have seen the police we'll try again. I have her friend Ava's number. We will try that later."

They got into the car. Their journey would only take a couple of minutes, and they could have walked it. But Colin wanted to make sure that Maddie was safe in the car in case of any problems with the two women. He could hardly believe what she had told him. His nightmare had come back, and was it all starting again? Maddie was not aware of what he had gone through with the Drakens before. People had nearly died.

He had managed to save them on that occasion, but would he be in time to save Sam? He prayed silently to himself. He hoped Sam would be found as soon as they got to Low Row. As the car stopped at Low Row Colin turned to Maddie and said,

"I am going to check the cottage. Lock the windows and doors and stay in here. Only get out of the car if you see the police. They are due any minute. Do you understand, Maddie? Stay in the car, and do not get out unless I tell you to."

"Yes, Colin," came the nervous reply.

Colin got out of the car and walked up the path. There was a full moon, which seemed to shine directly on the cottage. The unearthly silence was disconcerting.

The cottage door was open. Colin shouted Sam's name and went inside. Because she was alone in the car Maddie suddenly felt frightened. She hoped and hoped that Colin would be able to find Sam in the cottage.

"Please, please let Sam be safe," she prayed to herself. It seemed significant that it was Anna's cottage that Colin was going in, and she felt really bad because Sam had saved her by helping her escape.

The repetitive tapping of what she thought was rain on the side window by the passenger seat eventually made her look up. The window misted up, and out of the haze Maddie could see long, curled claws scratching at the window.

The face peering into the car was that of Agnes, Katharine's mother. Her ice-blue eyes looked at her as if she was surveying an insect, and she even moved her head to one side to see Maddie's reaction. The car seemed to puzzle her as her huge hands attempted to pull at it. Maddie realised that the witch did not know how to get the car door open, and she hurriedly checked the windows and doors. They were definitely locked. Then she sounded the horn.

She prayed and prayed that Colin would hear and come out of the house. The loud noise distracted the witch but Agnes's pale eyes continued to gaze hypnotically through the glass at her. Then she murmured some expletives under her breath and moved away from the car. She seemed to disappear into thin air, leaving a spiralling white smoke in her wake. Maddie watched this in fear, and then finally gave a sigh of relief and put her head in her hands as she tried to block out what she had seen.

Sam had found the door open to the middle cottage at Low Row. She ran in and closed the door behind her. Her eyes scanned any potential hiding places. The ground floor was too bare. She ran upstairs and found a large, old fireplace in one of the bedrooms. She climbed up into it. She heard scratching noises and saw a rat, which scuttled down the stairs out of her way. The soot falling down made her sneeze. She put her hand to her mouth to stifle the noise.

As she climbed higher into the chimney she spotted a shelf. She jumped up and managed to hang onto it. It had to be the safest place in the house to be in. Dragging herself up on to it, she folded her arms, listened, and waited. Then she heard it ... the sound of the front door opening, and the noise that feet or paws make when a group of people or animals have scattered suddenly. She was breathing heavily, and she put her hand to her mouth to try and muffle the sound a little.

The soot of many ages fell on to her head, and she had to move her face from side to side to stop it getting in her eyes. It tickled her throat. She gulped air, and she kept swallowing back because the soot made her feel sick. The shelf made her feel trapped. She needed to move but did not dare to. The footsteps downstairs seemed to echo round the house. They became louder as they came up the stairs. She closed her eyes and prayed and prayed the witches would not find her. She muffled the voice out with her hands over her ears and expected the worst.

"Colin, please come in time," she prayed as she twisted her hands together nervously.

Then she recognised the voice. It was his distinct Scottish accent. She sighed with relief when she realised who it was.

Colin Appleby.

Hearing him shout her name she climbed down from the fireplace, half falling and landing in a sooty heap as Colin came into the bedroom.

"Are you all right?" he asked her.

She nodded, and he then guided her gently out of the bedroom down the stairs. Her sooty footprints left a trail behind her. Colin was still unable to comprehend what had happened in the past hour. He shivered and coughed once they were out in the cold air, then he placed his coat round her shoulders and hugged her and said,

"Maddie has told me what has happened. I phoned the police and told them that two women had attempted to abduct you both. I know, however, what the truth is."

With a grimace in response Sam replied,

"I suppose if you told them that those two ghosts abducted us they would send us to the loony bin."

Colin did not respond to this remark. Instead he pointed at his car. On seeing her friend Sam ran over to it. Maddie opened the door with relief written all over her face.

"I am sorry I didn't come back for you. I was so frightened."

The girls hugged each other. Maddie was now covered in soot.

"I didn't want you to wait for me, Maddie," said Sam.

"Colin … Agnes, one of the witches, tried to get in the car while you were inside the house. I sounded the horn, and it seemed to frighten her off."

"Agnes? Who is that?" asked Sam, butting in.

"Katharine's mother, Agnes Underville. They are the witches who kidnapped us. She might still be around here," said Maddie, shuddering and looking around. An intense look round the area proved negative. She was not there. All three of them gave an inward sigh of relief.

Chapter 28

The sound of sirens announced the arrival of the Police. A heavily bearded thickset policeman got out of the car with his colleague. Colin broke away from the girls and went to greet him, and introduced himself and the girls. An afterthought made him turn round to the girls, and he said to Sam,

"Here, take my phone and tell Josh where you are."

He threw the phone to Sam, who caught it and began dialling the number. The second policeman appeared to be asking a lot of searching questions, and Colin seemed to be struggling with his answers. Sam managed to contact her brother as Maddie stood beside Colin. When Sam spoke to Josh he began to swear down the phone at her.

"Josh, if you speak to me like that I'll put the phone down. The police are here at Low Row. Two women kidnapped us. I do not need you giving me a hard time," gulped Sam down the phone as she tried not to cry.

"What?" came the shocked response from Josh, but the police were now beckoning her to come over.

"I have to go, Josh. I have to speak to the police." Tears came into her eyes as she switched the mobile off. Colin put his arm round her and asked her if she was all right.

"Yes. Just thinking about it brought it all back. I really thought they were going to kill us." The second policeman, who was concerned for her, spoke gently and said,

"Sorry, Sam, but we have to ask you more questions. If you get upset we will stop. Take your time and tell us what happened." He paused, then went on to say,

"We have to ask these questions because we have to know who these two women are." His tone calmed her down.

Sam and Maddie told the police that two women had abducted them, and they had ended up at Brocket Woods.

"No," Sam said, "we do not know these women," in answer to the burly policeman's questioning. Nor did they know why the women would do this to them. She said that one had a knife.

"Did she?" said Maddie her eyes like saucers in horror as she butted in.

"Yes, but I didn't want you to know. I thought we had to get away from them."

"Well, you will both have to come to the station. We will let your parents know and they can collect you".

The bearded policeman, Sergeant Bell, continued to ask them more questions. Then he asked about Maddie's cut head.

"That will need to be seen to. It's a nasty cut," he said. "We will get you sorted at the station."

Julie Painter was not happy. Boy-Girl was nowhere to be found. Where was she? Her sister Linda had gone round the gallery at Cattingham Hall and checked the kitchen and the library, but she still couldn't find her.

"Come on, let's go and ask the lady of the manor," said Julie in a bitchy tone and speaking in her falsest posh voice. They found Lydia talking to the band.

"Hello, Mrs Underville. We were wondering where Maddie was."

"Maddie ... well, she was on door duty. Maybe she is in the kitchen."

"We checked, and she is not in the library either."

"I tell you what ... go to her bedroom. It's on the top floor. It's the door facing you as you come up the stairs. I am sure she won't mind. She will be really pleased to see you."

"Thanks. We will," replied Julie sweetly.

"Come on, let's find the little cow," whispered Julie once they were out of earshot.

On entering Maddie's bedroom Julie was disappointed. Maddie was not there. It was not what she expected. Where was all her posh stuff? The room was quite bare. When she opened the walk-in wardrobe she could only see jumpers, trousers, and jeans. Where was her jewellery? The only thing Julie could find worth taking was an owl scarf. She grabbed it and stuffed it in her large holdall.

"There is nothing here to nick," said Linda, disappointed.

"It must be all at her mam's. All her stuff is worn and crap. Hang on ... here is her mobile. We'll have a look at her texts ... we might find something. I bet she has been texting some drippy lad." The girls sat on Maddie's bed and read through her text messages.

"It's boring stuff ... and who is this Anna? Asked Julie. "I thought Sam was the only friend she had. I bet Anna is a swot just like her." Julie threw the mobile on the bed and yawned. She was getting bored.

"Oh, look, there's her laptop. There might be something on that." She opened it and said,

"Bugger. I need her password. Have a look in those drawers and see if she has written anything down," said Julie, and pointed to them. Linda went through them and said,

"Nothing here. But isn't it tidy? I think I'll mess it up." Linda spitefully picked up some stationery and scrunched it up. She took some pen tops off and buried them in between some sheets of paper. Suddenly she came across the Ouija board and said,

"Look what she's got." Julie grabbed it and started looking at it. She turned it over and poked at it. She said,

"What a little dark horse she is. I always knew she was a little witch. They say that Cattingham Hall has a ghost, don't they? Well, let's make sure she sees one tonight. She will have to come back up here sometime. We can hide in her cupboard.

"Can you imagine her face when she goes to bed and she sees the Cattingham ghost? Boy-Girl will wet herself. Who knows? We might even frighten her to death." Julie looked at Linda and tittered gleefully. She handed the Ouija board to her sister who placed it in her large tote bag.

Josh had finally found Hamish. The torch had been handy. He had heard his barking, but every time he thought he had found him it became faint. He had almost given up hope when a whimpering Hamish had run to him. When he bent down and stroked the dog he realised that his shaggy fur was quite damp.

Josh was more relieved than angry. Besides, he was too upset to be cross because he was thinking about his sister. He had phoned his mother, who was now at the police station. She was there with his father and Josh said he would meet them there. Why Hamish had taken off all made sense now. The dog had been looking for Sam.

"Good boy," said Josh. He felt guilty when he looked into the dog's sad blue eyes. "Shall we go and find Sam?" he asked Hamish. The dog cocked his head to one side. It was if he understood, and his tail began thumping furiously.

"Come on, boy," said Josh, and gave the dog one last stroke as they went through the woods. Josh was glad he had his torch with him. It was so dark that only the moon and his torch gave him any light. He would be glad to get out of there. As they walked along Josh noticed Hamish was limping.

"I bet you did that when you jumped over the fence," he said. The dog responded by giving a human-like sigh.

Something rustled in the bushes and Josh, who was deep in thought, hardly noticed until he heard Hamish growl. When he looked behind he could see nothing. He guided the dog through to the opening in the woods where his car was parked. He opened the back door of his car, and Hamish jumped in. There was mud all over it now. Josh was too tired to care, and he could not be bothered to get the towels out of the back for the dog to sit on.

He had tried to text Emma back, but she had not responded. She could be really moody sometimes, and she would not have been happy that he had not been at the fancy dress party despite all this serious stuff happening.

A whimper from Hamish made him turn round as he got in the driver's seat. The dog was licking his paw and looking at it. Josh wondered if he had sprained it. It would need to be checked, but he could not take the dog home as he was now going directly to the police station.

Hamish had never been athletic. To jump over the garden gate would have taken some doing. That might have been when he hurt his paw. Josh was feeling stressed. Those women might have killed his sister and Maddie. He could not understand why those two loonies had taken the girls. What did they want with them?

A deeply felt anger set in as Josh thought of someone harming his sister and Maddie. As hr drove away he thought he saw what looked like a long shadow coming out of the bushes, but was too concerned about getting to the police station to see Sam to take any notice of it.

The lumbering shapes came into the clearing. They were gigantic black dogs that had been woken up from their sleep by the witches, and they were now ravenously hungry because the witches had not given them their feed. The boy would have been a meal, but the barking dog had distracted them. They would have to find someone else until the witches fed them …

Katharine had searched the woods, but the girls had escaped.

"How could that have happened?" she said, cursing. She had sent her mother out to find them. Agnes had a great sense of smell. She would find them, then neither girl would be spared. At the back of her mind, though, something was worrying her. She had got the time wrong. The beasts would not have been happy at being awakened so early. They would have to be appeased. She had promised them food but given them nothing.

It frightened her. They would be uncontrollable if they had not been fed.

When Lydia arrived at the police station she was asked if she was Maddie's grandmother. She did not even raise a smile at this. When she remembered that she was in her Miss Marple garb she told the policeman at the desk that she was Maddie's aunt, and that her mother was abroad.

"Where is Maddie?" Lydia asked.

"She is still being asked questions. She shouldn't be long," came the policeman's reply.

"Well, I feel I should be in with her. Can I go in and see her?"

Judging by Lydia's tone the policeman knew that if she wasn't allowed to go into the interview room with her niece she would kick up a fuss. The policeman went through a door and returned a couple of seconds later.

"Yes, you can see her. Come through." Lydia followed the policeman and was introduced to Sergeant Bell. He talked her through what had happened. Lydia sat down with Maddie and gave her a hug.

"How are you?" she asked.

"I'm alright," replied Maddie, and she repeated what had already been said. Lydia looked at Maddie's head, which had now been bathed and had ointment put on it.

"If anything had happened to you ..." she started to say shakily, but Maddie touched her hand.

"Aunt Lydia, I am fine. Honest." As more of the story emerged the girls stuck strictly to the facts of their abduction. They knew that no one would believe them if they told the real version of what had happened. Sam mentioned the dagger.

Sergeant Bell glanced at his colleague, then turned back and asked Sam for more details. She tried to remember all she could.

"I remember the dagger sticking out of the cloak pocket one of the women. It had a black handle with skeletons on it."

Maddie broke in and said,

"I never saw it."

"I was glad you didn't," said Sam sombrely, pulling her sweatshirt down as she said this because it kept riding up.

She looked odd wearing an old sweatshirt on top of a white paper suit. The legs were so long that they collected concertina like around her ankles... Her clothes had been too damp to keep on.

Descriptions of the two women had now been circulated, and the police were searching for them. Colin had also been questioned, and then he too was finally allowed to go home. On seeing Maddie coming out of another room he patted her back and mouthed,

"It will be all right,"

As he went away Lydia was still asking Maddie more questions. She was totally perplexed as to why the women had taken the girls, and for what reason.

"Aunt Lydia, they must have just been loony people," said Maddie.

But Lydia still questioned it. She sensed that her niece was not telling the whole truth. But why was her niece lying? Lydia was determined to get to the bottom of this.

Sam's parents and Josh had arrived, which stopped her asking any more questions. The police were then bombarded with questions by them. As she watched Valerie, Lydia was amazed at how calm she was. The police had even allowed Hamish in – who charged at Sam, much to her delight.

"He took off and went looking for you," said Josh.

"Did he?" Sam replied as she looked up. She smiled as she stroked the excited dog and said,

"Good boy." She kissed his head, and was rewarded with wet ecstatic licks. But this action set off a coughing fit and she could not stop.

"Are you all right? " Josh asked for the second time.

"Yes. I think I still haven't recovered from falling in the river. I think I may have caught a cold. " Her coughing finally subsided.

Her brother went over to her and gave her a hug.

"I'm sorry I shouted at you," he said sheepishly.

"Oh, don't worry about that. I am just so relieved that Maddie and I are both safe."

More questions followed. Maddie and her aunt were finally allowed to go home. Sam and her parents stayed behind. Her clothes were sent off for DNA testing, along with Maddie's. Maddie was also now wearing clothes three times too big for her, with the hems of the trousers were trailing on the ground.

As Lydia was driving back to Cattingham she gave Maddie a few searching looks.

"She knows I haven't told the whole truth," thought Maddie guiltily. "But if I told her she would never believe me. I bet she thinks I've been involved in drugs or something."

Maddie finally broke the silence, and asked,

"What happened at the fancy dress party?"

"Oh, Ava took over, but I was there when they awarded the top fancy dress prize to Natalie Irwin."

"Did they? That's great. I really liked her costume. I was talking to her."

"She has moved near our house. They are a nice family. She is very quiet – a bit like you. She would make a nice friend for you ...

223

Speaking of friends, your friend Julie and her sister Linda came to the party. They went looking for you. I told them to go to your room."

"What?" came Maddie's annoyed reply. "You didn't let them go up to my room, did you?"

"Well, yes, Maddie. They will have gone home now. I thought you liked them. Why, what is wrong with them going up to your room?"

"Oh, Aunt Lydia, they are really horrible. They bully me at school, and everyone is terrified of them. I hate them."

"Maddie, why didn't you tell me about this? I thought they were your friends."

"No, they are not. I hate them. They bully everyone at school. I just thought you liked them, and I know you want me to have more friends."

"Yes, I do, Maddie, but not bullies. If I had known that about them I would not have let them come to the party."

"I know, Aunt Lydia. I should have told you. Sorry ... and sorry about everything else," Maddie replied, starting to feel emotional. A lump was forming in her throat ...

"Come on, let's get you home. You look tired. You are safe now. These women will be caught. Let's try not to talk about it tonight. Oh, yes ... I forgot to tell you that the fancy dress party raised £5,000. So that was not bad at all, was it?" said Lydia. She was trying to get Maddie to think about other things.

"No. That's really good," replied Maddie as she swallowed back her tears.

"How's your head?"

"It's still sore, but the antiseptic cream they put on it at the police station soothed it a bit."

"Well, we are nearly there. Ava was going to wait until we got back and saw the guests off. I think we'll just get the food put away, and I think we should call it a night."

Maddie didn't argue with that. She just wanted to go to sleep. Her head still ached, and sleeping would stop her thinking about what could have happened.

When they walked back into the Hall they saw that all the leftovers had been put away and all the tables cleared, to Lydia's amazement.

"I thought you had enough on your mind without thinking about clearing up. A few of us put things away for you, so it wasn't just me. Is everything all right?" said Ava kindly. She was looking in a concerned way at Maddie.

"Oh, thank you, Ava. I am sorry I had to rush out and leave you in the lurch. Yes, she is fine now. Maddie, put the kettle on and I'll be with you in a minute."

Maddie didn't need her to ask twice. She would have done anything to get away from Ava asking her questions. As she went into the kitchen she could hear them talking in low voices, and she knew they were talking about her and what had happened. However, once the kettle had boiled Ava went home.

The kitchen table was crammed with Tupperware boxes filled with food. Maddie grabbed a plate and helped herself to a piece of slightly warm leftover quiche as Lydia came into the room.

"I could do you a proper meal," Lydia suggested as she watched her wolf down the quiche.

"No, this is fine. I don't think I could eat anything else."

"Well, let me have a look at your head, and I'll get some more antiseptic cream to put on it." Lydia moved Maddie's head back a little and examined the cut closely.

"Well ... it's not deep, but it will be sore over the next few days." She hugged her niece, and then she sighed and sat at the table. Her care for Maddie showed in her face while she watched her drink her coffee.

When she glanced round the room Maddie saw that there were more Tupperware containers.

"Titch will be pleased," said Maddie. "Look at this tub. It's got some of your home-made apple tart in it. He loves that."

"Are you sure you don't want anything else to eat?" Maddie nodded

"No I'll just have the apple tart," came the reply. She picked up the tart and the frangipane melted into her fingers, which she licked off greedily.

"I think we should have an early night, then, shouldn't we?"

"Aunt Lydia, can I sleep in your room?" Maddie asked suddenly.

"Of course you can," responded her aunt in reply. She looked concerned at her niece's exhausted face.

She would talk to her niece in the morning about what happened, but for the moment she felt she needed sleep. Julia had been travelling across Africa, so it had been impossible to get in contact with her. That would be another thing she would have to do tomorrow. What Julia would say about what had happened didn't bear thinking about.

Lydia locked up and Maddie waited for her, then went up the stairs with her.

"I have to get my pyjamas and toothbrush from my room," said Maddie.

"I'll come up with you. You might be a bit wobbly going upstairs," replied Lydia.

When they walked into the bedroom they noticed that the light was on. Maddie's phone was on the bed.

"That was not where I left it. I bet Julie looked at my messages," thought Maddie. She noticed that the lid of her laptop was open, but it was not switched on.

"At least they could not get into that," she thought angrily, "because they would not have known my password." But Julie snooping in her bedroom was a horrible thought.

Maddie picked up her toothbrush and pyjamas, and her aunt switched the bedroom light off.

They left the bedroom. With her pyjamas under her arm Maddie headed for the large bathroom to wash her face and brush her teeth.

Once they had left Linda and Julie emerged from the wardrobe and switched the light back on.

"Why has she not come to bed?" Linda asked Julie. She sounded annoyed.

"I don't know. Maybe she is watching TV in Lydia's room. Hell, this is not working out the way it was supposed to work out. Her clothes are so tight."

226

For a joke Julie had put on one of Maddie's jumpers. It was so small that it only went to her midriff. She had even placed Maddie's navy beret on her head and tucked her blonde hair in it so it was completely out of sight. She then put on Maddie's cream cardigan and had to stretch it to make it fit her.

She saw a pewter hairbrush with a rose design on its back, and stuffed it in her bag.

"What are you doing now?" Linda asked.

"Nicking more of her stuff. I thought there was some jewellery, but there is only crap."

"Don't nick any more. She will know it is you. I think we should go. My legs have cramp, and Mam will be wondering where we are," said Linda. The joke was now wearing thin, and she was getting really fed up

"Linda, Mam thinks we are at Joanne's ... so she knows we are not coming home. If you think I am going home now after waiting for Boy-Girl all night you have another think coming, and you are not going anywhere either." Julie's voice sounded intimidating, and Linda decided to stick it out. Her sister could be very frightening sometimes, as the deep bruises on her arms had demonstrated in recent months. So they waited.

The clock in the bedroom read midnight.

"Bloody hell. Look at the time."

"Shut up, Linda. I can hear footsteps. Get back in the cupboard."

They switched the light back off and tiptoed back into the walk-in cupboard. The bedroom door opened slowly. Julie peeped out but could only make out a dark shadow moving about the room. The figure started grunting. Linda whispered,

"Eeh ... you would think a pig was in this room."

"Shut up. She'll hear you," said Julie, and put her hand over Linda's mouth.

Julie strained to hear what Maddie was doing. She was now on her bed muttering to herself. Julie crept out of the cupboard towards the figure and seized the opportunity. She smiled to herself. Maddie was going to be terrified, she thought, when Julie jumped on her back.

227

The girls had brought a white gown and a wig for Maddie to wear. They were going to force her to dress in it and take pictures. Then they would then send the pictures round the whole school. Everyone would think Maddie had been pretending to be the ghost at Cattingham Hall.

How everyone would laugh at her. No one would be friends with her. Boy-Girl would probably then want to leave the school.

Julie was still thinking about it when she jumped on the figure's back but instead of landing on a warm body she seemed to go through it. Because she thought she had missed Maddie she tried to land on her again and whispered,

"Boy-Girl ... Surprise, surprise ..."

But a smell came from the figure, a sickly smell. It smelt of the sea ... damp and smothering. When she looked into the figure's face in the dark she could smell rotting fruit. Then something clawed at her head. When she touched her head her hands met with sharp, curled claws and a warm liquid dripped down ... blood.

She screamed in terror and now realised something else. It was not Maddie.

Chapter 29

From out of the dark Linda heard a masculine voice say,

"You took her away from us. Now you will take her place."

Puzzled at hearing the strange voice Linda left the cupboard and switched the light on. Her sister lay half choking on the bed. A monk like figure lay over her and held her throat with long, curled nails. The figure looked up. The light blue eyes glittered and the corpse like figure, its blackened teeth visible even in the poor light, screeched out and cursed her.

The banshee-like sound rang through Linda's ears. She ran out of the room screaming. She was hysterical and began running down the stairs.

Lydia woke up on hearing the commotion. She got out of bed just in time to see Linda racing past her, still screaming as she ran half falling down the stairs.

"What on earth are you doing here?" she shouted after her. But Linda kept running, then once downstairs she started hammering on the front door. She was desperate to get out.

"That thing ... it's got my sister," she shouted at Lydia. Hearing the noise Maddie had by now got out of bed, and came downstairs

"What thing?" Lydia asked.

"It's upstairs. Oh, my God, it might come after us." Linda started to wail as she said this.

"This is ridiculous," said Lydia angrily. "If this is some kind of joke aimed at my niece it is not amusing."

"It's not a joke. There is something in the room with my sister," the tear-stained girl pleaded with her.

"Right. Stay here and I will go and see what's going on upstairs, but I will not be happy if this is some game you are playing," responded Lydia firmly, still thinking it was some prank that the girls were playing on her niece. She strode up the stairs, and Maddie started following her.

"Stay with Linda," ordered Lydia but Maddie refused – and so, sighing, Lydia went up the stairs. Linda remained behind. She was now sitting on the ground with her hands over her face, too frightened to follow them.

As they entered the room there was a loud humming, and what looked like an enormous black whirlpool seemed to be engulfing the whole room. The noise became deafening.

"What the hell is going on?" asked Lydia as she looked at Maddie.

She blinked at epicentre and found herself being sucked towards the rotating mass. As she was dragged across the room Maddie grabbed her waist and held on tightly. Their combined weight kept them both from moving forward. As Lydia looked across the vortex she could see a lifeless Julie Painter being held by a monk like figure.

"Hold on to me as tight as you can," she shouted back to Maddie above the noise. "I am going to try and get her."

Lydia edged forward, forced her hand into the whirlpool, and grabbed Julie's hand. The heat burnt her hand, but she kept on trying to grab Julie's hand. Finally she managed to clasp it, but avoided looking at the robed figure beside Julie. A long claw grabbed her hand and scratched the surface of the skin, but she held on tightly to Julie. This action, however, seemed to drag her deeper into the whirlpool.

"Keep holding on," she shouted back to Maddie.

Using all her strength she gave a pull, and Julie's arm came out of it.

"Drag me back," Lydia screamed out. Maddie did as she was told. The whirlpool seemed to be getting weaker. This was the opportunity Lydia needed, and she pulled an unconscious Julie out. It was just in time, because the whirlpool started to become smaller. An animal-like roar came from the whirlpool, and continued to screech as it decreased in size.

Finally it disappeared into thin air. Julie, Lydia, and Maddie fell backwards on the ground. Julie was still unconscious. When they looked around the room there was nothing else there. Maddie's aunt looked anxiously at Julie. She touched her face. The girl was still deathly pale and unconscious. She patted her face and spoke gently to her. She said,

"Come on, Julie … Wake up. You are safe. Wake up."

The girl slowly began to awake. She opened her eyes, which widened in horror, and she started screaming.

"Julie, you are safe. It's all right. You are safe with us."

Lydia cradled the shaking girl's head in her arms while the girl sobbed into her chest. She finally got her to stand up, and she beckoned to Maddie and said,

"Get some blankets. I am going to put her in my bedroom."

Lydia managed to get the girl to walk a little, so she guided her out of the room and held on to her as they came down the stairs and took her into her own bedroom. Julie grabbed her hand as Lydia placed her on her bed and said to her,

"It's Lydia. You are safe."

Maddie dragged some blankets out of the pine blanket chest at the foot of the bed and wrapped one round Julie's shoulders.

"Maddie, I am going to phone for an ambulance … and then I'll call Julie's mother. Can you sit with her? My phone is in my handbag downstairs."

Maddie nodded back in reply and held on to the trembling girl. Lydia came back into the room with Linda behind her.

"You two sit with her while I phone for an ambulance."

The girls did as she said. After phoning for an ambulance she asked Linda for her mother's number. She phoned their mother and simply said that both her daughters were at the Hall but Julie was ill, and that an ambulance had been called.

"Your mother is on her way," said Lydia to Linda.

"What are you going to say to the ambulance man?" Maddie asked.

"I don't know. We both saw it. How on earth am I going to explain that?"

"Aunt Lydia, look at your hand," Maddie exclaimed.

It was covered in blood. The skin on the back of her hand had been shredded.

"I think that may have happened when I grabbed Julie out of that whirlpool thing and that creature clawed at me," replied Lydia as she picked up a box of tissues on her dressing table and placed half a dozen tissues over her hand.

"It was one of the witches who took Julie. I think it may have been Katharine Underville," said Maddie, finally feeling that she was going to have to tell her aunt everything.

She then started telling the whole story, and left nothing out. After what had happened she knew that her aunt would now maybe believe what she was saying.

"All this has been happening and you have said nothing?" her aunt said at last.

"But how could I? You would never have believed me. Now you have seen it for yourself. That's why I am telling you now. Remember, I told you about things moving about the Hall but you thought I had imagined it."

"Yes, I am afraid you are right. I wouldn't have believed you. The whole story sounds like something out of a ghost story. Who would believe us if we told them? I am so sorry I didn't take you seriously," Lydia said, and patted Maddie's shoulder.

"Colin knew something was going on. He said that members of his faith did not believe in things like that, but he did give me a cross to protect myself," came Maddie's reply. She added,

"He is doing the service tomorrow for Anna, so she will be at peace. Can I go to the church, please, to be at the service?"

"Well, I suppose that because you have gone this far with your investigative work it would be churlish of me to not allow you to go. But I am coming with you. I do not want you out of my sight. Heavens knows what Sam's parents will make of all these strange goings-on. I trust she will tell them, won't she?"

"Er … I don't know. She might be worried about telling her mum about Anna after her mother being ill because of seeing the ghost."

Julie was now sitting up. She had been listening intently to what was being said. Linda had fallen asleep, and had heard nothing of the conversation.

"Come on, Julie. We will need to go downstairs for the ambulance. Your mother is coming shortly. Linda, wake up."

"Mrs Underville, could I have my bag please? I left it in the walk-in cupboard," Julie said. She stared with eyes as innocent as a baby's at Lydia. She looked much younger than her years.

"If we can get into the room we will get it for you. But we have to make sure it is safe to go back in first," said Lydia, confused that Julie was asking for her bag. Thinking the girl might still be in shock.

At the sound of Julie's whining voice Linda woke up with a jolt, snorting as she did so. If you looked at her face you could see that she was remembering what happened, shock was starting to register.

The girls got up off the bed. Slowly they all walked downstairs. Lydia held a wobbly Julie's arm as she led her downstairs. As they reached the front door they could see the flash of the ambulance's lights through the glass. Lydia opened the door and spoke to the ambulance man. Maddie felt sorry for her because she had to try and explain what had happened.

"I know it's hard to believe, but there appears to have been a supernatural happening here. Whatever it was it tried to take Julie. We managed to rescue her. I am concerned about her health, and feel she should be checked at the hospital. She has been very weak, and was unconscious for a short period."

The ambulance man looked at his colleague as she said this as if to say,

"We have a right one here." One of them asked Julie how she felt. She mumbled back that she felt dizzy, and swayed as she said this. Lydia stopped her from falling and said,

"I think she is still in shock. She has had a terrible scare."

But the ambulance man ignored this remark and said to Julie,

"Hello, pet. How are you? Are you on any medication?"

Julie replied,

"I just want to go home. No, I am not taking any tablets."

"Well, pet, we are going to have to take you to hospital. But first we are going to have to check your heart rate and your blood pressure. Is that OK?" he asked her then continued,

"We can do that in the ambulance. This will not take long. The doctor will then have a look at you when we get to hospital."

Julie nodded back.

The ambulance man smiled at her as he said this. Julie's mother arrived with a friend in a car. The minute the car stopped she ran towards her daughter and cried out,

"Julie!" Her daughter stumbled forward into her arms.

"She is all right," said Lydia as she tried to calm down the girl's mother, but needs to be checked out at the hospital".

The ambulance man told Julie's mother that they would have to check her heart rate and blood pressure, and moved her aside as they took Julie into the ambulance. Once they had done this they got her to lie down on a bed. They closed the ambulance door and the vehicle set off with Julie.

"I will explain what happened later, but first go to the hospital." said Lydia to Julie Painter's mother. She did not protest. She was too stressed to ask questions about what had happened, and said to Lydia,

"Thank you for calling the ambulance." Then she looked at Linda and beckoned to her to get in the car. Marjorie Bywater, the friend of Julie's mother's, helped her get into the car. Julie's mother had never learnt to drive. She had never been able to afford the driving lessons, so relied on lifts from friends in cases of emergency. They drove off and Lydia and Maddie went back into the house.

"I am definitely not staying in my bedroom, Aunt Lydia," said Maddie.

"Of course you are not. We'll lock the door to that bedroom, and you can sleep in my bed. I just need to get the keys for the room from the hook on the back door. Wait outside your bedroom while I go in."

Lydia locked up and went into the kitchen to get the keys. After returning from the kitchen they both went upstairs to Maddie's room. Curiosity made Lydia open the door. She turned the handle and peeped in. There was nothing out of the ordinary there. She remembered Julie saying she had left her bag in the walk-in wardrobe, and went nervously towards it. She grabbed the bag quickly from inside, but after checking behind her she ran out of the room.

"Good heavens. What on earth has Julie got in her bag?" thought Lydia. It weighed a ton. She left it outside the room, and now she was satisfied that the room no longer had anyone or anything in it she locked the door and they both went back to her bedroom.

"Come on, let's get some sleep. It's 2 a.m. now."

Maddie didn't need any encouragement. They were both still in their pyjamas, and sank into the bed. Lydia carefully wrapped the bedcovers round her niece, who was already sound asleep. Then sleep took over, and all that could be heard was the sound of Lydia's gentle snoring.

While they slept Anna watched over them. She had used all her power to drag Lydia and the girls away from the whirlpool, but it had sapped her strength. They had been unaware of her presence. Katharine had now gone. She had been dragged back to the dark side. But Anna could sense that Agnes was around. This troubled her. Agnes was a much stronger force to be reckoned with. She would need to find a soul to barter with to prevent the same happening to her. If only she could help them before she went into the light. But time was against her. She had also seen the dogs. Agnes would use them help her to collect souls.

Tomorrow she would be gone. She had to do all she could to protect Maddie and Sam.

Agnes paced up and down outside the house. Her second sight had shown her what had happened to her daughter. Mad with rage, she raked her claws down Lydia's car door. Everything had gone wrong. She had lost her daughter. It was supposed to be a soul for a soul. That was not going to happen to her. Katharine and Agnes had taken the hounds without permission. Agnes swore that if she was dragged down to the fires of hell she would spill blood before she went.

But once again she would have to be invited in.

She looked up at the Hall and could see that the light downstairs had just gone off. They must have gone to bed.

The creatures had still not been fed. They would come after her for their feed …

The aunt and her daughter would be a suitable meal for them. If anyone else turned up as well then that would be a further delicacy that the dogs could enjoy. She would guide the dogs to the Hall.

The dogs were restless, and they moved through the woods leaving destroyed trees in their wake. Raging hunger motivated them. Animals began to flee in terror. The shrill calls of birds echoed throughout the trees. There was a flutter of frenzied wings as the birds flew away in a compact mass.

The creatures sensed they were getting near to Agnes.

Heavy rain in the early hours of the morning had left the streets empty of cars. The hellhounds, a portent of death, continued with their gigantic steps. They thundered across the muddy cobblestones. The cloven hooves of the hounds clicked in unison as they touched the muddied stones. Their large poker red eyes glowed in the darkness as they snorted fire, making the misty air around them feel ice tremblingly cold. As the beasts went past the church a face peered from one of the leaded windows.

The man who looked out of the window had a face that registered fear and disbelief then recognition.

"They have come back again. Someone must have summoned them. It must have been one of the Drakens," he said to himself.

They had done this before. He had to do something. It was happening all over again.

It was now 3 a.m. Maddie and Lydia were sound asleep.

Agnes stroked the heads of the giant dogs as they reached Cattingham Hall. She spoke to them, calmed them down, and whispered soothing words to them.

"Be patient … you will have your feed shortly."

The creatures did not recognise the world they had come into. Where was their master? They had been summoned by the witches from the underworld. The witches had used old magic to bring them back to life …

Katharine's mother knew he would not be happy that his pets had been taken. The witches had only ever summoned them under his instructions until now.

Also … the time had passed for the initiation. She did not have much time left to protect herself from them.

Agnes went up to the door of Cattingham Hall and hammered with the door knocker. The creatures remained in the woods and waited for her command.

It was Lydia who first heard the knocking.

"What? What was that?" she mumbled as she awoke from her slumber. She gazed across at the clock radio and saw that it read 3.15 a.m. They had only just gone to bed. Whoever could be at the door at this time? As she became more awake she thought it must be the police, so got up to put her dressing gown on. This action woke up Maddie, who half stirred.

"What is it?"

"Nothing. Go back to sleep. There is someone at the door. You stay in bed. I'll go and see who it is."

With her dressing gown hurriedly put on Lydia went to the bedroom door, but her mobile phone started buzzing.

"Who on earth could be phoning me at this time in the morning?" she thought as she answered the phone and heard a Scottish voice, which at first she did not recognise.

"Who is it?" she asked, thinking it was a wrong number.

"It's Colin Appleby, the vicar of Cattingham Church. Is that Lydia?" he asked.

"Yes," she replied.

"Lydia, this is a peculiar request … but please do not answer the front door. I have seen someone knocking on your door. They mean you harm. Believe me, I would not be saying this if it was not true.

"Please, please do not answer the door. I do not have time to explain. I am going to the back of your house. Please let me in. I am trying to protect you."

"But who is it? Why would they hurt me?"

"I will explain later. Just do as I say. Please go down the stairs very quietly – I do not want the person knocking on the door to know you are there – and open the back door quietly so I can get in."

Maddie was trying to listen to the telephone conversation and had now sat up in bed. Seeing the look of fear on her aunt's face she started to get concerned.

"What is it, Aunt Lydia?"

"Nothing, Maddie. Please stay in the bed. I am going to go downstairs … There is nothing to worry about."

But Lydia had her hand to her mouth as if in shock. It was obvious that there was plenty to be worried about. Maddie got out of bed.

"I'm coming with you."

"No, you are not. Stay in bed. Do not argue with me. Do as I say. Do not question it. If I tell you to do something you do it." Lydia spoke harshly to her niece. Maddie obeyed her. She had never seen her aunt speak like this to her before...

"Darling, I am so sorry, but I have to see someone. Please stay here. If I do not come up the stairs within ten minutes lock this door and call the police."

Maddie did as she said. She was now beginning to get very frightened.

Lydia tiptoed quietly downstairs. The huge front door faced her as she came down the stairs. It had a small frosted glass window and she could see a figure against the door. The hammering began again. Strange noises came from outside the door. The person behind the door was muttering, and shouting strange words she could not understand. It almost sounded Gaelic. A barefooted Lydia ducked past the door and quietly opened the kitchen door. Then she opened the back door. Colin swept past her and locked the door. In his hand he held a carrier bag.

"We have to sprinkle salt round the house." He handed her a box of table salt. He had already started to sprinkle the contents of another box of salt round the back door.

"Colin, what is going on?" Lydia asked. Her voice was now calm, but inside she was full of fear.

"Hellhounds have been summoned up by the Drakens. They help collect the souls of humans, and are rewarded with the blood of their human victims. It is imperative that nothing gets into the house."

"It will be Agnes Underville who has done this," came a voice from the hallway breaking into the conversation.

It was Maddie.

"Maddie!" Lydia was stopped short speaking further by Colin.

"We do not have time to talk about this. I am going to go in the hallway. I need to chalk a pentagram on the inside of the hall door floor. It is called the demon trap. I am hoping this will keep them at bay. Take these candles and light them round the back door. Do you have any windows open?"

"No, I don't," replied Lydia.

"Good. They will not be able to find an opening to get in. The hounds can shrink in size. Stay in the kitchen. Continue to sprinkle the salt."

Maddie and Lydia did as he said and as he went out of the door a voice called from outside.

"Maddie, open the door. It's me, Sam."

Maddie got up to go to the door, but Colin came running back in and blocked her.

"That is not Sam. Demons imitate voices. Do not answer the door, no matter what. It's a trap." The voice of Sam still continued to speak. It pleaded at first, then got angrier and angrier. Then there was silence.

"What will they do next?" Maddie asked.

"Let's hope nothing," came Lydia's grim response.

Colin went back into the hallway. The person on the outside was now muttering strange words, but on sensing he was there they opened the letter box and whispered mockingly.

"Is that a way to treat me? Why don't you let me in? I just want to talk to you." Long claws started to come through the letter box.

"Yes, I know what you want to do, but we have protection," said Colin coldly to the voice on the other side of the door. "You want to destroy us and get your soul back. This will not happen. You have taken too many souls. You will not take these ones."

Colin was silent for a moment, and then he began to recite the Lord's Prayer. He crossed himself and sprinkled holy water round the front door and over the pentagram. He picked up the salt and scattered it liberally all over the letterbox and on to the clawed hand. A shriek that seemed to whistle through the air came from the other side of the door. The house almost seemed to quake with the screaming. Then came a deep voice that said,

"You pathetic creature. Do you think you can keep me out with your prayers and your salt? Fool."

The voice continued to ring out round the house and mock him. Maddie and Lydia came out of the kitchen. They were now past the point of being frightened.

"Is there anything you want us to do?" Lydia asked, trying to speak over the voice coming from the letter box.

"Continue putting the salt round the door, and I will go to the back door to try and exorcise the spirits from there. No doubt they will attempt to come round there. They will be looking for an unguarded place."

Colin had changed from the gentle vicar of Cattingham to a person with a voice of authority. His eyes were cold when he looked towards the creatures who were trying to get into the Hall, and his whole personality had changed. An aura of goodness and a kind of benevolent yet indestructible power seemed to surround Colin, and Lydia and Maddie were glad they were in the house with him and that he was on their side.

Lydia could now see why he had come to protect them, and was she grateful for it. It was as if he had come across these creatures before and knew exactly what to do. If it was not for him the creatures would most certainly have got into the house by now. She would have unknowingly opened the door to the person on the other side of the door. It did not bear thinking about what might have happened then.

Lydia shuddered inwardly. Maddie went into the sitting room looking for Hodge, and suddenly remembered that the cat had been outside when she came in. But where had she gone now?

As she came in the sitting room the bay window faced her. Peering in at her was a huge black dog that was stretched up from the ground. The sheer size of it was frightening. Its rubescent eyes did not blink as it watched her, and it was licking its black lips in amusement. The beast's shiny black coat appeared to reflect no light from the moon. It moved forward and hunched the front of its body up to get a better look at her. She then became aware that there was another of these creatures beside it. It was an even larger dog. This one pulled back its head and drew back its lips over it fangs, and a long red tongue came out which stretched up towards the window. .

Maddie let out a scream and went running out of the room. She ran into her aunt's arms and trembled as she told her what was outside.

"Stay in the hallway," said Colin as he came back into the hallway himself. He then began to recite the Lord's Prayer again. The house seemed to shake as he spoke...

"Oh, my God … look," Lydia said, and pointed. A long tongue from one of the hellhounds started to glide out of the letter box into the hallway. Colin picked up some salt and poured it over the tongue. Smoke started to come from it as it curled up and went back through the letter box.

"The pentagram will keep us safe," he said. He spoke gently seeing the fear in Lydia and Maddie's faces, then hugged them both.

"God will protect us. Do not worry."

"You have seen these creatures before, then, Colin, have you?" Lydia asked.

"Yes," came the terse reply. "A member of the Drakens used old magic to conjure them up. But we sent them back where they came from."

"We?" questioned Lydia.

"The vicar who was originally at Cattingham Hall. He left the area shortly afterwards. That's when I took over here. The whole thing had sadly affected his health. He had dealt with these creatures before. He has shown me how to act if it ever happened again, even though the church does not approve. I had hoped I would never need to do it again," came Colin's curious reply.

Agnes spoke again through the letter box.

"Give yourselves up. You have no hope."

"She is running out of time," came a voice from behind Maddie, Colin, and Lydia.

It was Anna. In her arms she held Hodge, and she was stroking the cat's silky back. The animal did not seem at all stressed by this action, and lay comfortably against her chest.

"She has until four o'clock to get into the house or her soul will be lost," continued Anna. Maddie came towards her.

"Lydia, Colin ... this is Anna Blackstock."

"Anna Blackstock," repeated Lydia. She appeared fascinated by the spirit.

"Do not worry ... I mean you no harm. Please listen to what I have to say. My curse against Katharine and Agnes is strong. It cannot be broken." As she spoke she stroked Hodge's head. "You will have to keep her out of the house until that time. Note that this Agnes is frightened of cats. I remember that as a child at school a cat appeared when she was visiting the school. She ran out of the door."

"Frightened of cats?" said an incredulous Maddie.

"Yes. She is only a half witch. Keep your cat in the hallway. That is one way she will not get in. The other thing is to light all your fires, and put salt in the flames. She may try and get down one of them if she is getting desperate, but she will be fearful of it."

Anna then disappeared.

"Oh, my God ... she can get in through the chimney?" said Lydia.

She raced off, and began hurriedly lighting the kindling that had already been prepared in the fireplace. When she remembered that she hadn't prepared a fire in the morning room she then ran in there. This time she had to light some fresh papers first. Then she laid the kindling over it. It would not light at first, but then slowly an orange flame came into view and it started licking away at the paper and kindling. Smoke came out of it because it had not been cleaned for a while. Half choking, she left it burning, and shouted to Maddie,

"One more room to do. Maddie, make sure the fires in the other rooms do not go out." She coughed loudly as she went into the sitting room.

Colin remained in the hallway to make sure that nothing came through the letter box. Maddie quickly ran into the library and checked that fire, and the fire in the morning room. As Lydia lit the kindling in the fireplace a black shape seemed to be coming down the chimney.

It was the silhouette of a large clawed hand. As it tried to grope its way down the chimney it forced its way further down with its curled-up claws.

Chapter 30

Lydia screamed and lit one match one after the other while she tried not to look at the shadow of the hand creeping further down the chimney. Finally the kindling started to burn, and she quickly scattered the salt. Long claws stopped coming down the chimney. Then came loud growling, and a voice starting screeching at her from up in the chimney. It was the same voice that had been behind the door. The hand then went back up the chimney as the fire began to get stronger. The flames went higher and higher up the chimney.

Lydia was now certain that the hand had completely disappeared, and she left the room. She shouted to Colin and told him what had happened.

"She won't attempt to come down again if the fires are all lit, he said."

After looking at his watch he told her that they had twenty minutes left.

"We must keep checking the doors and windows and the fireplaces."

"Do you think we should call the police?" Lydia replied.

"No," came the reply. "As I have said, we do not have much time left. The police would be in danger with the monsters. I do not want her to take any more souls. Too many have been lost."

"Has she taken many, then?"

"Oh, yes, Lydia, but not just her Draken followers."

"Won't the creatures try and get in?"

"No. She has summoned them to obey her. They have no power to enter the house. She has to gain entry. Then they will follow. Make sure there are no windows half open. The upper windows may be too high up for them, but it is best to check."

Maddie came into the hallway as Colin said this, and she said,

"I'll check, Aunt Lydia."

"Just make sure that you are thorough, and that they are all locked. Are you sure you will be all right doing this? If you feel frightened come downstairs."

"I will, don't worry. One of us has to make sure the fires are burning, and you have to stop her getting in through the front door."

Maddie went up the stairs and checked all the windows. It was reassuring that all the other fireplaces had been blocked up years ago when the house had been partially modernised. As she came into Uncle Akkoubian's bedroom she went to the window. It had already been locked. She pulled at the handle to make certain.

As she did this something rolled towards her on the floor. It was a coloured glass ball seven inches in diameter. Maddie picked it up and peered into it. The glass was in brilliant shades of aquamarine and navy blue. She stared at it in wonderment. As she turned it she wondered where it had come from. A small glass hook was attached to it, and threaded through the hook was a plaited gold cord. It was then that she felt hands stroking her hair, and the smell of King Edward cigar smoke.

It made her feel safe. She recognised the smell. It reminded her of Uncle Akkoubian. As quickly as it came the feeling went.

As she held on to the glass ball she knew that he had left this for her.

"But why?" she thought.

Maddie went through the last of the rooms and came to her bedroom. The door was locked. She was not sure if her aunt wanted her to check this room, but decided to anyway. She unlocked the door, put the light on, and went in. There had been no change in the room. She checked the window and ran out quickly, because she still felt frightened of being in this room. She held on to the glass ball and ran down the stairs.

"Colin, look at this. I found it in Uncle Akkoubian's room." Colin was at the front door peering through the letter box.

"What was that, Maddie?" Again she repeated what she had said. He picked it up and twirled it round.

"I know what this is," he replied. "It's a witch ball. Where has it come from?"

"I think from my Uncle Akkoubian," came her answer.

"Well, if it was from him then he is trying to protect us. It will have been used to entice evil spirits into it. The witch ball would then capture the evil spirit. So I think we will keep it within arm's reach".

"How safe are we, Colin?" Lydia broke into the conversation.

"I think, Lydia, that we are as safe as we can be for the moment. We just have to be strong, and be on guard all the time. There are only ten minutes left. Anna said it was 4 a.m. when, if Agnes didn't gain entry to the house, she would go back to the fires of hell. We just have to wait. Have faith."

Colin could see the worry lines now etched in Lydia's face.

"If anything happened to Maddie—" she began. Her voice was trembling as she spoke.

"Don't think about it. Have faith, and be strong," said Colin gently. "Come on, you will need to check the fires are still burning."

Maddie had gone into the kitchen to relight the candles that had gone out. Some of the candles took a while to relight, and she burnt her fingers on one of the matches.

"Ouch," she said as she dropped the matches. There was a tap on the kitchen door, and she looked up.

"Maddie, open the door. It's your mother. Let me in. I've come round the back. There was no light at the front door."

"Mum, is that you? Why didn't you tell me you were coming? Stay at the back door. The key is not in the door. Let me go and find it."

The key was on the dresser in the kitchen. Maddie was excited, and went to get it but tripped and fell flat on her face and banged her knee. She got up slowly. Her knee began to sting.

"Maddie, open the door. Why are you taking so long? Hurry up, girl. It's a bitter night," came the voice from the other side of the door. "I said be quick, girl."

Maddie got up. She placed the key in the lock, turned it, and started to open the door. But something came into her head. It was as if something cold was ripping into her heart.

Her mother never called her 'Girl'.

"What are you waiting for, girl? Open the door? Let me in," came the impatient voice behind the door.

"You are not my mother," said Maddie, quickly locking the door again.

"Yes, I am your mother. I demand that you open the door."

The handle on the door began to turn violently and make a clattering noise.

"No," Maddie defiantly shouted back.

The noise from the kitchen brought Colin rushing in.

"What's happening?" he asked as he looked around the room.

"I nearly let Agnes in," came Maddie's anguished reply. "I thought it was my mother. She spoke in her voice. It was only when she kept calling me 'Girl' that I knew it wasn't her."

"Well, it was a good job you realised that. But didn't I tell you not to open the door, no matter what? Agnes would have imitated your mother's voice in an attempt to get in. You could have had us all killed, and our souls lost forever."

Ashamed, Maddie hung her head. She had really thought it was her mum, because she was so desperate to see her. Why had she been so stupid? She had also nearly opened the door to who she had thought was Sam. Colin's temper subsided, and he said,

"Maddie, I am so relieved that you realised that it was not your mother in time. It does not matter now. Come away from the door and go and check all the fires with Lydia. I will stay here."

He gave a brief smile to reassure her, but Maddie still could not believe how stupid she had been and continued to look down. She was so angry with herself. Colin took her hand and went to lead her out of the room. Agnes's voice continued to screech outside. It did not sound so arrogant now she had started whining and pleading for the door to be opened. The tone then changed. You could hear more sobbing as she begged them to open the door.

"Open the door ... save me. Help me ... please help me," she screeched at them.

"Ignore it," said Colin coldly to Maddie. But after what had nearly happened she had no intention of opening the door. The voice spoke again and said,

"Please, please let me in. I beg of you, let me in."

It was then they heard a loud scream, and a heavy thud against the back door. The dogs started howling excitedly. The sound was something Maddie would never forget. It clung to her bones. Then came the sound of dogs snarling. They appeared to be fighting each other. Colin went to the kitchen window and looked out. Maddie went to join him.

"Keep away from the window," he rasped back at her in shock. Then horror registered in his face and he shielded her from the window.

"It is all over. You will be safe now."

The dogs stopped howling outside. Then there was total silence.

"Colin what is happening?" asked Lydia as she came.

"It is all over. We are safe. Agnes and the hellhounds have gone," came his terse reply as he sat down shakily at the kitchen table and wiped the dripping sweat from his brow.

"Over?" repeated Lydia as she looked searchingly at his face.

"Yes," he nodded back. His voice then went very quiet.

"Where has Agnes gone?" Lydia asked finally.

"Even she should not have suffered that way, no matter what evil she had done ... the poor woman." Colin stroked the unshaven side of his face. He was distracted, and was speaking to himself as if he had not heard Lydia's question.

"What happened?" asked Lydia, not sure if she wanted to hear the answer.

He was breathing heavily. He finally said,

"The hellhounds killed and ate her ... She had taken the form of Maddie's mum when she tried to get in and must have forgotten to change back. The hounds must not have recognised that this was Agnes. They then disappeared into thin air. They will have gone back to the underworld."

He stood up and went back to look out of the window.

"You can look out of the window now. There is nothing there to see. God has protected us." Lydia turned to Maddie and hugged her, then went over to Colin and simply said,

"Thank you. You saved our lives."

"No," he replied. "We all helped save each other," but he looked completely worn out as he said this.

"Can I stay in the house tonight?" he asked Lydia. "I would feel happier if I did. I have to make sure you are both safe."

"Of course you can. You can stay in Sam's room. I will just put some fresh bedcovers in there." Lydia disappeared upstairs.

"I really thought she was my mum," said Maddie solemnly to him.

"I know, but these witches have always been very cunning. That would have been Agnes's last card to gain entry into the house. She was looking for a weakness. She found it in you missing your mother. But she had run out of time. It was a terrible thing that happened to her." He rubbed his eyes and looked wearily at her.

"Would you like a coffee, Colin?"

"I would love one," he replied. Maddie made coffee for both Lydia and Colin and a hot chocolate for herself. When she came back into the kitchen Lydia said to Colin,

"Your bedroom is ready now. I should think we will all be sleeping in. It is 4.15 now. I will have to put all the fires out first, though. This house has never been so warm. It is wonderful, but I had better not get used to it. Back to cold and draughty from now on, I'm afraid."

Colin and Maddie gave tired smiles in reply. Lydia sat at the kitchen table talking to Colin. The food in the large sandwich box was made short work of with all of them eating: they were so distracted with their thoughts that they ate one thing after the other until half the food was gone.

"Those creatures will definitely not come back, will they?" Lydia asked worriedly.

"Only if they were summoned – and that would bring Katharine back, but Agnes will never come back. Let's hope Katharine never comes back either," said Colin and added, "Yes, she could come back."

"Never ever use the Ouija board again. Burn it. It has an imprint of the witch's evil on it," came a voice from the back of the kitchen.

It was Anna.

The glow round her was now dazzling, and it hurt their eyes.

"I prayed and prayed that you would be safe," said the ghost. "I will soon be able to go home. I never thought this would happen. I have waited so long. I cannot thank you enough. If it hadn't been for you I would have been here for ever." Her eyes misted over as she spoke.

"I will miss you," said Maddie. Anna smiled back and said softly,
"I will miss you too. I think we would have been good friends."

"It is not long now, Anna. You will be at peace and with your family. The service will be at 11 a.m.," said Colin.

"I cannot believe it is going to happen, Maddie. I keep being pulled nearer to the light. I hear my mam's voice telling me to be patient and that I will be with her … I will have to go. It is now dragging me to it. I cannot fight it. I am so sorry I am unable to stay. I have to go. Thank you all so much. You saved me, and for that I am eternally grateful."

Anna gave a lovely smile and tried to speak further, but the glow around her became stronger and she began to disappear before their eyes.

"I would like to have spoken more to her," said Maddie. She sounded disappointed, and added,

"I suppose that will be the last time I will ever see her."

"Never mind. You have done a wonderful thing for her. You have brought her the peace she has so long craved," replied Colin gently.

"Well, if the service is at 11 a.m. we will have to get some sleep – or you, Colin, will fall asleep doing the service … Or, worse, miss it all together. I will make breakfast at 10 a.m. I will have to set the alarm so we don't sleep in," said Lydia. She was speaking practically, and trying to think about other things so they could take away the sheer terror she had felt. Food was to her the only real comfort she could give them.

"Can I sleep in your bed again?"

"Of course you can, Maddie. I am going to lock your bedroom up for ever once we get all the furniture out. You can sleep in another room in the house … choose a different room for a bedroom. Ugh. That bedroom just gives me the creeps. Even thinking about it makes me feel sick," she said, and gave a shudder.

They all went upstairs to bed. Lydia showed Colin his room, and where the bathroom was. They all slept soundly.

When the alarm went off at 9.30 Lydia groaned and tried to put her slippers on her feet without success, because she was still half asleep.

"Maddie, wake up." Her niece had her pillow over her head and Lydia gently eased it off her.

"Come on, time to get a shower."

Maddie awoke with a start and half fell out of bed.

"We have come this far. This is the final thing we have to do for Anna. No time for a sleep-in," she said to her niece. Maddie was now wide awake after realising what Lydia had just said.

"You use my bathroom first. I'll go and wake Colin up," said her aunt.

With both Maddie and Colin now getting showers Lydia fed a hungry Hodge. The cat was grumpy that she was being fed so late. Lydia had been so tired that she had even forgotten to close the kitchen curtains.

Once in the kitchen she opened the back door to put an empty carton of orange juice in the dustbin. She peered round the door nervously and ventured out to place the item in the dustbin. When she looked out she saw that the sun was shining quite brightly. It looked as if it was going to be a nice day.

The only evidence of what had happened the night before was a small strand of brown cloth on one of the fruit bushes that quickly blew away before her eyes and went high up into the sky. Lydia shook her head, and tried to wipe out the image of the horrible death that Agnes would have suffered. She hurried back into the kitchen and busied herself setting the table and making breakfast. She thought that one of her special breakfasts was in order.

As she started frying bacon she could hear activity from upstairs and smiled. It was amazing how quickly people staying at her house got up when she made a fried breakfast.

After Colin, Maddie, and Lydia had had breakfast Lydia went upstairs to shower. Both Maddie and Colin went out of the kitchen door with the same caution as Lydia. After checking outside and finding nothing there they both relaxed.

"I am going to throw the Ouija board away when we come back from the service. I will never use it again," said Maddie.

"I think that's very wise. But I would do as Anna said. Burn it," came Colin's reply.

Lydia came downstairs half an hour later with her hair still damp, but fully made-up and dressed. She then tucked her blue check shirt in her jeans and put her gilet on. Then sat down and put on her leather riding boots.

As they went to go out of the front door the three of them were hesitant, but again there was nothing there. As they walked down the drive Lydia glanced at her car and said,

"Oh, my God. Look at my car." Long slash marks ran across the paintwork along the passenger door.

"That will have been Agnes. Only her claws could have made those marks," said Maddie. Lydia shook her head in despair at Maddie.

"How on earth am I going to explain those marks to the garage?" No one replied. They all thought the same thing. No one would believe the truth.

"Come on," came Colin's reply. "We need to get over to the church."

They walked over to the church. As they entered, one of the volunteers, Mrs Hounslow, was at the door looking agitated.

"I couldn't get in, Colin. It was locked. I was going to arrange the flowers."

"Claire, I am so sorry. I had an urgent appointment I had to go to." His apology to Mrs Hounslow did not seem to work on her as she pursed her lips and looked at him disapprovingly, as if to say,

"The last vicar would never have done that."

This made Maddie smile to herself. It would have been funny if he had told her truth – for which he was sorry, but he had been delayed as he had had to ward off some hellhounds from the underworld and a witch who was trying to steal their souls.

Now that would have been something for Mrs Hounslow to think about.

The undertaker's assistant had arrived, and was at the back of the church in the churchyard as they walked around. Anna's wooden coffin lay on the ground beside the family burial plot, which already been dug up. The smell of fresh damp earth was strong in the air.

The coffin was lowered into the ground. It was a stark reminder of what had happened to Anna.

Colin began by saying,

"We are gathered here to say farewell to Anna Blackstock.

"Lord, our God, you are the source of life.

"By your grace lead her into your kingdom, through your son Jesus Christ, our Lord.

"In the name of God the Holy Father we commit this body of Anna Blackstock to the peace of God.

"Amen."

He then picked up some loose soil, threw a handful of it into the coffin, and said,

"From dust you came, Anna Blackstock.

"To dust you shall return.

"Jesus Christ is the resurrection of life."

He then made a sign of the cross. Then prayers were said.

The inscription on the Blackstock family headstone had been changed so that Anna's name was now beside her parents'. Maddie smiled and looked at Colin.

"Did you do this?"

"Of course. I had to give the poor girl a proper headstone when she went to join her family."

"Thank you," Maddie responded. Her eyes were shining brightly.

Hearing a flutter of wings made her look up. It was Antrabus. He made croaking noises to her, then he stretched out his wings and soared high into the sky. All at once he disappeared from the view.

Lydia and Colin did not notice this strange sight, but Maddie knew what had happened. The bird had found its mistress.

Colin was slightly ahead of them as the undertaker's assistant continued to cover the coffin in soil with his spade. Lydia caught up with Colin. Maddie walked slowly behind them. Her head hurt, and she was beginning to feel very strange. When she touched her forehead it felt hot.

Trying to catch up with the others seemed impossible. Exhausted, she gave a shout and then collapsed on the ground. As she turned Lydia saw her niece lying unconscious.

Chapter 31

Maddie had not been hurt when she had fallen. It was if it had been meant to happen. She had slipped back into one of her dreams.

In this dream she was on a grass verge. It was if she was about to take a photograph. Warm sunshine touched her face, and there was a smell of fresh meadow flowers. The sky was brilliant blue. Faces appeared before her that she did not recognise.

She felt safe. A sense of belonging engulfed her.

Then a line of people began walking together hand in hand – some young, some old. Two girls were laughing as they walked along. When she looked at them she realised who they were now. They were Anna Blackstock and Ursula Underville.

"This was the only way I knew to get you to see me," said Anna as she turned to speak to Maddie warmly. The girl with Anna was small in stature, and she smiled back at Maddie. When she got closer to her Maddie realised that she was older than she had first thought. .

It was Ursula Underville.

Older people followed behind.

There was a feeling of immense warmth and love. Anna came towards Maddie and stroked the side of her face. She did not have the scar on her face when she looked into Maddie's eyes tenderly. The sadness in her eyes was gone. She held something out in her hand.

"Take these, Maddie. It is a gift to remember me by. There is one for you, and one for your friend Sam," she said. She pressed two golden rings into her hand, and then kissed her cheek gently.

"I am at peace. I owe you a great debt. Both you and your friend must wear these rings always. They will protect you from any danger. Once they are on you they can never be removed."

Something began to pull at Maddie, and she was being dragged backwards.

"I will never forget you," she shouted back to Anna.

"Nor I you," came the reply.

A bird swooping down made her look up. It was the raven. Anna lifted her arm up, and the huge bird landed on it. It began clucking as she spoke to it.

"Come, Antrabus. It is time to go."

The bird flattened its feathers and lay across her shoulder. Its bright eyes lovingly watching its mistress's face intently.

Anna gave a smile, waved to Maddie and turned away...

The image before Maddie became dim, and a fine mist spread over her eyes.

"Maddie, wake up. Please wake up."

A desperate voice broke into the dream. Maddie opened her eyes to find her aunt holding her on the ground. On seeing her she said,

"I am all right. I saw Anna. She wanted to show me that she had found peace."

Something sharp cut into her palm, and when she opened her hand she found the gold rings Anna had given her.

"Look. She gave me these to remember her by." Lydia looked at her palms.

"How beautiful they are. Look, signet rings they even have a bird in a tree on their seals/"

"Yes, they will have. It's the medlar tree, I think. The bird will be Anna's raven Antrabus."

Lydia hugged her niece then helped her slowly to get up.

"She is fine, Colin," said Lydia to the vicar, who had been looking on anxiously.

Maddie told them all she had seen, and the three of them walked to the church. So many strange things had happened to them that no one was surprised by what she had to say.

"Anna wanted you to see her world and show you that she had finally found the peace she desperately craved," said Colin, and continued by saying,

"Remember what she said. Place the ring on your finger, and make sure Sam puts hers on. Never take them off. These gifts are Anna's protection for both you and Sam."

Three months later it was if the whole episode had been one long dream. Only the signet rings seemed to be a reminder of it all. Once they were on the girls fingers they could not as Anna had said be removed, no matter how hard the girls tried. . The fact they could not be removed did not bother them, as they gave Sam and Maddie a sense of comfort because they knew they were somehow protecting them.

When Julia returned from abroad Maddie's Aunt Lydia had spoken to her about what had happened in hushed tones. Not surprisingly Maddie's mum had found it hard to believe, but was more worried by the effect it might have had on her daughter.
She needn't have worried. Maddie seemed more confident.
It was as if the shy, lonely teenager had changed dramatically. Of course the strange women who had abducted Sam and Maddie had never been found, despite an extensive search by the police.

Over the following months Maddie was busy with schoolwork. There was so much of it that she felt she would be swallowed by her schoolbooks at any minute. She had not wanted to throw away her research papers on her Cattingham Hall project. They now lay in an old packing box in the attic. One day she would read them again. She just wished she did not have so much schoolwork.
It would soon be Christmas, and she was so looking forward to the holidays to get away from all the work. Her school project had been a great success, and she had been presented with a fountain pen and some book vouchers as the best student. As her mum had said, all her hard work had paid off.
Sam, Maddie, and Natalie were now firm friends. At the moment Sam was trying to persuade the other two to join the school's amateur dramatics group, but not with much success.
"Just humour her," murmured Maddie to Natalie. "She has these ideas. I have no acting talent whatsoever. I bet if we joined she would get the leading role, and I would be cast as a pig or something."
"Yeah, me too," said Natalie.

"Oh, you two are so pathetic. It's only amateur dramatics. Think of the fun we will have." Maddie rolled her eyes at Natalie and said,
"As I said, just humour her.'"
"I heard that," said Sam. She continued trying to persuade them as they walked to school.

It was great to hear their friend's voice. Sam had been very ill. She had ended up in hospital, with the onset of pneumonia. Fortunately the care and medication from the hospital had managed to nip it in the bud. She had been off school for two months. She had now pulled through, but the cosseting from her parents especially her mother had on some occasions been a bit smothering for her.

School was much better. Julie Painter and her sister Linda now left Maddie alone. Sometimes when they saw her they would look at her strangely, but they never spoke to her. Having said that, Linda would give a half smile when Julie wasn't looking ...

The shock of what had happened to her had at first made Julie's hair go completely white, but then most of the colour came back and there was now only one white strip on her fringe left. It remained that colour for a long time before it went back to its original colour.

Maddie never did find the Ouija board – nor her owl scarf, for that matter. Her aunt had remembered to give Julie her bag back Lydia had now locked her old bedroom up, and even said that she might brick the room up so that the room could never be entered again.

There had been amazing news on the paintings front. Lydia's paintings had been valued, and one had been sold at auction for £1.2 million. It had been a rare painting by the sixteenth-century painter Joseph Mahler. Another of the paintings was due to go to auction in a month's time. Lydia was now in a position to maintain the Hall properly. It had been decorated, and was having a damp course treatment put in.

All the strange spiders and the mushroom-like spores round the house had gone. The Hall even had a huge rose garden and a maze built into the grounds. This brought in a lot of tourists, which helped with the cost of maintaining the house. Lydia was offered money to hold ghost tours, but refused. She could not be persuaded to do this, despite the large sums of money being offered to her.

To her one ghost had been enough, without finding any more coming out of the woodwork.

Maddie still did cat-sitting for the Dee sisters. Ophelia had been let off with a caution. Maddie no longer felt frightened when she entered the cellar. Margaret Dee still continued to express disgust at her schoolbooks, but Maddie was used to her rants now. It seemed as if she was only happy when she was complaining about something, which made Maddie wonder if she had been born moaning.

The Ouija board had never been found, because of course Julie Painter still had it – along with Maddie's scarf, and a DVD she had from Maddie called The Dwelling Place on the Hill.

"Don't you think you should give her them back?" Linda asked her one day.

"What, and be accused of theft? Not bloody likely. I still don't like the stuck-up cow."

"She helped save your life," said Linda sounding annoyed.

"Whatever. Anyway, fancy a game with this Ouija board? But let's stick her DVD on to get in the mood. If it's hers it will be boring, so we might have to switch it off." As she said this she wove Maddie's owl scarf in and out of her hands.

"I think I might sell this on eBay. What do you think?"

Linda looked at her disgustedly.

"You can watch the film on your own, and I'm not playing with your Ouija board," she said. She got up off the bed and left the room.

Chapter 32

"Suit yourself, Fatty," Julie shouted back at her sister. She put the film on. It began with a woman walking across a hill in a monk's habit. Julie sighed. She was bored already. She pulled a face and started playing with the planchette on the Ouija board. She said half-heartedly,

"Is there anyone there?" There was no answer.

"Is there anyone there?" she asked again. She took the chewing gum off the board and placed it back in her mouth. The planchette moved forward, and her hand began to be controlled by some force. It spelled out the word Yes.

"Bloody hell," said Julie, and half choked on the gum. She stuck the gum back on the side of the Ouija board, then jumped off the bed and ran out of her bedroom shouting,

"Linda, come upstairs. I've got a ghost. It might be a fit lad."

But there was no answer.

"Oh, suit yourself. I'll keep him for myself," shouted Julie down the stairs and, annoyed, went back to the Ouija board. The film was still running. Julie glanced at it and saw that it was still showing a woman walking on a hill, so she held the planchette asked the Ouija board another question.

"Who are you?" Her hand was moved by a much stronger force this time, but no word came up. With her back to the television screen Julie asked more questions.

"Are you a lad?"

No, came the reply.

She now had no control of her hand, nor of the words that were being spelled out. She was disappointed that it was not a boy, and was about to stop playing when her hand was dragged across the board and these words came up:

I can make you rich.

Greed was getting the better of her and she asked,

"How?"

Invite me in, came the reply.

Behind Julie's back the figure on the screen was still walking up what looked like a very steep hill. Then it appeared to change its mind, and turned around and walked forward down the hill as if walking towards the camera. The film was in black-and-white, and some of the images were crackly and obscured by odd shapes that were impossible to make out.

At first glance you would have thought that the figure walking down the hill was an old woman because the steps were slow, and she appeared to be dragging herself along the ground. That seemed to change and the figure started to walk rapidly, as if it had regained its strength. It was a woman, but her brown hood was pulled down over part of her face so you were unable to see many of her features. She appeared to be so close to the television screen that if looked as if her face was almost touching it.

Julie was oblivious to this, so engrossed was she in playing with the Ouija board. The next question she asked the board was,

"Who are you?" The planchette dragged her hand across the board and spelled some words out, which read,

I said I would make you rich. Why don't you invite me?

"How rich will you make me?" The planchette stopped and slowly moved again under her hand. It spelled out the words,

I will reply to that question if you invite me in.

Julie's heart began beating fast with excitement. She was going to be rich. That was all that mattered to her, so she quickly replied,

"I invite you in."

The room seemed to go very cold when she said this. It was almost as if she was outside. A chill crept into her bones. She sat up and began coughing, then a fine mist starting to gather round her body.

Something was wrong ... more than wrong. Something was badly wrong.

Julie became very afraid, but could not move.

There was a slight movement behind her, then a weight on the bed. It was moving up her bed towards her. It touched her neck. It felt like a claw. Then came a burning pain that ran through her body.

No one heard Julie scream. Her mother and sister were not in the house. They had both gone out to escape her rants and her spiteful tongue.

Then there was silence in the room. All that could be heard was the clock ticking in the bedroom.

On the television screen the cloaked figure had gone. It had simply disappeared. And all that could be seen was a fine white mist, nothing else.

Katharine Underville had collected the soul of Julie Painter.

Cattingham had not had much luck with the weather. Snow had replaced the gale-force winds. It was now two weeks before Christmas. On the 18 November the village lights had been put on. A huge Christmas tree had been placed in the centre of the marketplace.

The whole of the front street was now lit up as Maddie, Sam, and Natalie walked to the Christmas market. The carol singers had moved further up the village, but the street was still packed with people. The blanket of snow underfoot shone like diamonds, the white powder making crisp crunching sounds as they walked over it. It would have been a beautiful scene if it had not been for Sam twisting her face now and again as they walked.

She had bought new boots but they pinched, and even had when she had bought them. After wearing them for two weeks they still hurt. How she would have loved to have pulled them off and walked barefoot in the snow. On two occasions she had nearly fallen flat on her face when walking on the cobblestones.

"I hate these boots," she mouthed, irritated.

She knew what it was. It was those weird sixth toes she had. The doctor had looked at them and said they could be removed by surgery, but she would go on a waiting list as it was – they said – a purely cosmetic operation. The growth on the side of her toe had got bigger, and now actually did look like a toe.

Sam found it embarrassing, and now no longer went barefoot round the house. She so hoped the operation would be soon.

Remembering Katharine Underville's remarks on it as if she was a freak had made her very self-conscious of it.

This was now the second year for the Continental Christmas market. It had an almost fairground atmosphere about it. The air was thick with cinnamon, mulled wine, and chocolate. It seemed as if the whole of Cattingham Village had been taken over by the market. What looked like religious people in brown robes walked in a line through the market.

"Why are they there?" wondered Maddie.

One of them was speaking to people, but she could not hear what was being said... On seeing her looking, he came up to her and handed her a leaflet. It was about joining the Drakens. She looked angrily at it and pushed it back into his hand.

"I don't think so," she said, and glared at him.

Surprised at her attitude he walked away, and pointed her out to his colleague.

"He has probably put me down as a troublemaker," said Maddie to Sam.

"Well, he is right on that, I would say," said Sam and nudged her in the ribs. "And why are those people never good-looking?" sighed Sam.

Maddie didn't answer. She had spotted a stall selling hand mirrors. She walked over to it and picked up a pewter hand mirror. She had lost the mirror she had bought as a birthday present for her aunt. She could have sworn she had put it in her walk-in wardrobe.

The mirror she picked up was heavily embossed, with a picture of a mermaid on it. Her silver fishtail continued over from the front of the mirror to the back, and finally went down to a curved handle. It was beautifully made, but the mermaid's hair was made of snakes and it did not look as nice as she had at first thought.

After all that happened she did not want anything creepy around her. Instead she picked up a wooden mirror with a hand-painted white rose on it. She handed her money to the stallholder and placed the wrapped package in her owl tote bag.

She looked around for Sam and she saw her at a chocolate stall buying truffles. Sam waved Maddie over and mouthed, "Free chocolate," and proceeded to put a large white chocolate strawberry in her mouth.

The stall had an amazing array of chocolates, from marshmallows to orange peel chocolate truffles. A large white box filled with coconut ice in the layers of pink tissue paper was open on the counter.

"Go on. Try one," said the stallholder, who spoke in what sounded like a French accent. Maddie happily took a piece of the pink confectionery. When she saw some violet creams wrapped in cellophane with a large purple bow on them Maddie bought them for her Aunt Lydia.

"Isn't it weird about Julie Painter?" said Sam as the girls left the stall.

"I think she went off with a lad," said Natalie, who had just come over from the candle stall.

"Yes, but to leave everything and not take anything with her … Do you know that the police said she didn't even take money out of her speed bank?" said Sam. She was licking the sugar off her lips as she popped a chocolate marshmallow into her mouth.

"Oh … knowing her, she will turn up. You know what she's like: anything for attention," replied Natalie.

"Well, I think it's a cruel thing to do to her mum. Her mum was really kind to me at the Hall. It's her I feel sorry for," said Maddie.

"Well, you shouldn't feel sorry for her," replied Sam. "A couple of weeks without that horrible daughter of hers must be a hell of a treat for her."

They all laughed. Sam had a point, thought Maddie, but it was still a strange thing to do. According to the Bickleberry Post when the police had interviewed Linda she had no idea that her sister was going to run away.

"I spoke to Linda at school," said Natalie as she gazed into her sweet bag. "She said her sister had been playing with the Ouija board, and that was the last time she saw her."

Maddie had only caught the end of this part of the conversation, as she was busy looking at another of the Drakens who was handing out leaflets. They were noticeable because of their trademark brown robes. They were also wearing brown leather sandals in the snow, and she could not understand why they were not affected by the cold.

"What did you say about the Ouija board?" Maddie asked, a strange feeling coming over her.

"Just that Linda said she was playing on the Ouija board and that they had a falling-out, so Linda went out ... and that was the last she saw of Julie."

Shocked by this piece of information, Maddie dropped the bag of sweets she was holding and bent to pick them up.

"Maddie, are you all right?" Sam asked.

"Yes, I am fine. It's just that the Ouija board went missing – and she was at my house, if you remember. I think she stole it. Do you think there was something in the Ouija board – like an evil spirit, or something – and that's why Julie has disappeared?"

"No, Maddie. All the evil went. It's all over now. It's just a coincidence the Ouija board went missing. We didn't really have time to search your room. Your aunt was obsessed with boarding it up. It was probably left in there. It might even be under your bed. Julie will turn up. You'll see," replied Sam.

"I suppose so," said Maddie. "I am just paranoid about everything. Do you know that I even have bad dreams about Katharine?"

"So do I" said Sam. "We'll get over it. Come on, forget about it."

"Hey, guys, look. There is a fortune-teller's stall over there. Shall we go in?" Natalie asked, butting in.

"No, I don't think I will," said Sam. She caught Maddie's eye as she added, "Count me out. I am keeping well away from that sort of thing in future."

"Me too," came Maddie's reply.

"Oh, well, I'll go myself. Catch you later," Natalie replied, disappointed because they wouldn't come with her. She took her purse out of her pocket and counted her money.

The tent had a table outside with leaflets piled on top of it. It promoted the Drakens. Standing at the table was a pale-faced youth with bad skin. He handed her a leaflet. She stuffed it in her bag without looking at it and asked him,

"How much are the fortune-telling readings?"

"Only £1. You will have to wait, though. There are two in already," he replied, almost zombielike.

"OK," she said. And she waited, pleased it was so cheap.

When she looked around she noticed that the makeshift tent did not seem to fit in with the other stalls. She had not noticed it when they came into the market. She heard a low growl and noticed a black shadow coming out of the tent. It was a huge dog, which looked like a cross between a Great Dane and a Dobermann Pinscher. It was completely black, with small ears flat on its head.

The dog would have easily have been seven feet on its hind legs. Its eyes were black, with what looked like a red reflection in them. The look it gave her was not pleasant, and it had an almost wolfish glint in its eyes. It had coarse and mangy black fur that covered its body in a zigzag-like fashion.

When it looked into her eyes it gave another growl. Natalie backed away from it, deciding not bother with the fortune-telling reading, and began to walk away.

"Where are you going?" a voice coming out of the tent asked. Behind the dog was a woman in a brown dress and fawn shawl.

"Er … I think I have changed my mind. I don't think I will have a reading," Natalie stammered back. The woman's tone was intimidating. The tent flap was now completely open, and there did not appear to be anyone else in the tent.

"I thought there were two people having a reading," she said to the woman as she walked further away.

"No. So I am free to do a reading. Come in," the woman replied.

On seeing Natalie looking at the dog the woman said,

"He will not hurt you. Do not be afraid of him. Move, Rane." The huge dog moved away from the tent but still did not take its eyes off Natalie.

The woman was much older than she first thought. Her eyes were pale blue; almost white. It was like looking into a blind person's eyes. In between her eyebrows were three warts, which made it look as if she had one long eyebrow. It was not a friendly face, and it made Natalie feel nervous.

"I said to come into the tent. I will do you a reading. Don't be shy, girl. I don't bite. What a pretty girl you are … such lovely hair."

The woman moved nearer to Natalie and touched one of her thick brown plaits. The large hand appeared to be wearing black gloves. The fingers were long and came to sharp points. Natalie wondered whether they were joke hands. Perhaps they were made to make you feel she was a witch. The woman smiled at her and displayed yellow teeth. Her breath was foul, and it made Natalie feel a bit sick.

"No, I don't think I will bother," came her reply.

"Don't be silly, girl. I can make you rich. Do you not want to be rich?" Natalie laughed at this.

"No, it's OK. I said that I have changed my mind," she said, and backed away from the woman.

"Get in the tent, girl. It will only take a few minutes," the woman insisted. Her tone had changed and become threatening.

"No. I said have changed my mind." As she said this Natalie realised that the man behind the stall had moved and was now at her side.

When she realised that they were going to make her go into the tent she looked around, but there was no one walking by. She became frightened and pretended to see someone she knew. She shouted out,

"Hello, Susie. I'm over here," and smiled back at an imaginary person. Natalie caught the man and woman off guard and ran away, pushing the man as she went, and ran to look for her friends. A wind began to blow as she ran off as if it were trying to drag her back to the tent. She had to force her body forward. The wind began to howl.

She struggled to move further and further away from the tent. Finally the strange wind subsided, and she managed to get to the end of the market. But it was cold, and the struggle had made her gasp for breath. Her mouth felt icy, and her lips were now very cold with the biting wind.

"Maddie and Sam," she shouted, but her voice came out in a whisper.

They did not see her. Crowds of people were pushing them further away from her. She finally managed to find her voice, and let out a shriek. When a man behind Maddie saw that Natalie was shouting to her he touched Maddie on the shoulder and pointed Natalie out to her. Maddie and Sam waded through the crowd to her.

As they came to her Natalie gasped,

"That fortune-teller, that … that woman … She tried to drag me into the tent even when I said I did not want a reading." As she tried to get her breath she continued,

"There was a man with her. I think he would have forced me in the tent. I have never been so terrified. They are a pair of nutters, and that dog was like something out of a horror film. Do you think I should tell the police?" She began coughing as she finished speaking.

"What did the woman look like?" asked Maddie, who was looking visibly shocked.

"Old … with pale blue eyes, and warts in between her eyebrows."

"Oh, my God."

"Maddie, what is it?" Natalie asked, on seeing the colour drain from Maddie's face.

"Do you think, Sam …? Oh, Sam, do you think it's Katharine?" Sam replied,

"But it can't be. Didn't you say she was sucked into a whirlpool?"

"Yes, but Anna said she could come back if she was summoned."

"Who would summon her?" Sam asked.

"I don't know. But a woman with warts between her eyebrows trying to drag Natalie into a tent … It can't be a coincidence."

"Where is the fortune-teller's tent?" asked Sam.

"I'll show you," came Natalie's reply. The three of them walked back down to the bottom of the market.

"It's on the far left," said Natalie. "Wait a minute. I must have got it wrong. It's not here. It must be further along." They walked to the very end of the market with Natalie screwing up her eyes and looking around her.

"It must be here. It had a man handing out those Draken leaflets. I must have got my bearings wrong."

They went round the whole of the market, but it seemed as if the fortune-teller's stall had disappeared into thin air.

"I think we should go and see Colin," said Maddie finally.

The Christmas market no longer appealed to them. The other two nodded in agreement. As they walked around to the church heavy snow began to fall, making it slippery underfoot. Thick, melting droplets of snow dropped off their faces and hair like tiny diamonds as they finally reached the church. Colin was talking to a volunteer. They waited until the woman had gone and then Maddie, Sam, and Natalie walked up to him.

"Hello, girls," he said, amused at the sight of the snow-covered girls. But the three of them could not even muster a smile.

"Why so serious?" he asked Maddie.

"Colin, something happened at the Christmas market. I think Katharine may be back. Natalie, tell him what happened to you." Natalie repeated what had happened to her.

"But this could just be a coincidence," said Colin.

"But the woman had warts on her eyebrows," replied Maddie.

"Yes but a lot of people have warts on their faces. The woman may not have made much money on fortune-telling, and just wanted Natalie's money. Did she try and follow you, Natalie?"

"Well, no, but I felt that something was trying to drag me back to the tent," replied Natalie. Colin looked at Maddie and said,

"After all that has happened anything like that is going to make you nervous. Put it out of your mind. I will however investigate the Christmas market just to put your mind at ease. Actually, Maddie, you are just the person I wanted to see. I am having trouble with my spreadsheets again. Can you have a look at them?"

This broke the ice, and Maddie laughed. She felt more reassured that maybe he was right and Katharine had not come back, and it was just her being paranoid.

Soon she forgot about the incident. She followed Colin, along with Sam and Natalie, to the church study. He said to her,

"I spoke to your mother. I believe you are having your Cousin Phillip come to stay over at your aunt's during the Christmas period. That will be nice for you."

"Yes. Aunt Lydia invited him. He is on his own for Christmas because Uncle Julian is in Africa." Maddie would have loved to have added,

"Yes, Uncle Julian is in Africa with some woman who is about forty years younger than him," but decided not to.

Recently she had begun to feel sorry for Cousin Phillip. She had not seen her uncle for a while now. After Uncle Julian had gone away Phillip had spent more time at Lydia's. At first Maddie had been very jealous and annoyed about it. But he had been so nice to them both that she had mellowed towards him.

"You should feel sorry for him," her aunt had said, and told her off one day for being nasty about him.

"He has no mother, and his father has gone off and left him on his own. He will be very lonely at Christmas. Would you want to be on your own for Christmas? Remember also that he has just split up with his girlfriend, and his father has gone to Africa for two months."

Guiltily, Maddie had said sorry to her aunt. She was still thinking about it when she became aware that Colin was asking about her mother, and then he mentioned Maddie's Aunt Persephone.

Maddie replied that her mother had received a letter out of the blue from Aunt Persephone asking if they would like to visit her. Her mother had replied that they would visit her in Scotland after the Christmas period. Aunt Persephone – who was on Maddie's Uncle Accoubian's side – was, according to Aunt Lydia, a bit of a recluse, and lived in a house in the middle of nowhere. There was talk that she even had a Scottish wildcat as a pet. They continued talking about it as the three girls and the vicar went into to his study. Maddie, Sam, and Natalie now more preoccupied with helping Colin with his spreadsheets.

Chapter 33

Mr Hind, the new headmaster of Mount High Senior School, had walked the whole length of the school. The caretaker had gone home, and all that could be heard was the headmaster's footsteps as he walked along the highly polished floors. After going into each classroom with his clipboard he tutted, and made notes of what improvements could be made for each class.

He was a very methodical man, who even had his Faber-Castell pencil standing to attention in the breast pocket of his cardigan. There was no heating on in the school, so he had had to put his black buttoned-up cardigan on over his black and white dog-tooth shirt as he walked around. Because he was very tall he had to stoop into the doorways of some of the rooms.

What was annoying him at the moment was the school cleaners. He could see grease stains on the walls. He walked over to one particular stain, measured it using his pencil and made a note.

"This will not do," he muttered to himself. His small pinprick-black eyes missed nothing.

When he looked into the cleaning cupboard he found that everything was in disarray. One bucket even had traces of dirty grey water in the bottom. He placed a green sticker on the offending item. After glancing back at the wall he placed a green sticker over the grease stain.

He had formerly been the headmaster at Alvaston Boys School. Discipline had been paramount, but the school had then closed. The cleaners at the school had known their place. He had given them lists of projected targets, and given marks for their cleaning and efficiency. This would have to happen at Mount High.

Engrossed in his thoughts, he went back to his the headmaster's room. He opened each of the desk drawers and pulled a face at what he could see: dust. He picked a packet of wet wipes out of his briefcase and placed it on the table. Then took everything out of the drawers and placed every item on the top of the desk. Some of the pencils looked dirty, and had suspicious-looking chewed ends. He picked them up in disgust and threw them into the bin.

He was concentrating so much on sorting out what he considered to be disorder in the drawers that he did not at first hear the knock on the door. That was until the person on the other side knocked again. He thought it was the caretaker, and shouted,

"Come in," with his best authoritarian voice. But no one came in. Irritated, he shouted, "Come in," again but still they did not come in.

He stood up and opened the door.

It gave rheumatic creaks as it opened.

To his surprise there was a woman outside the door who was possibly in her late fifties to sixties. She was thickset, and dressed in a brown gabardine dress.

"Are you Mr Hind?" she asked him. She was not smiling. He had a good look at her, and going by the manner in which she had spoken to him he thought she was possibly a school governor whom he had not met before. Even worse, possibly, he thought that she might have come to spy on him.

"Yes," he replied, and beamed back in what he hoped was his most pleasant smile.

She was not an attractive image to look at. She was almost mannish, with a wide jaw and a thin crease for lips. As she stared at him from the doorway one of her feet moved slightly impatiently as it prepared to step into the study. Mr Hind looked down at this action and saw thick brown stockings encasing her wide feet in chocolate brown lace-up brogues.

"Are you inviting me in?" she asked slowly.

"Certainly. Come in, Mrs … Er, what did you say your name was?"

"My name is Katharine Underville," came the amused reply.

Her small blue eyes studied the headmaster with amusement as she walked into his study. Once she had collected this soul she would be free at last.

Outside the main door an enormous black dog howled and scratched impatiently with its cloven hooves as it tried to get inside the school.

#0103 - 040416 - C0 - 210/148/14 - PB - DID1411314